He was very

Montana
Dreaming

Three satisfying romances from three beloved
Mills & Boon authors!

He was only interested in her...

Montana Dreaming

KAREN ROSE SMITH

Three satisfying romances from three beloved
Mills & Boon authors!

Montana Dreaming

JUDY DUARTE

KAREN ROSE SMITH

CHERYL ST JOHN

First published in Great Britain 2010
Harlequin Mills & Boon Limited,
Eton House, 18-24 Paradise Road, Richmond, Surrey TW9 1SR

MONTANA DREAMING © by Harlequin Enterprises II B.V./S.à.r.l 2010

Their Unexpected Family, Cabin Fever and *Million-Dollar Makeover* were
first published in Great Britain by Harlequin Mills & Boon Limited in
separate, single volumes.

Theirm Unexpected Family © Harlequin Books S.A 2005
Cabin Fever © Harlequin Books S.A 2005
Million-Dollar Makeover © Harlequin Books S.A 2005

Special thanks and acknowledgement are given to Judy Duarte, Karen Rose
Smith and Cheryl St John for their contribution to the MONTANA series.

ISBN: 978 0 263 88049 6

05-1110

Printed and bound in Spain
by Litografia Rosés S.A., Barcelona

THEIR UNEXPECTED FAMILY

BY
JUDY DUARTE

An avid reader who enjoys a happy ending, **Judy Duarte** always wanted to write books of her own. One day she decided to make that dream come true. Five years and six manuscripts later, she sold her first book to Special Edition.

Her unpublished stories have won the Emily and the Orange Rose and in 2001 she became a double Golden Heart finalist. Judy credits her success to Romance Writers of America and two wonderful critique partners, Sheri WhiteFeather and Crystal Green.

At times, when a stubborn hero and a headstrong heroine claim her undivided attention, she and her family are thankful for fast food, pizza delivery and video games. When she's not at the keyboard or in a Walter Mitty-type world, she enjoys travelling, spending romantic evenings with her personal hero and playing board games with her kids.

Judy lives in Southern California and loves to hear from her readers. You may write to her at: PO Box 498, San Luis Rey, CA 92068-0498, USA. You can also visit her website at www.judyduarte.com.

To Emalee Rae Colwell, who made her appearance in time to give Grandma a refresher course on birthing rooms and the miracle of childbirth.
Welcome to the world, baby girl!

In addition, I'd like to thank Christine Rimmer, Allison Leigh, Pamela Toth, Karen Rose Smith and Cheryl St John, the other authors in the MONTANA series, for making this book a pleasure to write.

Chapter One

Juliet Rivera had always favored the aroma of grilled onions and green peppers, but tonight, the kitchen smells of the busy bar and grill triggered a wave of nausea.

"Are those fries up yet?" she asked, arching her back and trailing her fingers along the contour of her distended womb.

God, she hoped everything was all right. The baby had been unusually quiet today, which increased her concern about working after Dr. Hart had recommended she take it easy. She didn't want to risk triggering premature labor, but she needed to support herself and the child she was going to bear.

Buck Crowley, the burly cook who'd once practiced his culinary skills on navy seamen, slid the plate toward her and grumbled. "You tell that fortune hunter that I'm not making them any crisper than this. French fries aren't supposed to be as hard as matchsticks."

"Thanks, Buck." Juliet made her way through the dining room of The Hitching Post and placed the well-done fries in front of the lanky customer who'd asked her to take them back to the kitchen.

She watched him poke a finger at the heaping platter of extra-crispy potato strips, apparently checking to see if they were made the way he'd requested.

He wasn't going to send them back again, was he?

If he did, she could imagine Buck storming out of the kitchen and into the dining room. The retired military man wasn't prone to confrontations with the customers, but he, along with some of the other Thunder Canyon locals, didn't appreciate all the strangers who'd flocked to the charming Montana town with hopes of striking it rich.

Years ago, several other gold rushes had lured their share of prospectors into Thunder Canyon. But the Queen of Hearts mine had played out, and Buck believed the contemporary gold-seekers would end up disappointed.

Juliet crossed her arms over the shelf her belly made and shifted her weight to one foot, waiting for the customer's approval.

Dios mio, señor. Cual es su problema? With just under six weeks to go until her due date, she'd probably give birth before he decided whether the fries were good enough.

Juliet was dead on her feet and ready to clock out,

especially after her visit to the emergency room two days ago. But she couldn't leave yet. The Hitching Post was hopping like a Saturday night, and it was only the middle of the week.

The persnickety customer finally shrugged his shoulders, then reached for a fry. When he popped a second one into his mouth, she turned to go, pausing as her boss approached.

Martha Tasker, a matronly woman who wore her silver-streaked hair pulled into a topknot, placed a hand on Juliet's shoulder. "I'm worried about you. How's it going?"

Other than sore feet and a twinge of nausea whenever she neared the kitchen? Juliet forced a smile. "I'm fine. Thanks."

"No more fainting spells?"

"Not since Sunday afternoon."

Mrs. Tasker studied her, as though trying to make her own assessment. "This is your just first night back on the job. We can try to handle the load without you. Why don't you call it quits until tomorrow?"

Because Juliet's small nest egg was only enough to see her through delivery and a few weeks after that. What would she do when it was gone? She'd been told there would be a workman's compensation settlement that would go to her brother's estate, but that could take years, and she wasn't counting on it.

She flashed her employer another smile, one she hoped boasted more confidence than she felt. "As soon as the dinner crowd thins out, I'll go home."

"Good," Mrs. Tasker said, as she began to wind her

way back to the cash register she manned. "We don't want that baby comin' into the world too early. That fainting spell nearly gave me a heart attack."

"*What* fainting spell?" a husky baritone voice asked.

Juliet glanced over her shoulder and spotted Mark Anderson, a reporter for a major news service who'd been sent to Thunder Canyon to cover the gold rush. Apparently, he'd just entered the dining room and had overheard her conversation with Mrs. Tasker.

She guessed him to be just shy of six feet, although he looked monstrously tall with his hands on his hips and glaring at her like a highway patrolman who'd just snagged a reckless driver. His dark hair, a bit long and unruly, bore a tinge of gray at the temples, so she judged him to be in his late thirties.

"It was nothing," she told him, although the fainting spell and ambulance ride to the hospital had been pretty scary.

The reporter eyed her carefully. "Have you seen a doctor?"

Juliet wasn't sure why he asked, why he cared. But she couldn't see any reason not to answer honestly. There were too many people in this world who didn't tell the truth, people who kept secrets. And she'd be darned if she'd be one of them. "I have a doctor. And I saw a resident obstetrician in the emergency room at Thunder Canyon General. Everything is fine, although I'm supposed to take it easy."

"Then what are you doing here?" His husky voice, with the hint of a soft southern drawl, settled over her like a drizzle of melted chocolate. But his probing eyes weren't nearly as sweet and comforting.

A strand of hair that had come loose from the gold clip she wore while at work tickled her cheek, and she swiped it away with the back of her hand. "What does it look like I'm doing?"

"You're certainly not taking it easy." His whiskey-brown eyes swept over her again, no doubt spotting the exhaustion in her expression that a dab of lipstick and mascara couldn't hide.

She wasn't sure whether she should be angry with him for butting in or pleased that he gave a darn about her health and the baby's welfare. But for a woman who'd grown up in a small, close-knit family, she'd been alone and on her own for too long to completely shrug off his concern.

He pulled out a chair and sat at the nearest table—on the dining room side, rather than closer to the bar where he usually parked himself for the evening. His gaze lingered on her, and he continued to study her with more interest than any of the other male customers.

At one time, she might have wondered if the reporter found her attractive. But how loco was that? With a belly that seemed to grow bigger every day, there wasn't much for a man to find appealing—not that she cared anyway. Her baby was the one and only priority in her life.

Wanting to break the intimacy of his gaze, to distance herself from his interest, she asked, "Can I get you something to eat?"

"Not yet. But I'll have a drink."

Since coming into town last week on assignment, he'd had several stiff shots of bourbon every night—at least, that's what he'd ordered when she'd been working. Then he ate dinner before heading across the street to the inn, where the news service had put him up.

She doubted he had a drinking problem, since his cynical yet flirtatious personality remained constant, and he appeared unaffected by his alcohol consumption.

"Bourbon and a splash of water?" she asked.

"Good memory."

"Predictable customer."

He grinned, and she headed for the bar, which sat on the far side of the room, near the dance floor that saw a lot of action on Friday and Saturday nights.

The Hitching Post had once been the town saloon, and although renovated many years ago into a respectable eatery, its history lingered in the old photographs that dotted the walls, the refurbished bar that still boasted scars and scratches from yesteryear and a painting of a nude woman, who was rumored to have been the original owner—the Shady Lady, as the locals called her.

Juliet always found it difficult not to stare at the image of the voluptuous blonde who sported a teasing grin. More straitlaced folks might disagree, but she thought the nineteenth-century piece of art added to the charm of The Hitching Post.

When the bartender handed her Mark's drink, she

returned to his table, placed a cocktail napkin in front of him, then served the glass of nearly straight bourbon.

He lifted his drink in a mock salute. "Thanks."

"You're welcome."

His eyes continued to study her, but she couldn't seem to make herself move, get back to work.

"Can you take a break?" he asked.

If she were inclined to think like a single woman on the prowl rather than an expectant mother wanting to nest, she'd consider it. "No, I'd better not. I'm still on the clock."

"There are laws about companies giving their employees a break during the workday." He glanced at her tummy, then caught her eyes in a mesmerizing gaze.

Juliet's grandmother, *Abuelita,* had taught her to search a person's expression—especially the eyes—to try and spot the secrets one kept. Of course, with Juliet's history, she wasn't very good at character assessment. And for some reason, she suspected she'd be just as lousy at guessing what drove Mark Anderson, what caused him to mellow out at night with alcohol instead of a cup of decaf and a slice of pie.

"Excuse me. I'd better get back to work." She turned to go, but he caught her by the hand.

Mark wasn't sure what had compelled him to touch the pretty Latina with sparkling caramel-colored eyes and long black hair she'd swept into a twist. It wasn't like him to be forward, but he'd been drawn to her since the first day he'd stepped into The Hitching Post hoping to while away the hours until his story developed.

Sure, there was a little attraction involved, he supposed. She was a beautiful woman, in spite of her condition. And her spunky personality made him sit up and take notice. But it was more than a case of Latin blood and genetics that caught his eye and held his interest.

He loosened his grip on her wrist, letting her go. "It wouldn't hurt for you to sit down for a while."

"I shouldn't," she said, but slowly took a seat anyway. "It's almost time for me to go home."

Mark couldn't remember any Hispanic families in the area when he'd lived in Thunder Canyon. But that had been twenty years ago.

"Where's home?" he asked.

She nodded at the ceiling. "I live here. In the apartment upstairs."

He hadn't expected her to reveal more than an "I live northeast of town," or "In that new housing development off White Water Drive." The women he knew liked to play cat-and-mouse games, never saying what was really on their minds, holding back and not revealing too much.

Was Juliet that young and inexperienced? Or were there a few women in this world who were still honest and open?

Either way, he found her innocence refreshing, to say the least.

He glanced at the ceiling, as she had done, and a grin tugged at his lips. "Did you know that the second floor of The Hitching Post used to be a whore-house?"

She smiled, a flush coloring her cheeks. "Mrs. Tasker, my boss and landlady, told me that, although she referred to it as a 'house of ill repute.' But you'd never know it now. One of the previous owners converted the upstairs into a living area for his family back in the 1950s."

Mark had heard the second floor was now an apartment. But when he'd lived in Thunder Canyon as a teenager, legends of the saloon and whorehouse held more interest for him and his friends than the renovations had.

"I lucked out," she told him. "I got a job and a place to live all in one day."

Lucky for her, maybe. Mark was glad he'd left Thunder Canyon. And just being within city limits made him uneasy and gave him reason to throw back a couple of bourbons before turning in. The booze helped pass the time and keep the memories at bay.

She shot him an unabashed grin. "I love it here."

"Here?" He scanned the dining room.

"Yes, working at The Hitching Post and living in Thunder Canyon, especially the old part of town. I love the Wild West charm."

Mark chuckled. "What are you, a history buff?"

"In a way." She fiddled with the unused napkin in front of her. "My dad and brother used to love those old shoot-'em-up westerns. You know, *Bonanza* reruns, *Gunsmoke*. John Wayne movies. And before long, I was hooked, too."

"Really?"

She leaned forward, her eyes flashing impishly, and grinned. "And when the TV is on the blink, I'm a big fan of Zane Grey and Louis L'Amour."

"No kidding?"

She lifted up her right hand in a Boy Scout fashion. "Honest. But don't tell." She smiled again, suggesting that she didn't really care what people thought of her choice of reading material. Caramel-colored flecks sparkled in her brown eyes. "On my days off, I walk along the wooden sidewalk here in Old Town and study the false-front buildings." She slid him an enchanting smile. "Sometimes, if I close my eyes, I can see a cowboy in a spun woolen shirt, leather vest and dungarees, walking along the dusty western streets."

"You don't say. That's a pretty vivid imagination you've got. Do you hear his spurs go jingle jangle jingle?"

"Of course." The mirth in her voice taunted his cynical nature. "You mean you haven't ever envisioned a prim lady dressed in calico and wearing a splash of lemon verbena?"

"No. Never." He leaned back in his chair, extending his legs, as his gaze swept her pretty face. "Not even a pretty *señorita* with flashing dark eyes."

Her lips, with only the hint of rose-colored lipstick, quirked as she made a tsk-tsk sound. "That's too bad. Life must be boring for a man mired in reality."

That was for sure. What little imagination Mark had was spent deciphering puzzles, weeding out lies and digging for the meat of a story. And although his life was normally far from dull, that wasn't the case on this assignment.

Covering the gold rush was a waste of his time, and it chapped his hide that his boss had sent him here because he'd once been a local boy. But Mark was a professional. He'd get the damn story written, make Thunder Canyon look remotely interesting, then get the hell out of town. As long as he could stay a step ahead of the memories he'd like to forget, he'd come out on top.

"My life isn't dull," he told her. "Not by a long shot. But I've got to admit I'm bored in Thunder Canyon."

She leaned back in her chair. "You're a stick in the mud."

"And you're a romantic."

Her smile drifted and the light in her eyes faded. "About some things, I suppose."

His gaze fell to her belly, to the swollen womb where her baby grew, and he realized the conversation had taken a personal turn for her. A heavy turn?

"What's your husband do?" he asked, curious about the guy and hoping he was supportive and making sure she didn't do too much in her condition.

"I'm not married. I'll be raising my child alone."

God knew he didn't want to go *there*. Mark would be in and out of town long before she had the baby. At least that was his game plan.

"Soooo," he said, trying to get them both back to an impersonal level, at least when it came to the lover in her past. "You fell in love with Thunder Canyon and settled here."

She nodded.

"Amazing. And I couldn't get out of town fast enough." The minute the words slipped out, he wanted to take them back.

There were some things Mark Anderson was hell-bent to forget, some memories he refused to discuss. Some guilt, that if left unchecked, would stealthily creep back in the dark of night, pointing a finger and reminding him how he'd failed his sister, his family.

But he'd be damned if he'd let the reminder haunt his dreams tonight. So he gamely changed the subject. *Again.* Back to *her* past. "Where are you from?"

"Originally? San Diego."

"That's a long way from Thunder Canyon."

"The distance was part of the appeal."

Mark nodded, as though he knew something he couldn't possibly understand. The reporter in him wanted to question her, to learn why she was running, but this wasn't another work-related interview. And he didn't want to encourage self-disclosure when turn-about *wasn't* fair play.

"My baby's father didn't want our child," she offered without being asked, then shrugged and cast a smile that didn't convince Mark that the guy's rejection hadn't done a number on her. "So I left town with the intent of settling down in the first place that felt like home to me."

The lover who'd fathered her baby was a fool. But Mark kept the thought to himself. "And you just ended up here?"

"I stopped at a restaurant near Sacramento and

chatted with a couple of tourists who'd come from Montana. They told me how quaint and charming Thunder Canyon was, and I decided to visit."

"And then you decided to stay." An easy assumption.

"That's about the size of it." She scooted her chair back and stood, her belly and the baby stretching between them.

"Where are you going?" he asked.

"Back to work."

"Shouldn't you go upstairs and put your feet up or something?" He didn't know why he was feeling so protective of her.

God knew he didn't have any intention of getting involved with any local women, not to mention a pregnant one who was a good ten to fifteen years younger than he was. But that didn't keep him from feeling sorry for her. After all, the father of her child wasn't in the picture, and considering her job, money was obviously an issue.

She shouldn't be working so hard this late in her pregnancy. Something could go wrong.

A momentary flash—lightning quick—thundered in his chest, reverberating in his mind and threatening to shake the memories free from their dark hiding place.

Kelly lying on the floor. The gray pallor of her death mask. The distended belly. The pool of blood.

Mark could tap dance around the truth all night. But he knew where the urge to protect the pretty waitress had come from.

His sister had been about Juliet's age when she and her unborn son had died.

As Juliet slid the chair she'd been sitting in back to the table, obviously ending their chat and the short break she'd taken, he couldn't keep quiet. "I hope you're turning in your apron for the evening."

"Dr. Hart told me to take it easy. And she suggested I stop work. But that's not an option right now."

"You need to take the doctor's orders more seriously." No one understood how something could go wrong better than Mark.

"I did take the doctor seriously. I took off two days from work, I've cut back my hours a bit and the other waitresses have tried to make my job easier."

Before Mark could stop her, she made her way to another table, leaving him to ponder the easy banter, the subtle flirtation that went on despite her circumstances.

And the overwhelming urge to take care of a woman he hardly knew.

He took a drink of the bourbon. And then another. He hoped the alcohol would drown the memories Juliet's pregnancy had invoked. But it didn't seem likely.

The godawful guilt had reared its head, and it was too late to turn back the clock, to right a wrong he'd never forget.

Chapter Two

As was his custom, at least while in Thunder Canyon, Mark ended each day of interviews by downing a couple of drinks and having dinner at The Hitching Post.

He didn't feel any better about the value of his work on this story or feel any closer to wrapping it up than he had on his first day back in town. For the most part, all he could come up with was human-interest type stuff.

Public opinion, it seemed, was split when it came to the gold rush and the influx of fortune hunters.

Some townspeople had gotten so excited by the fervor, they'd locked up their homes and drained their bank accounts in order to buy prospecting gear. Others—mostly business owners—were pleased by the increase in revenue the newcomers brought to town.

But then there were the vocal locals, those who hated the publicity and the swarm of strangers who'd turned the quaint little town topsy-turvy. Juliet, with her love of history, probably fell into that group.

Mark scanned the room and found her near the cash register, talking to her boss. Why didn't Martha Tasker trade jobs and let the pregnant waitress sit on a stool while collecting payments and making change? It wouldn't hurt the older woman to take orders and serve customers for the time being.

As Juliet walked away, she massaged the small of her back with both hands.

Damn. It grated on Mark to see her working so hard. And hurting.

But hey, he reminded himself. That really wasn't any of his business. He ought to be relieved that she hadn't waited on him this evening. That she hadn't made any effort to stop by his table—in spite of the friendly conversation they'd shared last night.

Yet the fact that she hadn't come by bothered him, too.

He missed her smile, her wit. Her company.

But then why wouldn't he? Juliet was about the only person, place or thing in this town he found interesting or appealing.

And she hadn't looked his way this evening.

Was she avoiding him? Had he been too intrusive last night? Offering his opinion and advice without being asked?

Maybe so, but that was just as well.

Last night, following their chat, he'd gone back to

the Wander-On Inn and, when he'd finally dozed off, he'd slept like hell, tossing and turning all night long like a trout trapped in shallow water.

He glanced up from the trace of meat loaf and mashed potatoes on his plate and saw her coming his way.

Well, what do you know? Speak of the pretty devil who'd triggered his insomnia.

When she reached his table, she smiled. "Mary Sue had to go home because of a family emergency. So I'm going to be taking care of you from here on out."

"You're the one who should be cutting out early. And someone ought to be taking care of *you*."

She arched, grimaced, then rubbed her lower back. "We've already talked about that."

They had. And he hadn't meant to get her all riled up. After all, it wasn't his place to harp on her. And even if she appreciated his concern, he wouldn't be around long enough to nurture a friendship. Besides, he damn sure didn't need to get involved with a single mother and her child, especially when they lived in a town he'd been avoiding for twenty years.

"I'm sorry, Juliet. I'll let it go."

"Thanks." She offered him an olive-branch smile. "I'm trying to take it easy, Mark. But I've got to keep working a little while longer."

He nodded. She was concerned about finances, which was understandable. Once she gave birth and went back to work, the cost of a babysitter would probably put a crunch on her paycheck.

Maybe he ought to give her some money. Five hundred dollars might make life a bit easier for her. And then he could let it go. Ease off. Let her be.

"Can I get you some dessert?" she asked. "Buck made his blue-ribbon peach cobbler today. And everyone's been raving about it."

"Sure. I'll take some." Mark placed his napkin on the table and pushed aside his dinner plate. "Will you join me?"

"Maybe for a minute." She glanced over her shoulder at Martha, who appeared preoccupied with sorting bills in the cash drawer. "I've had a nagging backache all afternoon."

Mark couldn't hold back a grumble. If he were a violent man, he'd slam a fist on the table in frustration. Was a backache normal for a woman in her condition? Or was it an indication that something was wrong? Something terribly wrong? Something that put her life and that of her baby at risk?

Like Kelly.

Damn the memory that wouldn't let him alone.

No matter what he'd told himself, no matter what kind of truce he and the waitress had drawn, Mark couldn't shake his concern. "I'm glad you're going to take a break, but come on, Juliet. You really need to go home and put your feet up. Think about the baby."

"I am." Her eyes locked on his in rebuttal, although they appeared a bit glassy, like they were swimming in emotion and barely staying afloat. "I don't have a family to fall back on. It's just the baby and me. And I can't help worrying about making ends meet, about keeping a roof over our heads once he or she gets here."

"Yeah, well unless you want that baby to get here too soon, you'd better heed the doctor's advice and quit work."

"Tonight, when I clock out, I'll ask for a couple of days off. Okay?" She lifted a delicate brow, as though cueing him to agree.

He merely blew out a sigh, giving in—so it appeared. He didn't usually offer unsolicited advice. It wasn't normally his style. But then again, he wasn't reminded of Kelly that often. Of her unnecessary death.

Juliet seemed to accept his silence as acquiescence, which it was. But her weary smile didn't take the edge off the exhaustion in her expression. Nor did it erase the dark circles he hadn't noticed under her eyes last night.

"I'll have two peach cobblers," he said. "And a glass of milk."

"I'd think the milk might curdle in your stomach with the bourbon you drank earlier."

"The milk is for you."

She nodded, then went after the dessert. When she returned, she took a seat. "How's your story coming along?"

"What story? This assignment is a joke." And it was, compared to the bigger stories he'd covered in the past. Important events that made him feel as though he'd reached the professional level he'd strived for, that level where one man—a reporter—could make a difference in people's lives.

"You think the gold rush is a joke?" she asked.

"Writing a story about a bunch of loony-tune prospectors who've flocked to a possible gold rush in Thunder Canyon can't even come close to a story about a major flood or fire." He dug into the cobbler and scooped out a gooey bite. Hmmm. Not bad.

When he glanced up, he caught Juliet's eye, her rapt attention.

"You'd rather write about disasters?" she asked. "Why such depressing news?"

"It touches hearts, confronts our deepest fears. Stirs up emotion."

"We had a fight in here last Saturday night. There was plenty of emotion stirring then." Her lips quirked into a grin, and he realized she was teasing him, trying to chip away at the cynical armor it had taken him years to build.

"A fight, huh? I'm sorry I missed the entertainment. But not to worry. I can go down to the E.R. at Thunder Canyon General and watch them stitch up the scalp of some idiot who tripped over a pickax and split his head open."

"So this is small tomatoes for you."

"Small potatoes," he corrected, unwilling to reveal his disappointment, his frustration. His desire to make a difference, to help people—victims of disasters. And to better prepare people who hadn't been stricken by major calamities yet. He shrugged. "I'll get the job done."

"You know," she said, licking a dollop of peach cobbler from her fork. "There have been some gold nuggets found. So one of the prospectors *could* strike it rich."

"Maybe. But I think the biggest story I've got is the hullabaloo about the ownership of the old mine."

"I thought Caleb Douglas owned it. That his great-grandfather won it in a poker game with the Shady Lady."

"That's the legend that's been circulating for years. People have just assumed that Caleb was the owner. But he hasn't produced the deed."

She furrowed her brow. "What about the county records?"

"They're not available right now. Harvey Watson, the clerk who's been transcribing all the old records into the new computer system, is on vacation." Mark slowly shook his head. "Can you believe, in this day and age, that Thunder Canyon would be so far behind the times?"

"Like I told you before, I think this historical old town is quaint."

He leaned back in his chair, watched the innocence dance in her eyes and smiled. "You must have some Amish in your genes."

"Sorry, no Amish. Just a little Basque, a drop or two of French. But mostly, a healthy blend of proud Mexican and Old World Spanish." She smiled and gave a little wink. "Maybe I was born in the wrong century."

She was definitely unique. A novelty. And as far as he was concerned, her bloodlines were damn near perfect.

"So, who do you think owns the Queen of Hearts

mine?" she asked. "You ought to have an idea. After all, you're a local boy."

Not *that* local. Mark hadn't moved to Thunder Canyon until he was thirteen. And he was long gone five years later. "I think Caleb Douglas owns the property, and it's just a matter of a misplaced deed and some backward record keeping in a land office. Anyway, that's my guess."

She took a sip of milk, and he watched the path of her swallow. She had a pretty neck. Regal and aristocratic. The kind of throat and neck a man liked to nuzzle.

When she lowered the glass, she wore a spot of white at the edge of her mouth. Unable to help himself, he reached out and snagged it with his thumb.

Her lips parted, and something—he sure as hell didn't know what—passed between them. An awareness. An intimacy. Something he hadn't bargained for.

"I…umm…I'm sorry. You had a little milk…" He pointed to her cheek.

Juliet swiped her fingers across her mouth, trying to remove any trace of milk that still lingered. Or maybe she was trying to prolong the stimulating warmth of Mark's touch. The flutter of heat his thumb had provoked.

For goodness' sake. She was acting like a schoolgirl with a crush on the substitute teacher, a handsome young man fresh out of college and thrown into a classroom of adolescents. Or on a guy who was way out of her league. And that was crazy.

With the healthy sense of pride Papa and *Abuelita* had instilled in her, there weren't too many people— or men—Juliet would consider above her reach.

Of course, being nearly eight months pregnant certainly left her out of the running when it came to romance.

She glanced across the room, eager to break eye contact, or whatever was buzzing between her and Mark, and spotted Mrs. Tasker sitting in the swivel seat at the register. The older woman wore a frown that made the wrinkles around her eyes more pronounced.

Were her ingrown nails giving her trouble again tonight? Or did she think Juliet had a crush on the handsome older man, that she was trying to strike up a relationship with a customer?

Maybe she was thinking Juliet ought to get back to work.

"Oh, for Pete's sake," Mark said. "Tell Attila the Hun to back off and let you have a decent break."

He was right—not about Mrs. Tasker being a barbarian, but about Juliet needing to quit for today. This darn backache was getting to her. "I'll take the rest of the night off, all right?"

"That's better yet." He caught her fingers in a gentle squeeze before releasing them. But the brief connection remained, humming between them as though he hadn't let go.

She shook it off, blaming her hormones and the loneliness that seemed to haunt her at times, ever since her brother's accident.

It had been two years, although time had eased the

pain and dulled the shock, as Father Tomas had told her it would. But time hadn't done a darn thing to ease the loneliness or to change the fact she didn't have a family anymore.

She brushed a hand along the contour of her tummy, caressed the knot that sprung up on the left side. A little foot? A knee? A fist?

As she stood, the muscles of her back gripped hard, causing her to bend and grab the table for support.

"What's the matter?" Mark jumped to his feet.

"I'm not sure."

For a woman with bad feet, Mrs. Tasker was by her side in an instant. "Are you in labor?"

Juliet froze as the possibility momentarily hovered over her like the calm before the storm. "No, I don't think so." At least, she hoped not. It was still too early.

As the ache in her back continued, she closed her eyes. *Dios, por favor.* Don't let it happen now. It's too soon.

"Are you having a contraction?" Mrs. Tasker asked, glancing at her wristwatch, as though she meant to start timing the pains.

"It's just a backache," Juliet said, willing it to be true.

The older woman crossed her arms in an all-knowing fashion. "That's how my labor started with Jimmy. All in my back."

Juliet lifted her gaze, looked at Mark, expecting him to blurt out a gripe, a complaint, an I-told-you-so. But the only sign of his response was a tense jaw, a pale face.

"No need for us to take any chances," Mrs. Tasker said. "I'll call an ambulance."

"Don't bother." Mark reached into his back pocket, took out his wallet, withdrew a twenty-dollar bill and dropped it on the table. "I'll take her to the hospital."

Juliet began to object, to tell him to finish his dessert. But he slipped an arm around her and led her to the front door.

Mark followed White Water Drive to Thunder Canyon General, then veered toward the separate emergency entrance. He stopped under the covered portico, close to the automatic glass doors, and threw the car into park. "Wait here."

Leaving Juliet in the idling car, he dashed inside past a security guard, his heart pounding as though he had a personal stake in this—and he sure as hell didn't.

But Mark knew firsthand how things could go wrong during labor. And he wasn't going to leave Juliet, who didn't have anyone to depend on, to fend for herself. Neither was he going to let her ignore any symptoms that might be serious.

He spotted a nurse behind the reception desk. "I need help. Now. I've got a woman in my car who may be in premature labor."

The nurse grabbed a wheelchair and followed him outside. But rather than take Juliet right to a room, she stopped at the reception desk.

"Can't this wait?" Mark asked, growing more agitated by the second. He wanted to hand over Juliet to a qualified professional, then get the heck out of here.

"I'm sorry," the nurse responded. "This will only take a minute."

She was wrong. But while the customary paperwork was filled out, Mark managed to not pitch a fit about the amount of time it took.

Finally, Juliet was given a temporary bed in the E.R. Her only privacy was a blue-and-white striped curtain that didn't reach the floor.

Before long, she'd had her temperature and blood pressure taken—all within normal range.

Mark really ought to loosen up. Normal was a good thing, right?

"Did you notify your physician that you were coming in?" the nurse asked Juliet.

"I didn't have time to think about it." Juliet glanced at Mark and blew out a sigh. "Can you tell Dr. Emerson that I'm here?"

The nurse, a matronly blonde, placed a hand on Juliet's shoulder. "Dr. Emerson had a heart attack last night and is in ICU."

Juliet gasped.

"But don't you worry," the nurse said. "We have a top-notch resident obstetrician who will take good care of you."

"Dr. Hart?" Juliet asked.

The nurse smiled. "That's right."

"I saw her on Sunday afternoon. I'd had a fainting spell. And you're right. I felt very comfortable with her."

"Good," the nurse said. "I'll give Dr. Hart a call and see whether she'd like us to examine you down here or send you to maternity on the second floor."

Juliet uttered an okay. She might be comfortable with the resident obstetrician, but Mark could see the worry in her eyes. The anxiety in her face.

"In the meantime," the nurse said, pointing to a chair beside the bed. "Why don't you have a seat, Dad?"

Dad? She had that all wrong. But before Mark could explain, Juliet did it for him. "This is my friend, Mark Anderson. He's not the baby's father."

The nurse smiled. "It's nice for a woman to have someone she trusts be her birth coach."

Birth coach? Whoa. Not Mark. He'd just brought Juliet here to make sure she saw a doctor, that she was someplace safe. Maybe he could stick around and hold her hand for a while. But if things got hairy, if she was really in labor, he'd wait in the cafeteria until she gave birth. Heck, he might even hang around long enough to look at the baby behind a glass window and tell her the kid was cute—even though he'd seen a couple of newborns and thought they looked more like aliens than humans.

Then, after that, he'd be on his way.

When the nurse stepped out, Mark took a seat, but he couldn't seem to relax. What was taking so long? He glanced at his watch. The minute hands seemed to be moving slower than usual.

A while later—he didn't know how long—another nurse arrived. A friendly, thirty-something woman with short, dark-hair and wearing a pink smock dotted with teddy bears. "Ms. Rivera? I'm Beth Ann. Dr. Hart has asked me to take you to maternity."

The nurse fiddled with the bed, making it mobile, then began to push Juliet out of the E.R. and into the hall. She slowed her steps just long enough to glance at Mark. "You can follow us."

He opened his mouth to object, to say he'd be having coffee in the cafeteria, but for some reason, he fell into step behind the rolling bed.

They took an elevator to the second floor, then the nurse wheeled Juliet toward the maternity ward, where she paused before the ominous double doors.

Mark's steps slowed, too. But not because he was tagging along behind them.

What the hell was he doing? Juliet was in good hands. Competent hands. He didn't need to go in there. They didn't need *him*. Besides, he'd done his duty. His good deed for the day.

But when Juliet turned her head and looked at him, those misty, mahogany eyes locking on his, he saw the fear, the nervousness. The need.

He offered her a wimpy smile, and when she turned her head away, he ran a hand through his hair. He didn't have any business going in there with her. He wasn't the baby's father. Or her husband.

But Juliet didn't have a mother or a sister. She was new in town. And he doubted she'd made any friends, not with her schedule. Hell, none of her co-workers had jumped in to help.

Right now, she only had him.

The nurse pressed at the button that automatically swung open the doors, then pushed Juliet through.

Mark followed behind, like a clueless steer on its way to a slaughterhouse.

They plodded along the hall, his Italian loafers clicking on the spanking clean floor, the nurse's rubber soles making a dull squeak with each step. They passed several open doorways Mark was afraid to peek into and continued along a glass-enclosed room that held incubators for the tiniest and sickest of patients. All of the little beds were empty, thank God.

Would Juliet's baby be placed in one of them?

The possibility jolted his heart, jump-starting his pulse.

Oh, for cripes sake. Mark wasn't a worrier. Not by nature. It was just the pregnancy, the vulnerability of both woman and child.

And his own fears brought back to life.

He swore under his breath. Juliet was just having a backache, right? From working too hard and carrying the extra weight of a baby. She hadn't been especially worried until Martha Tasker popped up like a jack-in-the-box, with the tale of her own labor, stirring things up. Making something out of nothing.

Mark followed the bed into a room that looked more like a bedroom than a private hospital room. Pale green curtains graced the window that looked out into a frozen courtyard that was probably colorful and vibrant during the summer.

Decorated in pink, green and a touch of lavender, the color scheme and homey touch of the room probably helped ease the nerves of laboring expectant mothers. But it didn't do a damn thing to ease Mark's

anxiety, not when he spotted medical gaskets and giz-
mos that reminded him of where they were, what they
faced.

"Here's a gown," Beth Ann said. "As soon as you
slip it on, I'll examine you."

An examination? Oh, cripes. Not an internal exam.

The nurse asked Juliet, "Would you like him to stay
in here?"

Oh, hell no. Not on a bet. Mark cleared his throat,
then started backing toward the door. "Why don't I
step out of the room for a little while. You can come
and get me when it's all over."

When it was *all* over. Not just the exam.

The nurse nodded as she reached for a box of rubber gloves.

Mark couldn't get out of the birthing room fast
enough. If he ever had a kid of his own, he wouldn't
be hanging around and watching that kind of a pro-
cedure. No way.

He ran a finger under the collar of his shirt, then
scanned the hospital corridor, where a floral wallpaper border softened the sterile white walls.

If there'd been anyone else who could be here for
Juliet, he'd be out of here faster than a sopping-wet
dog could shake its fur.

But she didn't have anyone.

And that's why he stayed.

Moments later, the nurse poked her head out the
door. "You can come in now."

He nodded, then stepped inside. But before he reached
Juliet's bed, an attractive woman dressed in medical garb
approached and introduced herself as Dr. Hart.

"I think she's in the early stages of labor," the nurse told the obstetrician. "And she's about two centimeters dilated."

Dr. Hart nodded, then approached Juliet. "I'd feel better about delivering your baby a couple weeks from now. So I'd like to give you something to stop labor and another medication that will help the baby's lungs develop quicker, in case your labor doesn't respond to treatment."

When the doctor and nurse left them alone, Juliet shot Mark a wobbly grin. "You don't have to stick around. I'll be okay."

Hey, there was his out. His excuse to leave. But he couldn't take it, couldn't walk away knowing she was all alone. "What if you need a ride home?"

"I can take a cab."

"Don't be ridiculous." Then he sat back in his chair, unsure of what the night would bring.

And hoping to hell he could step up to the plate. *This time.*

Chapter Three

Juliet stretched out in the hospital bed, wishing she could go back to sleep. The medication Dr. Hart had given her last night seemed to have worked. The backache had eased completely within the first hour of her arrival.

But that didn't mean she'd rested well. And neither had Mark, who'd stayed by her side the entire night.

More than once she'd told him he could go back to the inn, but he'd refused. And she had to admit, she was glad he hadn't left her alone.

She suspected hanging out with a pregnant woman at the hospital hadn't been easy for him. A couple of times, he'd gotten a squeamish I'd-rather-be-any-where-but-here look on his face. But he'd persevered like a real trooper.

Now he dozed on a pale green recliner near the window, hands folded over the flat plain of his stomach, eyes closed, dark hair spiked and mussed. He lay there for a while, unaware of her interest. And then he stirred.

She watched him arch his back, twist, extend his arms, then cover a yawn with his fist. When his eyes opened, he caught her gaze. "Good morning. How are you feeling?"

"Tired, but the backache is gone."

"That's good news." He gripped the armrests, manipulating the chair to an upright position, and stood like a knight in rumpled armor.

And that's how she thought of him. Real hero material—in the rough.

With a wrinkled cotton dress shirt and tousled hair, the cynical reporter might not make another woman sit up and take notice this morning. But another woman hadn't appreciated him pinch-hitting for the men she no longer had in her life.

Her brother Manny had been a macho guy, tough and gruff on the outside. But he'd also been a softy in the middle—at least, when it came to his little sister. And Mark appeared to be cut from the same bolt of cloth—a comparison made without any effort on her part.

There were men, as Juliet had learned the hard way, who wouldn't stand by a pregnant woman.

Her baby's father was one of them.

For a moment, as Juliet watched a sturdy, broad-shouldered Mark walk toward the window, she pretended that she had someone in her corner. Someone who cared enough to stick by her.

And, at least for the past twelve hours, that had been true. Mark had been there for her when she needed a friend. And that was something she'd remember long after he'd taken another assignment and left Thunder Canyon.

She watched as he drew the floral curtains aside, allowing her to peer into the dawn-lit hospital courtyard. She wondered what the grounds looked like in the summer, when the patches of snow had all melted and the rose garden bloomed.

The door to the birthing room cracked open, and they both turned as Dr. Hart entered. The slender woman with light brown, shoulder-length hair approached the bed. As in the past, she exuded professionalism and concern. Yet last night Juliet had noticed something different about her. A happy glow that lingered this morning.

"Good morning," the doctor said. "Did you have a restful night?"

"I didn't sleep too well," Juliet admitted, "but I'm feeling all right. No apparent labor."

"Let's make sure there hasn't been any silent dilation going on," the doctor said, as she headed for the sink.

As before, Mark left the room to give her privacy.

After washing her hands, Dr. Hart donned a pair of gloves and nodded toward the closed door. "That's some friend you have."

"It looks that way." Juliet closed her eyes during the

exam, whispering a prayer that all was well. That she hadn't dilated any more, that her baby was safe in her womb for the time being.

"Good," Dr. Hart said, removing the gloves and tossing them in the trash. "Nothing's changed since last night."

Juliet blew out the breath she'd been holding, as Dr. Hart opened the door to call Mark back into the room.

"I think we're home free," the obstetrician told him. "This time."

"Thank goodness." Mark blew out a little whistle and slid Juliet a smile, providing a sense of camaraderie. Teamwork. Something she hadn't experienced since her brother's accident.

The doctor made a note in the chart, then glanced at Juliet. "If you promise to stay off your feet, I'll let you go home."

"That's great." Juliet knew she'd feel better in the privacy of her own little apartment, close to her photographs and memories. "Thank you."

"But I'm talking extreme bed rest," the doctor stressed.

Mark cleared his throat. "Juliet doesn't have anyone to look after her, so maybe she ought to stay here."

For several weeks? Was he crazy? "That's ridiculous, Mark. I'll rest better and be happier at home."

Dr. Hart glanced up from the chart. "I'm not sure how your insurance carrier will feel about you staying here for more than a day or so. Do you have someone who can stay with you?"

"No, I live alone. But I promise to take it easy."

"Oh, yeah?" Mark made his way to Juliet's bedside. He'd seen the way she'd been "taking it easy" at The Hitching Post. "Doctor, you can't trust her not to get up and do the dishes or scrub floors or clean out closets or something like that."

"Then maybe we'd better keep you here." Dr. Hart, attractive even in green hospital scrubs, leaned her hip against the bed and crossed her arms.

Disappointment swept over Juliet's face, and Mark felt like a real spoilsport. But she didn't have anyone to look after her. He doubted Mrs. Tasker, who liked to park her butt by the cash register, would volunteer to help.

Juliet looked at him and frowned, tossing a guilt trip on him.

Mark supposed *he* could check on her. After all he was staying across the street.

"I can look after her." The comment popped out before Mark could think about the ramifications. And when Juliet and the doctor faced him, he realized backpedaling would be next to impossible now. He was committed. And he'd taken a stand. But that didn't mean his gut wasn't twisting.

Juliet shot him a wide-eyed stare. "You can't be serious about staying with me."

"Why not?" The question couldn't have surprised her any more than it had him. Hell, Mark had not only volunteered to babysit a woman who was on the verge of going into labor, but now he was trying to convince her—and maybe even himself—that it was a good idea.

"You can't waste your time taking care of me." Juliet pressed the control button that raised her up in bed. "You've got work to do."

He shook his head. "I don't have anything pressing to do."

"That's not true," she countered. "You've got a news article to write."

"The story, as I've told you before, is a joke. And the article can practically write itself."

"So, what's the verdict," Dr. Hart asked. "Do I sign these release papers or not?"

Mark crossed his arms. "Sign them."

"All right," the doctor said. "I'll have the paperwork processed. Then I'll send an orderly to take you out in a wheelchair."

When Dr. Hart left the room, Mark ran a hand through his hair. Juliet's back might feel much better this morning, but his hurt like hell.

What he really needed to do was get out of here, shower and maybe take a nap.

He glanced at Juliet and saw reluctance in her expression. Resentment, too? He wasn't sure. But she'd been overruled, and he had a feeling it didn't sit well.

Strangely, for a guy who liked to come out on top himself, he wasn't feeling too happy about winning this argument.

And he hoped to hell he hadn't bitten off more than he could chew.

Thirty minutes later, Mark brought his rental car to the curb at the main entrance of the hospital. Then he helped Juliet into the passenger seat.

He was taking her home. And that fact brought on a flurry of other concerns, things he hadn't considered when he'd volunteered to look after her.

There was no way around it. He would have to put in a significant amount of time with her. He'd told the doctor he'd take care of her, not pop in and out several times a day.

What if something went wrong in the middle of the night?

He'd have to stay there until she was no longer at risk for premature labor.

But how big was her place?

Where would he sleep?

On the sofa, he supposed.

The crick in his back, the one he'd woken up with, ached all the more, just thinking about being camped on her sofa for the next week or so. Damn. He was going to have to see a chiropractor when this stint in Thunder Canyon was over.

As they drove past the newly constructed Ranch View Estates, Juliet peered out the window, studying the pine tree-lined entrance, the bright, colorful flags and a sign announcing that Phase I was now available.

"That's a nice housing development," she said. "One afternoon, on my day off, I looked at the models."

Mark nodded, but didn't comment. He didn't have any inclination to set down roots, to purchase a home and landscape a yard. Especially not in Thunder Canyon.

At thirty-eight, he'd yet to buy a place of his own.

And why should he? He was always off on assignment, living in hotels that the news service paid for.

He turned left onto Main and followed it until they neared The Hitching Post.

"Can you drive around to the rear entrance?" Juliet asked. "I don't feel like going through the dining room looking like this."

"Sure." He didn't think she looked bad at all, not after what she'd been through. But he didn't argue. He swung around to the back, where a black Chevy S-10 pickup with a vinyl cover on the bed was parked next to a trash bin.

Mark nodded toward the custom truck with a lowered chassis. "Whose is that?"

"It's mine."

"You drive a pickup?" He chuckled. The lady was full of surprises. "Somehow, I figured you would drive a racy red sports car or a flashy white convertible."

"Hey, that little truck is special to me. It was my brother's pride and joy."

Was?

She'd told him the baby was her only family.

Unable to quell his curiosity, he asked, "What happened to him?"

"He died about eighteen months ago, and since he'd listed me on the title, I inherited his truck."

"I'm sorry," Mark said, the words feeling inadequate but necessary.

"I'm sorry, too."

A heavy silence filled the interior of the car, and Mark wanted it to end, wanted to lighten the mood.

To make her feel better. But it was hard to know what to say to someone who'd lost a loved one. He knew how impotent sympathetic words could be. No one had been able to ease his grief after his sister died. Not when her death had been his fault.

His parents had never forgiven him for what had happened that stormy evening. But he supposed that was to be expected. He'd never forgiven himself, either.

"It's tough not having a family," Juliet said, breaking the stifling stillness that had nearly choked the air out of the sedan. "But I focus on the memories we had. It's what Father Tomas, our parish priest, advised me to do. And it helps."

Mark was glad she had memories to rely on. He didn't. At least not the kind that made him feel better. In a way, he'd lost his entire family, too, even though his parents were still alive and kicking.

When his mom had learned he was in town, she'd called him at the Wander-On Inn. She'd sounded hurt that he hadn't chosen to stay at the motel she and his dad had owned and operated for the past twenty-five years.

Mark had told her it was because the company had prepaid his room without knowing his family could provide him free lodging. But to be honest, Mark had been very specific with the company's travel agent when they'd talked about where he wanted to stay— *anywhere but The Big Sky Motel at the edge of town.*

After parking beside Juliet's pickup, he spotted the stairway that led to the second floor.

He supposed he shouldn't be surprised that The Hitching Post didn't have an elevator, not when the county land office was just beginning to convert their records to a computer system. He bit back a swear word, but couldn't stop the grumble that slipped out.

"What's the matter?" she asked.

"I'm going to have to get you upstairs."

She opened her mouth, as if to object, then closed it again. Apparently, the recent bout of premature labor had made her realize how vulnerable she was.

He slid out of the driver's seat, circled the car and opened her door, intent upon carrying her.

She put her hand up to stop him. "Maybe if I take the steps really slow—"

He shook his head. "No way. Climbing stairs isn't a good idea. It's too strenuous."

"I can't let you carry me." She glanced down at her belly and frowned. "I'm too heavy."

She might be pregnant, but she was a petite woman. Small boned.

"Don't be silly. You're a lightweight."

"Open your eyes, Mark." She stroked her stomach.

Heck. Women could be so testy about their weight— even when they weren't pregnant. As he opened his mouth to argue, he caught a glimpse of skepticism in her frown.

Hey, wait a minute. Was she doubting his ability to carry her?

His male pride bristled. "Listen, sweetheart. I'm probably ten to fifteen years older than you, but that doesn't make me over the hill yet."

She balked momentarily, as though contemplating a fight, but she slipped an arm through the shoulder strap of her purse, swung her legs over the side of the seat, draped a hand around his neck and let him scoop her up.

She was heavier than he'd expected, but she was all belly. How big was the kid?

As he lifted her from the rented sedan, he choked back any sound she might consider a winded effort. But once he'd straightened and kicked the passenger door shut, it wasn't so bad. In fact, he kind of liked holding her in his arms and feeling like some kind of kick-ass hero.

Her arm looped around his neck. Holding on. Holding him.

He carried her up the steps, nails in the wood creaking under their combined weight. Damn, he hoped that whoever had built this stairway had made it sturdy. And that it hadn't been the original staircase. No telling what more than a hundred years of wear and tear had done to the structure.

"Mark, wait. I'm really uneasy. That can't be good for the baby, either."

She was right. He let her down, then helped her walk the rest of the way. Slowly. Carefully. Step by step.

When they reached the top landing, she dug through her purse for the key, but instead of unlocking the door, she turned to him instead. Her belly brushed against him, tempting him to touch it. To see what it felt like. But he refrained.

Her eyes sparked with sincerity. "I can stay alone. Really. Maybe, if I give you a key, you can stop in and check on me several times a day."

The idea had merit. But Mark had promised the doctor he'd look after her. And that's what he intended to do. "If it's okay, I can stay with you. Besides, I'm stuck in town anyway—at least until the county clerk returns and I can have a look at those old recorded deeds."

Her eyes widened and her lips parted. "Are you going to move into my place?"

No. He couldn't do that. Ever since his wife had left him and filed for divorce—way back when— Mark had learned to protect himself, his freedom. His secrets.

Even when he was seriously dating someone, he'd maintained a distance. He didn't like the idea of having his toothbrush and razor claim space on someone else's bathroom counter or on a shelf inside a medicine cabinet. Unless, of course, it was in a hotel room on a lover's getaway weekend.

But this was different.

Still, he couldn't bring himself to check out of the inn completely. It wasn't a matter of saving money. It was saving his space. His privacy. His ability to slip away before things got complicated.

"No, I'm keeping the room at the inn." As an explanation, he added, "With all the fortune hunters who've clamored into town, rooms are limited. And if I give up my place across the street, I might not be able to find another one."

And that was true. Mark sure as hell wouldn't ask his folks if he could stay with them. Not at the small mountaintop home they owned. Not even on a couch in the office of The Big Sky Motel.

"If you'll be okay for a while," he said, "I'll go across the street and bring over a few personal items. A change of clothes."

She flashed him a battle-weary but confident smile. "I'll be fine. Remember, I'm the one who wanted to stay alone."

He nodded, waiting as she turned her back and slipped the key in the lock. After she opened the door, he followed her inside.

The scent of cleaning products mingled with a hint of paint, as he entered a living room that didn't have any walls separating it from the kitchen or dining area. He glanced around, eyes adjusting to the darkened interior.

She flipped on a switch, turning on a goofy wagon wheel chandelier that lit the room, revealing a brown tweed sofa, a black recliner and a maple coffee table.

A trace of old cigarette smoke that a good scrubbing and a paint job hadn't been able to hide lingered in the gold drapes and the green shag carpet.

"Why don't you lie down," he said. "I'll be right back."

As he turned to go, she grabbed the sleeve of his shirt, those rich mahogany eyes snaring his, setting his nerves on edge, making his heart rumble in his chest.

"Thanks…for…you know…" She gave a little shrug. "For everything."

"No problem." But as he stepped into the crisp, cool morning air, he wasn't so sure he'd done anything commendable.

Juliet wasn't in a hospital—where she belonged.

And Mark, who had volunteered to be her private duty nurse, didn't know squat about pregnant women, childbirth or babies.

What in the hell had he set himself up for?

Juliet stretched out on the sofa, her head propped up on two pillows. As she thumbed through a *Parents* magazine, a knock sounded at the door.

She glanced up from an article on breast-feeding that had caught her eye. "Mark?"

"Yeah. It's me."

"The door is unlocked. Come on in." She fingered the fringed lapel of her blue robe, hoping he wouldn't give her a hard time because she'd taken a shower and shampooed her hair. But she'd been careful and had taken it slow and easy.

Mark, who looked shower-fresh himself, strode into the room with a newspaper tucked under his arm and carrying a gray duffel bag in his hand. His gaze zoomed in on her, and he frowned. "Why is your hair wet?"

"I took a quick shower. No strain, no stress."

"I don't think that's what the doctor meant by extreme bed rest."

"Maybe not, but I'll rest easier if I'm clean."

He scanned the interior of her apartment, as though noting the Early-American-Garage-Sale decor, the mismatched furniture, the decoupage wall plaques that served as artwork.

So the apartment was a little drab. She was happy here. She lifted her chin, prepared to defend her home from a remark that didn't come.

He nodded toward the wagon wheel chandelier that hung over the dinette table. "Those are low-watt bulbs. Do you mind if we have some more light in here?"

"No, go ahead."

She expected him to turn on another lamp, but he strode toward the window and paused in front of the ugly gold drapes.

The droopy, rundown condition wasn't her fault. And there wasn't anything she could do about it. The rod was missing some of those little plastic thingies the metal hooks poked into.

But, hey. As long as she had privacy, she could live with them. After all, she'd lived with worse and been happy. When love and laughter filled the interior of a home, nothing else mattered.

He glanced over his shoulder. "You need to ask your landlord to replace the curtains."

"I'm not going to push for anything like that right now. Not when Mrs. Tasker is going to be shorthanded in the diner and might have to replace me."

He started to say something, but turned toward the curtain rod. He fiddled with the cord until he opened the drapes a couple of feet.

"I rented this place furnished," she told him. "So I can't be too fussy."

Again, he withheld a comment, although she

wished he hadn't. She was prepared to argue. There was no need for him to feel sorry for her. She was glad to be in Thunder Canyon. Glad to have a job and a home for her baby. There was a lot to be said for counting one's blessings.

She reached for the soft green *covijita* that draped over the back of the old sofa and pulled it close, brushing it against her cheek. Her *abuelita* had crocheted the small blanket, and Juliet cherished it.

"How many bedrooms do you have?" Mark glanced at the two doors along the east wall.

"Just one. The bathroom is on the left. The other door is the bedroom. Go ahead and put your bag in there. I'll take the sofa."

"No way." He crossed his arms, standing sentry-straight, brow furrowed as though she'd suggested they run naked in a snowstorm.

"Shall we compromise?" She figured they could share turns.

"Sure. You take the sofa by day, and I'll take it by night."

She could argue, but what was the use? Mark was only looking out for her best interests. Besides, there would probably be plenty of times in upcoming days when they'd disagree. It was best if she chose her battles with this man.

Mark moved toward the bookcase where Juliet displayed her family photos instead of books. Her father had built it years ago. As far as quality, the wood was rustic and slightly flawed, but the piece of furniture was priceless.

He lifted a silver framed photograph of *Abuelita* holding Papa when he was a toddler.

"Did these pictures come with the place?" he asked.

"No. That's my father when he was just a little boy. And that's his mother. My *abuelita*."

He replaced it and chose the one of Manny in his baseball uniform.

"That's my brother, Manuel. He loved sports."

Mark studied the photo for a while. "What kind of accident did he have?"

"It happened at the warehouse where he worked. A freak industrial accident, they told me. Involving a forklift." She laid the magazine across her lap and tried to focus on something more pleasant. Something that didn't remind her of her brother's death, the lawsuit. Something that didn't trigger thoughts of Erik Kramer, the attorney who'd volunteered to handle her interests in the workman's compensation case. The jerk.

Mark replaced the silver frame, then turned away from the shelves. "I'm sorry your family isn't around for you now."

She shrugged and mustered a smile. "I have a lot of happy memories. Of the good times. And the unconditional love." She ran a hand along the contour of her tummy, caressing her child. "And I have a new baby to look forward to. Life goes on."

He merely studied her, looking skeptical. Hopeful. Concerned. A hodgepodge of emotion she found hard to decipher played havoc with his expression. But it didn't do a thing to lessen the attraction that continued to build—in spite of her circumstances.

Dios mio, the man was handsome. Or maybe she found him more appealing, now that she'd gotten to know him better.

It felt weird to have him here. But at the same time, it was kind of nice. And she found it hard not to stare.

He slipped off his black leather jacket, hung it over the back of the recliner and sauntered toward the sofa. He'd dressed casually today, sporting a pair of worn jeans and a long-sleeved chambray shirt.

As he drew close, she caught a whiff of mountain-fresh cologne, menthol shaving cream and peppermint toothpaste. It was a taunting scent. Mesmerizing in a way. Her gaze locked on his, her pulse kicking up a notch. Did he know? Could he sense her inappropriate interest?

He cleared his throat. "It's nearly nine o'clock, so we'd better think about breakfast."

The husky sound of his voice, more graveled than usual, made her wonder if he'd ever been a smoker. If so, he'd given up the habit.

"You've got to be hungry," he added.

She was. But she hadn't realized it until now.

"Can I get you anything?"

"I'll have a glass of milk. For the baby."

He walked to the kitchen, opened the fridge and pulled out a carton of milk. Then he rummaged through the cupboards, looking for a glass. She could have helped him out, she supposed, telling him where to look, but she watched him instead, her interest and curiosity piqued. There was something about a man in the kitchen. Especially that man.

There was so much she didn't know about Mark, other than he was a reporter who'd once been a local boy.

"Do you still have family around here?" she asked.

His movements slowed. "Yeah. My parents."

That was nice. "Do you see them often?"

"No." He filled the glass until the milk frothed at the top. "My folks and I had a falling out years ago."

"That's too bad."

He shrugged. "We were never that close anyway."

"Have you tried a reconciliation?" She knew the value of a family, the value of turning the other cheek. Of appreciating each individual personality, in spite of the differences. And the value of appreciating what you had, while you still had it.

"We talk, if that's what you mean. But we aren't very close. And I like it that way." He brought her the milk. "Do you have anything I can use to make breakfast?"

He was going to cook? By himself?

Her father and brother couldn't have fixed themselves a meal—maybe because *Abuelita* had claimed the kitchen as her territory. And even after she passed away, they hadn't stepped foot near the stove. So, at the age of ten, Juliet had taken over. And eventually she became a pretty decent cook.

"I have eggs and bacon in the fridge," she told him. "Orange juice, too. And the coffee is in the small canister on the counter."

"Okay. I'll fix something for us to eat. You just rest."

Actually, she thought watching Sir Rumpled Knight in the kitchen might prove to be entertaining.

And touching.

If she let herself dream, she could imagine falling for a guy like Mark. But Juliet knew better than to let any romantic, fairy-tale notions take root. Her heart had already borne more than its share of grief, and there was no need to set herself up for a fall that was easy to foresee.

Besides, Juliet came from sturdy stock. She was a survivor. And she didn't need to be rescued, didn't need anyone to look after her once the baby got here.

Especially not a globe-trotting reporter who'd made it clear that he was just passing through.

She returned her attention to the magazine she'd been reading, to the article on breast-feeding dos and don'ts.

And she remained focused on the words—until she caught a whiff of burning bacon and heard the squeal of the smoke alarm, as it ripped through the room.

Chapter Four

"**D**ammit!" Mark shut off the flame under the frying pan and turned on a fan that didn't work.

A giggle erupted from Juliet, who sat on the sofa, but he ignored it as he hurried to place the smoking skillet in the sink, dump out the grease and burnt bacon and turn on the faucet. The water hit the hot pan, roaring and sputtering like someone had entered the gates of hell.

As the smoke alarm continued to blast, he looked up at the archaic safety device that didn't have an on or off switch, then swore under his breath as he hurried to open the window, to let fresh air into the room, to allow the smoke to dissipate. All the while, the alarm continued to shriek like a drunken banshee.

By this time, Juliet's giggle turned into a laugh,

triggering a rush of embarrassment. Frustration. And anger at himself for getting distracted.

"What's so funny?" he asked.

Grabbing a dish towel from the countertop, he began fanning the smoke away from the kitchen, hoping it would clear the air and make the stupid alarm shut up. When that didn't seem to work, he reached up, jerked open the plastic contraption and removed the batteries.

Silence.

Except for Juliet's laughter.

When he glanced over his shoulder, he watched her belly jiggle with mirth. "Hey, stop that. Do you want to shake the baby loose?"

She placed a hand on her enlarged womb, as though trying to hold back the tear-provoking laughter, but it didn't work. Between her chuckles, she managed to say, "I assumed you knew how to cook."

"I do. But I'm not used to this stove."

Her gaze scanned the kitchen and lingered on the newspaper spread over the gold Formica countertop—no doubt realizing what he'd been doing when the bacon got away from him.

The editorial had caught his eye, dragging him into small-town politics, the debate about the gold rush, and the fortune hunters who'd converged on Thunder Canyon with hopes of striking it rich.

Consequently, Mark had neglected to watch the stove, the flame, the sizzling meat.

"Anything interesting going on in the world?"

"Undoubtedly," he said. "But I was reading the

Thunder Canyon Nugget, which is chock-full of nothing."

"Well, something obviously caught your attention."

"Not really. The paper, like this town, can't compete with the real world." He turned off the kitchen faucet and nodded toward the sink. "I'm afraid that was the last of the bacon. And the pan needs to go in that Dumpster outside."

"Don't throw it away. There's cleanser and steel wool under the sink."

"I'm not going to scrub this thing." He chucked the pan into the trashcan. "I'll buy you a new one as soon as I get the chance."

She swiped at the moisture under one eye, evidence of her amusement. But she couldn't hide her grin. "I've got cornflakes in the cupboard. And there's a banana on the counter. You can slice it—if you like fruit on your breakfast cereal."

Mark didn't like bananas, didn't like the taste or the texture. He'd eat his cereal plain, although he preferred a manly meal like bacon and eggs.

As he rummaged through the kitchen, looking for bowls and a box of cornflakes, he tried to shake off the image of what would have made a hearty breakfast going up in smoke. Of course, with all the fast food he'd scarfed down in his travels, his body could probably use the fiber from the cereal. Better to flush those arteries than clog them.

"It was really sweet of you to try and cook for me," she said.

Yeah, well, he didn't feel sweet. Or funny. And if

someone downstairs heard that damned alarm and called the fire department, he was going to feel stupid.

A few minutes later, after the smoke had begun to clear, he fixed her cereal, adding the sliced bananas on top. Then he placed her bowl on the coffee table so she wouldn't need to get up and walk any more than necessary.

"Thanks." She tugged at his sleeve, drawing his attention. "And I'm sorry for laughing."

"No you aren't." He tossed her a laid-back grin, sliding back into the easy banter they shared.

"Okay, I'm not." She giggled again. "You should have seen the look on your face when that alarm went off. And the way you frantically swung that dish towel around like a dime-store cowboy trying to lasso the horse that had thrown him."

"I think you enjoyed seeing me screw up."

"Let's say I found it entertaining. I'm competitive by nature. Maybe it's a little sister/big brother thing."

Was she saying she thought of him as a big brother? He supposed that ought to be kind of nice. Or touching. But for some reason it irked him that she thought of him that way. As if he were too old for her to consider as a lover—well, if she weren't having a baby and all.

Nah. She couldn't have been thinking about him as lover material. Mother Nature probably disconnected all the sexual urges when a woman got pregnant. In fact, he doubted Juliet thought about making love at all—especially now.

So why had sex crossed *his* mind—even briefly?

Maybe because it had been a while since he'd had time to spend on a relationship—as noncommittal as his were.

She swung her feet around to the floor and sat up to eat, making room for him to take a seat beside her on the sofa.

Actually, when Mark put his frustration and embarrassment aside, he had to admit it was nice seeing her smile, hearing her laugh. He shot her a crooked grin. "I looked like a cowboy, huh?"

"Roy Rogers at his worst." Her eyes glimmered and her lips twitched, as she used her spoon to snag a slice of banana and pop it in her mouth.

Although he enjoyed a good joke, a part of him didn't like her laughing at him. But he chided himself for being sensitive about something so minor and took a sip of coffee. As he savored the rich brew, he realized he'd done something right this morning.

He glanced at the ceramic cup—white, with a pink carnation trim along the edge. The pattern was bright and cheery, unlike the other things in the house. And he wondered if she'd had a hand in choosing the dishes. "Was the kitchen furnished, too?"

"The dishes are mine. I packed Mrs. Tasker's set in a box and put them in the closet."

Mark looked at his cup. "I'll bet these are nicer than the ones she had."

"I think so. They're not fancy, but they were my grandmother's, so they're special."

Yeah, well he was beginning to think Juliet was

special, too. Over the years, she'd lost her family. Yet she didn't seem beaten.

His gaze dropped to her stomach, to where she carried her child. Why hadn't the father of her baby stepped up to the plate? Why hadn't he wanted a pretty woman like her? Maybe, over time, the guy would change his mind.

"Tell me something," Mark said. "Does the baby's father know where to find you?"

"No." She dabbed her lips with the paper towel he'd given her to use as a napkin.

Mark might not have any desire to be a husband and father, but if Juliet—or rather some other woman—was having his baby, he'd want to know about it. And he'd want to know where she and his child lived. "Don't you think you should tell him? In case he needs to see the baby or send money?"

She thought for a moment, as if trying to find the words to defend her move out of state. Or maybe she was trying to decide whether Mark had been right, whether she ought to let the baby's father know where she was residing.

After studying the pattern on her cereal bowl, she caught his gaze. The bubbly smile that had seemed permanently fixed moments ago had drifted. "I grew up in the barrios of San Diego. But I was raised in a loving home, and we were happy."

He didn't know what that had to do with anything, but he'd been curious about her past. So he shifted in his seat, facing her, letting her know he was interested in what she had to say.

"I never knew my mother. She left home when I was just a baby. But my grandmother moved in to help raise my brother and me."

Mark wasn't sure where she was going with this. Why was she skirting his question?

"My father worked at a neighborhood *tortilleria* to support the family. It was a small, family-owned business that didn't provide health insurance for the employees. And even though my dad insisted Manny and I visit the doctor whenever we were sick, he didn't like spending the money for himself." She paused for a moment, her gaze drifting back to the pink carnation trim on her bowl. "When I was fourteen, he died of cancer. It had been a treatable case that went undetected until it was too late."

"I'm sorry."

"Me, too. But Papa was a man of great faith. And I know he's in Heaven." She offered him a sincere smile, one that held feeling, conviction and victory over grief. "It was tough back then, but Manny and I did all right. We took care of each other. And we held on to the values we'd been taught."

Manny was her older brother, Mark realized. The young man who'd died in an industrial accident. Without meaning to, Mark glanced at the bookshelf, at the silver frame that held a smiling boy in a red baseball uniform.

"About four years ago, after I graduated from high school, I got a job waiting tables in a San Diego suburb at a small Mexican restaurant called La Cocina.

And Manny took a night job as a stock clerk in a discount superstore. We pooled our resources and moved out of the barrio, where we could create a home together and start a new life. We'd dreamed of buying a house. It had been a dream of our father's, then it was ours. Now it's mine."

Juliet, he realized, was made of sturdier stuff than she seemed.

She leaned back into the sofa. "Manny's death was a real blow."

And not just because of his youth, Mark realized. They'd been close. And her brother had been the last family member she had.

Mark struggled not to take her hand, to pull her into his arms. To provide a hug. Something. But he'd never been a touchy-feely kind of guy.

"One of the regulars who frequented the restaurant where I worked, an older guy who was a lawyer, volunteered to help me. To take care of the legalities resulting from my brother's estate and the workman's comp lawsuit that's still pending."

A nice guy? Mark wondered. Or an attorney looking for a cut of a settlement she was bound to get?

Juliet ran a hand over her belly. Over her child. "I needed a friend. Someone to talk to. Someone who cared. And Erik Kramer was a charmer who promised to be there for me. I believed him, and before long, we became lovers." At that point, she looked up, caught Mark's eye. "He was my first."

If the attorney had been in the room, Mark might have considered punching him. Charming a young virgin when she was grieving smacked of unethical behavior. And since she'd already mentioned that the baby's father hadn't wanted the child—or her—it made Kramer seem like more of a jerk.

There was a certain responsibility a man ought to have after taking a woman's virginity, especially when she was vulnerable, as Juliet had been. And the man should have been there for her when the chips were down. Like he'd promised.

"When I found out I was pregnant, I broke the news to him. I knew he'd be surprised. Like I was. But I assumed we'd make the most of it." She offered Mark a wistful smile. "You know. That we'd get married and live happily ever after."

Mark could guess the end of the story. "Apparently, Kramer wasn't into marriage."

"Oh, but he was." Juliet smiled wryly. "He and his wife of fifteen years were planning a Mediterranean cruise to celebrate their wedding anniversary."

Mark might be hell-bent on remaining single after his disappointing divorce, but that didn't mean he approved of married men having affairs. A commitment—if a man or woman were inclined to make one—ought to mean something.

Juliet peered at him with misty eyes. "If Erik would have been honest with me, if I'd known he had a wife, I never would have slept with him. He gave me every reason to believe that he was free to pursue a relationship. That he loved me."

"He lied to you. The guy's a bastard, Juliet." Mark wished Kramer was standing before him so he could knock his lights out. "I hope he's agreed to pay you child support."

"He gave me nearly a thousand dollars in cash, telling me to get rid of the 'problem.' Then he encouraged me to get a little something for myself with what was left over."

Mark reached out, took her hand and gave it a squeeze. But it didn't seem to be enough.

"The pregnancy had come as a surprise to me, too," Juliet said, caressing her womb again. "But there was no way I'd consider aborting my baby. He or she is the only family I have left."

"So you left San Diego. But what about the lawsuit?"

"For that reason, I'll eventually call and give his law firm my address. But I wanted to put some distance between us. Emotionally, as well as physically."

It made sense, he supposed.

"I didn't want the baby to find out that its father didn't want him or her, that he had another family that didn't include us. So I pocketed the money he'd given me, gave notice at La Cocina, had a garage sale, packed my belongings into Manny's truck and headed north. I wasn't sure where I was going, but I was eager to create a family of my own."

"And you ended up in Thunder Canyon."

"I wanted to find a small town where people knew their neighbors, where there were no secrets, no one who could betray my trust."

Mark wasn't so sure she'd found that here, but he wasn't about to splash a wave of cynicism on a young woman struggling to embrace a buoy of hope.

"That's probably way more than you wanted to know," she said. "But I didn't want you to think I'd intentionally hook up with a married man. That I'd normally be that stupid. That my father and the church hadn't taught me better than that."

Mark flicked a strand of hair away from her cheek, and cupped her jaw. His thumb made a slow, gentle stroke of her skin. "You're a special lady, Juliet. And someday, a lucky man is going to figure that out. And then you'll have a family again, the family you deserve."

Funny thing was, Mark the cynic actually believed that to be true.

For her.

But unlike pretty Juliet, a family wasn't in his cards. He'd tried to recreate his broken family once, but his ex had doused that dream years ago.

Not about to go another round with the kitchen or the stove for at least another day, Mark ordered two take-out dinners from The Hitching Post. He hoped Juliet would be pleased with his choice—pork chops, mashed potatoes and gravy, green beans and lemon meringue pie.

He carried the cartons of food upstairs and, while Juliet turned off the television, set the dinette table. The doctor had said she could get up to use the bathroom, so Mark figured it wouldn't hurt to sit for a couple of minutes.

As he poured them two glasses of milk, she crossed her arms over her belly and arched a brow. "What? No bourbon?"

"Not tonight."

It's not as though Mark was a lush, even though he could understand why she might think so. She'd seen him having nightly cocktails ever since he'd arrived in town. But that was liquid courage to face the memories he couldn't seem to shake while in Thunder Canyon.

And this evening, he had an intriguing young woman to keep his thoughts off his past. Off the rebellion that had led to his sister's death.

Juliet reached for a butter horn roll, tore off a piece and popped it in her mouth. When she swallowed, she placed her elbows on the table and leaned forward. "So, tell me about the assignment that's going to write itself."

"Actually, it's going to be a big spread. A Sunday paper special."

"Impressive." She smiled, and he felt a surge of pride, of pleasure. "What kind of spread? What will be the focus?"

"I'm going to write about the gold rushes, past and present. The willingness of naive miners to pursue a hopeless dream."

"Why not focus on the positive, on the excitement, the thrill of striking it rich?"

Maybe because Mark's hopes and dreams had died in Thunder Canyon, and he'd had to move away to get his life back. To make a future for himself.

"Do you realize how many miners actually hit pay dirt?" he asked.

"Some do. That's what makes it so exciting, so interesting."

"Come on, Juliet. You really don't believe anyone

is going to find any significant amount of gold in Thunder Canyon, do you? By the early 1900s, the mines in the area had played out."

She took a bite of the crab apple garnish. "There could be another vein of gold. And someone might find it."

"Do those rose-colored glasses ever fog up?"

A grin tugged at her lips, creating a dimple on one cheek. "I choose to look on the bright side of life."

That was growing more and more apparent. "The chance of a big strike is pretty slim. Ever since the 1860s, when the first gold rush started in this area, miners swept the hills, finding nuggets here and there. And yes, some people did get rich. But there weren't too many big fortunes made for the little guys. And most people were disappointed, if not devastated after gambling their savings on lady luck."

"You're more pessimistic than most of the people around here."

She wasn't the first woman to point out his cynicism. But he liked to think of himself as realistic.

"When I was in high school, I wrote a paper on Fourteen Mile City, a stretch of settlements amidst the gold fields." Mark had received an A+ on that report, along with a budding interest in journalism. "My history teacher praised me for pointing out the downside of mining and exposing what greed did to people. Back then, gullible investors bought stock in fraudulent ventures, sometimes bankrupting themselves. And I won't even go into what the gold rush cost the Indians and the Chinese."

"I can see that there's a downside. But I think most people would rather read about dreams, possibilities, hopes."

"The best I can do is write realistically. But it should make you feel better to know that I'm going to also include the history and the legends of Thunder Canyon." He stole a glance at her.

A growing fascination lit her face. "What kind of legends?"

"Supposedly, this canyon was sacred to the Indians, although I'll have to research that for accuracy. And there's also that story about Amos Douglas winning the Queen of Hearts gold mine in a poker game."

Juliet turned toward him, brushing her knees against his thigh, shooting a tingle of warmth and awareness through his blood. The way she looked at him, her eyes wide, hanging on his every word, made him puff up like a toad that thought he was king of the pond.

"Was Amos related to Jason and Caleb Douglas?" she asked.

"Yeah. Amos was the original Douglas settler in Thunder Canyon."

"And what's the story about the poker game? Who did Amos win it from?"

"I don't know. Maybe a prospector with a drinking and gambling problem. It's hard to say. When I get some time, I'm going to head over to the museum and see if they've got more information."

She sobered. "I'm sorry, Mark."

"About what?"

"Keeping you from your research."

"Don't worry about it. I can place a few calls, if necessary, and can research the Internet. Maybe by the time I get back to my interviews, Caleb will have found the deed." His explanation seemed to appease her, and he was glad, although not entirely sure why.

She placed a finger to her lips and clamped down on a nail, puzzled by something. "If the Douglas family owned the gold mine property, what do you think happened to the deed?"

Mark shrugged. "Who knows? It's been over a hundred years. Maybe Amos or one of his descendents misplaced it. They probably thought the land wasn't worth anything."

"Not even in sentimental value?"

He reached up, stroked a silky strand of her raven-black hair and gave it a gentle tug. "Most people see land for what it is. Real estate. Money in the pocket."

"I'm not most people."

"So I'm learning." For a moment, something passed between them. Something tender and intimate. Something that ought to scare the hell out of him. Something that *did*. He dropped his hand and studied his empty plate.

"Well," she began, "from what I've gathered from mealtime chitchat at The Hitching Post, Caleb seems more focused on finding that deed than in the ground-breaking of the ski resort he's developing."

"He's probably no different than the others. Each time another gold nugget is found, folks want to believe there's an untapped vein out there. The idea of sudden riches stirs the blood of some people."

"But not yours?"

"No."

"What stirs your blood?"

He looked at her, caught the gold flecks in her eyes that glimmered in the lamplight when she teased him, spotted the cute nose that turned up slightly. Noticed the fullness of her bottom lip, the softness that begged to be kissed.

His blood was moving along at a pretty good clip now, but he'd be damned if he'd let her know that.

Damn. He definitely needed to get laid. How long had it been? Surely not long enough for his libido to contemplate putting the moves on an expectant mother, for cripes sake.

"You really are a stick in the mud." She patted his thigh in a gentle, we're-good-friends way. But it didn't seem to matter to the rush of his bloodstream. "You have no imagination, Mark. Can't you tap into your heart?"

His heart had fizzled out a long time ago. After his sister had died. And whatever had been left shriveled up when his wife filed for divorce and moved out of their apartment while he was away on an assignment.

Juliet tugged on the sleeve of his shirt again, which seemed to be her habit. Her way of touching him without actually doing so.

"Can't you let go once in a while?" she asked.

Let what go?

His past? His guilt? His pessimism?

"What do you mean? I know how to have fun." At least, he used to. It had been a while—about as long as it had been since he'd had a wild passionate, no-strings-attached night.

"Close your eyes," she said.

"Why?"

"Just do it."

For some dumb reason, he did. "Okay, now what?"

"Think about The Hitching Post. About a building that's been around for ages. Can't you almost hear the plunking sound of a piano? The voices of people who once lived and played here?"

He squinted, opening one eye and then the other. "I'm not sure we ought to be listening to *those* voices. This floor was a brothel, remember?" He chuckled. "Did you still want me to imagine the tales these walls could tell?"

Her face flushed, although the Pollyanna glimmer remained in those mahogany eyes. And she shrugged. "It might be interesting."

"Interesting?"

"I thought most women in the olden days didn't particularly like sex."

"I'm sure plenty of them did." He grinned. "What makes you think they didn't?"

"Well, once when I was in the fourth grade, I overheard my *abuelita* and an older neighbor lady talking about sex."

"Oh, yeah?"

"My grandmother said she wouldn't walk across the room for it."

"That's too bad. It sounds as though your grandfather didn't know how to pleasure her."

Juliet didn't respond. But then, what was there to say?

Mark wondered whether Kramer had been good to her, whether he'd given her the kind of first-time experience she should have had. "Tell me, Juliet. Would *you* walk across the room for it?"

"Probably. If there wasn't anything good on television." Her eyes glimmered, and he couldn't tell if she was serious or pulling his leg.

"Then Kramer wasn't any better at pleasing a lady than your grandfather was," Mark said, taking a guess.

Her eyes widened, as if he'd hit the G-spot and set off her first orgasm.

Sexual awareness filled the room, settling over him. Over her, too, he suspected.

Her lips parted in an enticing way, almost as if inviting him to close in on her, to give her the kind of kiss that made blood pound, race, demand.

What was happening to him?

He ought to pull away. Let it go. Laugh it off, like a guy with any sense would.

But Mark had never been very heroic.

And when Juliet ran the tip of her tongue along her lips, he was lost.

Chapter Five

The kiss started innocently, sweetly. A tender promise of sugar and spice.

But before Mark could decide whether to pull back or press on, Juliet placed an angel-soft hand on his cheek and leaned forward—into the kiss.

Her lips, parted, and he savored the taste of her, a unique, tantalizing flavor that went beyond a hint of lemon and meringue. He cupped her jaw with one hand, fingers delving toward the back of her neck, the strands of her hair brushing his knuckles in a silky cascade.

As the kiss intensified, ever so slowly, his tongue explored the wet velvety softness of her mouth, tentatively seeking and savoring until he craved more of whatever captivated his senses.

Desire smoldered under the surface, warming his blood in a steady rush, urging him to give it free rein, to let it build and surge.

But something ensnared him, held him in a mesmerizing spell that slowed their motions, while intensifying sensual awareness.

Whatever it was seemed to have caught her, too, he realized, as she whimpered softly and her fingers threaded through his hair.

So much for Mother Nature disconnecting sexual urges in women who were in her condition.

Oh, for cripes sake.

Her condition.

She was *pregnant.* And he was supposed to be taking care of her, making sure she took it easy—not doing something reckless that could jeopardize her health.

He broke the kiss, his hand dropping to his side, useless and empty. "I'm sorry, Juliet. That was crazy. Stupid. And so damn out of line."

"That's okay. I lost my head, too."

That was obvious, as well as unexpected—just as his impulsive response had been. He wasn't sure what had come over them, but his libido had been primed and ready to rock.

A mischievous sparkle lit her eyes, as a slow smile curled her lips. "And just for the record, that kiss was definitely something I'd walk across the room for."

He didn't know if he should feel flattered or guilt-ridden. In self-defense, he thought about changing the subject, but his male pride wouldn't let him ignore what she'd said. "So you liked my kiss, huh?"

The twinkle in her eyes intensified, highlighting the flush of her cheeks. "Yes, I did like it."

A goofy urge to pound on his chest Tarzan style swept over him. He tried to laugh it off with what sounded to him like a dorky chuckle. "That's probably because the television is off and there aren't any TV specials to distract you."

"Maybe," she said, her eyes glazed with...

With what?

Passion? Embarrassment? Annoyance at him for making light of the inappropriate but sensual kiss they'd just shared?

He wasn't sure. But if things were different, if she were someone else, someone not so young—so virginal in spite of her condition—he would have kissed her again, just to see where it led.

But things *weren't* different.

She was expecting a child. And nesting in Thunder Canyon, while Mark couldn't pack his bags and leave town fast enough. Getting involved with Juliet, romantically speaking, was senseless.

So what kind of fool would be tempted to put the moves on her, even if it was one little kiss?

A jerk of a fool who wasn't much better than that married attorney who'd jumped her bones when she was just as vulnerable as she was now.

He raked a hand through his hair. "Listen, I've got to go back to the Wander-On Inn."

"Why? I thought you were spending the night here."

Was she disappointed that he might leave?

Or pleased?

And why, pray tell, should he care either way?

Hell, he really ought to sleep at the inn. Things were way too awkward here. Kissing Juliet had triggered a flight-or-fight response.

She nodded toward the bathroom. "It's just that you left your shaving kit in there."

Yeah. He had. Packed, zipped and ready for a fast getaway. He caught her gaze, saw the question in her eyes. The vulnerability.

Oh, God. What if she went into labor? There wouldn't be anyone with her. And Mark couldn't take that risk.

"I'll be right back," he told her. "I just need to get my laptop so I can do some research on the Internet this evening."

What a crock that was, but her nod told him she'd bought his explanation.

"Take your time," she said. "I'll just leave the door open."

"I don't plan to be gone that long." He just needed a breath of fresh air, a little break. Something he could focus on, other than a casual kiss that didn't mean anything.

"All right. If I'm not on the sofa, I'll be reading in my room."

"I'll just let myself in." He stood and shoved his hands in his pockets, then forced a smile before heading downstairs.

But the "meaningless" kiss followed him, taunting him long after he shut the door and sucked in a deep breath of crisp night air.

* * *

Several minutes after Mark left, Juliet continued to stare at the closed door, her fingers pressed softly to her lips.

What had just happened?

She wasn't sure, but it was more than the kiss that had her heart and mind singing. It was her response to it. That and the overwhelming urge to kiss Mark again. To make sure she hadn't imagined how sweet, how special, how arousing his mouth had been.

Mark's kiss had been so different from those Erik had given her.

Erik's mouth and tongue had been urgent, insistent. The kind of kisses that took her a while to warm up to. On the other hand, Mark, who seemed to know exactly what he was doing, had taken things slow and easy.

She hadn't been lying when she'd told Mark that she'd *probably* walk across the room for sex. It had been nice with Erik. Pleasant, once she caught up to his speed. But more than the act itself, she'd enjoyed the intimacy. The embrace, the touch of someone she'd cared about. But now Erik's lovemaking skills paled.

If the promise in Mark's kiss was an indication of what had been lacking in Erik's, Juliet suspected making love with Mark might prove to be very special indeed. A stimulating opportunity she'd not only walk across the room for, but, in anticipation, would turn off a perfectly good television show along the way.

But how likely was that?

Her hand slowly dropped to her swollen womb, reminding her to focus on motherhood and the new baby she'd soon hold in her arms.

But if Juliet weren't pregnant, she might be tempted to find out what Mark knew about pleasuring a lady that Erik hadn't known.

The next morning, Juliet woke to the aroma of fresh-brewed coffee.

Mark was proving to be an intriguing man, in spite of his cynical nature. The kind of man who made a woman smile when he wasn't around. The kind of man who provoked dreams of romance.

But Juliet knew better than to let silly romantic notions do anything but drift by the wayside. She and Mark had nothing in common.

So why had she spent so much time thinking about him last night? Dreaming about long, lingering kisses that stirred the blood and made her want to slip on a pair of track shoes so she could sprint across the room for another taste of his lips?

She blew out a sigh and climbed from bed. What was wrong with her? She didn't have any business thinking about Mark, his kiss or romance.

For goodness' sake, she was going to be a mother. And if she ever became involved with any one else, it would be with a man who'd make a good husband and father. A man who would take pride in his wife and child while barbecuing in the backyard on Sundays. Someone who held the same family values that she did.

And Mark Anderson, a pessimist who disliked Thunder Canyon and wasn't concerned over the falling out he'd had with his parents, wouldn't fit the bill.

Sure, he'd been good to her, a true friend. He'd also been a great listener, although he hadn't told her very much about himself.

Maybe she ought to quiz him a bit. Find out about the rift he'd had with his parents. Then maybe she could help facilitate a reconciliation.

Families were special.

More than anyone, Juliet knew that. And, if she could get Mark to see the value of a nurturing, loving support system, it would be one way to pay him back for being so good to her.

She slipped on her blue robe and strode into the living area, where he sat at the dinette table, his laptop open, a coffee cup at his side.

"Hey," he said, offering her a smile. "Sleep okay?"

Not really. She'd stewed for way too long about the kiss they'd shared—so long that she couldn't get into that book on pregnancy and childbirth she'd picked up at the library last Saturday. But there was no way she'd make a confession like that. "I slept all right. How about you?"

He glanced at the sofa, where the folded blanket rested on his pillow. "Not bad."

She noticed that he'd taken a shower and shaved. His hair, a bit long and unruly, was still damp. He'd put on a fresh white T-shirt and a pair of worn jeans, but his feet were bare.

He'd made himself at home, which was interesting. Comforting, she supposed.

In the six months she'd dated Erik, he'd never spent the night. Never made a pot of coffee. Never left a shaving kit in her bathroom. She hadn't thought anything about it at the time. Nor had she realized he'd been holding back on their relationship.

So, in a way, it pleased her to know that Mark had settled in, that he'd slept on the sofa. That he'd felt comfortable enough to take a shower in her bathroom. That he'd carefully put away his things, zipping the small leather bag closed. How neat and thoughtful was that?

With the morning sun at his back, blessing him in a glowing aura, he looked as though he belonged here—in her living room with his work spread out in front of him.

He scooted his chair back, the metal legs snagging on the matted green carpet. "I can fix cereal again. And after you've eaten, I'll head to the market and do some shopping."

"Okay." She made her way into the room, taking a seat at the table, and nodded at his laptop computer. "How's the research going?"

"I guess it's going all right. I'm learning some things about the early days of Thunder Canyon, things I remember my history teacher telling us in school. Things I didn't care about back then."

"What kind of things *did* you care about?" she asked, wanting to know more about Mark, his youth, his life.

"Football. Parties. Girls." He slid her a wry smile.

"The stuff that an adolescent surge of testosterone produces."

She returned his smile, as if she understood the typical teenage lifestyle. But she hadn't gotten caught up in any high school activities. Not when she was working after class let out so she could help Manny pay the bills.

"Were you a good student?" she asked.

"Not as good as my dad thought I should be."

Ah, an opening she could zero in on. "I'm sure he was proud of you, too."

"Not that I can remember." The sixties-style dinette chair squeaked, as Mark leaned back in his seat and stretched out his feet. "My mom said that from the time I chucked my first bottle out of the playpen, my dad and I were constantly butting heads."

"What kind of things did you argue about?"

"Everything. About my grades. The way I swung the bat during a Little League game. The hairstyle I chose. The music I listened to. The friends I had. My lazy-ass attitude around the house."

Was the relationship between Mark and his dad just a normal part of adolescent rebellion? A result of that surge of testosterone he'd mentioned earlier?

If that were the case, would their relationship be better now—if given a chance to start fresh?

She placed her elbows on the table and leaned forward, as far as her belly would allow. "Now that you're grown, do you think that maybe your father had a point about any of those things?"

He paused for a while, pondering her question, she supposed. Or maybe reevaluating his memories.

"He was right about my attitude. But it was tough to live with constant criticism, and eventually I got sick and tired of it."

"So you rebelled."

"That's about the size of it. But things got worse after he uprooted the family. My sister and I wanted to stay in Texas with my grandmother."

"Why did he decide to move here?"

"Because some great-uncle we'd never met died and left my dad a motel at the edge of town and a cabin-style home about ten miles up Turner Grade." Mark shook his head. "And to make matters worse, my dad insisted upon living in the mountains. It was hard not having neighbors, especially when my parents were in town all the time."

"I can see how it would have been more convenient for everyone involved if they'd lived closer to the motel."

"Yeah, well that was just another thing we argued about. And even though I think my mother agreed with me, she didn't press him about it."

"And so you're holding all that over his head now?"

Mark tensed. "That and a few other things."

"Like what?"

He fiddled with the keyboard of his computer, as though he hadn't heard her. And she wondered if the discussion was over on his part.

Then, as if her question wasn't still lingering in the air, he signed off the Internet and shut down the computer. "I'm starving. Are you ready for a bowl of cereal?"

"I guess so."

"Good. Once I fix your breakfast, I'll do the laundry. I'm running out of clothes, and I figure you are, too."

"You're not going to do my laundry," she said without thinking. If Mark didn't help her with it, who would? She was supposed to stay off her feet, and she didn't think the doctor would approve of even a simple activity like throwing her clothes into a washer and dryer.

"What are you going to do?" he asked. "Wait until your clothes are all dirty and buy new ones?"

She couldn't do that. But she felt funny about him washing her things, especially her bras and panties. Maybe she could set her undies aside and wash them in the bathroom sink. That wouldn't be any more strenuous than washing her hands, would it?

"Now that we've got that settled," he said, "do you want cornflakes again? Or the granola stuff?"

Apparently, he'd decided not to try and cook again. And she got the feeling he wasn't comfortable in a kitchen. He probably ate all of his meals out. But she was getting tired of cereal every morning.

"A toasted bagel and cream cheese sounds good for a change."

"Okay."

She watched as he puttered around the kitchen, preparing breakfast.

He'd been so good to her. Just like Manny or her father would have been.

When the baby was here and life was back to normal, she'd cook for him. That is, if he was still in Thunder Canyon.

Maybe she shouldn't hold back her thanks. "I appreciate what you've done for me, Mark."

"No problem." He pulled the jug of milk from the fridge. "You don't have anyone else to look after you."

And neither did he, which was sad, especially since his parents were still alive and nearby.

She realized he was avoiding them, something that didn't feel right to her. She opened her mouth to quiz him again, but thought better of it. For now anyway.

In a day or so, she'd bring it up again, because she intended to learn more about that falling-out they'd had. And given the chance, she would encourage him to mend that rift.

Mark might balk at her interference, but she was only looking out for his own good.

Juliet and Manny might have loved each other and been close, but they hadn't always seen eye to eye. But it was love that held a family together, in spite of the differences of opinion.

If anyone knew how to handle stubborn men when they were wrong, Juliet did. And she knew how to get her point across.

Especially when it was in a man's best interests.

For the next couple of days, Juliet let the subject of Mark's family ride. But on Saturday afternoon, after he'd gone across the street to the inn to check for telephone messages, she realized she couldn't avoid it any longer.

When he entered the apartment, he wore a blue flannel shirt under a brown leather jacket, which he peeled off and hung on the coat tree by the door. "I never could get used to this unpredictable Montana weather. It's supposed to be spring. But I swear we're in for another storm."

"Did you get what you needed at the inn?"

"Yeah." He kicked off his shoes, then checked the thermostat.

"You know," she began. "Something is puzzling me."

"What's that?"

"You told me that after that falling-out you'd made peace with your family."

"We talk." He strode toward the window and peered outside.

"Then why, if your folks own the Big Sky Motel, are you patronizing the Wander-On Inn?"

He turned and crossed his arms. "Because the inn is more convenient. It's in the middle of town."

That might be true. But she knew there was more to it than that. "Have you seen your parents yet?"

His movements slowed; his expression tensed. "No. I haven't had time."

But why had he been able to find time to come into The Hitching Post each evening and chill out at the bar first?

"Have you called them?" she asked.

He shrugged and headed for the kitchen. "I talked to my mother a week or so ago."

"Maybe you ought to drop by the motel for a visit."

"They're pretty busy." He opened the refrigerator and pulled out a can of soda.

"Do you know what I think? That the falling-out isn't over at all."

"So what if it's not?" He pulled the tab and took a long, steady swig before setting the can on the countertop. "Not every family is close, Juliet. And some of us prefer it that way."

"How about your sister? Do you talk to her?"

He stiffened, then touched the hole on the top on the aluminum can, his index finger circling the sharp edge. "My sister is dead."

"I'm sorry. How did it happen?"

He caught her gaze, but didn't speak. His eyes swept down to her lap, where her hands rested around the bulge of her tummy.

He finally said, "It doesn't matter."

"Why not?"

The muscles in his cheek twitched, and his jaw tensed, as though he was holding back.

"Were the two of you close?"

He shrugged again, but the tension didn't leave his face. "I guess so."

Juliet had told him about Manny's death. Her dad's, too. So it seemed only fair to ask. "Was it an accident?"

The question hung in the air, making it hard for Mark to breathe. "Yeah. It was an accident."

And it had been. Sort of. Mark hadn't meant to screw up. But he wasn't going to go there, wasn't going to discuss it with Juliet.

"That's too bad," she said.

Yeah. It was.

She probably figured it was a car accident or something like that. But Mark wouldn't correct her. Hell, even if he felt like opening up, revealing his guilt and pain, an expectant mother sure as hell didn't need to hear how his sister and her unborn baby died during labor.

"If you're the only child your parents have left, I imagine they would welcome a reconciliation."

How could she be so damn optimistic all the time? So naive?

"Things are more complicated than that," he explained. "More complex. And I'd rather not talk about it."

"Families are a blessing, Mark."

Oh, for cripes sake. Why couldn't she just let it go? Quit nagging at him?

He didn't need a ration of guilt to upset his lunch. To ruin a quiet afternoon.

"Why don't you approach them first? Maybe ask them out to dinner?"

Mark bristled. He'd kept his guilty secret bottled up inside for so long that he wasn't going to relive it, not even in dialogue.

"You know what?" he asked her. "I've got cabin fever. Maybe I ought to take a walk before it starts snowing." As he made his way to the door, she followed, grabbing him by the sleeve of his flannel shirt.

"I'm sorry, Mark. I'm just trying to help."

"Well, don't." He raked a hand through his hair. "I need some fresh air."

As he reached the doorknob, she sucked in a breath. His feet slowed, but he kept a forward motion.

"Oh, my God," she said. "Wait."

He turned to acknowledge her voice—not her command—but she was looking down, her lips parted, her eyes fixed on a dribble of water running down her legs.

A gush splattered on the floor, and she looked up at him, eyes wide and frightened. "My water broke."

Chapter Six

Mark wasn't exactly sure what "my water broke" meant, especially when a woman had a good month or so to go. But it couldn't be good.

A jolt of fear shot through him, reminding him of his sister's death, of how he'd failed her. Reminding him of his recklessness. His guilt. "I'll call 9-1-1."

"Doc Emerson told me to call his office if something like this happened."

"Isn't he the guy who had the heart attack?"

She nodded, her eyes transfixed on the floor, on the wet puddle.

"If your doctor is still in ICU, he's not going to be any help. Isn't there someone on call for him?"

"Yes," she said. "But I don't know him very well. Maybe if I go to Thunder Canyon General, Doctor

Hart will be working. I'd feel better if she were in charge."

"I don't care who we see, as long as he or she has a medical degree. Come on." He grabbed her jacket from the coat tree and held it open as she slipped her arms inside. He wanted to bundle her up, even though it wasn't that cold outside, but there was no way he would be able to button it around her stomach.

As he reached for the doorknob, she asked him to wait. "I'd better get some towels to sit on. And the overnight bag. It's already packed and in the closet."

"I'll get them." He wasn't going to waste any time getting her to the hospital. Wasn't going to risk something going wrong before he placed her under a doctor's care.

When Mark had the towels and the gray canvas bag, he opened the door, then paused on the stoop. "Should I carry you down?"

"No. That's okay. The stairs aren't going to be too strenuous for me. The baby is coming now. Let me walk."

He wasn't sure what to do, but at this point, she sounded kind of confident. And since he was scared spitless, he thought it best to defer to her—as long as they were hospital-bound.

Mark followed her down the creaking stairs, his feet hitting the steps like he had on a pair of ski boots. The afternoon sun had broken through the clouds, melting whatever snow had been left the night before. Maybe spring was really on its way. He was ready for green buds, warmer days and the kind of sunshine that made a guy want to be out-doors.

As she reached the white sedan, he opened the pas-senger door and waited for her to adjust the towels. So far, so good.

"Are you sure the baby's coming?" he asked.

"Yes. Once the water breaks, contractions are more or less imminent. And according to the pregnancy book I've been reading, they won't try to stop labor this time."

A million fears hit him in the gut, nearly knocking him breathless, and all he could think of was getting her to the hospital, of passing the baton to medical professionals. Yet at the same time, he wanted to pro-tect her, keep her safe—not an easy task for a man who meant to remain detached.

He circled the car to get in on the driver's side, his heart pounding in his ears, stirring his fear, as well as his reluctance to be involved. He stole a glance at her, saw her pursed lips, her furrowed brow. She had to be more frightened than he was.

As they pulled out onto Main, her breath caught and she rubbed her stomach.

"What's the matter?" he asked, hoping she hadn't heard the panicky edge to his voice.

"I'm having a contraction."

Oh, no. He'd read horror stories of kids being born in taxis and cars. But surely they didn't just pop out. Didn't the labor process take a while?

He glanced at his wristwatch, then stepped on the gas, trying his best to zip through the lazy Saturday afternoon traffic. A lady honked at him, and he had half a notion to flip her off, shake a fist and swear at her. But he had to admit he hadn't seen her vehicle, hadn't realized he'd cut her off.

Damn. He'd better slow down and get his head out of his ass. A car accident wouldn't do Juliet or the baby any good. But he didn't want to waste precious time and found it hard not to speed.

As they turned onto White Water Drive, his pulse seemed to settle into a steady rush, rather than a frantic race. He stole a look at her, saw the apprehension in her eyes.

Do something, he told himself. *Make her feel better.*

Hell, he had to do something to make them *both* feel better. But he didn't have a clue what.

He gripped the steering wheel as though he could control the situation as well as he maneuvered the rented sedan.

Up ahead, he spotted the colorful flags that lined the entrance of Ranch View Estates, the development that she'd pointed out to him the last time they'd traveled this road.

"How big are those homes?" he asked, hoping to stir up a conversation that might take her mind off her worries. Off his, too.

She looked out the window, but her face didn't light up. Not like it had when she'd first made a fuss over the housing development and mentioned that she'd gone to see the models. "I'm not sure. I think the smallest one is about twenty-eight hundred square feet."

"How many bedrooms?" he asked, trying his damnedest to keep the casual conversation going.

"Three to four, I think. The biggest model has a den that can be used as an office or another bedroom."

"Those sure are nice-size lots. I guess a guy would have to buy a good mower."

She nodded, her eyes fixed on something he couldn't see.

But Mark continued to keep up the lame conversation. "And I like the ranch-style architecture."

"Uh-huh."

"It sure would be nice living in a gated community." That is, if he ever got the urge to put down roots. Then it would be nice.

She started rubbing her belly with her hand and breathing weird. Was that normal?

He glanced at his watch again. They'd been on the road for about five minutes. Only three or four more miles to go. Then he could pass the responsibility on to someone else. He tried to think up something else to say, but what was the use? He had a feeling she didn't appreciate his efforts to chat, and they were almost at the hospital.

Moments later, they pulled into the entrance of Thunder Canyon General. By this time, Mark knew the drill, but that didn't make him feel any less nervous. Any less afraid.

As he parked the idling car under the covered portico, Juliet reached a hand across the seat and tugged at the sleeve of his leather jacket. "Thanks for bringing me here."

"No problem."

Had voicing her appreciation been her way of letting him off the hook? Of telling him he could just leave her here?

He hoped so. But he'd wait until he got her settled, until the doctor stepped in and took over. Then he could walk out the door and get on with his life, knowing he'd done his good deed. That he'd made sure at least one pregnant woman had gotten to the hospital safely.

Moments later, Mark brought a nurse and a wheelchair to the car. And for the first time in what felt like forever, he was able to hand over Juliet to someone medically trained. Someone competent.

Still, he followed her and the nurse through the double glass doors, past the security guard. Mark acknowledged the uniformed man, and the guy nodded in return.

While the E.R. clerk handled the paperwork and phoned the maternity ward to give them a heads-up, Mark continued to hang out, to make sure the admission process was complete and that Juliet didn't need him anymore.

"Who's the head of the department?" Mark asked, wanting the best for Juliet.

"Dr. Chester is the head of Ob-Gyn," the clerk responded. "She's out of town on a speaking engagement at the Montana Women's Health Fair. But Dr. Hart is here."

"Oh, good," Juliet said. "I was hoping Dr. Hart would be working."

As long as she was comfortable with the resident, Mark supposed it was okay. But he'd have felt better with the head obstetrician.

Before long, a heavyset man dressed in hospital greens stepped behind Juliet's wheelchair to take her to the elevator and up to the second floor.

She glanced at Mark. "Are you going with us?"

It was just a question, he told himself. Not a request. He could tell her he'd take a rain check this time around. Besides, it was a perfect time to cut whatever flimsy connection they'd built over the past few days, a perfect chance to escape before she expected something from him. Something he couldn't— or wouldn't—provide.

But what if she wasn't out of the woods yet? What if she needed him—or rather someone—to be with her for a little while?

"Yeah," he told her. "I'll stay for a bit."

She nodded, as the orderly pushed her down the hall, and Mark fell into step behind them.

When they reached the heavy double doors that required someone to buzz them in, the orderly pulled the wheelchair to a stop.

"What's the deal with the password and the locked door?" Mark asked.

"A year or so ago, a woman tried to kidnap one of the newborns. She didn't get away with it, but we tightened our security, hoping to prevent something like that from ever happening again." The orderly punched in a code, and the doors swung open.

Mark glanced at Juliet and saw the wide-eyed

expression. Was she concerned that someone might try to take her little one?

"You and the baby will be just fine," Mark told her.

Then he forced a smile, hoping to high heaven that what he'd told her was true.

When Dr. Hart donned a pair of gloves, Mark slipped out of the birthing room. Juliet wondered whether he'd say goodbye before leaving. There wasn't any reason for him to stay, she supposed.

She held her breath, waiting as Dr. Hart examined her.

"You're about two to three centimeters dilated already," the doctor said. "And the head has dropped down nicely."

"But it's too soon for me to deliver." Nervous fear shot through her. "Is the baby going to be all right?"

"I think everything is going to be fine, even though it's more than four weeks early. When you were here last Sunday, we gave you medication to help the lungs develop. And we've managed to keep the baby in the womb for nearly a week. At this stage, every day helps." The doctor placed a hand on Juliet's shoulder. "Don't worry, Mom. We'll do our best to get that baby delivered safely and in your arms."

Juliet wasn't sure if Mark had already left the hospital or if he was waiting outside the room until after she'd been examined. Of course, she couldn't blame him for leaving—if he had. And it was okay. She'd never planned on having a birth coach or anyone to support her during labor.

But when Dr. Hart stepped out of the room and Mark popped his head inside the door, she felt a rush of relief.

He made his way to her bedside. "How's it going?"

"I'm nervous," she admitted. "And scared."

"Are you hurting?"

"It's tolerable."

He took the seat beside the bed. When the back of his chair swayed in movement, a little-boy smile lit his face. "Hey, it rocks."

Before she could respond, Beth Ann, the dark-haired nurse she'd had last time, entered the room. She greeted them, then started an IV and hooked up a monitor to Juliet's tummy.

Mark looked a bit sheepish at first, but before long he was asking questions about the screen that graphed the baby's heart rate and another squiggly line that reflected the length and duration of the contractions.

"What's normal for the baby's heart rate?" he asked Beth Ann.

"She's sleeping, so one-twenty seems to be normal for her. But when she wakes up, that will increase to one-forty or so. And you'll see some little black lines along this area that will indicate her movements." The nurse handed Juliet a remote call button. "I'll leave you two alone for a while. And I'll come back and check on you in about two hours."

"You're leaving for two hours?" Mark stood and raked a hand through his hair. "What if something goes wrong?"

Beth Ann smiled. "We're constantly monitoring

her from the nurse's station. We can see this screen in there. And if anything changes, I'll be right in."

Mark shoved his hands in his pockets. A grimace indicated he wasn't pleased that the nurse was leaving. He slid a look at the monitor.

"Hey, wait," he called to Beth Ann. "There was a little green light that looked like a bell. And now it's yellow. What does that mean?"

"It means that something is happening in one of the other birthing rooms."

"Is someone in trouble now?" he asked.

"It doesn't necessarily mean trouble. It means that something is happening. In this case, the woman in birthing room three is being prepped for delivery."

"Oh." His words indicated understanding, but his expression was clearly one of concern, worry. He glanced at Juliet, a fish-out-of-water expression in his eyes.

She would have loved to have taken a picture of him at that moment, something to keep forever. But another dull pain began in her back, then spread to her stomach, as the womb that had once sheltered her baby began to force the child out into the world.

Juliet closed her eyes, breathing with the contraction like she'd learned from the birthing video she'd checked out of the library. She wasn't sure whether the Lamaze techniques worked or not, but it did keep her mind focused on something other than the pain.

"It's winding down," Mark said, coaching her to hang on, to stay on top.

He'd said he would stay for "a bit," and she appreciated whatever time he shared with her.

But that didn't mean she wouldn't miss him when he decided to leave.

Thirty minutes later, Mark had gotten into the swing of the labor routine. He kept track of the contractions, telling Juliet when to expect another, when a pain was peaking and when it was starting to ease. He even found himself breathing with her, which was probably goofy. But what the heck?

More than once, he thought of his sister, Kelly. Thought of her going through this by herself. Alone. Frightened. In pain. Bleeding.

But if he focused on that, if he allowed the guilt to slip back in, he'd drive himself crazy. So he forced the image from his mind, zeroing in on the petite woman who held his hand and the child who was struggling to be born.

Time was measured by the minute lines on the monitor, as Juliet's contractions came quicker and lasted longer. Still, he repeatedly looked at the clock, hoping the two hours would be up and the nurse would return. Juliet was really hurting, and he hoped they would give her something to ease her pain.

As the door creaked open, Beth Ann entered the room. "I think I'd better check you. Your contractions are getting closer and appear to be quite strong."

"I hope I'm four centimeters," Juliet said. "Dr. Hart said she'd order an epidural then."

Mark stood, but instead of leaving, he pulled the

curtain, giving Juliet privacy. Surprisingly, he was feeling more comfortable about being in the room. And she seemed to be glad he was there and had thanked him more than once.

About an hour ago, she'd asked him to massage the small of her back, something she'd said helped. So they'd fallen into a routine. Each time a contraction started, she'd roll to her side and he'd rub until the pain eased.

"Well, I'll be darned," Beth Ann said.

"What's wrong?" Mark flung back the curtain and stepped forward, just as the nurse was removing her gloves. "That was quick, Juliet. You're almost eight centimeters dilated."

"What's that mean?" Mark asked.

"It means I'm in transition," Juliet said. "And it's too late for an epidural."

"It also means her labor is progressing faster than usual, especially for a first baby. I'd better call Dr. Hart. It could be a quick delivery."

Mark's heart dropped to the floor. The baby was coming?

Now?

The nurse hadn't seemed too worried, but then she was probably trained to stay calm in front of patients. But before Mark could give the scary situation much thought, Dr. Hart entered the room and things began happening at a pretty good clip.

He probably ought to slip out during the hubbub and let everyone do their job, but a particularly hard contraction struck, and Juliet's pain-filled gaze latched onto him like a drowning woman grasping for lifeline.

Mark couldn't move, couldn't leave. As if having a mind of their own, his feet slowly made their way to her bedside. "Hang on, honey. You're doing great. The baby will be here soon."

That ought to be a comfort for her, but it brought on another flurry of anxiety for Mark. Would the baby be okay? Would it have all its fingers and toes? Would they whisk it away to some baby ICU?

He didn't know how much time had passed. It didn't seem like very long to him. All he knew was that Juliet didn't appear to be hurting as bad.

"I feel like I have to push," she said.

"Hold on a minute." Dr. Hart prepared for delivery, then glanced at Mark. "Are you going to stay in here?"

"Who me?" Mark asked.

"I'd…like you…to stay," Juliet said, her voice coming out in huffs and puffs. "If you're…okay with it."

Hell, he ought to escape while he had a chance. But he'd been with her throughout this ordeal. And he'd never been one to cut out in the last ten minutes of a movie—especially one that kept the audience on the edge of their seats.

"Sure," he said. "I'll stay."

Beth Ann got on one side of Juliet and asked Mark to stand on the other. "We're going to help her push."

Help her push? What in the hell had he gotten himself into?

"I'll show you how." The nurse watched the doctor, like a runner on second looked at the third base coach.

"All right," Dr. Hart said. "Let's go."

Mark wasn't sure what was happening, but he stayed by Juliet's side, holding her legs, helping her push and strain. Before long, he could see the dark hair of a little head emerging, and his pulse surged with excitement. "Good job, honey."

About four contractions and a whole lot of pushing later, a tiny baby girl slid into the doctor's hands. She was kind of purple, and her head was misshapen—a scary mess, in Mark's opinion. He thought they ought to hide it from Juliet, but everyone was oohing and aahing, like everything was just the way it was supposed to be.

When the baby let out an angry wail, Mark realized he'd never seen a more beautiful sight. Nor one that was more precious.

"Is everything okay?" he asked, assuming that it was, since everyone continued to smile and make light of the baby's color and the shape of her head.

"They're doing fine." Dr. Hart laid the naked infant on Juliet's stomach. "Do you want to cut the cord, Mark?"

He glanced at Juliet, saw her beaming like a blessed Madonna. He couldn't very well pass on what appeared to be a special opportunity. "Sure."

The doctor handed him scissors, indicating where to cut, and Mark snipped the cord, freeing the tiny baby and making her an individual.

"Time?" Dr. Hart asked, as she continued to work on Juliet.

"Nineteen twenty-eight," another nurse said.

It was enough to make a grown man choke up. God, had he ever felt so blessed to be a part of something so special?

Beth Ann whisked the baby to a little bassinette-type bed. All the while, the little one screamed.

Mark made his way to the infant's side, just to make sure she was all right. Not that he could be of any help, but he wanted to see for himself.

After suctioning out the little mouth, Beth Ann went to work, listening to the tiny chest, among other things. Then she placed the baby on a scale. "Four pounds, eleven ounces."

Was that big enough? Mark wondered. She looked awfully tiny to him.

Beth Ann took a paper tape measure and stretched out the poor little girl, making Mark think of Popeye and Bluto tugging on Olive Oyl as they fought over her.

"Seventeen and a half inches long," Beth Ann said.

"She's petite," Dr. Hart said. "But she sounds spunky."

"Like her mother," Mark said, admiring the tiny head of thick dark hair, the button nose, the rosebud lips. What a precious little face.

He wasn't sure how long he'd stood there, marveling at the baby girl, while making sure she had just the right number of fingers and toes. But he remained long enough for the doctor to finish tending Juliet and for another nurse to put the room back in order, just like there'd never been a delivery.

A young woman with auburn hair entered the room and introduced herself to Juliet as Dr. Hodsman, a pediatrician. Then she proceeded to flip the newborn around like a rag doll, or so it seemed to Mark. He wondered if he ought to say something, tell the doctor to be more careful.

Weren't people supposed to hold a baby's head and neck? Watch out for soft spots? Not that he was an expert.

The pediatrician listened to the little girl's heart and lungs, then bent her legs at the knees and hips. The baby continued to fuss, and Mark couldn't help thinking the doctor might break a bone or pop a joint out of the socket.

"She may be nearly five weeks premature," the pediatrician said, "but her lungs are fully developed. She does have a little foot that turns in, probably because of the way she was curled up in the womb."

Something was wrong with her little foot?

Mark peered into the clear plastic bassinette where the baby lay naked, legs and arms reaching out for someone. Her mom. Or him. But no one seemed to notice.

Her right ankle turned in. Was Juliet's baby going to be crippled? Would she need surgery to correct it?

"It's nothing serious," the pediatrician said. "Her bones are soft and pliable right now. A corrective shoe will straighten it within a few months, but I don't think she'll even need that much treatment."

That was good, wasn't it?

The doctor pulled the foot. "See how easily it bends back to normal? You can work with it, helping it to bend correctly while she's eating or when you're holding her."

Mark glanced at the young mother. Even in her exhaustion, there was no denying her beauty, especially now. "The baby is beautiful, Juliet. Just like you."

"Thank you." She beamed at him, turning him inside out. "I don't know what I would have done without you, Mark."

A warm glow lit his heart, causing his chest to swell as though he'd had a hand in creating a miracle, as though he'd actually done something to bring this precious child into the world.

After the baby had a sponge bath and was bundled up like a little burrito in a flannel blanket, the nurse handed her to Juliet. "Let's try to get her to nurse."

Mark might have stayed for the birth, but he thought it would be best if he slipped out for a while now. "I'm going to get a cup of coffee before the cafeteria closes."

"You may as well get something to eat while you're there," Beth Ann said. "We're having dinner brought up to the new mommy."

"All right. I'll be back, Juliet."

After having the Salisbury steak special and a slice of chocolate cake, he savored a cup of coffee, taking time to reflect on the awesome experience he'd just had.

If Mark were a church-goer, he might whisper a

prayer of thanksgiving. But he wasn't. Still, he couldn't quell a sense of wonder, of awe.

"Hey," he whispered, his voice raspy with emotion. "Thanks. For the miracle."

Then he put his plate, cup and utensils in the plastic receptacle and headed back to maternity to tell Juliet that she'd done a great job. That she'd make a wonderful mother.

When he stepped into the birthing room, the baby was nestled in Juliet's arms. The doctor had gone, and Beth Ann was preparing a little bassinette near the hospital bed.

Mark plopped down on the chair, although he wasn't sure why. Moments later, Beth Ann left them alone.

"Are you going to stay?" Juliet asked.

He glanced up. "Here?"

"You don't have to."

Did she want him to spend the night? He tried to read her expression.

She bit on her lip, then clicked her tongue. "It's just that I was thinking about what the orderly said. About that woman trying to steal a newborn. And I know they've got security and all." She glanced at the sleeping baby in her arms. "But I'm not going to rest very well tonight. I'll keep looking at her, checking to see if she's breathing. Checking to see if she's still here."

He figured it was just a typical case of maternal anxiety. Both mother and child would be safer here than anywhere. But he wasn't going to tell Juliet she was a worrywart. Not after what she'd been through.

"I'm sure you'll both be fine. But I'll stay, if it makes you feel better. And I'll keep an eye on you both."

"Thanks." She offered him an appreciative smile. "It may sound weird, but this is the first time she hasn't really been a part of me. And it will make me feel better if you stayed."

He nodded. "You try to get some sleep. If she cries, I'll wake you."

Juliet chuckled. "If she cries, I have a feeling I'll hear her."

"Maybe so. But just in case, I'll stick around."

She stroked the little girl's cheek, then looked at Mark. "Can you lay her in the bed?"

What?

Hold her?

Well, he supposed it would be tough for Juliet to maneuver. And maybe she wasn't allowed out of bed. "Okay."

Juliet handed him the tiny bundle. The sleeping baby, still warm from her mother's embrace, felt like a bit of nothing in his arms. An empty bundle of flannel.

He tried not to spend too much time fawning over her, marveling over the healthy pink color and the way her mouth made little kissing movements, but it wasn't easy. He actually had to make himself place her in the bed.

Then, without thinking, he brushed a kiss across Juliet's brow, an affectionate gesture he hadn't planned.

It didn't seem to bother her, which he supposed was good.

"Don't worry," he told her.

"I won't." She smiled, then nestled her head into the pillow and closed her eyes.

He watched her for a while, saw her grow easy and suspected she'd fallen asleep. He'd promised to watch over her and the little one.

And he would.

He just hoped to God that he'd been right when he told her not to worry. That nothing would go wrong.

Especially on his watch.

Chapter Seven

Juliet sat up in the hospital bed, a tray of breakfast before her. Mark, bless his heart, had gone to the cafeteria. But he'd stayed with her the entire night.

He had to be exhausted, because each time she'd wakened for a feeding, he'd handed the baby to her.

She couldn't believe how helpful he'd been, how supportive. Nor could she believe how much she'd grown to appreciate having him near. Or how his smile could make her feel as though she didn't have a worry in the world when that wasn't the case. Her finances were still shaky, especially since she would need to hire a sitter after her disability ran out.

The baby whimpered, and Juliet turned to see her daughter scrunch her sweet face. Throughout the night, Mark had called her Sweet Pea, referring to the crawling infant in a Popeye cartoon. But the little girl needed a real name.

Over the past few months, Juliet had tossed around some ideas. At one time, while contemplating girls' names, she'd thought about calling the baby Manuela, after her brother. Or maybe Maria Elena, after her *abuelita*. But before making a final decision, she'd decided to wait until her daughter arrived.

It seemed logical to make sure the baby looked like a Manuela or a Maria before dubbing her with a name that would stick for the rest of her life. And now that Juliet had seen the baby and fallen in love with her, neither seemed to fit.

But around two o'clock in the morning, she'd gotten another idea. Something that felt more appropriate and more fitting.

The door swung open, as Mark entered the room. He carried a newspaper and a disposable cup she assumed was coffee.

"Looks like Sweet Pea is giving you a chance to eat breakfast in peace," he said.

Juliet smiled and glanced at the precious little one lying in the bassinette. "So far so good, but I think she's starting to wake up now."

He made his way to the baby's bedside and studied her while she squirmed. "What are you going to call her?"

Juliet didn't respond until his gaze caught hers. "I'd like to name her after you, Mark. What do you think of Marissa?"

His eyes widened, and his lips parted. "You're going to name her after *me*?"

He seemed genuinely touched, and she was glad. "I'm not sure how I would have managed without you this past week."

Before he could respond further, a blond candy striper popped her head in the door. "Are you finished with breakfast?"

"Yes," Juliet said, taking one last sip of milk.

The bright-eyed teen crossed the room with a spring in her step and picked up Juliet's tray. "Did you hear the news?"

Mark, who'd managed to doff the sentiment from his expression the minute the candy striper entered the room, slipped into reporter mode. "What news?"

"A couple of guys hunting for gold near Turner Grade found several large nuggets. They showed the E.R. staff, and everyone said they were the biggest ones yet." The teenager smiled, revealing a set of rainbow-colored braces. "My grandpa left us a piece of property that used to be a gold mine in the olden days. And my dad is going to get a second mortgage on our house so he can buy the equipment and hire a crew to start working it again."

Juliet glanced at Mark, knowing what he was thinking—that the poor candy striper's father was wasting his time, as well as risking the family's financial security.

Mark didn't comment, didn't deflate the young woman's hope, which was good. And Juliet, who always tried to keep a positive outlook, was glad he'd held his tongue. But she had to admit even she found the man's enthusiasm a bit scary. After all, Mark had been right about something. Most of the gold hunters would end up empty-handed.

"What were the prospectors doing in the E.R.?" Mark asked.

"Apparently, they'd been celebrating their find at The Hitching Post last night. On the way to the parking lot, one of them tripped and cut his hand on a bottle of beer he'd been holding. So he came in for stitches."

"Crazy fools." Mark glanced at Juliet, with a see-what-I-mean look in his eye, which silently pointed out the downside of the gold rush.

It was amazing. Juliet and Mark had actually communicated in a look, a glance. Just like married couples seemed to do.

For a moment, she wondered what had happened between them in the past week. What had changed? Had they forged some kind of a bond? And if so, what direction would their friendship take?

But rather than get carried away, she shrugged off her question, deciding to take one day at a time.

"The E.R. gets a lot of gold-rush related injuries," Mark said.

"They sure do." The candy striper grinned. "Just this morning, someone came in with a gunshot wound."

"That's a lot more serious than a cut or broken bone," Mark said. "Was it another prospector?"

"Uh-huh. My friend is a nurse's aide, and she told

me it was a property dispute or something like that." The teenager lifted Juliet's tray. "Well, I'd better get back to work." Then she left the room and went on her way.

Juliet glanced at Mark, saw his furrowed brow.

Was he contemplating the value of the candy striper's gossip? Or the importance of the land dispute?

"It looks like your story is taking off without you," Juliet said. "Marissa and I are doing okay. Why don't you take some time to yourself?"

"Maybe I will." He glanced at the baby, watched her squirm and fuss. "Mind if I pick her up? I think she's hungry."

Juliet could just as easily take care of the baby herself, but she had a feeling Mark liked being helpful. "Please do."

He held the child against his chest for a bit longer than necessary, which Juliet thought was sweet. That fish-out-of-water expression hadn't completely disappeared, but he'd grown more confident.

"Have a nice breakfast, Sweet Pea." He ran a knuckle along the baby's cheek, then handed her to Juliet. "I'll be back later this afternoon."

"That's fine. Dr. Hart was just here. She wants to keep us at least another night, just to make sure Marissa is nursing well and doesn't develop any problems related to her premature birth."

"Ma-ris-sa," he said, enunciating each sound. His eyes lit up, as he smiled. "I'm not sure if I told you, but I like that. It's a pretty name for a pretty little girl."

Then he grabbed his coffee, rolled up the newspaper and headed for the door. Off to work. Just like a typical new father.

Stop that, Juliet told herself. *Soy la tonta del barrio,* the biggest fool in town.

Mark had been a good friend—that's all. And she couldn't let those kinds of silly thoughts take root.

Lord knew she didn't need to set herself up for any more disappointments in her life.

The newspaper office was located along South Main, just a few blocks from Town Square. It wasn't a big building, but then again, the *Thunder Canyon Nugget* was only a weekly.

Mark had come by twice before, not long after he'd arrived in town. But the publisher and editor, Roy Canfield, had an Out To Lunch sign on the door. And the sign had remained there all afternoon.

But today Mark was in luck—no sign and the door of the white-stucco building was unlocked.

He entered the small front office and caught the heady scent of newsprint and ink.

A heavyset, salt-and-pepper-haired man in a tweed sports jacket sat at a desk near a door leading to the back. His leather desk chair squeaked as he turned from his work. "Can I help you?"

"My name's Mark Anderson. I'm with Golden Eagle News Service. Are you Mr. Canfield?"

"Yes, siree." The sixty-something man stood and reached out a hand in greeting. "But call me Roy."

They shook hands, and Mark cut to the chase. "I

read your latest editorial. In fact, I was a bit surprised that it was so well-written and thought-provoking."

"Because you agree with me? Or because the *Nugget* is just a weekly?" Roy crossed his arms above an ample belly, but his smile indicated he hadn't found the comment offensive.

Mark returned his smile. "Actually, I disagreed with you. And I plan to write a letter in rebuttal."

"Good!" Roy stood as tall as his five-and-a-half foot frame would allow, putting quite a strain on his red suspenders. "I'm always up for a heated debate."

Mark smiled. "I must admit the issue I read was better than I expected."

"I bought the *Nugget* two years ago, after I retired from a big-city press. And I've tried to make it a quality newspaper while maintaining the small-town appeal."

"You've done a good job. I expected to see something about a two-headed cow or a fifty-pound rutabaga."

"That's what I've tried to get away from ever since I bought this rag." Roy's blue eyes glistened. "It's not always easy to find real news in a small town. Do you know what the last editor ran on the front page the day before I took the helm?"

Mark shook his head. "Hard telling."

Roy chuckled, his belly shaking with mirth. "Elmer Godwin, who was suffering from a godawful case of gout, got drunk and, in his frustration over the pain, tried to cut off his big toe and damn near bled to death."

A wry smile tugged at Mark's lips. "Sorry I missed that issue."

"Bet Golden Eagle would have paid you plenty for a newsflash like that." Roy indicated a chair in front of his desk. "Why don't you take a seat? It isn't often we get a hotshot reporter from the city in town."

There was something about Roy Canfield that Mark liked, that he could relate to, although he sure as hell didn't know what it was. The fact that they were both journalists, he supposed.

"I've been sent to write a big spread on the gold rush," Mark told the older man. "But I doubt there's anything worthy of a story."

"You gotta believe, son." Canfield's blue eyes sparkled.

"Come on, Roy." Mark took the seat across from the heavyset older man. "The fortune hunters are spitting into the wind."

"What about those two brothers who found themselves a couple of good-size nuggets yesterday?"

"You mean the two guys who celebrated at The Hitching Post and ended up at the E.R. getting stitches in one of their hands?" Mark clucked his tongue. "Sure, there might be a few nuggets out there. But the real story lies in the broken dreams of those foolish enough to sell their homes and buy prospecting gear, especially when they don't know squat about mining gold."

"You know who Caleb Douglas is?" Canfield asked.

"Yeah. He's a wealthy businessman and cattle baron who's developing that new ski resort."

Canfield nodded. "And right now, the man is more interested in finding the deed to the Queen of Hearts mine."

"I'd heard he was still having trouble locating the deed. Are you saying he's caught gold fever?"

"For years, that boarded up mine was considered worthless, except as a piece of real estate. And more recently, as you probably know, Caleb has been focused on that fancy new ski resort and the groundbreaking ceremony next month. But that's not the case anymore." Canfield leaned back in his chair, leather creaking and wood squeaking as he rocked. "When a couple of squatters began to hunt for gold on Caleb's property, he was concerned about liability, more than anything else. After all, enough of those foolish gold hunters have already ended up at the Thunder Canyon E.R. So he posted No Trespassing signs."

"Makes sense. Besides, any gold on the property belongs to him."

"But now, Caleb realizes that just because the Queen of Hearts played out years ago doesn't mean there's not a new vein."

"Okay," Mark said. "Let's say there is still gold in the Queen of Hearts. How's that going to help all those prospectors combing the hills?"

"It won't. But that's not where your story is, son."

"What do you mean?"

"Yesterday, a squatter challenged Caleb, spouting rumors about mine ownership and questioning who actually had the legal right to run off anyone from the property." Roy leaned forward, resting his elbows on the desk. "If you've kept your ears open, you know there are a lot of rumors about how old Amos Douglas won the Queen of Hearts in a poker game a century or more ago. And there's a lesser known story that some prospector won it back."

"I went to high school in Thunder Canyon, even though I haven't been back in twenty years. So I'm familiar with the rumors. You think there's anything to them?"

Roy shrugged, reached for a pencil and twiddled it through his fingers. "Who knows? Caleb hadn't been able to find the deed before, thinking it just wasn't handy. But since then, he began to hunt diligently, and so far, he's come up empty-handed."

"How about a title search down at the courthouse?"

"He's having trouble with that, too. Especially with Harvey Watson out of town on vacation."

Watson, Mark realized, was the clerk who was trying to computerize the old ledgers.

The semiretired journalist chuckled. "You look bumfuzzled. If I were still at the *Tribune,* I'd probably scoop you on this one. But I'm not."

"What are you thinking?" Mark asked, finding himself interested in the old man's take on the situation.

"If Caleb can't find the deed, it makes me think at least one of those old rumors must be true. That Amos sold off the property, thinking it was worthless. Or that he lost it in a card game. Or that it was stolen out from under his nose." The editor grinned like a cat in an aviary. "And that's where your story is, son."

Mark pondered what the older man had said. And he found his interest stimulated. Maybe Canfield was right. Maybe Caleb Douglas didn't own the property. And if there was a new vein, someone else stood to profit. Someone who might not realize it.

"Well," Roy said, getting to his feet. "I hate to rush you. But I've got to run home and eat lunch. My wife has been on my case. She hates every minute I spend down here, although I think she's more resentful of the money I invested. But what the hell would I do with my time if I retired completely?"

Mark sure didn't know what to tell him.

"The smell of ink is in my blood. I love my work. And I can't see myself on one of those Caribbean cruises she's been pestering me to take, even if I could find the time. I finally got her to take one with her sister, Mildred."

Canfield didn't need to explain. Mark understood how the newspaper got in a man's blood. And how a woman could get upset about the time a man spent away from home.

Hell, Mark had a divorce decree to prove it.

His marriage to Susan, of course, had been years ago. And it hadn't lasted very long. Just long enough for him to learn how unhappy his travels had made a woman whose only goal in life was to create a home and be a mother—until she got fed up and threw it all away.

But that was all right. Mark loved his job, and having a family would have only tied him down.

As he followed Roy to the door, his thoughts

drifted to Juliet and the baby, although he wasn't sure why. Because they'd spent so much time together, he supposed. Because he probably ought to check on them and make sure things were still okay.

"By the way," Roy said, as he flipped over the Out To Lunch sign and locked the door. "Are you the reporter who's been looking after the pregnant waitress at The Hitching Post?"

"Yeah. News travels fast."

"Hey, Thunder Canyon news is my business, even if it isn't Pulitzer material." Roy grinned. "So, did that pretty young woman have her baby?"

"Yeah," Mark said, a warm glow building in his chest. "Juliet had a tiny little girl. Four pounds, eleven ounces."

The older man blew out a whistle. "That's small. Mother and baby doing well?"

"Yeah. They're doing great."

"What'd Juliet name the child?" the editor asked. "I might write up a little blurb for the paper."

"Marissa."

"Pretty name."

"Thanks," Mark said, wondering why he'd felt as though he'd been given a compliment.

Juliet and Marissa stayed in the hospital for two nights and most of the next day. After promising to make an appointment for the baby to see a pediatrician for a weight check in three days, they were released around dinnertime, and Mark took them home.

Then, while mother and baby settled in, Mark went

downstairs and purchased dinner at The Hitching Post, even though he was a bit sick of their meals.

He returned to the apartment and let himself in.

"It's me," he said, setting the bags of food on the table.

"I'm in here," Juliet called from the bedroom.

He entered and found her placing the baby in a secondhand cradle and covering her with a green crocheted blanket. He wondered if she'd brought the cradle from San Diego, but didn't ask. He was too caught up in the scene before him.

Juliet wore a white cotton nightgown, the thin material and the lamplight allowing him a glimpse of her silhouette. The way her breasts seemed fuller, the nipples pronounced. Her belly hadn't gone back to its normal size, yet she looked beautiful standing over the baby's bed, her hair glossy and hanging free.

He scoffed at himself for staring. And for finding her still attractive. "I…uh…got pot roast this evening. And strawberry shortcake for dessert."

"Thanks. That sounds delicious." She cast him a smile, one that lit her face and made him realize how pretty she was without makeup and any special effects.

He raked a hand through his hair and leaned against the doorjamb. "Mrs. Tasker sent up a bottle of sparkling apple cider in celebration."

"That was nice of her."

"She'd also like to come up and see the baby, but I told her tonight wasn't a good time." Actually, he didn't like the idea of having people breathe over the baby. Not yet. She was too tiny, too vulnerable. What if Marissa caught a germ and got sick?

"I'm a bit tired," Juliet admitted. "Tomorrow would be better."

Mark hoped she didn't think he was moving in, or something. He had every intention of taking his shaving kit back to the inn and staying where he belonged. "If you don't mind, I'll join you for dinner. Then I'll head back to the inn."

"All right." Her smile faltered, waned. Was she disappointed that he'd be leaving? Afraid she couldn't handle the baby alone yet?

"Unless you'd rather I stayed one more night," he added.

"No, that's all right. I think we'll be fine." She tucked a strand of hair behind her ear, then glanced at Marissa's sleeping form. "Give me a minute, and I'll be right there."

He nodded, then returned to the dining area. Moments later, she joined him. But she'd slipped on her blue robe and a pair of scruffy white slippers.

Was she getting shy all of a sudden? Or just chilled?

"Should I turn up the heat?" he asked.

"No, I'm not cold."

Okay. So she wasn't wearing the robe to ward off a chill. But Mark let it drop.

They ate dinner in silence, an awkwardness settling over them. Mark didn't have a clue what had caused it. Not exactly. The fact that they'd been playing house maybe. That they'd been a couple for nearly a week. And now playtime was over.

He opened the bottle of sparkling cider and poured them both a glass. Lifting his, he said, "To Marissa."

Juliet clinked her glass against his, then took a sip. He watched the movement of her swallow, admired the shape of her neck, as he had before. Swanlike. Pretty.

She stood and moved toward the bookshelf that held her family photos, then picked one up, communing with her family the only way she could. She lifted another silver frame, then swiped a hand under her eyes. Her shoulders trembled.

Oh, hell. She was crying.

His mind told him to stay seated. To let her grieve alone. To mind his own business. To find a reason to leave. But for some inexplicable reason, he stood and made his way to her side.

"Are you okay?" he asked.

She turned, eyes red and watery. A tear slid down her face. "I'm so sorry they couldn't see Marissa. That they can't be a part of her life."

Mark wrapped her in his arms and drew her close, breathing in the citrusy scent of her shampoo. Offering her his strength. Hoping his embrace was enough.

Her tears continued to fall, so he continued to hold her.

"I'm really sorry," she whispered into his cotton dress shirt, making it warm and moist. "I haven't done this in a long time."

"It's the baby. And hormones," he said, although he had no idea if that were true. It sounded reasonable, he supposed.

His mother used to say that to Kelly, when she locked herself in her room for days at a time. Mark had always figured his sister was depressed because the SOB she'd married had left her barefoot and pregnant. But his parents had been too busy to seek help for her, counseling. Something.

"You're probably right," Juliet said, causing him to wonder what it was that he'd said. "It's normal to have some depression after birth. Some people call it the baby blues."

She sniffled, as if the crying jag were all over.

Whew. This childbirth stuff was so new. So out of his league.

As he loosened his embrace and let her go, she glanced at the bookshelf, ran her hand along a watermark on the wood. "Manny made that stain. He…"

She sniffled again, then batted away a new tear. And then another.

The next thing Mark knew, he was holding her again. And she was trembling in his arms. "Come on, honey. Let's take a walk into the other room."

Of course, the only other room was the bedroom, where Marissa slept. This apartment was so damn small there was no escape from the memories of the past. But maybe the baby would offer her a promise of the future.

When they reached the bed, he used his thumbs to wipe the tears from her eyes. "Why don't you lie down? You ought to rest while the baby is sleeping."

"Will you lie down with me? Just for a minute or two?"

He nodded, willing to do anything to make her feel better. To see that pretty Pollyanna smile again.

"Sure." He joined her on the bed, fully clothed, his loafers still on his feet.

He tried his best to comfort her, as they lay there for the longest time, not talking. Not needing to.

When she finally fell asleep, he continued to hold her.

And he didn't have the foggiest idea why.

Chapter Eight

Juliet slept better than she had in years.

She'd missed human contact, the warmth of a touch, the comfort of an embrace, the steady beat of a heart. So she nestled in a sweet dimension, somewhere between dreamland and reality, relishing a peaceful slumber.

Until Marissa fussed and began to root into the sheets of her cradle.

Juliet opened her eyes, ready to reach for her daughter and feed her. But she couldn't move.

Mark had one arm under her neck and the other around her waist, holding her close.

They'd left a lamp on in the other room, which allowed her to see, and she sought the lighted dial of the clock on the dresser.

Almost midnight.

They'd lain like that for nearly three hours, like lovers. Like husband and wife. New parents.

For just a moment, she let herself go, let herself pretend that Mark loved her, that she loved him in return. And that her daughter had a devoted family in which she could grow up.

But love was a game of pretend Juliet didn't dare play.

"Mark," she whispered softly.

He grunted, then drew her closer. His chin nestled in her hair, the faint mountain-fresh scent of his cologne riding gently in the night air.

"Mark," she said again, this time louder. "I need to feed the baby."

"Huh?"

Marissa let out a cry, and the poor guy nearly jumped through the ceiling.

The mattress wobbled as he braced himself on an elbow and scanned the room. "God, I'm so sorry. I fell asleep. I must have been more tired than I realized."

Juliet smiled, as she climbed from bed and retrieved her hungry daughter. "That's okay."

He glanced at the clock and blew out a sigh. "I guess it's too late to go back to the inn. But I... uh...can go out to the sofa."

She smiled at his sheepish expression, at his thoughtfulness. "Don't bother. Go on back to sleep."

"Are you sure?" He sat on the mattress and glanced at the single loafer he wore, probably wondering where he'd kicked off the other one.

"I'm not sure what's happened between us," she said, as she shushed Marissa. "But it's pretty safe to say we've become close friends in the past week or so."

He raked a hand through his sleep-tousled hair. "I guess you're right."

"So if you don't mind if I nurse her, I don't mind if you're in the same room. After all, you've seen me at my worst."

He kicked off his remaining shoe, which thumped onto the floor, then laid back down, on top of the comforter, and rested his head on the pillow.

As Marissa cried, anxious to eat, Juliet unbuttoned the front of her gown, releasing a breast and offering it to her child. Within moments, the baby latched on. Juliet's milk was just starting to come in—at least she suspected it was. Her breasts were fuller, and Marissa seemed to be swallowing more than she had before.

The lamplight from the living room cast a dull glow through the bedroom door, making it easy to see, easy to marvel at her pretty, dark-haired baby.

Juliet looked over her shoulder, saw Mark lying in bed, eyes open, watching her. She wasn't sure there was much to see, other than an outline of her breast. And interestingly enough, she didn't feel shy or embarrassed.

She felt womanly.

"Do you want me to get you anything?" he asked. "A diaper or a glass of water?"

She offered him a smile that came from her heart. "How did I ever get by without a friend like you?"

He didn't answer. And that was just as well, because the underlying reality echoed in her mind.

Once Mark was gone, she'd have to get by on her own again.

Ever since Mark had fallen asleep with Juliet and wakened with her in his arms, he'd gone back to the Wander-On-Inn each night at bedtime.

In the past, he'd always enjoyed the quiet hours before turning in. But lately, he worried about what was going on at the apartment across the street, about whether Juliet was okay, whether the baby was sleeping longer between feedings.

He supposed Juliet had been right about their friendship. They'd definitely forged some kind of a bond in the past two weeks. A bond that was just as frightening as it was appealing.

Somehow, the pretty young mother had touched his heart—as a friend, of course. And her daughter had done the same thing.

So that was why, a week after Marissa was born, Mark drove Juliet and the baby to the clinic for a weight check.

Juliet had said she could probably drive herself, since she'd had an easy birth and hadn't needed any medication or an episiotomy. But Mark had still insisted on going. To be honest, he wanted to make sure that Marissa was gaining weight and that everything was all right.

He secured the car seat in the back of his rented sedan, while Juliet carried the baby down the steps.

And moments later, they were on their way to the Lone Pine Medical Building, which was located on White Water Drive, just past the entrance to the hospital.

Several different doctors, including Doc Emerson, Juliet's primary physician, housed their offices in a single building that shared a large, single waiting room. A registration desk sat in each open doorway. They signed in at the pediatrician's office and took a seat near the entry.

Their appointment wasn't supposed to take long, since it was with the nurse and not a full-blown checkup.

About ten minutes after they signed in at the pediatric desk, a grandmotherly blonde wearing a blue smock with a Noah's ark print called Marissa's name.

"I'm Karen," she said, as she led them back to a small exam room.

Juliet was asked to undress the sleeping baby— something Marissa didn't like. Her wail of protest soon filled the air.

Karen placed the naked, crying baby on the scale and fiddled with the dial. "There we go. Four pounds, eleven and a half ounces."

Uh-oh. Only a half ounce? That wasn't very much, was it? At this rate, Marissa would be in kindergarten before she hit the ten-pound mark.

"Good job, Mom." Karen picked up the unhappy baby and handed her to Juliet. "She's already regained her birth weight."

"That's good," Juliet said. "She'd dropped down to four pounds, six ounces when we left the hospital."

Oh. So she was making up for lost weight. Mark blew out a sigh. "When do we have to bring her back in?"

The "we" slipped out without him realizing it.

Damn, he was going to have to step back and let Juliet and Marissa get on with their lives. He'd be leaving town shortly—just as soon as he finished the story.

"Since the baby was a good four weeks early and small," the nurse said, "we'd like to see her in another week. But so far, so good. She's doing just great. Do you have any questions?"

"When can she take a bath?" Juliet asked.

"The cord is just dangling. So as soon as it falls off, you can bathe her."

Mark didn't like the thought of the tiny girl in the bathtub. "Isn't she too little for the tub?"

The nurse smiled. "If you don't have one of those plastic baby baths, you can bathe her in the kitchen sink."

"Oh," he said. There was a lot about babies he still didn't know.

The nurse led them to the desk where they could make an appointment. When they settled on next Friday at two, the receptionist said, "There's a ten-dollar co-pay for this visit."

Mark reached for his wallet.

"What are you doing?" Juliet tugged at his shirt-sleeve. "I can pay that."

"I know." But he wasn't going to let her. She had a lot of upcoming expenses—a babysitter, for one. He whipped out a twenty. "Let me take care of this."

The woman at the desk gave him change and they returned to the car. All the while, Marissa made quite a racket, and no amount of shushing or gentle swaying seemed to help.

"Do you mind if I feed her first?" Juliet asked.

"No. Go ahead." Mark hadn't meant to watch, to see her unbutton her pink cotton blouse and offer a breast to the child. But he couldn't turn away.

It's not as though there was anything sexual about it. Well, not really. But the attraction, the appeal, was just as strong, just as powerful.

For a moment, he wondered if he would ever be part of a family—like this one. But he quickly shook off the crazy notion.

After all, he'd *been* married once. To a pretty coed he'd met in college, a homebody with a teaching credential. The kind of woman who wanted to be a mother and create a family. A sweet, twenty-two-year-old redhead who'd morphed into a whiny nag after the first six months. And then she'd offered him an ultimatum—either his marriage or his career.

Mark had told her that he couldn't walk away from the job he loved, especially not while on an assignment. And when he got back to town, she was gone—along with the furniture and all the wedding gifts.

The failure of the marriage had hurt, even though he'd sensed it coming. But he hadn't fought the divorce, letting his ex have all the stuff they'd acquired in the short time they'd been together.

What the hell. He would have had to put everything in storage anyway.

After Marissa had been burped and placed into the car seat, Mark headed home along White Water Drive.

The sky was a vast, springtime blue, and the sun promised to warm the wintry chill in the breeze and carry them to summer. Yet Mark had learned the weather in Montana could turn stormy on Mother Nature's whim.

As they neared the colorful flags that lined the entrance of Ranch View Estates, a hell of an idea began to form.

Mark's accountant had been after him for years to buy a home—as an investment, as a much needed tax write-off. But Mark had dragged his feet.

Hell, he'd let the execs at Golden Eagle know that he was willing to go anywhere the company sent him. So why have a house when he was never home?

Instead, he'd socked away the cash he would have spent on a mortgage and put it into a money market account that had been growing steadily. With his globe-trotting lifestyle, complete with a hefty expense account, he didn't have much opportunity to spend his earnings.

Still, he thought about what his accountant had said.

What if he bought one of those ranch-style houses? Just a small one, of course. He could let Juliet and the baby live there, and she could take care of the property for him—in lieu of rent. After all, he'd be taxed on rental income anyway, wouldn't he?

And she certainly didn't need to be wasting money that was better spent elsewhere. Her wages and tips from The Hitching Post couldn't possibly be very much, and he suspected she would have a difficult time making ends meet, especially if she had to hire a sitter.

And speaking of babysitters, they'd better find someone good. Someone competent. Mark didn't like the idea of just anyone looking after Marissa.

"It's a pretty day," Juliet said.

"Yeah. It is." And it was too nice for her and the baby to stay cooped up in that drab old apartment. "I was planning to go by the museum today. Would you and Marissa like to go with me?"

"Sure. We'd love to. On my days off, I used to spend a lot of time there." She crossed her arms and slid him a questioning look. "But why do *you* want to go to the museum? I thought history didn't interest you."

"Normally, it wouldn't. But I'm looking for information about the Queen of Hearts that will add a little color and flavor the article I'm writing. And while I interview the docent, you and Marissa can wander around and enjoy the place all you want."

"We will." Then she flashed him a pretty smile that turned him every which way but loose.

Damn. He was growing a little too fond of the mother and her baby. Too concerned about their welfare.

It was definitely time to finish his story and get the hell out of Dodge.

The Thunder Canyon Museum was located on two acres of land on Elm Street, in a barn-red clapboard structure that had been a schoolhouse in the late eighteen hundreds. Originally, it had been built in the classic, one-room style, with a foyer/mudroom and big closet in front, the schoolroom in the center and a kitchen/workroom in back.

But over the years, outbuildings had been added until the community outgrew the facility. And when the new schools were built on the other side of town, the historical society had taken over the original structure and created a museum.

From what Juliet understood, townspeople had donated money and different artifacts over the years, which allowed the museum to include various exhibits that showed how the early settlers lived. And the biggest contributor had been Caleb Douglas.

There was also a roped-off area that displayed clothing, accessories and toiletries that once belonged to Lily Divine, the Shady Lady.

Juliet had always found that particular display to be the most interesting. Or maybe it was the woman's occupation as a saloon owner and possibly a madam that set her curiosity soaring. She wished she could have met Lily. And that she could have lived in the late nineteenth century.

That period in history had always fascinated her, which was why she'd spent so much time at the old schoolhouse museum.

And on each visit, she'd enjoyed her many chats with the various docents, all volunteers and members of the Thunder Canyon Historical Society. In fact, she'd even thought about joining the interesting group.

As Mark parked the sedan on the side of the building, Juliet spotted the old shed-style barn in back. It didn't look like much now, but on her last visit one of the docents had mentioned a plan to make it into a blacksmith exhibit. Juliet thought it would make a nice addition.

She got out of the car, and as she opened the passenger door to take Marissa from the car seat, a soprano voice sang out.

"Yoo-hoo! Mark Anderson, is that you?" A heavyset woman in a yellow, floral-printed dress wiggled her fingers in greeting.

Mark made his way toward the smiling matron. "Yeah. It's me, Mrs. Eagleston."

"Why look at you. All grown up. Of course, I would have known you anywhere, even if your mother hadn't told me you'd come into town on that big assignment. She's so proud of you."

"You're looking well, Mrs. Eagleston."

"Well, thank you, Mark." She fingered the side of her lacquered hairdo, where mousy-colored strands had been swept into a beehive. "But after all these years, you'll have to drop the formality and call me Gladys."

Mark smiled, yet his iceberg stance convinced Juliet that he wasn't happy about seeing his mother's friend.

Juliet pulled Marissa from the car seat and adjusted the blanket, blocking the sunshine and the cool breeze from her face.

"I'll bet your folks were tickled pink to see you," the older woman said.

Mark didn't respond.

Because he had yet to visit them, Juliet suspected. And apparently, the Andersons hadn't told their friend that he hadn't. Were they all pretending that a falling-out hadn't occurred? That everything was fine? And that their family interactions were normal?

"I hope that new medication helps your father's arthritis. It's a shame that he's had to quit bowling. He and your mother used to enjoy the Wednesday evening Gutter Busters. And I gotta tell you, we all miss them. Jess and Anne-Marie were a hoot to bowl with. Of course, they still come watch. But it's not quite the same."

Mark maintained a detached smile.

Juliet wondered if Gladys knew about the family rift, if she'd noticed the lack of warmth and affection in Mark's voice or if she suspected his discomfort when talking about his parents.

It broke Juliet's heart to think Mark was going to allow that estrangement to continue. Especially when she'd give anything to have her family back.

Mark didn't appear to appreciate what he had—two parents, Jess and Anne-Marie Anderson, owners of the Big Sky Motel. A couple who enjoyed bowling on Wednesday nights, a man and woman whose friends thought they were a hoot.

Had Mark even known that his mother was proud of him? Or that his father suffered with arthritis?

"Well, it was good to see you, Gladys." Mark placed a hand on Juliet's shoulder. "But we'd better get the baby inside."

"The baby?" The older woman brightened and edged closer to Marissa. "Oooh. Can I take a little peek?"

"Of course." Juliet unfolded the blanket to reveal her daughter's face.

"Well, bless my soul. What a beautiful baby. And such a tiny one. A preemie, it looks like. How much does she weigh?"

"Four pounds, eleven and a half ounces," Mark said. "And we really ought to get her inside. It's a bit breezy out here."

"Of course." Gladys studied Juliet. "I'm afraid I haven't met your wife, yet."

Mark's hand, which had warmed Juliet's shoulder, dropped to his side. "She isn't my wife. This is Juliet Rivera. A friend."

"Oh," Gladys said, her eyes growing wide. "You're the waitress at The Hitching Post, aren't you?"

Juliet nodded.

"It's nice to meet you dear." The breeze whipped a strand of hair from Gladys's upsweep, and she batted it away. "For a moment, I thought I'd have to get after Anne-Marie for not telling me she was finally a grandma."

Mark threw back his shoulders like a Buckingham guard with hemorrhoids. "Take care, Gladys." Then he ushered Juliet and the baby out of the parking lot and to the museum.

Juliet opened her mouth to complain, to tell Mark that he could have been nicer to the lady, but she bit her tongue, deciding to put some thought into her comments, especially since she intended to help him mend fences.

Mark had made his parents sound like ogres. But after listening to Gladys, that hardly seemed the case.

Juliet would do whatever she could to help him make things right. After all, it was the least she could do. Mark had proven to be a good friend.

A very special friend.

Or was it more than that?

The kiss they'd shared crossed her mind, as did the night he'd slept by her side, arms holding her as though they'd become much more than friends. But as pleasant as that thought was, she shoved the possibility aside.

The kiss as well as the embrace had only happened once.

Mark hadn't ever kissed her again. And the morning after they'd slept together in her bed, he'd moved back to the Wander-On Inn as soon as the sun rose.

No, Mark wasn't into families and commitments. He loved his job and traveling on assignment. And he'd made no secret that once his work was through he'd leave Thunder Canyon for good.

Before long, he'd leave Juliet behind.

Just as he'd left Jess and Anne-Marie Anderson.

Chapter Nine

As Mark and Juliet entered the building through the front door and stepped into a reception area that had once been the old mudroom, he caught a musty whiff of worn fabric, old paper and faded memories.

They continued to the central part of the museum, which had been the original schoolroom. The windows had been closed up and walled over. And two rooms had been added to each side.

Through the open doorway on the left, Mark could see a display of gold panning equipment and what looked like Native American relics.

He ought to head for the gold mine and prospecting display, but his feet didn't move. Instead, he studied Juliet.

With the baby in her arms, she moved slowly

through the room, browsing various display cases and wearing a smile that only a history buff could appreciate—or a man who found the beautiful young woman intriguing.

Mark might not share her interest in antiques and dusty exhibits of outdated memorabilia, but he enjoyed watching her run a hand lovingly over a glass case, seeing interest light her eyes.

"Folks, I'll be with you in a minute," a man's voice called from the back. A familiar voice?

"All right," Juliet responded. "We'll make ourselves at home, Ben."

Ben Saunders?

Mark's old high school teacher? Now there was a *real* history nut. And just the guy Mark needed to talk to.

"Why, Juliet Rivera," Mr. Saunders said, making his way from the back room to the center of the museum. "I didn't expect to see you so soon after your baby's birth. The last time I stopped by The Hitching Post, Martha Tasker told me you had a little girl and were on maternity leave."

Obviously, Juliet hadn't been kidding about spending a lot of time in Old Town. And at the museum.

"Did you bring that little baby to get her first taste of Thunder Canyon history?" Mr. Saunders asked.

"I sure did." Juliet cast a loving smile on the baby she held in her arms. "But she'll probably sleep through it."

Mr. Saunders laughed, still unaware that Mark was in the room, and peered at Marissa. "I heard she was a few weeks premature, but I had no idea she was so small. Or that she was just as pretty as her mama."

Ben Saunders hadn't changed much, Mark decided, even though the former high school teacher was probably pushing seventy. He'd grown a bit heavier, and his hair had turned white. But he seemed just as friendly with those who shared his interest in history.

In the classroom, Mark hadn't been one of them.

When Saunders finally scanned the room and spotted Mark, recognition flashed in his eyes. "Why if it isn't one of my old students. Mark Anderson. The cocky kid who used to sit in the back row and shoot spitballs when I wasn't looking."

Mark grinned. He'd never been caught in the act. But he'd had a feeling Mr. Saunders had figured out who the culprit had been. "How do you do, sir?"

As they shook hands, Mr. Saunders beamed. "You know, it didn't surprise me when I heard you became a reporter."

"Why's that?" Mark asked.

"You wrote a heck of a paper on the devastating effects gold rushes have had on some people, especially the Indians and the Chinese. It was more like an exposé than a report. And I knew you had real talent putting your thoughts into words."

So, his former history teacher had remembered his work. Mark couldn't help a soaring sense of pride in a ten-page paper he'd thrown out years ago. "I'll admit full responsibility for the paper, sir. But not the spitwads. I can't remember anyone in my class doing something so tacky and disrespectful."

"Well, I can. Sometimes I'd go home and find one stuck in my hair." Mr. Saunders chuckled. "Would you like a private tour of the museum? Or do you want to wander around on your own?"

"Juliet may want to wander, but I'd like the tour. I have some questions I'd like to ask you about the Queen of Hearts."

"I'll tag along, too," Juliet said, holding the sleeping baby in the crook of her arm. "It's always so interesting when you share those tidbits of Thunder Canyon history."

"Great." Mr. Saunders took them through the museum, stopping at each roped off section. They saw a typical parlor, the replicated interior of a one-room pioneer home and a fancy bedroom suite made out of mahogany, complete with a heavy, four-poster bed, matching bureaus, chairs and a vanity. A velvet patchwork quilt covered the mattress.

"This bedroom set was donated by the Douglas family," Ben said. "Notice the fine workmanship, the detail in the pineapple finials."

"It's beautiful." Juliet stroked the grain of the wood.

"This furniture belonged to Amos and Catherine Douglas," the older man added. "And it once graced a guestroom at the Lazy D."

Mark paused, not ready to move on. "Speaking of Amos Douglas, how did he really acquire the Queen of Hearts?"

"Well," Ben said. "There are several legends, none of which has been proven. Most people believe Amos won the property in a poker game from a prospector with a drinking problem."

"And what about you?"

Ben smiled. "I favor the story about him winning it from a renegade outlaw."

That one was new to Mark. "Which outlaw?"

"A redheaded fellow folks claimed was as crazy as a patchwork quilt." Ben chuckled. "Of course, in this day and age, we'd probably say he suffered from post-traumatic stress syndrome, caused by cruelties of the Civil War."

Mark's interest piqued. "Tell me about him."

"Crazy Red Phelps was once a Confederate soldier who fought alongside the Rafferty brothers, a couple of natural born hell-raisers who didn't care whether the war was over or not. They formed a ragtag outfit of renegade soldiers and vigilantes, but that didn't last long. They soon moved on to robbing trains and banks in Colorado."

"I've heard of the Rafferty gang," Juliet said. "They weren't as big or well known as Frank and Jesse James or the Daltons, but they did their share of robbing and killing."

"That's right." Ben tugged at the waistband of his slacks. "Crazy Red and Bobby Joe Rafferty, the head of the gang, fell for the same woman, a widow named Sally McKenzie who ran a stage stop about fifty miles outside of Denver. The fight over the woman created some bad blood between the two, and a shoot-out resulted."

"Who won?"

"Sally, if you ask me." Ben chuckled. "When Crazy Red shot Billy Joe between the eyes, she pulled out her shotgun and blasted Crazy Red in the shoulder, then ran him off. He went on to pull a few armed robberies by himself and eventually ended up in Thunder Canyon, looking for gold and a piece of the action."

"And you think Crazy Red got a hold of the Queen of Hearts?" Mark asked.

"An old newspaper quoted Crazy Red as claiming the mine rightfully belonged to him. And that he meant to have it, one way or another."

"And you believe the claim of a thief who'd been dubbed with the nickname of Crazy?"

"Nope. But he was the kind of man who might have stolen the deed." Ben slipped his hands into the pockets of his gray dress slacks. "And that could explain why Caleb Douglas can't find it."

Before Mark could respond, the telephone rang.

"Excuse me," Ben said. "I need to answer that."

Juliet, who held Marissa with one arm, tugged at Mark's shirtsleeve, a habit that always amazed him. Why didn't she just grab his hand or touch him?

"I want to show you something." She led him to the small room with the Shady Lady display and pointed to a tall case that held a mannequin wearing a faded red satin dress with a scooped neckline and trimmed with black lace. "That dress belonged to Lily Divine, the original owner of the Shady Lady saloon."

Several ropes of fake pearls looped around the

mannequin's neck, and a big black ostrich feather adorned the fake hair.

"I like the black fan the mannequin is holding," Juliet added. "See the workmanship? It's edged with chantilly lace and a purled braid."

She sure knew her history of ladies doodads.

"And look at that." Juliet nodded at the display case, where several colored bottles and a powder puff sat among other personal items once used by the notorious lady. "See the tortoise shell comb with a gold floral design and studded with rhinestones? Isn't that pretty?"

"I guess so, but I think those black garters are more interesting." Mark nodded toward the mannequin, who held up the hem of her red skirt, revealing red and black petticoats and a black silk garter with a gilt buckle and roses made out of ribbons. "The Shady Lady must have been one sexy woman."

Juliet swatted at him, grazing his arm and making him yearn for more of her touch. When she laughed, the lilt of her voice settled over him like fingers on an angel's harp. "You would find her undergarments intriguing."

"You're right about that. I don't know why she didn't wear those garters in the portrait that's hanging over the bar at The Hitching Post."

Juliet smiled impishly. "She probably knew the men would find her more appealing with that bedroom smile and only that gauzy thing draped over her."

Mark slid her a crooked grin. "Not me. I'm a black garter man."

Juliet arched a brow, brown eyes glimmering.

Was she making note of that tidbit of information?

He hoped so, then admonished himself for allowing his thoughts to drift in a sexual direction. For cripes sake, she'd just had a baby. And even if she hadn't, they were just friends.

"You know," Juliet said, "Lily Divine was an enterprising woman in her day. And I find her fascinating."

"Me, too," Mark said. Because she ran a whorehouse and a saloon, profiting from a man's lust. "But why do you find her so interesting?"

"Mr. Saunders told me that she was considered a troublemaker in her day. But I think that's probably because she was involved in the fight for women's suffrage."

"Well, that makes sense. I'm sure she had an interest in women's rights, especially since she was a businesswoman. After all, she owned the hotel, as well as the saloon. And then there was that private business she ran upstairs."

"Lily was only suspected of being a madam, since the previous owner of the saloon had run a brothel," Juliet argued. "No one really knows for sure. But I have a feeling that, more than anything, her forward-thinking caused folks to look down on her."

Before they could continue the conversation, Ben returned. "I'm sorry for the interruption. That call was from Matilda Matheson, an elderly lady who has a trunk full of memorabilia in her attic. She would like to make a donation, if we're interested."

"Is she bringing it in today?" Juliet asked.

"Oh, no. Tildy has arthritis and doesn't venture far from her house. And even if that weren't the case, she can't donate anything until her niece takes time to climb into the attic and go through the trunk."

"What's in it?" Juliet asked, obviously interested.

"Tildy can't remember," Ben said, with a chuckle. "Bless her heart."

Eager to get back to the discussion of the gold mine, Mark asked, "So who do you think is the legal owner of the Queen of Hearts?"

"Most of the rumors don't amount to much. And even if Crazy Red ran off with the deed, the old archives ought to prove that the title wasn't ever transferred properly. So I have to believe the mine was handed down to Caleb. And from what I understand, he's hired a lawyer to defend his claim."

Caleb certainly had the money to put up a legal fight for the land.

"Of course," Ben added, "Some of the old-timers would like to see Caleb Douglas get his comeuppance. But as far as the Thunder Canyon Historical Society and the museum go, we appreciate his generosity in helping us preserve our early history."

Mark and Juliet completed the tour, but instead of finding answers, Mark was left with more questions.

But one thing was true. Roy Canfield, the editor of the *Nugget* had been right. The real story revolved around the deed of the old gold mine.

And Mark planned to find out who really owned the Queen of Hearts.

* * *

"Do you mind if we stop at Super Save Mart on the way home?" Juliet asked.

"No. Not at all." Mark pulled out of the museum parking lot onto Elk, then turned south on Pine.

Juliet planned her speech carefully, trying to maneuver the conversation in the direction she wanted it to go. "Your parents sound like nice people."

"I suppose so." His eyes remained focused on the road.

"Maybe we should pay them a visit. Marissa and I could go with you. I think it would be a nice outing."

"Not today."

She slid a glance at him, saw that same hardened expression he'd worn when Gladys discussed his parents. But Juliet wasn't afraid to stand up to him. To push when necessary. "Maybe another day, then."

He didn't answer, and she realized he wouldn't commit. And that he had no intention of discussing his family situation with her.

Juliet was trying to be sensitive to his feelings. She really was. But his stubborn side was frustrating her to no end.

"I've never bowled," she said. "But it sounds like a lot of fun, especially in a league called the Gutter Busters. Maybe we could go watch some Wednesday. Or even play a game or two."

"I used to bowl once in a while," Mark said. "But I play golf now, whenever I get a chance. And the pro who gave me some pointers said the bowling was affecting my swing."

She wasn't sure if she wanted to prod him further or throw something at him. But she let it go.

For now.

Moments later, they parked in front of the grocery store. This time, Mark carried the baby, while Juliet filled the cart with things she needed to prepare a special dinner. She didn't know about Mark, but she was getting sick and tired of The Hitching Post meals. And even if she weren't, she didn't like him paying for everything.

She hadn't made a list, so they wandered from aisle to aisle, picking up pinto beans, rice and tortillas.

In the produce section, she selected tomatoes, green chilies, cilantro and onion. And in dairy, she grabbed a half gallon of milk, sour cream and a bag of Monterey Jack cheese.

As they neared the butcher case, a woman wearing an oversize black sweatshirt with a sunflower appliqué gasped and placed a hand on her chest.

Was something wrong?

The woman's gaze had locked on Mark's, and subsequently, so did Juliet's.

"Hello, Mom."

"Hi, Mark."

Juliet froze, a package of chicken breasts gripped in her hand. She studied mother and son, saw their tension-filled stances, felt the awkwardness. And it broke her heart. The reunion should have been exciting, something worthy of a hug, a bright-eyed smile.

"I...uh...was hoping you'd come by the motel," Mrs. Anderson said. "We've missed you. We both have."

"I've been busy."

The woman's eyes dropped to the bundle of pink flannel Mark held. Then she glanced at Juliet, a hundred questions in her gaze.

"This is my friend," Mark said. "Juliet Rivera."

"How do you do?" The woman reached out a hand. Her eyes begged for answers, for more of an explanation, for something Mark wasn't providing her. But she remained silent. Watery eyes told Juliet she was hurting, but not because Mark's presence had disturbed her.

"This is Juliet's baby," Mark said. But he didn't unwrap Marissa. Didn't reveal her sweet face.

Juliet stepped forward and withdrew the edge of the pink flannel blanket. "Her name is Marissa. And she's a week old today."

Mark's mother smiled, sentiment glistening in her eyes. "What a precious baby."

"She certainly is. Thank you." Juliet should have been pleased that Mark had introduced them, but she suspected he'd merely meant to avoid any of the questions that hung in the air.

How have you been?

Why haven't you called?

When will we see you again?

"I was just picking up things to make a special dinner to celebrate Marissa's birth," Juliet said. "Do you like Mexican food, Mrs. Anderson?"

"Yes, I do." The woman's green eyes grew wide and bounced from Mark to Juliet and back again. "My husband and I don't get a chance to eat it very often, especially when it's homemade. Having been brought up in Texas, we miss a good Mexican-style meal."

"Then maybe you'd like to join us for dinner," Juliet said.

Mark tensed.

"Why…" The woman paused, then looked at Mark as though wanting him to second the invitation.

He held his tongue.

Juliet wanted to kick him in the shins. Couldn't he see the woman was hurting? Maybe more than he was?

"My husband isn't feeling well," Mrs. Anderson said. "Perhaps another time."

"Of course." Juliet offered her a sincere smile, which was far more than her son had offered.

As Mrs. Anderson turned to leave, Juliet stopped her. "Wait, please." She reached into her purse, pulled out a slip of paper and a pen, then jotted down her telephone number. "Let me know when your husband is feeling better."

The woman took the paper, holding it close. In that moment, Juliet knew they'd all been hurt. Deeply. And by something she didn't understand. Something that needed to be fixed.

"Well, I'd better get back to the motel," Mark's mother told him. "Your father is working the front desk by himself, and it's been very busy today."

Mark nodded. "I'll stop by and see you before I leave town."

"Please do." Mrs. Anderson's lip trembled, then she looked at Juliet. "It was nice meeting you. And I *will* give you a call."

Juliet flashed her a sincere smile.

Then the woman pushed her empty cart away.

Mark's jaw locked, like the Tin Man's after a heavy rain.

But Juliet had a feeling he might not be silent when they got back to the car.

Chapter Ten

Mark gripped the steering wheel and stared straight ahead. He didn't want to fight with Juliet, but he didn't want her getting chummy with his folks, either.

Not while he was still in town.

He wasn't up for a family reunion. Not yet. And maybe not ever.

"I didn't mean to put you on the spot," Juliet said. "Are you angry with me?"

"No, not really." He was just frustrated, especially since he refused to share enough of his past to make her understand.

Years ago, Susan had tried to push him to reconcile with his family before their wedding, since Mark had refused to invite his parents.

"I don't want to chance ruining a day that's supposed to be happy," he'd told her.

Like Juliet, his fiancée hadn't understood the falling-out and had thought the absence of the groom's family would look weird to people. When Mark had finally leveled with her, opening his guts and explaining why he and his parents didn't have a close relationship, she'd backed down.

It might have been his imagination, but she'd never seemed to look at him the same after that. So, from then on, he'd intensified his resolve to keep his shameful secret to himself.

Still, Mark didn't want something from the past to affect his relationship—or rather his friendship—with Juliet. "It's your apartment, and you can socialize with anyone you want. But I don't appreciate you inviting my parents to dinner without talking to me first. That's all."

She nodded, as though she actually understood his feelings rather than the filtered half-truth.

"I'm sorry it bothered you." Juliet turned in her seat, facing him. "I should have waited to say something. But your mother seems very nice. And since I'm a new resident of Thunder Canyon, I like meeting people who live in the community."

He could understand that, but he still didn't like being pushed. Forced to do something that chapped his hide. "Why don't you invite my parents to dinner after I'm gone?"

She didn't respond right away, which made him think the conversation had died a slow death. Thank

God. But as they neared The Hitching Post, she brought it up again. "I wish you weren't so stubborn."

He bit back a hard-ass retort. It wasn't Juliet's fault that he didn't want to be around his parents. Well, his father, anyway. And she had no inkling of the kind of cruel accusations that had been slung at Mark years ago, accusations that still hurt, that still echoed in his mind.

You no good rebellious bastard.

You son of a bitch.

You let your sister die.

You killed her.

Get the hell out of my house. And don't ever come back.

To this day, he could still feel the grief, the guilt, the pain of rejection.

There probably weren't too many sixteen-year-olds who, after an outburst like that, would've dropped their heads and plodded to their rooms with their tails between their legs.

Mark certainly hadn't.

He'd thrown a few belongings into a knapsack, grabbed his jacket and stomped off into the stormy night, determined to either escape the godawful guilt or die in the process.

But he hadn't done either.

Around midnight, the sheriff found him thumbing a ride out of Thunder Canyon, sopping-wet and chilled to the bone.

"I can't believe you'd run off at a time when your family needs you," the uniformed officer had said.

Mark clamped down his shivering teeth, refusing to say anything in his own defense. And after a speech about minors and curfews, the sheriff had taken him back home.

It didn't take an honor student or an Eagle Scout to figure out his dad wasn't particularly pleased to see him walk in the front door, even though he hadn't said a damn thing. The hateful scowl his old man had worn was an image Mark would never forget.

"Sorry to hear about the loss of your daughter," the sheriff had told his parents. "It's a damn shame."

Jess Anderson had merely grunted, then climbed into the old family station wagon and driven down the mountain to the motel, where he'd holed up until the funeral.

His mother had burst into tears again, leaving Mark to face the sheriff alone. He'd actually wished the police officer would have pressed charges against him. Manslaughter. Negligent homicide. Something.

But he hadn't.

Still, every time his old man looked at him, each time his mother went into his sister's empty room and cried, whenever someone in the community whispered behind Mark's back, a gavel in his head pounded out his guilt.

And he couldn't blame them. It had been a tragic, rebellious mistake that couldn't be corrected.

Mark slid a glance at Juliet, and a jab of remorse struck him in the chest. She didn't know the demons he wrestled with, and he damn sure wasn't about to reveal them to her. But she didn't deserve the harsh words he'd lashed out at her. "I'm sorry, but my dad made it clear years ago that I was a disappointment to him. That he wanted me out of his house and his life for good."

"Maybe time has changed things."

"Not my memory."

"What about your sister's memory?"

His heart pounded in his chest, and his hands grew clammy as they gripped the steering wheel. "What about it?"

"Did your sister find it hard to forgive and forget, too?"

Juliet had no idea how badly the past haunted him. But he wouldn't let on. He couldn't. "No, my sister always got along fine with my parents. They favored her."

And he could now understand why. Prior to her wedding, she'd always done whatever they asked, whatever was necessary to keep the home fires burning while they worked at the motel from dawn to dark.

On the other hand, Mark had resented being stuck on the mountain, so far away from town, especially when his dad could have made life easier by living within city limits.

"I'm sure your parents miss her," Juliet said.

No doubt about that. His mom had been looking forward to being a grandma, even if Kelly wasn't too keen on being a mother. But Mark didn't want to go there, didn't want to encourage Juliet's curiosity.

"And since you're all they have left," she continued, "I'm sure they'd welcome a reconciliation."

"For cripes sake, Juliet. You don't know them. You don't know me. You don't know anything about what tore our family apart."

"You're right," she said. "But I'm just trying to help. Sometimes getting things out in the open gives a person a new perspective."

He felt badly about snapping at her, but wouldn't apologize. Why encourage her to push harder, to probe deeper? So he held his tongue, hoping to assuage the guilt. Hoping to end the conversation. But Juliet's eyes drilled into him, lancing the wound and releasing a brand-new assault of pain, guilt. Regret.

"What did they do to hurt you like this?" she asked. "To make you hold a twenty-year grudge?"

"They didn't do squat."

"Then did you do something?"

The truth of her question pierced him to the bone, but he refused to answer. "I'd rather not talk about it."

"Why not?"

"Dammit, Juliet. Would you get off my case?"

The words had no more than left his mouth, when he cringed at the sharp edge, at the bark, at the way he'd hurled them at her.

God, she wasn't going to fall apart on him and start sniffling, was she? He hoped not. He didn't deal well with tears—especially when he couldn't tell if they were real or fake. Susan, his ex, had been able to shed tears on demand.

When he snuck a glance across the seat, Juliet's gaze slammed into his.

Sharpened flecks of topaz blazed in her eyes, as she

pointed a finger at him and raised her voice. "Don't talk to me like that. I only meant to help. Not stir the guilt you feel."

So much for expecting her to fall apart.

He stole a glance in the rearview mirror, wondering how she'd come to that conclusion. Had she read the shame in his expression or his mind?

"If they didn't do squat," she pressed, "then I'm led to believe you're the one who's responsible for the rift."

"Yeah. In a way, I am."

"Your mother is hurting," Juliet said. "And you're hurting, too. Only you're covering it with anger and an I-don't-give-a-damn attitude."

She was probably right about his mom. And about him, too. But he wasn't going to discuss what happened that night, nor was he going to relive it.

On his eighteenth birthday, he'd finally left that mountaintop prison Jess and Anne-Marie Anderson called home, hitched a ride to the bus depot and took the old gray dog to Bozeman.

Before this damned assignment, he'd never looked back. And resurrecting old memories and pain wasn't something he intended to do now. Leaving home, leaving Thunder Canyon, had kept him from drowning in guilt. From reliving that fateful afternoon when a selfish decision on his part had led to his sister's death.

He slid another glance at the young woman across the seat, saw her furrowed brow, the pretty lips turned into a frown.

She had to know he was looking at her, but she didn't respond.

Well, so what?

He didn't need her sympathy.

Or her unspoken verdict.

When they arrived at her apartment, she maintained her silence, striking another blow to their friendship—or whatever the hell it was.

And right now, a bus ticket to Bozeman looked pretty damn appealing.

As soon as Mark had escorted Juliet and the baby inside the apartment, he left.

He hadn't said where he was going, and she hadn't asked. Nor had she mentioned her frustration, which was out of character for her.

Juliet had never been one to mince words when it came to expressing herself or her emotions. Feelings existed, and she didn't make a secret of hers.

Like her *abuelita,* she was quick with a hug when she felt love and affection. And she had no problem voicing an objection when crossed or slighted.

But this was different. She found it difficult to understand what had caused the ache in her chest or the tears that welled in her eyes. And she couldn't explain the guilt she felt over losing something she'd never really had.

This cold war she and Mark had silently declared made her uneasy and sad. And that didn't make much sense.

After all, Mark planned to leave Thunder Canyon as

soon as his story was finished. Only the town fool, *la tonta del barrio,* would expect their relationship to continue. Besides, she'd only known him for a couple of weeks. The secretive man was still a stranger in many ways.

So why did it bother her to think she'd lost his friendship?

Surely it wasn't because she'd fallen in love with him. She knew better than to let herself do something that crazy.

She just didn't like seeing him hurt, that's all. He'd proven to be a good friend—her only friend right now. And she'd only meant to help him in return. That's why she'd tried to get him to reconcile with his family.

Okay, so he'd been right. It wasn't her business. And her efforts had backfired. She knew better than to push him any more than she had.

But she cared for Mark, more than she dared admit—even to herself.

A *lot* more.

Oh, *Dios mio.*

Was it possible? Was she falling in love with the tortured, cynical reporter who had stepped in when she needed a friend the most?

It sure felt that way.

Great. Just what she needed. Another absent loved one.

Juliet put away her groceries—all but the items she needed for dinner—then soaked the pinto beans in a pot of water. Before she could do anything more,

Marissa began to cry, announcing it was chow-time again and causing Juliet to prioritize.

Her baby needed her, and their mother-daughter relationship was the only one that mattered.

For the past twenty-five years, Juliet had gotten along fine without Mark Anderson in her life. She could certainly survive the loss of his friendship, even if that meant never seeing him again, never seeing that teasing, flirtatious glimmer in his eyes, the way his lips quirked in a rebellious grin. Never hearing his graveled voice, his baritone laugh.

Grief and regret tore deep in her heart.

But she wouldn't let it mar her future or that of her daughter.

After feeding Marissa and getting an extraloud burp, Juliet laid the baby in the cradle she'd purchased at Second Chances, the thrift store down the street, and covered her with the light green *covijita*.

She marveled at the precious miracle that grew bigger each day and whispered a prayer of thanksgiving. Then she caressed her daughter's head, felt the downy fine hair. *Duerme bien, mi angelita.*

After leaving the bedroom and entering the kitchen, she put the beans on to cook, and lost herself in the sounds and aromas of a meal meant to be therapeutic. All the while she hummed a medley of mariachi tunes that *Abuelita* used to sing.

She prepared several chicken breasts, soaking them in a sauce of tomatoes and chilies, taking care to make the salsa especially mild. The lactation expert at the hospital said that if a food made Juliet gassy, it would probably do the same to the baby. Of course, the spices in this dish had never bothered her.

While the *pollo* marinated, she chopped additional chilies and tomatoes, along with onions and cilantro. It seemed like an awful lot of trouble to go to for a meal she'd most likely eat alone, but it didn't matter. She felt at home in the kitchen, and the scent of beans and fresh salsa reminded her of her grandmother. Of love and laughter on Sunday afternoons at home in the barrio.

Juliet might be the only one seated at the table, but she would prepare a meal that would make *Abuelita* proud. A meal that would heal her frazzled emotions and fortify her heart. After all, she was creating a new home in Thunder Canyon, one based on love, family values and a hint of Old World culture.

And she darn sure didn't need a stubborn, globetrotting reporter to turn her life upside down.

Even if he already had.

An hour later, Mark stretched out on the king-size bed in his room at the Wander-On Inn. Using the remote control, he turned on the television set and surfed the channels, looking for something to take his mind off his work and the argument he'd had with Juliet. But he'd be damned if there was anything on that even came close to handing him an easy escape.

Watching the evening news made him long for another assignment, one that would allow him to make a difference in people's lives. One that would enable him to ride off in the sunset and leave Thunder Canyon in the dust.

A *Gunsmoke* rerun triggered thoughts of Old Town and of Juliet's love of the Wild West.

Bowling For Dollars reminded him of her silly urge to visit Buckhorn Lanes and watch the Gutter Busters do their thing. Or—God forbid—join the league his parents belonged to.

Trading Spaces merely made him think about how badly Juliet's apartment needed a remodel.

Dammit. He turned off the TV and stood. There wasn't anything worth watching, anything that didn't remind him of Juliet in one way or another.

He didn't like fighting with her. Didn't like stomping off and leaving things unresolved—a defense mechanism that had always worked well for him in the past.

And he damn sure didn't like thinking that their relationship—or whatever the hell it was—had been irrevocably damaged.

He probably ought to go to her place and tell her he was sorry. Not about being stubborn and refusing to socialize with his parents, but about snapping at her.

She'd only meant to be helpful.

But apologies didn't come easy for Mark.

He strode into the small bathroom and turned on the spigot, setting the shower in motion. Then he stripped off his clothes and climbed under the steaming spray.

The steady pulse of water helped some, but not enough. As he toweled himself dry, his thoughts remained on the argument they'd had, on the way Juliet's eyes had flashed in anger. And on the pain he'd spotted in her gaze when he'd taken her home. That last, sorrow-filled glance that had nearly torn him apart.

He blew out a ragged sigh. Damn. He didn't want her angry. Or her feelings to be hurt.

Against his principles, he threw on a pair of jeans and a shirt, then brushed his teeth and ran a comb through his hair. He didn't see any need to shave.

Five minutes later, he stood at Juliet's door, feeling like a kid who'd hit a baseball through his neighbor's window, asking for the ball and promising to replace the glass with a hard-earned allowance.

He knocked, and several moments later, she answered, wearing a pair of black slacks and a pink blouse, its buttons pulled taut by her breasts.

A shy but pretty smile made him momentarily forget why he'd come, so he just stood there. Their gazes locked. Caught up in something he couldn't explain.

The scent of peach blossoms and spice taunted his senses, making him take a second whiff.

And a third.

She ran her tongue across her bottom lip, and sexual awareness slammed into his chest, taking his breath away, along with the words he'd intended to speak.

She swung open the door, allowing him inside.

A part of him wanted to rewind, to start over. To head back to the Wander-On Inn and pretend he hadn't come to talk to her.

But he had. And he realized how much he'd missed their easy banter, their camaraderie. How much he'd missed *her*.

"I...uh...came to..." Oh, for cripes sake. Why couldn't he just spit it out? Why this awkward, adolescent reaction to the sight of her?

Her hair was loose and hung like a veil of silk past her shoulders, the glossy strands begging to be touched.

She didn't speak and merely stared at him in the same way he looked at her. Why wasn't she making this easier on him?

"I'm sorry," he finally said, his voice coming out soft and hoarse at the same time. "I didn't mean to be so hard on you."

"I'm sorry, too. My brother used to get mad at me when I didn't mind my own business. It's tough to keep quiet, though, when I care about someone and want to help."

He raked a hand through his hair, realizing now wasn't the time to tell her he didn't need anyone's help. He was ready to put this argument behind them. For good.

"Go ahead and invite my folks to dinner," he said. "That is, if you want to."

"And you'll come, too?" Hope glistened in a bright-eyed smile that dimpled her cheeks.

"Yes," he said. "I'll come, too, just as long as it's on my last night in town."

She didn't respond to the stipulation he considered a hell of a compromise. Still, he stepped over the threshold and closed the door behind him.

Once inside, the warm, fresh aroma of chilies and spice waylaid him, and his stomach growled in response.

Had she expected him? Had she made enough for two? Would she ask him to stay?

His stomach growled again, this time too loud for her to have missed.

"Dinner will be ready in a minute or two. Will you join me?"

Maybe she was just trying to be polite, but right now, he didn't care. The meal smelled incredibly good, and he was too hungry to be sensitive. "Yeah, I *would* like to eat with you. Thanks."

He watched in silence as she set the table. Then, taking a seat across from her, he relished one of the best chicken dishes he'd ever had. The sauce was on the mild side, but it was tasty just the same.

Throughout dinner, they seemed to tap dance around the sticky subject of his parents and the rift they'd had, which was a big relief. Mark preferred to glance up from his plate and see her smile, rather than frown.

After they ate, she stood and began to clear the table.

He reached for her arm and stopped her. "Let me help."

"All right."

They carried plates, silverware and glasses to the kitchen, and when they got to the sink, they reached for the faucet at the same time, fingers brushing, gazes locking, hearts pounding. Awareness flaring.

Time seemed to stand still, and a megadose of adrenaline blasted his libido, sending it into overdrive.

Mark didn't know why he did it. Didn't know why he couldn't keep his hands to himself. But he wanted to kiss her in the worst way.

And in the best way.

He cupped her jaw, his thumbs caressing the silky skin of her cheeks. Her lips parted, but she didn't speak. Didn't step away.

So he drew her mouth to his.

Chapter Eleven

Juliet knew better than to kiss Mark again, but her knees turned to mush when he cupped her jaw with gentle hands and placed his lips on hers.

And even though she knew it was foolish to encourage a relationship destined to end before it started, she couldn't fight the attraction or the desire.

The light bristle of his beard scratched against her skin in a pleasurable way. And she threaded her fingers through his hair, still damp from the shower, and drew his face closer still.

His hands stroked her back, her hips, and his tongue swept the inside of her mouth.

The musky scent of his mountain-crisp cologne drove her wild. She couldn't seem to get enough of him, of his taste, of his caress.

A whimper escaped from somewhere deep in her heart, which only seemed to enflame him, to urge him on. And his growing desire only heightened hers.

Their tongues mated in a desperate hunger, giving and taking. And when he moaned and drew her hips flush against him, she reveled in her power to excite him, pressing into his erection, wanting him. Wanting this.

An ache grew low in her belly, reminding her how long it had been since she'd had sex. And how recently she'd delivered her daughter.

Making love was out of the question, at least for another week or so. But that didn't mean she couldn't enjoy the taste of him and the overwhelming passion that blazed between them.

As he intensified the kiss and the gentle assault on her senses, she realized something special had happened. Something powerful.

If there were ever any question whether she'd fallen in love with Mark before, she knew the answer now. She loved his rebel grin, his wounded heart, his awkward but sweet efforts to look out for her and the baby.

And she certainly loved the effect he had on her body.

God help her, she was falling—heart first and eyes closed—for a man who would soon leave town, who would ride off into the sunset without her.

She ought to push him away, to put a stop to the passion that continued to build, but she wanted Mark and whatever he had to offer. And she meant to make the most of a kiss that rivaled anything she'd ever known.

No, she wouldn't put an end to the heated embrace until he did. And she certainly didn't sense any reluctance on his part.

Mark didn't know what had caught hold of him, but he didn't want it to end. Not the kiss, not the fire that raged in his blood.

Passion flared between them, promising a breathtaking sexual experience that would take them to places few people had reached. And that's just where he wanted this heated exploration to progress—to bed, where he could make love with her all night long, where he could bury himself in her softness and hear her cry out in a fulfilling climax.

The baby cried out from the bedroom, reminding Mark that they weren't alone, that things were far more complex than he'd let himself believe.

He couldn't allow their desire to run its course, so he pulled back, wanting to do the right thing, yet filled with regret. "I...uh...guess we shouldn't be kissing like that."

"I suppose not." A flush on her neck validated his suspicion—that she'd been just as carried away as he'd been.

He tried to clear the awkwardness from his throat. "Aren't you still...healing and stuff?"

"I feel back to normal, but Dr. Hart suggested I wait three weeks for...you know, sex. But I told her I'd be waiting a whole lot longer, since I haven't been... hadn't been...seeing anyone like that."

Until now.

Mark ran a hand along his jaw, felt the bristles he should have shaved, had he known they were going to kiss. A bucket of cold reality splashed over his head, and he wasn't sure what to say. He damned well couldn't start making promises about the future.

His game plan certainly hadn't changed.

And it wouldn't.

But that didn't mean they couldn't have a brief sexual relationship, assuming she was agreeable.

If she hadn't been told to wait another week for sex, would they have made love tonight? Would he have eventually realized he didn't have any condoms on him?

He might have one or two in his shaving kit, which was back at the inn, but a hike across the street would have diffused the moment.

He blew out a ragged sigh. This was a hell of a time to risk an unplanned pregnancy.

Talk about complex complications.

He cleared his throat, hoping it would clear his head. "I guess we've got another week to think about it then, don't we?"

"It seems that way." Her smile was a bit hard to read. Hopeful maybe?

Or was it remorseful?

Mark wasn't sure. But maybe in the next week or so, he ought to think of a way to casually bring his shaving kit back to Juliet's place.

Just in case he was invited to stay over for breakfast.

* * *

Several days later, Mark sat at the desk in his room at the inn, going over his notes. The scope of his story had changed in the past few weeks. And over the course of his stay in Thunder Canyon, he'd interviewed a slew of people, some more interesting than the rest.

Caleb Douglas had been the first he'd spoken to. At the time, the wealthy rancher and businessman seemed more interested in the grand opening of his ski resort, but that had changed with the influx of fortune hunters. Now, after talking to Caleb several more times, Mark had learned that the man was frustrated about the snafu with the land records down at the town hall.

And who could blame him?

Harvey Watson, the clerk who'd been transcribing all the old records into the new computer system, was on vacation, and rumor had it he might not be coming back anytime soon.

Mark slowly shook his head and clucked his tongue. In any other town, he would be able to access the records via the county computer system. But not in good old Thunder Canyon, which was still rooted in the early twentieth century when it came to modern technology and innovation.

So, early on, Mark had focused his research elsewhere, starting with respected members of the community, like Mayor Phylo T. Brookhurst.

He'd even interviewed some of the prospectors who'd come to town, looking to make their fortunes.

One of the wackiest interviews had been with Miles "Mickey" Latimer, a crusty old miner who seemed to be losing it. But it wasn't just the fact that Mickey was tottering on senility that had made Mark come to that conclusion. Latimer had probably been goofy all of his life. For years, the old man had continued to mine for gold, never finding much of anything, but still working with a pickax and a mule and looking for a mother lode that probably didn't exist.

What made guys like that practically turn their backs on society? Hell, no wonder Latimer seemed so out of touch.

Mark flipped the pages of his notebook. He'd also interviewed knowledgeable men like Roy Canfield, the editor of the *Nugget*. And Ben Saunders, the high school teacher and museum docent who knew just about everything there was to know about the town's history.

But maybe he ought to focus his attention on some of the older folks in town and see if they could shed some light on the ownership of the Queen of Hearts.

Ben had mentioned Tildy Matheson, a woman in her eighties who'd lived in Thunder Canyon all of her life. She might have a better handle on some of those rumors and legends.

Mark picked up the phone, dialed 4-1-1 and asked for Miss Matheson's number. He jotted it down, then gave her a call and introduced himself. "I'd like to interview some of the citizens who've lived in town for a good number of years. I think it would help me get a better understanding of the history of Thunder

Canyon. Would it be all right if I came by and talked to you?"

"I'd be delighted," the elderly woman said. "I don't get many visitors."

"When would it be convenient for me to stop by?"

"If you'd like to come now, I'll put on a pot of tea."

Mark wasn't the tea and crumpets sort, but he hated to offend the elderly woman who didn't get many visitors. "I might bring someone with me, if that's all right with you. She's just had a baby and doesn't get out too much."

"That would be lovely," Miss Matheson said. "The babies in my family have all grown up. They sure don't stay little for long."

After setting an appointment for thirty minutes from now, Mark called Juliet and invited her to go along. He was glad when she agreed.

Twenty minutes later, they were on their way. Several times, Mark glanced across the seat, admiring his attractive companion.

Juliet looked especially pretty today, dressed in a pair of boots, a midlength black skirt and a cream-colored blouse. In fact, if she didn't have Marissa with her, most people probably wouldn't believe she'd just had a baby.

When she spotted him looking at her, she smiled, a rosy flush coloring her dimpled cheeks.

Mark found it hard to keep his mind on driving and hoped having the pretty mother and child come along on the interview wouldn't prove to be a distraction. They'd almost reached their destination, so he'd find out soon enough.

Miss Matheson's house was located on Chinaberry Lane in the old part of town.

Juliet pointed to the Victorian home bearing the address the woman had given Mark. "Is that two-story house hers?"

"I believe so."

"Just look at that architecture," Juliet said. "Isn't it charming?"

As far as Mark was concerned, the house might be interesting, but it needed paint and a handyman's touch.

The yard was a bit overgrown, with rosebushes that hadn't been pruned in at least a year and a lawn that needed mowing. It was a shame the elderly woman didn't have anyone to help her maintain the place.

Juliet peered out the window at the grounds. "I'll bet her yard was a floral wonderland at one time."

Her optimism was amazing, but she was right. In its day, the Matheson house had been a showcase.

After they parked, Juliet lifted the baby from the car seat, and Mark carried the diaper bag. They climbed the steps, and when they reached an old, ornate door that needed varnish, Mark knocked. But he beat Juliet to the punch. "Probably handcrafted. Nice workmanship, huh?"

"Beautiful," she said, studying the stained glass window that adorned the carved oak.

The door opened, and they were greeted by a gray-haired woman wearing bright pink slacks, a pastel-striped blouse and a white sweater.

"Hello, Miss Matheson. I'm Mark Anderson, and this is Juliet."

"How do you do?" She glanced only briefly at the adults on the stoop, her tired gaze immediately settling on Marissa. "Oh, what a beautiful baby. And she's a perfect blend of her mother and father."

Juliet glanced at Mark, as though allowing him to correct the woman, but for some dumb reason he held his tongue.

He told himself it wasn't necessary to complicate matters. Or was it more than that?

Did he, deep down, like the idea of being mistaken for Marissa's father? Or of being thought of as Juliet's husband?

Impossible. He wasn't a family man. Nor was he good husband material. His ex-wife could certainly attest to that.

"Please," Miss Matheson said. "Come in."

Mark waited for Juliet to step inside first, then followed her into the house that held a unique fragrance of timeless memories and lilac sachets. His grandmother's house back in El Paso had a similar lingering smell—one he found comforting.

Miss Matheson walked slowly, a cane in her gnarled hand to steady her steps, and led them into a living room, where a silver tray and china tea service sat on the coffee table. "Have a seat while I pour you some tea."

"Please," Juliet said, to the elderly woman, as she handed the baby to Mark. "Let me help."

"Why, thank you, dear."

Mark sat on the sofa, which was upholstered in a blue and green floral print that matched the drapes. He rested Marissa in the crook of his arm.

Miss Matheson placed her cane near the armrest of an easy chair, then carefully lowered herself into the seat.

"Thanks for seeing me," Mark said.

"I don't get out much," the older woman said. "So I'm always glad when someone stops in."

Juliet picked up the teapot that was adorned with a pink floral trim. "What a beautiful china pattern. Is this an antique?"

"Yes, it belonged to my grandmother. And it brings me a great deal of pleasure to use, even more so than having a perfectly steeped cup of tea." The old woman smiled wistfully. "But you probably won't understand that."

"Oh, but I do." Juliet returned her smile. "I lost my grandmother when I was ten and still have the quilt she made and several other personal items. They each remind me of her."

"Then hold on to those memories," the older woman said.

Juliet handed her a cup and saucer. "You have a lovely home, Miss Matheson."

"Thank you, dear. But let's not be so formal. My name is Matilda and everyone calls me Tildy."

Juliet smiled and nodded, but continued to peruse the room.

Next to a Tiffany floor lamp was a bookcase adorned with framed photographs, many of them yellowed by time. Mark suspected they were Tildy's family members, some of whom had probably passed on, yet remained as precious memories.

He wondered what Juliet was thinking and suspected the two women, one just beginning her life and the other facing the end, had a lot in common.

"I'm glad you came today," Tildy said. "I'm planning a trip to visit my sister in Billings, and I'm not sure how long I'll be gone."

Mark balanced the baby in the crook of one arm, while holding the delicate handle of the china cup in the fingers of his other hand. He studied the hot, amber liquid, but didn't take a sip. Instead, he addressed Tildy. "Do you know Caleb Douglas?"

"Of course. I've known the Douglas family for years. My grandmother used to be a friend of Catherine Douglas." The elderly woman smiled and added, "Amos and Catherine were the original Douglas settlers in Thunder Canyon."

Mark hoped he was finally getting somewhere. "Then I'm sure you're aware that the Queen of Hearts mine is supposed to belong to Caleb."

"Yes. It's been in the Douglas family for years."

"Did you know Caleb is having difficulty finding the deed?"

"No." Tildy took a sip of her tea. "I don't have much time to socialize anymore."

Mark wondered if this visit had been a waste of time. "Do you think it's possible that Amos may have forgotten to file the necessary paperwork?"

"That doesn't seem likely. From what I remember being told, Amos was a stickler for details."

If that was true, then where the hell was the deed? Could one of Amos's descendants have misplaced it?

He studied the woman who sipped her tea. Did she actually know anything about the mine or deed?

"Who do you believe owns the Queen of Hearts?" he asked her.

"Why, Caleb Douglas."

That certainly seemed to be the assumption of everyone in town.

Just then the telephone rang, and Tildy reached for the portable receiver resting on a small table to the left of her chair. "Excuse me, please."

"Certainly." Mark took a sip of sweetened tea and tried not to grimace at the taste. He preferred a hearty brew of coffee—black and loaded with caffeine.

"Hello?" the older woman said. "Oh, dear. Is today Tuesday?"

Mark wasn't sure what was being said on the other end of the line, but he figured Tildy had obviously forgotten something.

"What time will you be coming for me?"

So much for the interview.

"Twenty minutes? I'll have to hurry, but I'll be ready when you get here." She ended the call, then apologized. "That was my niece. I'm afraid I'll have to cut our visit short. I've got a doctor's appointment today."

"That's okay," Mark said. "I understand. But before I go, I want to ask you another question. Have you ever heard of Crazy Red Phelps?"

"The outlaw?" Tildy asked. "Sure, I've heard of

him. He was before my time, of course. But he once shot up the saloon. And if I remember correctly, he had some kind of feud with Amos, although I'm not sure what it was all about."

"According to Ben Saunders, Crazy Red once claimed that the Queen of Hearts belonged to him and that he meant to have it, one way or another."

Tildy took a sip of her tea. "I'm afraid my memory isn't what it used to be. But from what I was told, that outlaw was as crazy as they made them and twice as ornery. He might have imagined that he had a prior claim on the mine."

"That's possible. And maybe he stole the deed from Amos."

"I have no idea."

Mark sat back in his seat. Tildy Matheson hadn't offered him anything new or solid, but she'd sure set his mind spinning.

"Maybe we ought to let Tildy get dressed for her appointment," Juliet said, picking up the teacups and placing them on the tray. "I'll just carry these into the kitchen for you."

"Thank you, dear." The older woman slowly got to her feet and pointed a crippled finger toward the dining room table and beyond. "It's through that doorway."

Mark stood, too, and waited for Juliet to return from the kitchen. Researching Crazy Red Phelps would be his top priority.

And maybe, in the process, he'd learn who held the deed to the Queen of Hearts.

* * *

The next afternoon, Mark drove out to the Ranch View Estates on White Water Drive. He turned into the entrance on Stagecoach and followed the flags to the models at the end of the cul-de-sac.

A sales rep looking like a dime-store cowboy in a pair of shiny boots, a bolo tie and a black hat handed him a brochure, along with a map of the subdivision. "Just take your time. And if you have any questions, or if I can help, just let me know. My name is Bill Jarvis."

Mark nodded, then set out on the walkway to look over the professionally decorated houses.

Wouldn't Juliet be surprised if he handed her the keys to one of these new homes? A small one, of course, although they all looked fairly big, especially to a man who'd lived out of a suitcase and spent most of his nights in a hotel.

As he wandered through the first couple of models, he wasn't sure what he was looking for and wondered if he should have brought Juliet with him. But in the third home, the decorator had made one of the smaller bedrooms into a nursery.

The walls had been painted an airy, cotton-candy pink. A crib, made out of light wood, sported a fluffy comforter with pretty, pastel-colored butterflies. A matching frou-frou over the window was a nice touch. And so was the toy box full of stuffed animals and the baby doll perched on the dresser.

Yeah, Mark knew that decorator stuff wasn't included in the house he planned to buy. But that didn't mean this model wouldn't be a great home to raise a little girl in.

He strolled through the last two, but by the time he entered the sales office, his mind was practically made up.

Or should he include Juliet in the decision?

After all, she and the baby would be the ones living in the house.

The wannabe cowboy/sales rep was busy talking to a silver-haired lady who was visibly shaken.

She dabbed at her eyes with a tissue. "Bill, I don't understand why you can't let me out of the deal. I don't need the house now. My husband passed away last Friday, and my daughter wants me to move in with her in Colorado."

"Ma'am, I'd like to help you. I really would. But your escrow closed two weeks ago, and it's out of my hands. That house is your problem."

The woman, her eyes red and watery, sniffled. "I don't know anything about real estate, or escrows or mortgages. My husband and I were married for nearly fifty-two years, and he always handled those sorts of things for me."

When the lady wiped her tears again, the dime-store cowboy rolled his eyes and flashed a can-you-believe-this-old-lady? look at Mark before continuing. "I'm sorry to hear about your husband, Mrs. Grabowski. But I sell houses. I don't buy them back. Now, why don't you go home, skim the yellow pages and find yourself a good Realtor?"

Mrs. Grabowski sniffled again and lifted her chin,

then as Cowboy Bill opened the door and ushered her out in a manner that was just a tad more polite than booting her in the butt with those fancy boots, she turned to him.

Her tired blue eyes flashed a look of betrayal. "You were sure fussing over us when you wanted us to buy the house, saying things like, 'If there's anything I can do to help, anything at all, you just give me a whistle.'"

He lifted his palms in a slick, don't-get-me-dirty manner. "My hands are tied, Mrs. Grabowski."

She shook her head, then walked toward her car.

Mark couldn't help sympathizing with the grieving widow. He knew the sales rep couldn't very well buy back her house, but he didn't have to roll his eyes and make light of the poor woman's dilemma.

In fact, Mark wasn't sure he wanted to deal with a guy who couldn't be more sensitive, more respectful than that. So he sidestepped ol' Cowboy Bill and followed Mrs. Grabowski to the parking lot, watching as she climbed into a late-model Chevrolet.

She probably hadn't thought about things like probate, either. It could take a long while for her to sell the house. And Mark sympathized with her.

His grandma hadn't had much business sense, either. And when his grandpa had died, she didn't even know how to write a check or drive the car. That was one reason he'd resented moving from El Paso to Thunder Canyon and leaving his grandmother to fend for herself.

And that move to Montana, he realized, at that particular time, had been the turning point in his relationship with his dad. The moment when teenaged rebellion turned to resentment and disrespect.

Mark couldn't imagine how difficult it would be to survive the loss of a spouse and be slapped with financial decisions and problems all at once.

As he prepared to slide into the driver's seat of his rented sedan, he heard the woman's engine grind. Battery problems, he guessed. Car trouble was obviously something else she wasn't used to handling.

Mark couldn't very well leave her stranded like that. Cowboy Bill would probably tell her to call the automobile club, then make her hike to a payphone to do so.

The jerk.

So Mark climbed from the car and walked to her vehicle. "Sounds like you've got a bad battery."

"Oh, dear." The look on her face was enough to make a guy's conscience squirm.

"Do you have jumper cables?" he asked, knowing there weren't any in the sedan.

"I don't know. But my husband always kept tools and whatnot in the car."

"Let's look in the trunk."

With a little encouragement, she managed to flip open the lid. Sure enough, her husband had thought of everything—except ensuring his wife could get by without him. But Mark kept quiet about that.

Moments later, with her standing beside him and peering under the hood, he got the engine running. "You probably ought to drive straight to a service station and have someone check your battery."

"I will." She offered him a weepy-eyed smile. "Thank you, young man. I was just sitting there, praying that the engine would start. You've been a real blessing, an answer to a prayer."

Mark didn't know about that. He and God had never seen eye to eye, so he couldn't imagine The Man Upstairs using a hard-ass reporter to answer a grieving woman's request. But if she thought so, what the heck.

"My name is Iris Grabowski," she said.

"Mark Anderson." He reached out a hand to shake on it, and the woman offered him a hug instead, like he was some kind of hero.

"Bless you, young man. I'm going to be praying for you and your family."

Don't bother, he wanted to tell her. But he held his tongue. He sure as heck didn't need the poor widow to start crying again. "Thanks."

After she drove off, he climbed in the sedan and drove back to town. In the stillness of the car's interior, a pensive mood settled over him and he pondered all kinds of things—like widows and grandmas who'd been looked after all their lives and then thrust into a world they weren't prepared to handle. Of a stubborn son who shouldn't have moved his family thousands of miles away, leaving his widowed mother to fend for herself. Of an angry teen who resented leaving his grandmother all alone in the last years of her life.

Of the way a man's guilt and remorse seemed to ease when he helped someone less fortunate.

Then his thoughts took a philosophical turn.

If a guy did enough good deeds, could he eventually right his wrongs?

Not the unforgivable ones.

Chapter Twelve

After feeding Marissa, Juliet turned on the radio and found a classical station.

Music, she'd read, was good for babies. Maybe, with an early introduction, her daughter would grow to appreciate lyrics and rhythm and become a singer or musician someday.

Hey, it could happen. Papa had played the guitar, and Juliet, who'd sung in the high school choir one semester, had been invited to sing in the Troubadours, an elite high school group that performed in the community. She'd had to decline because of her job, but it had been an honor to be chosen.

She glanced at the small, plastic Tiny Tot mobile that rested on the dinette table. Mrs. Tasker had come by earlier today and brought the toy for Marissa. She'd told Juliet that her last grandson had used it when he was an infant, lying underneath it for hours and watching the colorful stuffed animals dangle overhead.

Juliet laid a quilt upon the living room floor, then after kissing Marissa's cheek, set the baby down and carefully placed the mobile-on-stilts over her.

Marissa blinked several times, noticing the movement of zoo animals that dangled over her head.

A knock sounded at the door, but before she could answer it, Mark let himself in.

"It's me," he said.

She could see that. A smile tugged at her lips as she admired his masculine form. He wore a pair of khaki slacks, a lightweight black sweater and a crooked grin that turned her inside out.

His hair was windblown, and he looked a bit tousled, in a most attractive sense. But then, everything about him seemed to appeal to her these days.

He held a maroon-and-green file of some kind at his side. As he opened his mouth to speak, his gaze landed on the baby. He cocked his head. "What's she doing on the floor?"

"She's playing. The child development book I checked out of the library said she'd stay awake a little bit more each week. So I thought it might be nice to offer her some stimulation. See how she tries to focus on the little animals?"

He nodded and studied the colorful zoo mobile. "Then I guess it's time we went shopping for some baby toys."

We?

Oh, cut it out, Juliet scolded herself. She shouldn't try to read into things Mark said.

"I imagine she'll need a lot more than toys," he added.

"You're right. And guess what." Juliet grinned, eager to share her good fortune, her acceptance in the community. "Mrs. Tasker came by to see us this morning. And she accidentally let it slip that on Saturday morning, before The Hitching Post opens, she's having what used to be a surprise baby shower for me. Isn't that sweet?"

"Yeah. That'll be nice." He looked up from the floor, where Marissa lay with her eyes closed, and flashed Juliet a smile. "Looks like Sweet Pea played so hard, she fell asleep."

"I suppose she's a little young for toys yet."

As Mark eased closer, she thought about giving him a hug in greeting, but kept her hands to herself.

Their relationship was at an awkward stage. She knew where she wanted it to go, but she had no idea how he felt, so it was probably best to let him take the lead.

For now, anyway.

He nodded toward the bookshelf, where the radio softly played a concerto. "Do you like this stuff? Or is the classical music for Marissa, too?"

"I want to introduce culture into her life early, and I don't think it's too soon."

He smiled, then lifted his free hand and ran his knuckles along her cheek, jump-starting her pulse and sending a rush of warmth through her veins. "You're going to make a great mom, Juliet."

Her heart soared. Did he think she'd make a good wife, too?

He dropped his hand, as though he'd done something out of line. He hadn't, though. And she wished she were bold enough to reach for his fingers, replace his touch and caress his face, too. But she decided it was best to wait until he gave her more encouragement.

So she asked, "Would you like something to eat or drink? I have iced tea and can make burritos with the leftover meat from last night."

"Not now. I ate while I was out."

All right. She'd try again. "How's your research going?"

"I'm plugging along. I talked to Ben Saunders earlier this morning, and he said various newspapers from the late eighteen hundreds were placed on microfiche and left in a box at the museum, although he couldn't remember where. He's going to call me when he finds it. The article he told me about, the one in which Crazy Red was quoted, is supposed to be in there somewhere."

Like a supportive wife who was interested in her husband's work, she asked, "What else is new?"

He flashed the file he'd been holding at his side, a brochure of some kind.

"What's that?"

He held the cover so she could see the words. *Ranch View Estates.*

"I'm thinking about buying a house in that new development." His words opened the floodgates, releasing a rush of hope in her heart.

Her unfulfilled dreams soared.

Had Mark changed his mind? Had he decided to stay in Thunder Canyon?

Apparently.

Did his plans to buy a house have anything to do with her? With them?

Oh, Dios mio. Could he be falling in love with her?

She wanted to say something, to babble her happiness, but she kept quiet, waiting. Waiting to hear the words she wanted him to say.

But his cell phone rang, interrupting their conversation. He flipped open the lid and spoke. "Anderson. Hey, Mary. What's up?"

Was Mary a co-worker?

The fact that she might not be echoed in Juliet's ears and thudded around in her chest.

"Sure. I've got a copy stored in my laptop, back at the inn. I can e-mail it as an attachment."

She blew out the breath she hadn't realized she'd been holding. The call was definitely work related.

"No problem." Mark disconnected the line, then placed the cell phone on the dinette table and opened the Ranch View Estates brochure.

"You were right about those houses," he said. "They're nice and the floor plans are roomy. And since I need a write-off, I think I'll buy one, which ought to make my accountant happy."

It would make Juliet happy, too. After all, it looked as though Mark had decided to make Thunder Canyon his base. And that meant, even if he had to travel on assignments, he would always come back home, and she'd get to see him again.

"Which model do you like?"

He wanted *her* opinion on the house? Was that because he wanted her to live with him? To marry him?

She had no idea, but even if he'd just contemplated the possibility that they might have a future together, it was a step in the right direction.

Trying not to let her optimism run amok, she said, "I like them all."

He pointed to a floor plan of the Sedona. "This one is a bit bigger than I wanted, but it ought to work."

Ought to work for what?

Before she could respond, his phone rang again.

"Hello." He frowned. "Right now? What's his rush?"

She bit her bottom lip, wishing they could get back to the discussion of the house.

"All right. But give me a few minutes to get back to my room." He disconnected the line and set the cell phone on the table. "Listen, Juliet, I need to send a file to my boss. Maybe we can go look at the houses together this weekend. Then, if I put a down payment on one, we can celebrate by having dinner at Sebastian's Steak House."

"Sure." She walked him to the door, afraid to dream, to believe. After all, he hadn't said anything about love. Or marriage. But he'd definitely decided to stay in Thunder Canyon—or at least establish residency here.

She couldn't wipe the silly grin from her face or the song from her heart.

Maybe she should be the one to mention love

first. After all, Mark might need a little encouragement—a gentle push that would have him admit falling in love with her, just as deeply as she had with him.

An hour later, while Juliet nursed Marissa, Mark's cell phone rang and rumbled on the dinette table, where it sat next to the Ranch View Estates brochure.

She wondered whether he'd realized he'd left it here. And if not, whether the call was important.

He hadn't invited her to his room across the street, and although she'd always wanted to see the inside of the hotel that had once been owned by The Shady Lady, she hadn't pressed for an invitation. When it came to men, Juliet had never been pushy.

But she had an excuse to visit now.

And if the opportunity arose, she would be honest about her feelings so he'd feel better about expressing his. And maybe, if things worked out the way she wanted them to, she could talk him into moving back to her apartment until the new house was ready.

Hope, which had always been something she'd latched on to, reared like a mystical, white stallion.

She went to the closet and pulled out the second-hand stroller. Then she carefully placed Marissa in the bed and used two rolled receiving blankets to support her comfortably. Then she knelt and placed a kiss on the baby's cheek.

"I'll wheel you into the bathroom, pumpkin. Mama's going to freshen up, then we're going bye-bye."

Twenty minutes later, Juliet pushed the stroller

around the side of the building, to the front of The Hitching Post and across the street.

The Wander-On Inn had been refurbished over the years, but it still maintained the charm of the other false-fronted buildings in Old Town. She'd heard it was more like a bed-and-breakfast than a hotel.

She entered the lobby, a small, cozy room with a couple of leather sofas, a fireplace and a decorator piece of carpet lying on top of hardwood floors. She made her way to the front desk, where a tall, lanky man with dark hair worked behind a computer screen.

When the clerk glanced up, Juliet said, "I'd like to see Mark Anderson. He's staying here."

"Just a moment, while I check to see if he's in."

"Thank you." She fiddled with the narrow strap of her shoulder bag. Maybe she should have called first. If Mark was out on another interview, she'd have to head back home.

"Mr. Anderson?" the man said into a house phone. "There's a lady with a baby here to see you."

"All right." The hotel clerk smiled at Juliet. "He's in suite 104, which is right through that doorway, the last room on the right. You won't have to take the stairs."

Juliet flashed him an appreciative grin. "Thank you." Then she wheeled the baby down the carpeted hall.

Before she had a chance to knock, Mark opened the door. He wore the same khaki slacks and black sweater that he'd had on before, but he'd kicked off his shoes. For a woman who'd been interested in looking over the hotel, she couldn't seem to keep her eyes off the man who stood before her.

"This is a pleasant surprise." His crooked grin warmed her inside and out, making her feel giddy and awkward at the same time.

A lock of his hair had tumbled onto his forehead, tempting Juliet to brush it aside.

Or did she just want an excuse to touch him?

She handed him the cell phone. "You left this at the apartment, and I wanted to return it to you, especially since you received at least one call that I know of."

"Thanks." He took the phone, then opened the door to let her and the sleeping baby into his room. "This is a first."

It was, she supposed. She'd never been bold enough to visit a man at work or at home. Erik had placed a lot of boundaries on their relationship, something that, in her naiveté, she hadn't questioned.

She scanned the small interior, realizing she'd entered a sitting room. "I didn't know the old hotel had suites."

"Originally, it didn't. But during the last remodel, the owner took two rooms and created this one. Depending upon the guest, they refer to it as either the bridal or presidential suite." He shrugged, eyes crinkling, a grin tugging his lips. "The company travel coordinator passed me off as a dignitary of some kind, so I got lucky. I can give you the grand tour, if you want to see it."

"Actually, I'd love to." She glanced at Marissa, saw her sleeping soundly and parked the stroller near the sofa. "From what I've been told, most of the hotel rooms have an old photograph or piece of furniture that has some history behind it."

"Maybe so," he said, "but I haven't found anything noteworthy in here."

She looked at the desk, where his laptop was connected to the Internet via the telephone. A take-out menu sat beside it, a brown smudge marring the print. The newspaper rested on the coffee table, next to a candy bar wrapper and a half-eaten bag of pistachios.

"I guess you could call this my office. Come on, I'll show you where I kick back and relax." He led her into the sleeping area.

Her eyes immediately lit on a blue-and-yellow spread that matched the drapes. It was a bit rumpled, and she could see the indentation his head had left on the pillow. He must have been kicking back before she knocked.

"Did I come at a bad time?" she asked.

"Not at all. I'm glad you're here."

So was she. Just being with him in his room, so close to the bed where he'd recently lain, was a bit heady. Exciting.

He tossed her a smile that tumbled around in her heart, stirring up all kinds of feelings—attraction and desire, to name two—and provoking a pressing urge to tell him she'd missed not having him sleeping at her place.

They stood there for a while, awareness growing. Hearts beating. That lazy shank of hair calling to her.

She reached up and bushed it aside, her fingers lingering a bit longer than necessary. Their eyes locked, and she couldn't move, couldn't speak. She was too caught up in whatever swirled around them—pheromones, desire. Sexual curiosity.

Surely, Mark felt it, too.

He reached out and stroked her hair, letting the strands sift through his fingers.

Her heart pounded in anticipation, waiting for him to make a move while contemplating making one of her own.

"It's been a week," he said, reminding her that the doctor had said sex was okay.

"I know."

"We were going to think about…some things."

"I haven't thought of much else," she admitted.

Was that making the first move?

His lips quirked into a crooked smile, then he bent to give her a kiss.

She lifted her arms, wrapping them around his neck, and leaned into his embrace. The kiss deepened, and she thought she'd die from want of him. From want of his love.

As tongues sparred and mated, she closed her eyes, oblivious to anyone or anything than this man who touched her in such a sensual way and held her heart in his hands.

Mark didn't want the kiss to end, didn't want to put a stop to the blood rushing in his veins. He relished the lady in his arms, each touch, each soft whimper.

No woman had ever moved him like this, provoking him to make love with a slow hand and a gentle touch, to prolong the pleasure for as long as he could hold out, making sure she enjoyed each moment in his arms, in his bed.

He wanted her. Badly. And with reluctance, he withdrew his lips—but not his embrace—and rested his forehead against hers. "I want more than your kiss, Juliet."

"I want that, too."

His heart thumped into his throat, and he tilted her chin and kissed her again. His tongue swept the inside of her warm, willing mouth—seeking, exploring, savoring, demanding. He caressed the gentle slope of her back, the curves of her hips, then cupped her bottom and pulled her against his demanding erection.

Their first time together should be special, but all he could think of was losing himself in her, which both scared and excited him.

He nuzzled her neck, placing open-mouthed kisses along her jaw and throat. At the same time, he slid his hand under her yellow cotton top, felt the warmth of her skin, the silky softness. His fingers slid along her ribs, finding her bra and the fullness of her breasts. "Is it all right if I touch you here?"

"You can touch me anywhere you like," she said, her voice edged with the husky tone of passion.

He fumbled with the buttons of her blouse, then slid the fabric over her shoulders, removing it and revealing a white cotton bra. It wasn't one of those slinky, little ones made of flimsy lace and silky cups meant to arouse a man beyond measure, but seeing her breasts nearly bare and that sweet anticipation in her eyes, nearly knocked him to his knees.

She was offering him a gift, something a man like him didn't deserve but couldn't refuse. "You're beautiful, Juliet."

"You don't have to say that." Her hands slipped to the slight bulge of her tummy. It had gone down significantly over the past few weeks—not that he cared whether it had or hadn't.

"I'm five or ten pounds heavier than I used to be," she said. "And I've got stretch marks, too."

He knelt before her, caressed her belly and placed a kiss near her navel. Then he gazed up at her. "Childbirth and motherhood have only made you more womanly, more appealing."

Juliet closed her eyes, relishing the words Mark said, the sweet kiss he'd pressed on her tummy.

As his sensual praise chased away self-consciousness and doubt, she pulled his shirttail from his pants, trying her best to undo the buttons. She wanted him naked, wanted to feel him skin to skin, wanted to feel him inside of her.

Before long, they stood before each other, partially clothed and fully aroused. He kissed her cheek. "I've got a condom in my shaving kit."

She smiled. "Get it, while I turn down the covers of the bed."

She went to the sitting room and took a quick peek at her daughter, who continued to sleep soundly, unaware of the step her mother and the man who had helped bring her into the world would take, a step Juliet was eager to make.

When she returned to the bedroom, Mark stood by

the bed, the spread folded down, a foil packet in his hand. She smiled and made her way to the man she loved.

Did he know how badly she wanted to give him her body, heart and soul?

Mark cupped Juliet's cheeks in his hands. Passion smoldered in her gaze, matching his own, he suspected. "I want this to be good for you."

"It's already been better than I'd ever imagined." Then she stepped out of her shoes and unzipped her pants.

He watched as she bared herself to him, and something stirred deep within him, something he had never experienced before. Something he didn't dare contemplate now.

She stood before him, naked, lovely, flushed with passion and desire, yet appearing to battle shyness.

"Are you sure about this?" he asked.

"Love me, Mark."

Her simple request was his undoing. He wanted to make love to her more than anything he'd ever wanted in his life.

Juliet watched as Mark undressed. He probably suspected she'd only been requesting sex. And she had been. But there was so much more to her words. She loved Mark deeply and wanted him to love her back.

He tore into the foil packet, protecting them, then took her mouth, his hunger not sated in the least, and drew her to the bed.

All right. So he hadn't said the words, hadn't pronounced his love. She'd be content with that.

For now.

If she only had this once, this afternoon, to make love with him, then she intended to give him all she had, and to take whatever he had to offer.

"I don't want to hurt you," he whispered. "So I'll try to be gentle."

She nodded, trusting him like she had no other.

He entered her, slowly at first. And it hurt briefly, but the urge to feel him inside of her was too great to care. She arched against him, drawing him deeper. The initial discomfort was surpassed by pleasure and fulfillment as he moved, giving, taking, driving her to the brink of some precipice she'd never before reached.

Her heart sang, as her body responded to each touch, each kiss, each thrust.

The loving rhythm built into a powerful rush, a crescendo that made them one, taking them to paradise and beyond. As they peaked together, a star-spinning climax burst across her vision, touching her heart and soul.

She'd read about orgasms and wondered why she'd never experienced one before, but now she knew. She'd never made love like this—not with a man she truly adored. So she held on to each wave of pleasure, wanting to keep him inside of her forever.

When their sweet joining was over, the loving didn't stop.

Unlike Marissa's father, Mark continued to hold her, murmuring how sweet she was, how beautiful.

An I-love-you could come later, she supposed. As

it was, she would bask in the afterglow of what they'd just shared and pretend that he'd said the words she longed to hear. That he'd committed to more than a one-time sexual fling.

As they lay in each other's arms, bodies glistening and the scent of their lovemaking lingering in the air, she was afraid to move, to speak. Afraid to break the magical spell that bound them together forever. Afraid to quell the sense of family and rightness that she'd been missing for what seemed like ages.

The ensuing silence grew heavy.

Over and again, words of love struggled to break free, but she bit them back for fear he wasn't ready to hear them yet. But that didn't mean she wasn't listening, waiting for him to share his thoughts about the future.

Mark, his passion spent and still reeling in the power of his release, felt the urge to say something, although he didn't know what. He was too afraid they'd have to discuss the turn their relationship had taken. And the fact that he'd be moving on to another assignment one day soon.

But he couldn't deny how good their lovemaking had been. How special. How unforgettable. And although he'd suspected she'd been just as caught up in the heat as he'd been, he needed to know for sure.

He rolled to the side, taking her with him, then ran a hand along the contour of her hip. "I hope that was something you'd walk across the room for."

She smiled. "I'd run a marathon for it."

"It'll be better next time." He brushed a strand of hair from her forehead. "I promise."

"Oh, yeah?" She brightened. "I'll have to hold you to it."

He liked the sound of that, the promise of another afternoon in Juliet's arms. And he hoped that she realized their sexual relationship, no matter how special, was just temporary. Mark didn't make commitments and promises he couldn't keep—although he had to admit, this was the first time he'd suffered even a pang of regret that he didn't.

"By the way," he said. "I didn't get a chance to tell you. But I'd like for you and Marissa to live in the house I'm going to buy."

"You would?" Her eyes glimmered, brighter still, and he could understand why. She'd probably give her right arm to move out of that rundown apartment over The Hitching Post.

"And you don't have to worry about rent," he added. "I'll need someone to look after the place, since I'll be gone most of the time."

Had the flicker in her eyes died down?

Maybe it was only the afternoon shadows that darkened the hotel room.

"So what do you say?" he asked.

Juliet pondered his question before responding. Something told her that she and Mark hadn't placed the same value on their relationship. It made her glad she'd held back the vows of love and forever she'd been tempted to utter during their lovemaking.

Well, glad and sad.

She finally managed to answer his question—sort of. "I'll have to think about it."

Hopefully, Mark was still tiptoeing through his feelings for her. Maybe he needed more time to consider something deeper, something stronger and more special.

But memories of her baby's father crept up on her. Erik Kramer had always sidestepped an I-love-you, and that fact didn't sit well with her.

Had she misjudged a man again? Given herself to someone who didn't want the same things in life that she did?

"I need the house as a tax write-off," Mark said, repeating something he'd already told her. "And since I won't be living in it, I'll need someone to take care of things for me."

She assumed he meant someone to take care of the house. But was he actually asking her to take care of his physical needs, too, while he lived another life that didn't include her?

Erik had wanted to set Juliet up in a condo. But he hadn't wanted to marry her, hadn't been free to do so.

Nor had he wanted to create a family with her.

She offered Mark a smile, but not a commitment of any kind. She needed some time to think. Some time to consider the ramifications of living in his house rent-free. Some time to see if his offer included stipulations she couldn't accept.

And, a Pollyanna voice reminded her, she needed time to see if there was a remote chance Mark might one day say the words she longed to hear.

Chapter Thirteen

Mark didn't move into Juliet's apartment, but his shaving kit sat on her bathroom countertop, and he'd spent the past two nights with her.

That had to count for something.

Sleeping in his arms was something Juliet could easily grow used to. In fact, it was something she hoped they'd both grow used to. And although she had some qualms about his lack of commitment, she decided to take one day at a time. She hoped that, given time, Mark would fall in love with her.

As she parked the Chevy S-10 pickup in the parking lot of the Lone Pine medical building, she glanced into the rearview mirror and checked her lipstick. Light and glossy. Hair was okay, too.

She took Marissa from the car seat and carried her inside.

Mark had offered to go with her to the appointment with the pediatrician, but she'd told him not to bother this time. He'd been researching the Internet and had just found an interesting site that listed the Rafferty Gang and brief bios of some of the outlaws, including Crazy Red Phelps.

As Juliet entered the central waiting room that several doctors used, she recognized a couple of regulars from The Hitching Post, most of whom thumbed through magazines, waiting their turns to be called.

But the attractive, salt-and-pepper-haired woman sitting near a potted palm stood out—Mark's mother.

Mrs. Anderson had recognized her, too.

Juliet smiled, mouthed a "hello" and waved at the woman. She wanted to be friendly, but was afraid to get too close. After all, challenging Mark about the falling out he'd had with his parents hadn't gone over well, and she was reluctant to do anything to put a strain on a developing romance.

Okay, so she was still hopeful that their relationship was moving toward happily ever after.

After signing in at the pediatric desk, Juliet searched for a chair. There was an empty seat beside Mrs. Anderson, but she chose one closer to the pediatrician's office. Surely, the woman wouldn't think that was odd or that Juliet was trying to avoid her.

Several minutes later, Mark's mother placed the magazine she'd been reading on a table, stood and made her way to Juliet. She nodded to an empty chair. "I hope you don't mind if I sit here."

Obviously, Mrs. Anderson didn't have anything to lose by striking up a conversation. And since Juliet had decided not to push Mark anymore about reconciling with his parents, what would it hurt?

"No, I don't mind at all." Juliet offered her a smile, then made sure Marissa's diaper bag was out of the way so the older woman wouldn't trip over it.

"Are you bringing the baby in for a checkup?" Mrs. Anderson continued to stand and study Marissa, a look of awe in her gaze.

"Yes. I'm curious to see how much she's grown, although I know she fits into her newborn gowns much better now."

"She's a beautiful baby."

"Thank you, Mrs. Anderson."

"It's Anne-Marie," she corrected, flashing Juliet a nervous smile. She took a seat and rested a black purse in her lap. "I'm not sure what my son has told you."

"Not much. Just that he's never gotten along with his father. And that you'd had a rift of some kind." Juliet didn't want to be disloyal to Mark, yet she was still curious as to what had caused the division.

"My husband and I would like to apologize for a lot of things, but Mark won't give us a chance." The older woman bit her bottom lip. "And I suppose, I can't blame him."

Juliet felt sorry for the mother who appeared to want to make things right with her son. And since

Mark was the only child the Andersons had left, Juliet could certainly understand that.

"I'm not sure how close the two of you are," Anne-Marie said, "but if you could talk to him, let him know that we love him, that we'd like to talk and try to put some of this behind us...."

"Mark is stubborn," Juliet said. "And I think he's been hurt deeply, although I don't know any of the details."

"It all started with the move," Mrs. Anderson said. "I should have leveled with the kids, but I was afraid to."

Juliet knew Mark didn't like Thunder Canyon and resented moving away from El Paso.

"Mark was always butting heads with my husband. And I was afraid that if he knew his father was having an affair with a young woman in town and that our marriage was on the rocks, he wouldn't take it well. That he would have rebelled. But now I think that may have been the wrong decision."

Juliet wasn't so sure about that. Did kids need to hear those kinds of details about the adults in their lives? Or should they be protected from things that really weren't their business?

"My husband's father had passed away, and his mother, although grieving and struggling to be on her own, came up with the idea. She begged Jess to give our marriage a chance, to leave town and the woman who'd come between us. A move was our only chance to remove the temptation and start fresh."

"And your husband agreed?"

"Reluctantly." Mrs. Anderson blew out a shaky sigh. "It was tough at first. Jess was so hard to live with. He'd made a sacrifice for the good of the family, but that didn't mean he was happy about it. And then we were struggling to make a go of the motel. The kids were miserable and missed their friends, their grandmother."

That still didn't seem like a good enough reason to stay angry, to maintain a grudge.

"But things are much better now," Anne-Marie said, a steady smile growing. "My husband and I have become involved in the community and in our church. I just wish Mark could get to know his father on an adult level."

So did Juliet. If anything, she was more convinced that the Andersons needed to have a heart-to-heart.

"My daughter's death is what finally tore our family apart," Anne-Marie added. "Mark felt responsible, and I'm afraid, in our anguish, we blamed him, too."

"Was it his fault?"

"No, it wasn't. But at the time, my husband and I were crazy with grief and frustration. We, or rather Jess, said some terrible things to Mark. And, obviously, those remarks are something my son can't forgive."

Juliet hurt for Mark, but she sympathized with his parents, too. Surely this was something that could be mended, patched up.

"I don't think there's a lot I can do to facilitate a reconciliation right now," she told the older woman, "but I truly believe Mark would be a happier man if he could make peace with his family. And when the time is right, I'll do my best to encourage him to talk to you and your husband."

"Bless you," Mrs. Anderson said. "Mark's wife tried to step in, right before their marriage, but Mark refused. And my husband and I weren't even invited to the wedding."

Mark's wife?

Juliet's heart pounded in her chest, but before she could comment or quiz the woman any further, a nurse called, "Anne-Marie Anderson."

"I have to go, but thank you so much for listening." Mark's mother patted Juliet's hand, then got up from her seat, leaving Juliet in the waiting room, feeling betrayed.

She'd been honest with Mark from the start. Why had he kept so many secrets from her?

And he had a wife? Was he married? Divorced? Separated?

He'd never said a word, never hinted.

Her pulse throbbed in her ears, as her anger built. Were all men jerks?

Or just the ones she was attracted to?

Mark sat before the laptop computer, typing some notes into a file.

So far, he'd learned that Willard "Crazy Red" Phelps, the Confederate soldier turned outlaw, had been born near Thunder Canyon. His father had died "in the prime of life," and his mother had taken him and an older brother to live with her parents on a small farm outside of Atlanta. That's where he'd grown up.

Stretching and trying to work a kink out of his shoulders, Mark glanced at the clock in the kitchen. Juliet was due home soon, unless she stopped by Super Save Mart.

He heard a car drive up and peered out the dining room window. There she was. Just her and the baby. No groceries to help her carry in.

After saving his work, he shut down the computer, eager to hear what the doctor had said, and opened the door for Juliet.

She trudged up the steps, her movements tense, all signs of a smile absent.

"Is something wrong?" he asked.

"Yes."

Mark's heart damn near jumped from his chest. He could have sworn Marissa was gaining weight and growing longer. "What did the doctor say?"

"Nothing much." Juliet carried Marissa into the bedroom and laid her in the cradle.

"Then what's the matter?"

As she returned to the living room, her hands plopped on her hips and a fire raged in her eyes. "How *dare* you keep secrets from me."

"What the hell are you talking about?"

"I told you everything. About my family. About Marissa's father."

The woman might be petite and soft-spoken at times, but a Latin temper had surfaced, one he'd only caught a glimpse of in the past.

He didn't know who had talked to her, what she'd learned, but he wasn't going to run at the mouth until he had an idea where she was going with all of this.

"Why don't we start over," he said.

"Why don't *you* start over by telling me about your wife."

"I have no idea what's got you so riled up. Susan and I were divorced years ago."

Juliet's stance didn't waver. What the hell did she want to know? It's not as though he was still married. As though he was trying to pull a fast one, like Marissa's father had done.

Mark raked a hand through his hair. "Not long after landing a job with Golden Eagle News Service, I married a young woman I'd met in college."

Juliet listened, although her silent anger showed no sign of abating.

Mark blew out a sigh. "Susan was a homebody and a schoolteacher by degree. She wanted a home and a family and didn't appreciate my itinerant lifestyle."

"Why didn't you tell me?"

"The marriage didn't last a year, but that was long enough for me to realize I'm not husband material."

His words seemed to crush her. Or enrage her. It was hard to tell. Whatever she was feeling had her wrapped tighter than a top ready to launch.

She crossed her arms and shifted her weight to one leg. "You've kept secrets from me."

So what if he had? He kept secrets from everyone. It was the only way he could live with what he'd done.

Had her informant told her about Kelly, too? About the part he played in her death?

"Our friendship," Juliet added, "hasn't been a two-way street."

Their *friendship?*

Whatever they'd shared was more than that, although he didn't want to go there. Didn't want to consider what he was feeling for her and why her anger bothered him so much.

He wasn't sure what to say in his defense. His emotions were swirling around like a Texas twister.

"Why did you ask me to live in the house you want to buy?"

"To help you out," he said. "You and Marissa need a better place to live. And I hoped we could work out something beneficial for both of us. I hoped you'd look after my interests."

"You can take your interests and shove them where the sun doesn't shine." Her eyes sparked in ire, then she unleashed a flurry of words in Spanish, few of which he could decipher when she spoke that fast. She threw up her hands. *"Soy la tonta del barrio."*

The fool of the neighborhood?

Mark wasn't exactly sure what had set her off. Or who had told her he'd been married before, albeit briefly. But there was no talking to her, no reasoning with her like this. So he kept his mouth shut, listening and hoping a clue would surface.

"I think it's best if you take your things and go back to the inn."

Her words sucked the air out of the small apartment, but it was too late for her to reel them in, too late for him to apologize and start over.

And he wasn't sure he wanted to. Wasn't sure what would happen if he did.

The old fight-or-flight instinct had kicked in, and he was afraid to fight for something he didn't think would last. So he packed his laptop and his shaving kit, and left the small rundown apartment.

And as he did, no one felt more of a fool than he did.

Back at the inn, Mark paced the floor, his anger and frustration pouring out of every cell in his body.

Thank God he hadn't signed on the dotted line for one of those damned houses, or he'd be in the same fix as Iris Grabowski—stuck with a home he didn't need or want.

Stuck.

That's how he felt. Imprisoned in Thunder Canyon on a fool's errand.

But he wasn't going to stay any longer. He was out of here.

He snatched his cell phone and dialed his boss. After several rings, Tom Detwiler answered.

"It's Mark Anderson."

"Hey, thanks for getting that file to me so quickly. You're the best."

Yeah, well Mark sure hoped he felt that way after he asked to be reassigned, or else he'd quit the news service. He couldn't stay in Thunder Canyon one more minute.

"Listen, Tom. This story isn't panning out. There's nothing here, and I'm not going to waste my time or your money by staying here any longer."

"Are you sure about the story?"

"Damn sure." He just wasn't sure about anything else. About why his heart was ricocheting in his empty chest with hollow thumps. About why that ever-present sense of guilt seemed watered down with regret.

"Okay," Tom said. "But sit tight, will you? I have a feeling something *big* is coming down the pike. And it might be your lucky day."

If anyone needed a turn of luck, it was Mark.

"What's up?"

"A political exposé, possibly. But I don't want to go into any more details yet."

"Okay. I'll wait to hear from you."

"Talk to you later."

Mark disconnected the line. There was hope of an escape from Thunder Canyon without quitting his job. Hope of a story that was worthy of his skill.

So why didn't that make him feel better?

He strode over to the honor bar in his room, unlocked the door and fished out a bottle of bourbon. Taking a glass from the bathroom, he made a stiff drink, using just a splash of water—his usual beverage of escape.

But this time, it wasn't memories of his sister that made him want to drown his sorrows. It was thoughts of a petite brunette with a Latin temper and a fiery kiss that he might never taste again.

A hot-blooded woman who had a death-grip hold on him and made the squeeze feel comfortable. Appealing.

And that scary thought was enough to make him want to jump in a vat of bourbon and never climb out.

He plopped onto the chair by the desk and took a drink. But the alcohol didn't slide easily down his throat, nor did it hit the spot.

Juliet wasn't going to be an easy woman to forget.

Swearing under his breath, he dumped the bourbon down the drain.

Chapter Fourteen

Over the next couple of hours, Juliet's anger slowly shifted from Mark to herself. She should have known better than to let him get too close, than to have pinned her dreams of love and forever on him.

I hoped we could work out something beneficial for both of us, he'd told her.

On the outside, that sounded like a generous offer. But when he added, *I hoped you'd look after my interests,* her suspicions had been confirmed.

Mark hadn't wanted any more from her than Erik had. And this time the revelation hurt more than it had before.

A lot more.

She'd hoped to stay mad at Mark, and even at herself; anger was so much easier to deal with. But by sunset, grief and loneliness trickled in, burrowing into her heart.

After a light dinner, she spent some quiet time with Marissa, then nursed her and put her to bed.

But that merely left Juliet alone with her thoughts, with her deep sense of loss.

Until a knock sounded at her door.

Uneasy since it was nearly nine, she peered through the droopy drapes. The glow from the single light in the rear parking lot lit a familiar form.

Mark.

She hadn't expected to see him. And although she had half a notion to either ignore him or give him another piece of her mind—a colorful, multilingual version—she opened the door.

"I...uh...wanted to talk to you about something," he said.

"All right." She stepped aside, allowing him in the apartment.

He nodded at the sofa. "Can I sit down?"

"Sure." She waited until he'd taken a seat, then, wanting to leave some distance between them without being obvious, she sat on another cushion.

"I'm going to be leaving Thunder Canyon soon," he said, "but there's something I want to tell you."

For a moment, she wondered if he was going to apologize and tell her he'd been a stubborn fool. That he hadn't realized how much he loved her, how impossible it would be to live without her. But she knew better than to give a loco fantasy like that the time of day.

"You've been open with me, Juliet. And I've kept secrets from you."

She merely stared at him, letting him continue.

"I'm not sure who you spoke to, who told you I was married before, but it was to a woman who wanted something I couldn't provide. A woman whose love began to die after I told her about the part I played in my sister's death."

"I'm not like other women. Not when I care about someone." It was the closest Juliet came to actually admitting her feelings. Feelings, she realized, that hadn't lessened just because Mark had disappointed her, hurt her.

"I hope you're right about that, because I've had a hell of a time living with what I did. And I'd hate to lose your friendship over it."

"Try trusting me," she said.

"I will. Our friendship means a lot to me. And I should have trusted you before, but I'd been on my own for so long, it was hard to let go." He looked at her with such a pained expression, it tugged at her heart.

Had he done something that unforgivable?

"My older sister, Kelly, married her high school sweetheart right after graduation. Daryl got a job selling cars, and they moved to Bozeman. We didn't see much of them, and I assumed they were happy. But a year or so later, after Daryl left her for another woman, Kelly came home heartbroken and five months pregnant."

Pregnant and betrayed.

Juliet knew the feeling well.

"My sister was miserable and cried all the time," Mark said. "She spent day after day sulking in her bedroom, with the door shut and the drapes drawn."

Juliet had been hurt, too, but she'd been able to cope with her situation. "It sounds as though your sister was suffering from some serious depression and needed professional help."

"You're right. Unfortunately, she didn't get help."

"Not even from her obstetrician?"

"I don't think she saw a doctor after coming back home. My parents were so busy at work that they didn't force the issue. In fact, I don't think they knew how much time Kelly spent locked in her room." Mark leaned forward, resting his arms on his thighs, his hands clasped together. "I knew, though. And I probably should have made a bigger deal out of it."

"How old were you?" Juliet asked, wanting to touch him, to comfort him, but afraid to intrude.

"I was sixteen."

"And at that age, you were supposed to have taken on more responsibility with your older sister than your parents did?"

He shrugged. "In retrospect, I wish I had."

"What happened?"

"One afternoon, a week before she was due to have the baby, my friends were getting together at the bowling alley." He looked at Juliet, his eyes begging to be understood. "You have no idea how boring it was at the house, especially with my sister holed up in her room."

She nodded, wanting him to feel free to continue.

"Before my parents had left for work, they'd told me to stick close to home because there'd been a storm warning. But I didn't plan to be in town that long and figured I'd be back before they got home."

Juliet felt a chill in the room, one that had little to do with the weather and a lot to do with Mark's tense demeanor, his pained expression.

"So I ignored their orders and took the family car into town. Shortly after that, the storm hit even harder than expected, creating a power outage and knocking down telephone lines." He glanced at Juliet, pain etched across his brow. Remorse. Regret. Guilt.

Juliet wished she could soothe them all away, but feared they'd been hiding under the surface for so long that it wouldn't be easy.

"At the time, I didn't realize babies don't always show up on the day they were supposed to. And Kelly went into labor when no one was home."

Juliet had the urge to slide closer, but was afraid to move, afraid to stop the flow of his memory. Still, she reached for his hand, felt a cool chill to his skin.

"When the roads were clear, my parents returned home and found Kelly on the floor in a pool of blood. Dead. The baby was still inside her."

Grief settled over Juliet's heart—for the loss of the young mother she'd never met, the child struggling to be born, the parents who walked into their home and found unspeakable horror.

And for the man who felt responsible for it all.

"The autopsy said the placenta had attached to the

cervix, rather than the uterine wall. Anyway, she hemorrhaged and died before the baby was born."

"It's called placenta previa," Juliet explained. In her studies of pregnancy and labor, she'd read about the condition. In a case like that, dilation of the cervix caused the placenta to rip away too soon, leaving the baby without oxygen and the mother at risk for hemorrhage. "With proper medical care, the prognosis is good. A doctor can schedule a C-section."

He nodded, processing her words. Or so she hoped.

Juliet gave his hand a squeeze, hoping to chase away the chill, the undeserved guilt he'd carried for years. "Your sister's death wasn't your fault. It was hers. And if she'd been too depressed to see to her own health and that of the baby, it was your parents' fault for not insisting she get the help she needed."

Just hearing Juliet absolve him from guilt helped, Mark supposed. But he still wished he would have done something, gotten Kelly to seek medical care, counseling. Something. And he wished he hadn't left her alone.

"When I finally returned home, my parents lashed out at me, blaming me for leaving my sister alone, for being so selfish and irresponsible." Mark didn't tell her the rest, the words her father had shouted as he slammed his fist into the wall, leaving a knuckle-bruising hole. A hole his old man had refused to seal up for the next six months as a constant reminder of what he thought of his son.

You no good rebellious bastard. You son of a bitch. You let your sister die. You killed her.

I didn't know she was in labor, Mark had tried to explain. *I didn't know she would need help.*

You were told to stay home and look after her. Jess Anderson paced the floor, looking like a madman. *Get the hell out of my house. And don't ever come back.*

"Kelly's death wasn't your fault," Juliet repeated. "And your parents know that. *Now.*"

"I was devastated by my sister's death. And wracked with guilt. And there wasn't a damn person in the world to talk to."

Juliet slid closer, then wrapped her arms around him.

Mark wanted so badly to lean into her embrace, to absorb her strength, her forgiveness.

For a moment, he gave in and clung to her. But that didn't change the fact that he wasn't a family man. That he was leaving on assignment soon.

And it was better that way. Really.

"Your parents are sorry about blaming you," Juliet repeated.

Maybe they were. But Mark wasn't sure he'd forgiven himself. Still, some of the things Juliet had said made sense. His sister's depression had gone untreated, and she'd neglected to see an obstetrician, at least after she'd moved home.

When it came time to deal out the guilt, there seemed to be a lot of players to consider. He didn't have to take the brunt of it alone.

"You're a good man." Juliet stroked his forearm, trying, he supposed, to soothe his conscience.

It worked. Her belief in him was like a healing balm.

She lifted her hand, placed it on his cheek. "I love you."

Her words blindsided him, causing his heart to race and a response to lodge in his throat. He merely looked at her, amazed. Unsure. Unbelieving.

"I don't expect anything from you," she added, as her hand slowly lowered, leaving his cheek cold. Empty. "I appreciate all you did for me and the baby. And no matter where you are, no matter what the assignment, I want you to know that Marissa and I will always be in your corner."

"Thanks." His voice came out raw. Hoarse. Laden with all kinds of things he couldn't put his finger on. Things her words had unleashed.

I love you.

What did she mean by that?

Did she love him like a friend?

Or was she *in* love with him?

He didn't know. Nor could he figure out why it seemed to matter. In the past, if one of his lovers got starry-eyed, he knew it was time to skedaddle. To turn heart and run. And now seemed like that time.

"I'm going on a new assignment soon," he said. "I'm just waiting to hear the details."

There. He'd done it. Cut bait. All he had to do was go.

"I know how much your job means to you," she said, her voice coming out soft and whispery. "And how much you disliked being in Thunder Canyon. I'm happy for you."

Was she?

"Thanks," he said. "I'm glad you understand. And that you're okay with my leaving."

She leaned toward him and placed a kiss on his cheek. "I wish you the best of luck."

He nodded, not exactly sure what was happening.

She was letting him go? With her blessing?

He'd tried to set some boundaries. And she'd agreed to them without tears or an argument.

So why didn't he feel like hightailing it out of her apartment and back to his place?

She stood, leaving him alone on the sofa. "Keep in touch, will you?"

Huh? Yeah. "Sure."

Why did he feel as though there was something more for him to say?

Before he got in too deep, before he said something that might screw up a perfectly good retreat, he got to his feet and headed for the door.

"Take care," she said, her voice whisper soft.

"You, too." He let himself out and closed the door.

But instead of feeling relief or a sense of escape, he felt caught up in something. And as he ducked into the crisp, Montana night, hoping to break free from whatever held him, the snare only grew stronger.

Juliet *loved* him?

All night long, Mark struggled with Juliet's admission of love, making sleep impossible.

He'd been afraid to ask what, *exactly,* she meant by "love." Afraid that he would be backed into an emotional corner. Afraid he'd be faced with something he didn't know how to deal with.

And now, as Saturday morning wore on, he regretted that he hadn't asked.

Did she love him as a friend?

Maybe. But friends didn't kiss the way they'd kissed. Didn't reach star-bursting, mind-spinning orgasms in each other's arms.

He stood before the bathroom mirror, looking at the unruly strands of hair that bore the brunt of his frustrated insomnia, and ran a hand over his bristled jaw.

Now that it was over—whatever *it* was—and now that he was able to get on with his life, he wasn't so sure that he wanted to.

Juliet had grown on him. And leaving town didn't seem nearly as appealing as it had last night—before his guilt-riddled confession. Before her unconditional acceptance.

Before she'd mentioned love.

Hell, they'd never even talked about the house he meant to buy. The house he'd planned to let her and Marissa live in.

There was a lot they hadn't discussed, a lot that needed to be said. After all, he was leaving soon—maybe even today.

A political exposé, Tom had called it. An assignment worthy of excitement.

But instead of elation, that rush of adrenaline when a new story broke, Mark felt...

Dammit. He didn't know what he felt, but it sure as hell wasn't excitement. Or happiness.

He was going to miss Juliet.

And her daughter.

Hell, Mark had watched Marissa take her first breath, had cut the cord. Held her.

Held her mother.

And now, the two of them had a heck of a hold on *him*.

That was it.

The trap. The snare.

Mark's heart did a death-defying loop-to-loop, soaring, pumping, thumping. Spinning.

But not on a quest to escape.

Oh, for cripes sake. He'd fallen hard for Juliet— head-over-sorry-ass in love.

Still, the realization wasn't nearly as scary as it should have been.

The only scary thing was packing up and leaving town. Leaving her.

He grabbed his cell phone and called his boss.

"Tom, I've had second thoughts. I don't want to pass the gold rush story on to another reporter. I want to write a scoop on the real owner of the Queen of Hearts mine. A story loaded with history and legend—poker hands, lost and stolen deeds. A story about a crazy old outlaw and a prospector with a gambling problem."

"You sure about this?" Tom asked.

Yeah. Mark was growing surer by the minute. "I don't believe that Caleb Douglas owns that gold mine."

"What makes you say that?"

"I talked to him yesterday," Mark said, pondering something the wealthy rancher and businessman had mentioned. "He's contacting Vaughn & Associates, a P.I. firm, to find the deed and verify his ownership."

"You might be on to something. Go for it. And keep me posted."

"I will." Then Mark disconnected the line. He really wasn't sure who the owner was, but he would soon find out, even if he had to dog the trail of the investigator Caleb hired.

In the meantime, he had a few more calls to make. The first was to Roy Canfield, the editor of the *Nugget*. After all, if Mark was dead set to be a homeowner and a family man, he couldn't very well be traipsing across the country on assignments.

When Roy answered, Mark introduced himself and said, "I've got a question for you."

"Shoot."

"How would you like a partner, someone who could help you make the paper all you want it to be and still allow you to take your wife on an occasional cruise?"

"You've got my ear," Roy said.

"I've got a full day planned, but can we get together tomorrow morning at the newspaper office? Maybe around nine?"

"That works for me," the older man said. "I'll make a fresh pot of coffee."

"Sounds great. I'll see you then." Mark disconnected the line.

Damn, that felt good. And it had been easy, too.

He just hoped his proposition to Juliet went over as well.

Just one more call to make—if he could find the number.

Fifteen minutes after getting off the phone, with his dreams soaring higher than they ever had, Mark headed for The Hitching Post to tell Juliet how he felt.

He sure hoped he hadn't read her wrong, but if he had, he wasn't going to take no for an answer. He'd just have to convince her that Marissa needed a father.

And that Juliet needed a husband.

But not just any husband. She needed *him*.

As Mark sauntered out of the lobby of the Wander-On Inn and prepared to cross Main Street, he was surprised to see how many cars were parked along the curb.

The diner didn't open for lunch until eleven. What was going on?

Unable to quell a nose for news, Mark entered The Hitching Post, rather than slipping around the back. He found the eatery filled with women. Giggles, chatter and plenty of oohs and aahs filled the air.

Juliet sat at a table in the middle of the room, a stack of presents and colorful gift bags surrounding her, while a rosy-cheeked, matronly woman held Marissa, swaying back and forth as though in an invisible rocking chair.

Oh, yeah. Her boss was throwing her a baby shower.

Mrs. Tasker met him near the door. "I'm afraid we're not open yet. Not until eleven."

"Do you mind if I interrupt for a minute?" His eyes locked on the woman he loved.

Yeah. *The woman he loved.*

His chest puffed up with emotions he hadn't even allowed himself to dream about in years.

"Why, I suppose it's okay," the older woman said, stepping aside and letting him make his way through the throng of ladies sipping coffee and pink-colored punch.

In the center of the room, the woman he loved was knee-deep in torn wrapping paper and little baby things. He tossed her a smile.

Juliet studied Mark, his crooked grin, the glimmer of sunshine that lit his brown eyes.

What was so important it couldn't wait? Was he leaving now, this very moment? Was this the only chance he had to tell her goodbye?

She'd managed not to cry last night, when she'd bravely let him go—but only until the door closed behind him. And since tears began to sting her eyes, she wasn't sure she could pull it off again.

"Juliet," he said in a voice loud enough to still the chatter and gain the attention of every woman in the diner. "I've got something to tell you."

She crossed her arms, bracing herself, as she waited for him to drop a bomb.

"I love you."

His words reverberated through the room, jarring the heart from her chest.

"And if you and Marissa will have me," he added, "I want to marry you and be a part of your family."

Emotion clogged her throat, making it hard to respond with more than tears. She swiped at the moisture under her eyes.

Was this real?

She blinked, hoping that, if this were a dream, she'd wake up.

But he continued to stand there, a hopeful look plastered on his face.

"You want to marry me?" she asked. "Are you sure?"

"Honey, since the first time you slid a menu in front of me, you grabbed a hold of my sorry heart and made me feel like someone special, someone worthy."

She swallowed the lump in her throat, afraid to speak, afraid to break the spell.

"I love you, Juliet. I love your rose-colored view of the world, the Latin temper you hide so well. Even your interest in history got a hold of me. Lady, I love *you*—plain and simple. Marry me and make my life complete."

Juliet couldn't hold back the tears, couldn't hold back the flood of happiness. She stood, wrapped her arms around Mark's neck and sealed her agreement with a kiss.

She knew she should hold back, make the kiss brief and discreet. But she was too happy, too much in love. And amidst cheers and applause, she offered Mark all the love in her heart.

When they came up for air, Mrs. Tasker was the first to officially congratulate them. "When's the wedding?"

"As soon as I can get the license," Mark said. Then he looked at Juliet. "If that's okay with you."

"That's fine."

"And you'll have to find another waitress to take Juliet's place," Mark told Mrs. Tasker. "My wife is going to take care of our daughter for a while."

Mrs. Tasker grinned. "I figured as much."

He scanned the crowded room, the half-opened gifts. "How soon will the party be over? I'd like to take you someplace."

"We'll need to clear out of the diner before eleven," Juliet told him.

"Good. We've got an appointment at eleven-thirty."

An appointment?

"Are you planning to go to the courthouse and find a justice of the peace?" She'd always wanted a church wedding. Just a small one, of course.

"We can decide on when and where we want the ceremony over dinner tonight. But I don't want to wait very long, not when it feels as though I've been waiting my whole life. But you deserve more than a few words spoken by a county official in front of a couple of witnesses we don't know. Besides, I thought it might be nice if we invited my parents."

His eyes glistened with sincerity, and her heart nearly burst. Her little family was growing by the minute. "I don't think you'll be sorry about including your mom and dad."

"I'm beginning to think you've been right about a lot of things." He nodded at the seat she'd been sitting in. "I'll let you get back to your baby shower."

As she sat, he grabbed an empty chair and parked it next to hers, looking eager to make that appointment he'd mentioned.

Her curiosity piqued. "Where are we going at eleven-thirty?"

"It's a surprise," he told her, a grin boasting of his excitement, his happiness. His love.

Juliet didn't know what he had planned, but it didn't matter.

The future was an adventure on which she was eager to embark.

After the baby shower, Mark took Juliet and Marissa for a drive, pleased with the surprise he'd planned and unwilling to spoil it.

"Where are we going?" she asked again.

"Just wait and see."

They drove to Ranch View Estates, but Mark didn't stop at the sales office. Instead, he turned onto Wagon Wheel Drive and parked in front of the house Iris Grabowski and her late husband had purchased.

The woman's Chevrolet was parked in the driveway.

As he slid from the rented sedan, Mark realized he'd need a new car—a family-style vehicle like an SUV or a minivan. But there was time for that.

He escorted Juliet and the baby to the front door and rang the bell.

Moments later, a beaming Mrs. Grabowski answered. Mark introduced the women, and Iris let them into a vast living room, just waiting for the furniture they'd need to buy. The focal point was a stone fireplace with a mantel for Juliet to display her pictures. At least, that's what he figured she'd do.

"Honey," Mark said, "Iris has agreed to sell her house to us. And while we're waiting for probate and dealing with escrow, she's going to rent it to us. We can start moving in this afternoon."

"God works in mysterious ways," the older woman told Juliet.

Mark wasn't sure what the Ol' Boy Upstairs had to do with anything. Mark was the one who'd come up with an idea that would help everyone out, but he didn't want to shake the widow's faith.

"My husband and I had put in a lot of upgrades," Iris said, as she led them into a roomy kitchen with Corian countertops and state-of-the-art appliances.

"The house is absolutely beautiful," Juliet said. "I love it."

"Well, let me show you what was going to be my sewing room," Iris said, as she led them down the hall and opened a door on the right.

Mark stepped into a room with pale pink walls and a white, built-in bookshelf near a window that looked into a sod-covered backyard.

"Pink is my favorite color," Iris said. "But I'm sure you can repaint it white or another color."

"Pink definitely works for us." Mark slipped an arm around Juliet, pulling his wife and daughter close. "It will make a perfect nursery for our baby girl."

"I'm so glad this has worked out for everyone," Iris said. "And I hope you don't mind if I leave you here. I'm meeting a friend for lunch."

"No problem." Mark was eager to take Juliet shopping for furniture, eager to hear what she thought about making this house their home. Eager to be alone with the woman he loved.

Iris handed him the key.

Just like that?

"We haven't signed anything," Mark told her. "But I'm good for the money."

"I know you are," Iris said.

The widow obviously didn't have a mind for business. Mark could have been a flake, trying to take advantage of her.

"You're more trusting than you ought to be," he told her.

The silver-haired woman smiled sweetly. "God wouldn't have sent you to me if I couldn't trust you."

Yeah, well her faith was a lot stronger than his. He took out a business card that had his cell phone number on it. "I'm looking forward to working with your son-in-law and the escrow officer he knows."

When Iris left them, Mark turned to Juliet—the woman he loved—and the baby she held in her arms.

His wife.

His daughter.

His life.

Being part of a family never felt so right.

Chapter Fifteen

On Sunday evening, Mark and Juliet drove to his parents' mountaintop home, ten miles up Turner Grade.

Mark had called his mother earlier in the day and asked whether a visit would be convenient, since he knew how much time his parents spent at the motel.

His mom's happiness had been hard to ignore, and she'd asked if they would stay for dinner.

His first thought had been to decline, but when he'd spotted Juliet packing the last of the boxes for their move, he agreed.

Now, they stood on the front porch of the house he'd always considered a prison. A pot of pink geraniums offered a bit of color to the white exterior of what had once been painted a drab, winter-gray, telling him that a lot had changed. Somewhat bolstered by the woman at his side, he knocked on the newly lacquered door.

His mother answered, wearing a yellow apron and an awkward smile. She started to lift her arms, as though wanting to offer a hug, then dropped her hands to her sides and fingered the material of her apron. "Please come in."

The aroma of pot roast filled the air, mingling with a hint of yeast and cinnamon. It wouldn't surprise Mark if his mother had cooked all afternoon. And the fact that she had, pleased him.

"I'm so glad you brought the baby," she told Juliet. "I'd love to hold her, if it's all right."

"Of course." Juliet handed the precious bundle of pink and white flannel to the woman who'd longed to be a grandmother for years. Twenty or more, Mark suspected.

A look of awe swept across her face, erasing years of stress, as she studied the sleeping baby in her arms. Then she looked up at Mark and Juliet with a smile. "Please, have a seat. Dinner is almost ready. Can I get you something to drink? Iced tea? Milk? I have beer and wine, too."

"I'm fine for now," Juliet said. "But milk sounds good with dinner."

Mark had half a notion to ask for a beer, but decided to face the evening head-on. "I'll pass for now, too."

At the sound of steps coming downstairs, Mark glanced up to see his father. It was the first time they'd laid eyes on each other in twenty years, so he shouldn't be surprised to see how time had put a slight bend to his old man's stance, more lines on his face, more gray in his hair.

He walked with a limp, Mark noticed. A result of the arthritis that plagued him?

His father reached out a hand that appeared a bit gnarled. "I'm glad you came, son."

Mark gripped him gently, but firmly. "Thanks. It's been a long time."

"Too long." His father smiled, then turned his attention to the woman Mark was going to marry. "It's nice to meet you, Juliet."

"Thank you. It's nice to meet you, too, Mr. Anderson. Thank you for inviting us to dinner. I'll have to whip up one of my Mexican feasts and return the favor."

"Please," his father said, "call us Jess and Anne-Marie. And we'd love to join you for dinner sometime, wouldn't we honey?"

His mother, pleasure glowing on her face, agreed.

Still, the past hovered over them, in spite of the awkward smiles and small talk.

"Anne-Marie, why don't you take Juliet into the den and show her what you've got for her," his father suggested.

"Of course. Come with me, dear."

As Mark's mother and Juliet left the room, his dad smiled. "Your mother told me your fiancée was pretty. But that was an understatement."

"Juliet's beauty runs deeper than the eye can see," Mark responded.

"Good. I'm glad to hear it. A wise man recognizes the inner woman early in a relationship."

Apparently, in recent years, his father had grown to appreciate his mother, which was nice to know. His parents' relationship had been strained when Mark was a teen.

Juliet had told him about the conversation she'd had with his mother at the clinic. The news that his father had been having an affair while the family had lived in El Paso had come as a surprise, although it shouldn't have. The signs and clues had been there all along—now that Mark knew.

His dad motioned toward the sofa. "Have a seat, son."

Mark sauntered toward the beige sectional and sat, as the past continued to permeate the room, the air they breathed.

There was no other way, but to face it. But before Mark could broach the subject, his father did.

"I owe you an apology son, one that's more than twenty years late."

"I owe you one, too."

"No," his father said. "You don't have much to apologize for. I had a hell of a temper and a shameful attitude years ago. I had my own demons I was wrestling with, and I took out my anger and frustration on my family. Especially you."

He had. And now that Mark knew about the affair that had placed a dark cloud on the family, he understood—even if he didn't appreciate—why the man had been so angry all the time, so ready for a fight with anyone who crossed him, especially a rebellious teenage son.

But Mark didn't bring up the affair. What was the point? His father and mother seemed to have reached a peace about it.

"When your sister died, I couldn't own up to my failure to look out for her. And in my grief, I lashed out at you, wanting you to bear the guilt that was mine alone. Your sister should have been seeing a doctor. And even though your mom thought we ought to push it, I didn't take the situation seriously enough."

"I've carried a lot of guilt over Kelly's death for years," Mark admitted. "I should have stayed home that day. And I'm sorry I didn't."

"Don't beat yourself up over it, son. From what your mother and I have learned, an emergency C-section would have saved Kelly. But with telephone lines down and roads closed..." He didn't finish, didn't have to.

"You're probably right. But I should have stayed home, like you told me. I'm sorry for being such a rebellious cuss."

"That you were. But, truth be told, you weren't any ornerier than I was as a kid." His dad took a deep breath, then blew it out. "Any chance we could start over, Mark? Pretend some of our past never happened?"

"I'd like to give it a try. Juliet has taught me a lot about love and family. And, if you don't mind being a grandpa to the most beautiful baby in the world, I figure we have a lot of catching up to do."

"I can't think of anything your mom and I would like better than to be grandparents." His dad smiled, brightening his face in a way Mark hadn't seen in a long, long time.

Before they could say any more, Juliet and his mother returned to the room. His mom carried the baby, while Juliet held a colorful array of cloth.

"Look what your mother made for Marissa," Juliet said, flashing some little baby outfits and dresses.

His mother, with a glow of pride, looked prettier and happier than Mark could remember.

"I love to sew," she said. "So Marissa is going to be the best-dressed baby in town."

"And I'm going to build us a playhouse for the backyard," his father added, a grin bearing testimony of his acceptance, his hope for the future. "Just like the one I built for Kelly while we lived in El Paso."

Mark remembered the little white house, where his sister used to spend hours with her dolls. His mom had made red-checkered curtains and placed yellow plastic flowers in miniature window boxes.

The memory, he realized, was one of many he had of the happier times, the times Juliet had urged him to remember.

"I'm sure Marissa will like a playhouse," Mark said.

"That's the plan." His dad chuckled. "Your mom and I hope, that if we make our home appealing and keep our cookie jar filled, Marissa will beg for you to bring her to visit."

"I have a feeling she won't have to beg." Mark flashed a grin at the woman he loved. "Family means a lot to Marissa's mommy."

"Juliet, as much as I hate passing this baby back to you," his mom said, "I need to get dinner on."

"Let me help." Juliet took Marissa from Mark's mother and held her out to Mark's dad. "Jess, why don't you take your first turn at being a grandpa?"

His father's eyes widened and his mouth dropped. "She's so little. And I don't know how to hold babies. Never even held my own till they could walk. Maybe I ought to—"

Before he could utter another word, Marissa was placed in his arms.

"Well, I'll be darned. Will you look at that." He marveled over the tiny girl, his eyes glistening. "She's no bigger than a peanut. And she's got her eyes open. Hey there, Angel, you don't know me yet, but I'm your grandpa."

A flood of warmth filled Mark's heart, seeking out every cold nook and cranny.

He'd been alone for so long, that love and family ties had become foreign. Remote.

But not anymore.

Before Juliet could slip away to the kitchen to help his mom, Mark stood and wrapped her in his arms. "I've got you to thank for making things right in my world."

She placed a lingering kiss on his lips. "Thanks for giving love and family a chance."

Five minutes later, they sat around the old dining room table, where love, laughter and forgiveness chased out the old memories, hurts and resentments.

"I know that we never used to pray before meals," his mother said. "But I feel so very blessed, I think it's only fitting to offer a prayer of thanksgiving."

"You've got a point." Mark reached for Juliet's hand and enfolded it in his. "For a guy who'd once been a cynical hard-ass, I gotta admit, I'm the luckiest man in world. And I have a lot to be thankful for."

Juliet returned the loving squeeze. "We all do."

As they bowed their heads, Mark couldn't help but chuckle.

If the future looked any brighter, he might have to shed his cynical nature and borrow Juliet's rose-colored glasses.

* * * * *

CABIN FEVER

BY
KAREN ROSE SMITH

Karen Rose Smith grew up in Pennsylvania's Susquehanna Valley and still lives a stone's throw away. Readers can write to her at PO Box 1545, Hanover, PA 17331, USA or e-mail her through her website at www.karenrosesmith.com

With thanks to Jessica Miller for her valuable help in describing Montana weather and scenery. Her love of the state easily inspired me.

To my continuity partners, Christine Rimmer, Allison Leigh, Pam Toth, Judy Duarte and Cheryl St John, who made working on this project a pleasure.

Chapter One

"I am *not* the father," Brad Vaughn stated in no uncertain terms.

The Chicago private investigation firm of Vaughn Associates was *not* where Brad wanted to have this discussion. However, with his dad standing in his office, newspaper in hand, Brad had no choice.

Phillip Vaughn, head of the firm, a man who was always right, a father who was grooming his son for his position, shook the newspaper at Brad. "Are you sure? Suzette Brouchard says—"

"I don't care what Suzette Brouchard says. We had a brief relationship, but I never slept with her without protection. From the information I have so far, her baby was born forty-two weeks after our last night together.

She'd moved on to someone else, and *that* man is the father of her baby."

Suzette was a beautiful, sexy model, but neither of them had expected more than a few nights of good sex. She'd faded into the background after they'd stopped seeing each other, and that had been almost three years ago.

"Why would she do this?" Phillip Vaughn asked, still in an accusing tone.

"Money. She thinks if she makes enough noise, I'll settle and give her a bundle."

Brad *had* a bundle. Not from the fortune his father had acquired but from his own sweat. He'd earned an MBA and opted out of his father's plans for him for a few years to work on Wall Street. He'd done well and invested most of it, not in the dot-com of the moment but in solid, stable companies he'd researched. At the height of the boom, he'd sold most of it, bought real estate, sold that, reinvested in conservative investments for the future and constantly turned over the rest for profit. At thirty-five, he had more money than he'd ever need.

Money certainly hadn't been the reason he'd joined his father in his firm. Taking over Vaughn Associates someday hadn't been one of his aspirations. However, when his mother had phoned him and gently suggested his dad wouldn't be around forever, Brad had wondered if he and his father could set aside the adversarial relationship they'd always had and forge real bonds they could build on. But Brad had been vice president of his dad's firm for two years now, and the bonds were as thready as they'd always been. He didn't know any more now what made Phillip Vaughn tick than he had when he was twelve and his parents had divorced.

"I've already contacted Suzette's lawyer and informed him I'll be giving a sample for a DNA test today. This will be settled within a month," Brad said decisively.

"The reputation of this firm could suffer a hell of a lot in a month if articles like this keep appearing."

"That's what Suzette and her lawyer are counting on."

"A settlement could shut it all down *today*," Phillip insisted.

But Brad wasn't about to settle, not when his reputation was at stake. "No. I want to clear my name. I won't be thought of as an irresponsible playboy who doesn't care if he gets a woman pregnant."

"That's not what you are?" his father asked with a bit of an amused smile.

His dad often frustrated him. Now his question rankled in a deep place that unsettled Brad. "I have *never* been irresponsible."

Silence reverberated in the office until his father broke it. "Maybe you should think about settling down," he suggested, throwing the newspaper onto Brad's mahogany desk.

"You know how I feel about that." Brad couldn't keep the acerbic edge from his voice.

When his father had kicked his mother out of their home after her affair, Brad had lived with her during the week and with his father on weekends. He wouldn't take the chance of doing that to any kid. Besides that, he simply didn't trust women. That might have started with his mother's infidelity, but in college he'd given the fairer sex a chance. That had been a mistake. His father had bought off the girl that he didn't deem appropriate for Brad, and Brad's eyes had been opened to exactly how little love mattered compared to the allure of money.

"With your paternity up in the air, what are you going to do about Thunder Canyon?" his father asked.

"Thunder Canyon can't wait," Brad answered, considering the client's case he was personally overseeing.

Thunder Canyon, Montana, was a small town near Bozeman. Since Vaughn Associates was acclaimed for its security work and all-around private investigation skill, the company's reputation was known across the country. Caleb Douglas, one of the most renowned citizens of Thunder Canyon, had hired Vaughn Associates to uncover the true ownership of a gold mine there.

"I got the history from Caleb Douglas yesterday," Brad went on. "Since the late eighteen hundreds, the Douglas family has claimed the property in Thunder Canyon that includes the Queen of Hearts gold mine. Now they can't find the deed. Caleb has always assumed he knew the truth and the land was his. I'm hoping I can wrap up the investigation in a few days."

A small voice on his shoulder, however, reminded him a missing deed could mean trouble.

"I'll need to find the deed or some proof of ownership. I'm going to ask Emily to go along."

"Your secretary? Is she necessary?"

"Caleb said he wanted this done quickly no matter how much it cost. If Emily's along, I can count on her to write up the daily reports and do preliminary interviews."

With a frown, his father checked his watch. "I have

an appointment across town. I'd better get going." He cast a disdainful glance at the newspaper once more. "Maybe if you're out of town for a few days, the hub-bub over that…situation…will settle down. I don't want to have to field calls about your personal life while you're away."

As if his father really knew anything about his personal life. "If you receive any calls, give the caller my cell number," Brad said curtly.

Phillip gave him a long look. "I'll do just that." Then he left Brad's office.

Crossing to the doorway, Brad's gaze didn't follow his father as he left the office suite. Rather, his eyes rested on Emily Stanton. His secretary sat at her computer, headset on, transcribing yesterday's reports.

Brad would never depend on a woman in his personal life. He knew the foolishness, the futility in that. But in his professional life, Emily was as dependable as a woman got. She was organized, punctual, thorough and sometimes uncannily able to read his mind. With her straight, dark brown hair—shoulder length and blunt—her bangs; her sedate, always-polite attitude, she didn't turn heads and she didn't flirt. She was just available when he needed her, straightforward in her manner and an asset he didn't want to contemplate doing without. She'd been with the Vaughn secretarial pool for two years. Then, six months ago, when his secretary had taken maternity leave, Emily had applied for the promotion. He knew from her personnel records she was twenty-seven, but he didn't know much else. They'd never had a personal discussion.

Engrossed in her work, Emily wasn't even aware of him stepping out of his office. Since she was wearing her headset, he clasped her shoulder, hoping not to startle her. "Emily?"

She gasped and came up out of her chair so fast her headset flew from her ears and landed on the computer keyboard. They were standing toe to toe and almost nose to nose, except her nose came to the knot of his tie. He suddenly realized how petite and fragile she seemed as he inhaled a flowery scent—lilacs, maybe? Yes, Emily Stanton smelled like lilacs. Had he ever been this close to her before?

Trying to back up, she bumped into the desk. "Mr. Vaughn! Did you call me? I didn't hear you come out of your office."

"No, I didn't call you." He motioned to the headset. "I didn't think you'd hear me."

She was wearing a two-piece black suit today, with a boxy jacket and a straight skirt. For the first time since he'd hired her, he noticed her eyes were the color of emeralds.

For a moment, neither of them spoke, just gazed at each other.

Then, feeling a bit unsettled and not knowing exactly why, Brad asked, "Can you come into my office? There's something I need to discuss with you."

Emily's cheeks were flushed and she didn't appear to be her calm, cool self as she reached for the legal pad on her desk and a pen in the holder. "Sure. I'll be right in."

Brad didn't wait but returned to his office and lowered himself into the tall, burgundy leather chair behind his desk.

Hurrying in after him, Emily took a seat in one of the two chairs facing him. She was composed again, her legal pad and pen ready to take notes or directions. Emily loved lists, he knew. She stuck them on her computer, on her keyboard, on her desk. He supposed that's how she stayed organized.

"I have a special assignment for you. Something out of the ordinary."

"A special assignment?" she repeated, looking perplexed.

"Remember those notes you typed on Caleb Douglas?"

"The man who thinks he owns a gold mine in Montana?"

"He's the one. By the way, thanks for staying late last night and deciphering my scribblings from the phone call with him."

There were still spots of color on her cheeks. "No problem. I knew you wanted to start working on his case today."

"There's some urgency in finding out whether he truly owns this mine or not. Supposedly the gold mine was abandoned in the late eighteen hundreds. But a couple of months ago, when a young boy fell down an erosion hole into a mine canal, gold nuggets were found. Caleb Douglas, of course, wants to mine any gold if it's there. The problem is, he and his family can't find the deed."

"And you're supposed to find it?"

"I'm supposed to find out who truly owns the Queen of Hearts mine. I doubt if I'll find the deed itself, but hopefully I can find some type of record that will prove Caleb Douglas is the rightful heir or the owner."

"What do you want *me* to do?"

As Brad's attention focused on Emily again and the expectant look on her face, he realized how cute she actually was. Was he looking at her differently because he'd be traveling with her? Because he was thinking about time they'd be spending together outside of the office? Because he was thinking about how she'd look in blue jeans?

Reminding himself that Emily wasn't the type of woman he dated for a multitude of reasons, he said evenly, "I'd like you to fly to Montana with me tomorrow. As I said, I need to tie up this case quickly. If you're along, the work might go faster. We might have to page through a lot of old records, and I may need to follow leads while you make calls."

Her gaze dropped to his desk and the newspaper lying there. Then she asked, "It would just be you and me? Alone?"

Brad had the reputation for being one of the most eligible bachelors in Chicago. He had been dubbed that when a reporter had written an article about him after he'd returned to his hometown. At the time it hadn't bothered him, but now he didn't like that reputation any more than he liked the column that had appeared about him and Suzette in this morning's paper.

Picking up the newspaper, he folded it in half and tossed it into the trash can beside his desk. "The allegations are false."

To her credit, Emily didn't play dumb. "It's none of my business," she said softly.

"You're my secretary. It's your business because I

don't want unfounded gossip to keep you from taking this trip."

"I'm surprised you're going away now," she admitted honestly.

"I'm not going to let an unsubstantiated accusation interfere with my work or with my life."

"I don't know, Mr. Vaughn...."

"It's only for a few days, Emily. There will be plenty of other people around. We'll be busy with interviews and public records."

"Where would we stay?"

"There's an inn and a motel. From what I understand, it's pretty much a little, one-horse town, but it's readying itself for a new ski resort."

Seeing indecision still on her face, he offered the one incentive he knew she'd understand and probably not resist. "If you take this trip to Thunder Canyon with me, I'll toss in a bonus." He named a sum that made her eyes widen.

"You're willing to pay that much for my help?"

"I'm willing to pay that for *good* help. I need someone dependable, and you're dependable. So what do you say?"

After a few moments of hesitation, she asked, "When should I be ready to leave?"

"Sorry, Mr. Vaughn, I simply have no rooms to rent you," said the motel manager with a Texas drawl that seemed out of place in Montana.

Emily couldn't believe what she and Brad were hearing. He had told her yesterday there was no need to make advance reservations since the tourist season

wasn't yet in full swing. They'd just arrived at dinnertime, and they were worn out from their flight—from
Chicago to Denver, then Denver to Bozeman. The foreman of Caleb Douglas's ranch had picked them up at
the airport and driven them to Thunder Canyon. When
he'd asked where they wanted to go, Brad had directed
him to the Big Sky Motel at the edge of town.

Standing to one side, the foreman of the Lazy D—a
man in his fifties with a stubble of gray beard and a huge
black Stetson—tipped his hat up on his forehead. "It's
because of the gold rush. We got more people coming
in than this town knows what to do with."

"Mr. Vaughn, maybe we should try to call Caleb
Douglas," Emily suggested.

"It's Brad, Emily. I told you that on the plane. And
Caleb Douglas is going to be meeting us here anytime
now." Turning back to the hotel clerk, he demanded,
"Let me talk to the manager."

Emily could tell Brad was getting impatient. He was
the type of man who was used to clearing his way no
matter what the obstacles in his path.

The man behind the desk looked a bit frazzled, too.
Emily thought he looked a little like Al Pacino. He wore
a name tag that said Jess Anderson.

Now the motel manager tugged on his bolo tie and
blew out a breath. "I'm the manager *and* the owner. I
don't have any rooms to give you."

Taking his wallet from his jeans, Brad removed a bill.
Emily's breath caught when she saw that it was a hundred dollars. Her employer laid it on the counter. "Are
you sure?"

Mr. Anderson seemed to draw himself up a little straighter, not that he was anywhere near Brad Vaughn's six-foot-three height. Emily sensed a tirade coming on.

With her best friendly smile and her calmest voice, she stepped up a little closer to Brad and then was sorry she did. Even at the end of the day, she could smell a trace scent of cologne. His short, black, curly hair was a bit mussed, and beard stubble darkened his jaw. She should know better than to get too close to him. She avoided men like Brad when they crossed her path, and she wasn't about to be stranded in a strange town with him with no place to sleep for the night.

Emily fingered the strap of the camera bag that was hanging around her neck. "Mr. Anderson, I can see you're busy, but we've come a long way. Could you recommend someplace else we could try? A bed-and-breakfast maybe?"

"No bed-and-breakfasts around here. There's a dude ranch on the edge of town. I sent some folks over there yesterday, but now they're full up, too. You should have called first."

"I never expected this place to be overflowing with tourists," Brad told the motel owner.

Mr. Anderson shook his head. "I've never seen anything like it. All this because a couple of people found a few little nuggets of gold." He glanced at Emily again. "Let me make a few calls, miss." Pushing Brad's hundred-dollar bill back at him, he said haughtily, "No need for that."

Putting the bill back where it belonged, Brad looked puzzled, as if he didn't understand what the hotel owner had just done.

When Emily had applied for the job with Brad Vaughn, she'd put her attraction to him aside, keeping her eye on the promotion. There had been a buzz about his return to Chicago. Everyone knew Phillip Vaughn was grooming him to take over someday, but Brad wasn't the kind of man to be groomed. She'd passed him in the halls, glimpsed him picking up work at the secretarial pool. Her heart had thudded riotously every time she had. He was the kind of man women noticed.

But she'd had her fill of that kind of man. As the old adage went, *Once burned, twice shy.* She'd emerged from her first and only serious relationship with more than a broken heart. She'd been devastated. Not because she'd found herself pregnant and the man had walked away but because a few weeks later she'd had a miscarriage. She didn't want handsome, wealthy, irresponsible men anywhere near her radar screen. She had a sister to finish putting through college and she had her own goals now. Nothing was going to interfere with them.

Not even her elemental reaction to her sexy boss.

"What seems to be the problem?" a booming voice asked over Emily's shoulder.

She turned and found a man in his sixties with silver hair, pale green eyes and a ruddy face that looked as if he spent a lot of time outdoors. His white Stetson sat high on his forehead and his turquoise-and-silver belt buckle caught the glimmer of the overhead lights as he unbuttoned his suede jacket.

Emily wished she'd brought along *her* suede jacket. She'd never realized May in Montana would not be the same as May in Chicago. It still felt like winter here.

The foreman pointed to Brad. "This here's your private investigator."

Caleb Douglas extended his hand to Brad. "It's good to meet you, son."

"It's good to meet you, too, Mr. Douglas." Then, to Emily's surprise, Brad nodded to her. "This is Emily Stanton, my assistant."

Caleb reached for her hand and pumped it, too. "How do you do, Miss Stanton."

"I'm fine, thank you. Anxious to get to work. But we do have a problem. There aren't any rooms. Mr. Anderson is making a few calls—"

Jess Anderson returned to the front desk to face Brad once more. "I'm sorry, Mr. Vaughn, there's just nothing in this town to rent. You might have to drive back to Bozeman."

"No sense in that," Caleb decided. "Under any other circumstances, I'd invite you to stay with me at the ranch, but my wife's family is visiting from back east. They haven't visited for ten years and all of a sudden they came roaring in like a herd of cattle gone crazy. All because of the gold rush. Anyway, like I said, you can't stay at the ranch right now, but I bought a cabin last month to get away from all this hullabaloo. It's about forty minutes out of town, up in the mountains. I've only been there a few times and I haven't had time to get it renovated yet. But the essentials are there. My wife's family should be leaving in a few days, and then you'll be welcome to stay with me. In the meantime, maybe Mr. Anderson will have a vacancy. What do you think?"

To her dismay, Emily felt as if she were riding a train

to an unwanted destination. It was going too fast for her to jump off. One minute she'd been sitting at her desk, typing up Brad's notes, and the next she was facing a night in a cozy cabin with Brad. Alone.

No way.

"I don't know if that would be a good idea," she began, trying to be calm, reasonable and professional.

To Caleb, Brad said, "Will you excuse us for a minute?" Clasping Emily's elbow, he pulled her aside.

After Brad had tugged her a good five feet away, he said in a low voice, "This offer's the best one we've got."

"I can't spend the night *alone* in a cabin with you. What would my family say? What would your father say?"

"You're twenty-seven, Emily. Your family cares if you spend the night alone in a cabin with a man?"

"I have an older brother who's protective. I have two younger sisters who I have to set an example for."

Brad was looking at her as if she'd landed in Thunder Canyon from another planet.

"They care about me, Mr.—" she felt Brad's warning look "—Brad."

"Do you think they'd rather have you spend the night in a car or maybe Caleb Douglas's barn?"

When Emily worked for Brad, she concentrated hard on her work and didn't let him distract her. Today she hadn't had work to concentrate on. Whenever he looked at her, her breath caught. The feel of his hand on her arm was making her whole body tingle. His presence sent her into a tizzy and that's why she couldn't think straight. She could see now they really didn't have any other options.

The fact that he couldn't convince her easily had made Brad's jaw set. If he was angry with her, he was restraining it well as the sparks in his eyes made butterflies dance in her stomach.

Finally he released her arm. "If you want to return to Chicago, I'll find someone to take you to Bozeman. But I doubt if there are any flights out tonight."

She was sure he was right about that and, darn it, she wanted that bonus. She needed it to help with the last of her sister's expenses. After Lizbeth graduated, Emily could save toward going to college herself. "I don't want to go back to Chicago. I came here to do a job with you and I'm going to do it. Let's tell Mr. Douglas we'll stay at his cabin."

"Are you sure?" Brad's deep voice held a measure of concern.

Before she lost her nerve, she responded, "Yes, I'm sure."

When Caleb's foreman dropped Brad and Emily off at the rental-and-used-car lot, Brad still had high expectations this trip would be quick and successful. Now he hoped so even more than before. Cooped up in planes beside Emily for most of the day, he'd been much too affected by her natural femininity. There was nothing coy about her, nothing flirtatious, nothing pretentious. But ever since yesterday, he couldn't keep the adrenaline from rushing through him whenever he inadvertently touched her. He couldn't keep the light scent of her perfume from teasing his libido.

However, self-restraint had never been a problem. So

they were going to spend the night in the cabin together. It was one night, and he'd pretend she was a backpacking buddy.

Emily had insisted on staying outside with the luggage and the laptop computer he'd brought along mainly for her use. Inside a small building on the car lot, Brad's expectations diminished as he spoke to the woman behind the desk. She'd just told him she had no SUVs to rent.

"If you don't have an SUV, what about a pickup?"

The frizzy-haired redhead frowned. "Mister, you've got to understand what's happening here. We've got more sightseers than you can count coming into Thunder Canyon. Up until a few months ago, we didn't have much call for rentals. Now we can't keep an SUV or a truck on the lot to rent or sell. I can take your name and number, and if one comes in I can call you. But for now, that blue sedan out there is as good as it gets. It was turned in yesterday and the mechanic went over it before he left today, so it's in good shape."

Peering out the window, Brad spotted the light blue midsize car. He produced his credit card, knowing he had no choice. "I'll take it."

When he emerged from the office ten minutes later, keys in hand, he noticed the big, blue Montana sky had changed. Gray clouds had covered the sun although dusk was still an hour away. He was starved and he supposed Emily was, too. She was standing by their luggage, her arms wrapped around herself.

She hadn't dressed for Montana weather. For their flight she'd worn tan casual slacks and a cream oxford shirt. But the blouse had short sleeves, and the sweater she'd thrown over her arms for most of the trip didn't look that heavy. He'd spent a summer in Montana over a decade ago, but he'd forgotten the weather here was as changeable as a woman's moods. He'd forgotten how even in summer the mornings could have a nip and the nighttime temperature could drop into the fifties.

He dangled the keys in front of her and lifted her suitcase, as well as his. "I have directions to a grocery store. We can pick up food and supplies and head out. Do you have the directions Caleb gave us?"

An open Jeep with four men sitting inside sped much too quickly down the street. The vehicle backfired as it turned a corner.

Hoisting her purse onto her shoulder, Emily took a slip of paper from her pocket as she tried to keep up with his long stride. "Right here. I went over them again. We're going to have to watch the odometer carefully. He said there weren't any road signs after the first turnoff. How rustic do you think this cabin is?"

"He said there's one bedroom and the place is furnished. There's water and electricity, but if the power goes out, we have to use the pump out back for water."

Emily was horrified. "If the electricity goes out?"

He stopped. "It's in the mountains, Emily. I guess anything can happen. Haven't you ever gone camping?"

Shaking her head, her expression told him that going on a camping trip was as foreign to her as signing up for a trip to Mars.

"Caleb assured me there's a fireplace. We'll be fine. We just have to remember to pick up some Sterno."

"Sterno?"

"So we can cook if the power goes out." He started walking again, came to the car and gave it a look-over. "It's not what I wanted but it should get us where we want to go."

"I hope so," she murmured, looking worried.

Before he thought better of it, he set the suitcases on the ground near the trunk and took a step closer to her. "We can handle anything for one night, right?"

A breeze whipped her hair across her face and a strand caught on her lip. Without forethought, he reached out and smoothed it away. Her skin was so soft under his thumb, her lips such a pretty natural pink, her eyes a shade of green that captivated him.

The hum between them that had seemed to come from nowhere kept him immobilized for a few seconds until finally she repeated bravely, "I can handle anything for one night."

But Brad was beginning to wonder whether *he* could.

A cabin in the mountains of Montana with a secretary he was suddenly finding very difficult to ignore. Bringing Emily Stanton along on this trip had been a monumental mistake. Now he just had to be damned sure he didn't make another one.

Chapter Two

Buying supplies took longer than it should have, Brad thought, as he drove away from the Old Town section of Thunder Canyon, with its frontierlike connected storefronts and boardwalk promenade. It seemed his taste and Emily's were decidedly different. She'd looked for food with few preservatives and spent more time in the produce section than he'd spent buying Sterno burners, matches, candles and a flashlight. While he'd snatched up a package of chocolate cookies, she'd weighed one apple against another. Now she was silent as the gray clouds faded into a dark sky and the wind picked up even more.

The interior of the car seemed much too confining with the heater blowing and Emily's perfume floating around him on the air currents. She was studying the map with a penlight attached to her key ring.

They were only a mile out of town when snow began to fall. It swirled lightly at first, then began hitting the windshield more densely.

"How can it be snowing?" Emily asked in amazement. "It's May."

"This is Montana."

"That explains it?"

"It's the altitude and the mountains and weather fronts. There *is* life outside of Chicago."

He hadn't meant to snap at her, but her dismay was evident, and he asked, "You're sorry you came, aren't you?"

"Aren't *you?*"

As tall firs collecting the swirling snow sped by, he realized he'd needed this break from routine. "Actually, I'm not. I get tired of sitting at the computer doing searches. I'm beginning to hate the politics of finessing important clients. And I'm thoroughly fed up with investigating one company stealing another's secrets."

In the darkness he could sense her gaze on him as she asked, "Isn't that what you want to be doing? Isn't that why you came back to Chicago and joined your father's firm?"

Emily had never asked him personal questions before. They'd never had a personal conversation, and he wasn't sure this was the right one to begin with. "I came back for lots of reasons," he answered, explaining nothing.

A few heartbeats passed as snow swept around the car in a squall, covering the road and everything else they couldn't see through the storm.

"Don't you like working with your father?"

Persistence with her work was one thing. Persist-

ence in digging personal info out of him was another.
"I came back to work with my father."

"That's not what I asked you. Sometimes you seem
so removed from it all."

Day after day he'd thought Emily had done her work,
not noticing much else. Apparently he'd been wrong.
"It's not always easy working with family. When I'm in
my office, I'm there to get a job done."

"You're good at what you do. You always find the answer, solve the problem, connect the right people together."

"But...?" he drawled, knowing there was one.

"But you do it so...impersonally."

"The same way you do your work?" he inquired
calmly.

Her hand brushed his question aside as she shifted
in her seat to look at him. "That's different. I type. I file.
I transcribe. I don't work with people. *You* do."

Thinking about it, he realized why he stayed impersonal. "It's no fun discovering that a wife is cheating on
her husband. Why would I want to get involved?"

"You don't normally take divorce cases. At least not
unless your client is rich and famous."

Brad remembered the talk-show host who had come
to him last year asking for complete anonymity. Brad
had met with the man where he could remain incognito,
and Emily had set up those clandestine appointments.

Through the illumination of the car's headlights,
Brad could hardly see ten feet in front of him. He slowed
the vehicle to a crawl and glanced at the odometer. "I
don't want to miss the first turn."

"I don't know how you can even see," Emily said

in a subdued voice, dropping the subject they'd been discussing.

Brad wasn't sure he *could* see, but somehow through the snow he spotted the high and square rock formation that Caleb had described as distinctive right before the first turn. However, as he attempted to turn left, the car skidded, then spun in a circle.

In the dark, suspended moment, he heard Emily's gasp.

"We're all right," he assured her as he managed to control the car and head in the right direction again. Reaching out, he laid his hand on her arm.

When there wasn't another peep out of her, he stole a glance at her. "Are you okay?"

"No, I'm *not* okay," she blurted out. "I'm scared. What if we get stranded out here?"

"The snow's letting up. We're not going to get stranded. Why don't you try to find something on the radio."

"Do you think that's going to distract me?"

"It might distract us both."

In spite of his attempt to keep his attention focused on road conditions, to his annoyance *she* was distracting him…more than the storm or the snow or the wind or the strange road at night. Her reactions were so damned honest. He wasn't used to honesty from a woman.

Emily fiddled with the channel-selection knob on the radio, but all she could produce was static.

"I could hum," he suggested, trying to lighten the atmosphere. But Emily's mind was obviously still on their drive and their destination.

"What did you think of Caleb Douglas?" she asked,

her voice not quite steady. He had to give her a gold star for trying to overcome her apprehension.

"I think he's a man with a lot on his plate. He has an office in town to run his new ski-resort project and he owns the biggest ranch in the area. But he still had to buy a cabin to find peace and quiet. That tells me his life is speeding by pretty fast and he's trying to put on the brakes."

Shifting in her seat again, she let go of her clench on the door handle. "Maybe. Or maybe he just needs a quiet place where he can get in touch with who he is, not who everyone *thinks* he is."

Emily's perceptive comment made Brad glance at her once more. Although he really couldn't see her by the luminescent glow of the dials, he was very much aware that she was there and that she had more substance than he ever expected. Still, he remembered the way she'd jumped at the offer of a bonus. He remembered the night his fiancée had let money take precedence over a life together with him. He remembered his lawyer telling him before he left Chicago, "Suzette Brouchard wants a settlement."

As Brad drove deeper and higher into the mountains, snow fell lightly most of the time. Now and then it became heavier and Brad could feel Emily's tension. That was an odd thing. He didn't consider himself particularly intuitive when it came to women because he didn't usually plug in that well.

By the time they reached the last turnoff on the directions, Brad felt relieved. "We're almost there."

Emily muttered, "Thank goodness," and he smiled. They'd laugh about this when they got back to Chicago.

In the next few moments, the smile slipped from Brad's lips. As he spotted the creek he'd have to cross before they drove the last half mile or so to the cabin, he realized the situation they'd be in if he did. In May, runoff from the mountains could cause flooding. As the road curved onto the bridge, he could see sloshing water had reached its snow-covered surface. The problem was, he couldn't turn back. With the snow accumulating steadily every mile they'd traveled, the car would never manage a trip back to Thunder Canyon tonight. At least in the cabin they'd be warm and dry. They'd brought enough food to last them a week.

Brad thought about the cell phone clipped to his belt. What were the chances he could still get a signal out here?

The car's tires swished through the slushy snow and water on the bridge.

As Brad covered the half mile, then veered off the road to take the lane to the cabin, he could tell that here the two or three inches of new powder that had fallen tonight covered patches of old snow that still hadn't melted.

The sedan's tires churned beneath them, and he couldn't make any more headway up the incline. "This is it. Why don't you stay in the car while I get the supplies unloaded. You'll be warm and—"

"I'm coming with you."

"Emily…"

"I'm not the damsel-in-distress type, Brad."

After he switched on the inside light, his appraisal of her was quick, from her off-white sweater to her flat tan leather shoes. "I may have to carry *you* inside, as well as the supplies. How far do you think you're going to get in those shoes?"

When she looked him over, from his jean jacket to his black boots, she mumbled, "I have sneakers in my suitcase."

"Good. You'll need them. Do you want me to get them out now?"

She shook her head. When she did, he couldn't help but follow the sway of her dark hair along her cheeks. He couldn't help but think how silky it looked and how he'd love to feel its softness in his hands.

"I'll keep the sneakers dry for tomorrow," she responded quietly. "Let's just get inside."

Blocking thoughts of touching Emily out of his head, realizing she was as stubborn as he was, he didn't argue with her. If she wanted wet feet, that was her choice.

As Brad exited the car, snow fell on his head and shoulders. He took in a couple of lungfuls of cold night air, surveyed the pines not far from the cabin illuminated by the car's headlights and realized he was glad he was here. He'd only be in Montana a few days, but already he was relieved he was away from the city…away from his father…away from Suzette Brouchard and a situation he couldn't resolve until the lab results came in.

Out here, all of that seemed very far away.

After he rounded the car to open the trunk, Emily appeared beside him. He'd loaded batteries into the flashlight after he'd bought it and now he used it to guide his key into the lock on the trunk. When it popped open, he shone the beam inside.

Emily reached for her suitcase, but his hand covered hers. "I'll get that."

His skin meeting hers sent an electric jolt to his system. When his gaze collided with hers, he saw she was as affected by the result of their contact as he was. Her expression was startled, her eyes wide with man-woman awareness. Snow was settling in her hair, falling onto her long, dark lashes unenhanced by mascara. They didn't need to be enhanced.

When she shivered, he ordered gruffly, "Just grab a bag with groceries. I'll take care of the rest."

Ignoring his instructions, she hung her camera bag around her neck, then picked up two bags and started the ten-yard trek to the cabin.

Brad swore softly, shook his head and decided the next few days were going to be damn interesting. For the past six months Emily Stanton had played the part of a dependable secretary who kept her opinions to herself. Now he realized there was a woman behind that facade—a woman with spirit and a mind of her own.

The rustic-looking log cabin didn't have a porch, simply two snow-covered redwood steps leading to the door.

Watching Emily as her small feet sank into the snow, Brad followed her. When the sole of her leather shoe sank onto the first step, her foot slipped. He realized he'd been expecting that to happen.

Dropping the suitcases, his arms went around her and the grocery bags to prevent her and their supplies from tumbling into the snow. Her shoulder brushed his chest as he caught her, and his nose grazed her hair—hair that smelled like flowers!

As she looked up at him, their faces were very close. Their white breaths in the cold air mingled as she said, "I'm fine," and he murmured, "I've got you."

For a long, silent winter moment, everything went still. Their body heat seemed to create a cocoon of warmth diametrically opposed to the elements surrounding them. With the headlights of the car shining toward the cabin, he could see her expression in the shadows. It was questioning now—surprised and even a little curious. He was curious, too, about the vibrations humming between them, the chemistry that had seemed to spring up out of nowhere yesterday outside his office. Snowflakes landed on Emily's bangs, on his nose. If he bent his head, their lips would brush. If he turned her to face him…

A gust of wind buffeted them.

He had to get a grip. This wasn't a fun getaway for two. They were in Thunder Canyon to work and nothing else. He and Emily weren't from the same world. In many ways she was very much like his ex-fiancée, Robin. She came from a blue-collar family, hadn't known many advantages and was trying to make the best of her circumstances. Robin had made the best of her circumstances by accepting his father's check and bailing out of Brad's life.

Years later, he knew he should never have gone after her. He should never have heard her say she had feelings for him but wanted the good life *now*. His father's money had given her freedom, and she wanted to experience it alone.

The good life. Freedom. He had both, but lately he'd felt more restless than satisfied or happy.

Releasing Emily, he said, "We're getting wet."

As another gust of wind and snow brushed across the front of the cabin, Brad used the key Caleb had given him, pushed the door open and stepped inside.

Emily watched Brad enter like a man on a mission. She could hardly keep her teeth from chattering now, but for those few moments when Brad had held her she'd been as warm as toast.

He hadn't held her. He'd caught her. And if she hadn't seen the desire in his eyes to kiss her...

She simply hadn't. Her imagination was working way past overtime.

Suddenly she realized Brad had probably gone into the cabin ahead of her to search for creatures. Were there bears in Montana? She'd seen those movies where animals in the wild had broken through windows and played havoc inside a vacationer's paradise.

This was not her idea of a vacation. A vacation destination for her would be a sunny beach on an island, swimming to her heart's content, dancing under the stars.

With whom?

Shaking disturbing visions of Brad from her mental images, she followed the glow of Brad's flashlight as he found the light switch.

The switch controlled the overhead light in the kitchen, and she took in the place where they'd be spending the night. They'd stepped into a living room with a wood floor, Native American patterned rugs, a hunter-green tweedy sofa and a tan leather club chair with a buffalo painted on its cushion. The log walls were devoid of decoration, but a bookshelf sat against one wall across from the club chair. The sofa faced the fireplace that was small but beautiful with its stone hearth and chimney.

Peering straight through the living room, she saw the small kitchen had an oven, burners and a compact refrigerator. To her left, she tried to see into the darkness of the bedroom, but she wasn't able to. She supposed the bathroom was in there.

Finding the thermostat on the wall, Brad went to it and heat clicked on. "I'll get the rest of the supplies. Don't even think about trying to help me," he said with a stern look. "Get warm."

For some reason, when he looked at her, she got *very* warm. But she'd never admit *that*.

Taking her suitcase from the floor, he carried it to the bedroom. She saw him turn on a small lamp and then he set her valise on the bed.

"You can sleep in there tonight," he said, emerging from the bedroom. "I'll take the sofa."

In the office setting, Emily hadn't glimpsed Brad's chivalrous side, though he did always open doors for her. She was a bit surprised by it.

When Brad opened the door to return outside, she heard the wind howl. He was going to freeze until he brought everything in. She knew he was probably used to fine brandy, but tonight maybe he'd appreciate hot chocolate.

As Brad brought in the last of the bags of supplies and placed them on the wrought-iron-and-glass kitchen table, he began unpacking them. After storing the cookies in an upper cabinet, he put milk and juice into the refrigerator. Emily couldn't help but watch his every move.

"What?" he asked when he caught her interest.

She felt color rise to her cheeks. She'd been admiring his height, his broad shoulders, his adaptability to the situation. Brad Vaughn had to be used to maid service, but he was putting his groceries away. "Nothing."

"What were you thinking, Emily?" His gaze pinned her to the spot, and she knew he wasn't going to let her evade him. Brad didn't let anybody evade him.

Choosing her words carefully, she selected the ones that were most diplomatic. "I was just surprised you were putting away the supplies."

Like a panther cornering its prey, Brad took a few steps closer to her. "Surprised?"

"Guys don't usually think about things like that."

To her relief, he didn't seem angry. "Guys? Meaning any guy in particular?"

His closeness unnerved her, and she quietly unscrambled her thoughts. "My brother, for instance. You'd think with three sisters and a mom he would have learned to pick up after himself after all these years. But even his wife says he's impossible."

Instead of focusing on her brother, Brad asked, "Did your parents divorce?"

"No. Dad died when I was ten. An aneurysm he never knew he had burst."

"I'm sorry. You said you have a brother and sisters?"

"Eric's two years older than I am. Lizbeth and Elaine are younger. What about you? Brothers and sisters?"

Brad shook his head. As the wind rattled the windowpane, he still studied her closely. "It must have been hard for your mom to raise you on her own."

"It was. We all had part-time jobs as soon as we could."

When he reached out and slid his hand down the back of her hair, she closed her eyes, amazed by the sensations coursing through her.

"It's still damp," he murmured.

"It will dry," she responded, opening her eyes again, gazing into his brown ones, suddenly wanting to feel his lips on hers more than anything else she'd ever wanted.

The windowpane rattled again, and she couldn't believe she was even thinking such a thought. Gathering her wits about her, she turned away from him and switched off the burner on the stove. "I'll have hot chocolate ready in a minute, and then we can think about supper."

"If we can agree on what to eat." His voice was a bit husky. "Your taste and mine seem to run in different directions."

"I don't eat a lot of meat," she admitted. "But if you want to pan fry that steak, I can make a huge salad—"

All at once, there was sudden and complete darkness and an all-encompassing silence. Then the wind whooshed against the cabin once more and the whole building seemed to quake.

"Damn," she heard Brad mutter. "Where's my flashlight?"

"I have a penlight on my key chain."

"But you'd have to find your key chain," he said in a wry tone.

In the pitch blackness she knew it would be hard to find anything. As afraid as she was in their present situation, Emily was concerned that if she moved she'd bump into Brad, and that seemed even more dangerous than standing in darkness in a strange place. So she stayed put, trying to remember where she'd dropped her purse. She thought it was on the buffalo chair, but she wasn't sure.

She heard Brad moving around, shifting bags on the table. Finally he announced, "Got it." A moment later, a beam of light streaked to where she was standing.

"I'm fine, but what are we going to do? Without the power, we don't have any heat."

"Slow down, Emily. We've got a fireplace. There's wood on the hearth and probably more out back. I think I spotted an oil lantern over on those bookshelves."

Dipping his hand into one of their bags, he produced matches. After he found the lantern, he lit it. The light vanquished some of the darkness in the living room area.

"There's a can of lantern oil here, but we should still probably conserve it. Why don't you make that hot chocolate while I go out and check the wood supply."

"Why check it? If we already have some here—"

"I have to see how much we have. We may have to make it last."

"Only one night." While he aimed the flashlight at the floor, she couldn't see his face in the shadows. "Brad? It's only going to be one night, isn't it?"

"Let's just take things as they come."

"What aren't you telling me? We can't get snowed in here for days, can we?"

"I doubt that, but I don't want to run out of wood, either."

"From what I could see, there were trees everywhere."

"There are. But even if I had an ax, everything's wet. Green wood smokes. I'm hoping there's a supply of covered logs out back. Make the hot chocolate."

He was keeping something from her—she knew he was—and she wasn't going to plead with him to tell her. She wouldn't plead with a man for anything.

Five minutes later, when Brad returned from checking the wood pile, his face looked grim.

Emily panicked. "What?"

He'd carried in a few logs and now he deposited them on the hearth. "This is it."

She was shivering again. She'd taken off her sweater because it was damp from the snow. The temperature in the cabin was only a little warmer than when they'd arrived. Her slacks were still wet and her stockings, too.

Shrugging out of his jacket, he hung it over a kitchen chair. He was wearing a western-cut, blue plaid shirt, and the truth was, he looked as if he belonged in Montana. *She* obviously didn't. Brad Vaughn was sexy enough in the suits he usually wore, but in jeans and a snap-button shirt...

She swallowed hard.

"What do you want to do first? Drink the hot chocolate or change your clothes?" He looked down at her slacks, which were wrinkled against her ankles. "You've got to get out of the wet clothes so you can warm up. I hope you brought something comfortable."

At the last minute, she'd thrown in a pair of sweats. "I did, but I don't really have anything warm."

"I've got to get the fire going. Once I do that, we'll

raid the closets and drawers and see what we can find. We'll both have to sleep in here tonight by the fire to keep warm."

Her gaze automatically slanted to the sofa.

"You can have that," he said generously. "I'll make a bedroll on the floor."

"That'll be hard."

"I've camped out before. I'll be fine. If it gets too uncomfortable, I can always try the buffalo chair. I can usually sleep anywhere."

Sleeping brought to mind beds. Beds brought to mind what men and women did in beds. Pushing away visions of her and Brad in a bed, she remembered the article in the newspaper yesterday morning. She remembered Suzette Brouchard and the claim that Brad was her baby's father. She remembered Brad's rich-bachelor lifestyle.

"Go on," he said with a nod. "Take your hot chocolate with you. Drink it while it's warm."

"We won't be able to make steak for supper."

"We're not going to starve. We have plenty of food and we've got the Sterno burners. Relax, Emily. You're going to get gray hair if you keep worrying about everything."

Suddenly the whole situation—Montana, the snow, being cooped up with Brad Vaughn in the cabin—got to be too overwhelming.

As she straightened her shoulders and lifted her chin, she said, "Maybe I've never been to Montana and maybe I've never gone camping, but you don't have to treat me like a child."

Picking up her mug of hot chocolate, she tried not to

let it slosh over her hand as she made her escape into the bedroom.

It would have been a good exit, but then Brad called to her. "Emily, you're going to need this."

When she turned, he held out the flashlight to her. "I can use the oil lamp. You won't be able to see in the bedroom."

Did she spot amusement in his eyes? Was that an almost smile at the corner of his lips?

Grabbing the flashlight, she mumbled, "Thank you," and headed for the dark room.

After she pushed the door shut, she hated the fact that tears pricked in her eyes. The attraction to Brad Vaughn that had plagued her ever since she'd started working at Vaughn Associates had been buried with a lot of effort. But this trip was bringing it to the surface, and she didn't want it. She didn't need it. As soon as Lizbeth graduated from college at the end of May, she was going to earn her own degree. Then she could become more than a secretary. She could become anything she wanted—except maybe the kind of woman Brad Vaughn dated.

That doesn't matter, she chastised herself.

After she fiddled with the flashlight, unpacked her suitcase and found the clothes she wanted, she changed, not anxious to go back into the fray with Brad. The violet sweats had been a Christmas gift from her sisters. They were comfortable, as were the crew socks she pulled onto her feet. With her wet clothes off, the room was still cold but she didn't feel quite as chilled.

Sniffing, she caught the scent of burning wood. She'd

lived in an apartment all her life and had never been in a house with a fireplace. That more than anything else urged her to open the bedroom door and go back out into dangerous territory.

But when she stepped into the living room, she froze.

Brad was standing in front of the fire, pulling a pair of jeans from his suitcase on the sofa.

He was stark naked!

Chapter Three

In spite of herself, Emily couldn't look away. Brad was
magnificent with the firelight flickering over his skin,
shadows playing in intimate places. Stunned and absolutely speechless, she noticed that with no shirt to hide
his muscles, Brad's shoulders seemed twice as broad.
His chest hair was black and curly, and as she followed
it down—

Either she made a sound or he sensed her presence.
Rather than looking embarrassed, though, he tossed her
a grin, obviously unashamed of his body.

She swiveled around, ready to run back to the bedroom, when she heard the rustle of jeans, the clank of a
buckle and the quick rasp of a zipper.

"You can turn around now. I didn't expect you to

come out so quickly. Women usually take a lot longer than that to change their clothes."

Maybe the women *he* dated.

Her hand went to her hair. She hadn't even taken time to brush it after she'd slipped on the violet top that went with her pants. "I guess I'm not your typical woman," she responded blithely.

Though her cheeks still felt as if they were on fire, looking straight ahead, she went to the kitchen, trying to pretend seeing him naked hadn't affected her at all. Although he'd pulled on jeans, the snap above his fly was still undone, his belt buckle was unfastened and he was shirtless.

"So what's for supper?" she asked him, her heart still racing as she kept her gaze away from his bare skin.

After he pulled on socks, he rummaged in his suitcase to find a flannel shirt. "Since we had the hot chocolate and we have a good fire, why don't we go with peanut butter sandwiches and a can of fruit for tonight. In the morning we can use the Sterno and try to cook eggs."

She knew he'd bought more than one Sterno unit. Nevertheless, she still had the feeling Brad was keeping something from her. Maybe he was concerned the snow would fall more heavily during the night and they wouldn't be able to dig themselves out.

"Peanut butter's good, but *you* can have the can of fruit. I'll eat an apple."

"A purist," he teased with a smile that almost made her toes curl.

"With some things," she tossed over her shoulder.

The kitchen was cold and getting colder. Only the living room held warmth, because of the fire. "I guess we could eat on the sofa."

"If you want to stay warm."

With him beside her on the sofa, she had the feeling she'd be plenty warm. While she made the peanut butter sandwiches—two for him, one for her—he popped the top on the can of fruit and then hunted in the cupboard for the cookies he'd stowed there. He'd let his shirt hang out over his jeans, and she had the disturbing urge to slip her hands under it and touch his bare skin.

What in the world was happening to her?

With a quick twist of her wrist, she closed the jar of peanut butter. "You never did tell me how you learned to clean up after yourself."

Leaning against the counter, holding the bag of cookies, he casually crossed one foot over the other. "No, I didn't."

The sound of his voice was unusual. "Does that mean you're *not* going to tell me?"

"You're different here than you are in the office."

If that was his way of not answering her question, it wouldn't work. She wasn't going to let him turn the tables on her. "And *you're* changing the subject."

The oil lamp on the kitchen table flickered, as if a sudden draft had given it renewed life. Its light was reflected in Brad's eyes. He seemed to stare at the flame for a few seconds before his gaze finally met hers. "Kids pick up habits out of necessity."

The statement seemed incongruous with his background. It was well known that Phillip Vaughn had come from money, even if he hadn't been successful in his own right. As a boy, Brad should have had every advantage, as well as a maid picking up after him.

Uncrossing his ankles, the casual pose forgotten, Brad set the cookies on the counter as if he'd suddenly lost his appetite for them.

As she thought about his statement, she said softly, "I know what you mean. After Dad died, Mom was scattered. Since Eric was the oldest and a boy, she looked to him to do some of the things Dad had done—everything from taking out the garbage to helping sort through her finances. Lizbeth, Elaine and I had to pretty much fend for ourselves. Since I was the oldest of the three of us, I took care of them and also took over a lot of the household chores. Mom had to work longer hours to make ends meet."

"Did you resent it?"

"I'd like to say I didn't, but sometimes I did when my friends could do things I couldn't. But most of the time I just felt needed. I learned how to manage time, leftovers in the refrigerator, even the girls' activities. What about you? Did you resent what you had to learn?"

"My situation was different from yours."

Waiting, she hoped patience would encourage Brad to go on. It did.

"My parents divorced when I was twelve. I lived with my mother during the school week, and on weekends I lived with my dad in the house where I'd grown up. In the beginning I would forget a schoolbook at one place, a favorite toy at another. I couldn't depend on anyone to know exactly what I needed except for me. It became important for me to find a place for everything— then I could lay a hand on it at a moment's notice."

"That must have been so hard having two homes but not a real home." Brad must have constantly felt as if he were being pulled in two directions.

He shrugged. "I got used to it, but no child should have to."

Picking up the two paper plates with the sandwiches, he nodded toward the sofa. "Come on. Let's eat."

In the living room Brad set the plates on the wrought-iron-and-glass coffee table in front of the sofa. He'd brought along a can of soda with the cookies, and Emily had picked up a bottle of water.

Instead of sitting, Brad moved the coffee table to the side and pushed the sofa closer to the fire. "If you're cold, I could pull a blanket off the bed."

She curled in a corner of the sofa closest to the fire. "I'm okay for now."

When Brad sat beside Emily, there was half a sofa cushion between them, and it seemed like no space at all. They made polite conversation as they ate, and Emily began to relax. To her surprise, Brad was easy to talk to as she explained she'd like to go to college. He drew her out about courses she was interested in. When she asked him about his years on Wall Street, he told her stories that made her laugh.

As the fire burned lower, the windowpanes stopped rattling, and she hoped the storm was over.

Brad had opened the pack of chocolate cookies and now he held it out to her. "Want one?"

Her apple had disappeared after her peanut butter sandwich. The chocolate-covered cookie with marsh-mallow in the center *did* look good. Pulling one from the bag, she took a bite. Then she closed her eyes and savored it.

Brad's voice was low and deep as he said, "There are a lot more. You don't have to spend so much time on that one."

After she opened her eyes, she realized he'd been watching her. She'd been enjoying the cookie as if it were the most sensual experience on earth, and he'd apparently seen that. He'd apparently *liked* seeing that.

When he looked at her as if she were one of those chocolate cookies, her breath almost stopped. For two years she'd watched Brad from afar, wondering what he was like. Six months ago, when he'd given her the job as his personal secretary, she'd told herself any attraction she felt had to be swept under a rug. She'd warned herself against feeling anything for him. Her relationship with Warner Bradshaw should have taught her that men like Brad, men like Warner, thought they ruled the world.

But tonight she'd seen a different side to Brad and she liked it. Her thoughts slipped back to seeing him naked by the firelight, and she knew more than anything in the world that this moment she wanted him to kiss her. She'd shifted from her corner of the couch in the course of their conversation and now her knee practically brushed his.

"Emily." Low and husky, his voice fell over her as his gaze roamed her face.

Her mouth went dry as she managed a small, "What?"

Moving closer to her, his thumb stroked over her upper lip. "Chocolate crumbs."

When her hand went to her lips, it was caught by his. "Since yesterday," he began, "there's been a buzz between us. Do you feel it?"

She could only nod.

He leaned even closer. "I'm going to kiss you."

It was a declaration of intent, and she realized why he'd made it. She could move away. She could run to the bedroom and shut the door. She could pretend she wanted another chocolate cookie more than his kiss. But that wouldn't be true.

For months she'd wanted to run her fingers through his hair. For months she'd seen his beard shadow at the end of the day and wondered what it would feel like against her cheek. His stubble now made him look even sexier than usual, if that was possible.

As his hand came up to cup her cheek, she kept perfectly still, afraid she'd break the spell.

His long, warm fingers slid into her hair as he brought her face closer to his.

The fire crackled in the hearth as a different fire that had lain dormant for months came to life inside of her. When Brad's lips covered hers, tiny rockets exploded all through her body and she wanted one thing—to experience more.

Brad's tongue slipped inside her mouth, and after a few moments of pure erotic pleasure, he pulled back. He was breathing raggedly and so was she as he smiled at her. "You taste like peanut butter and chocolate."

She couldn't speak because the kiss had been too short—an appetizer when she wanted the whole meal. That must have shown in her eyes.

With a groan, his head bent to hers again, and this time there was no holding back as he let his hunger show.

Brad Vaughn not only looked sexy, he *was* sexy. She'd never experienced anything like his kiss. It was intense and demanding and seductive. Her hand went to the nape of his neck and she inhaled his scent. She inhaled Brad.

The longer they kissed, the more the strokes of his tongue inflamed her. The longer they kissed, the more her thoughts scattered. The longer they kissed, the more she forgot about everything but Brad.

As he laid her back on the sofa, she embraced him, eager to stroke his back, eager to lift his shirt and feel his hot skin.

At her touch, he shuddered, then he stilled and broke the kiss. Propped on his forearms, he stared down at her. "Do you know what you're doing?"

The question brought Emily back to the real world, and that wasn't the cabin where they were stranded. He brought her back to her life in Chicago and who she was and who he was. Then she remembered the pain when Warner had left and she remembered the devastation when she'd lost her baby. For goodness' sake, Brad had been accused of fathering a woman's child! Didn't that show her the writing on the wall?

When she tried to scramble to a sitting position, he lifted himself off her and sat on the sofa. "That's what I thought," he muttered.

Although she was upset, flustered and still longing for more of his kisses, she asked indignantly, "What does *that* mean?"

He ran his hand over his face. "Nothing. We both just got caught up in the moment."

But she couldn't let it go. She had a feeling he was making comparisons and she didn't like it. "I guess I've had a lot fewer of those moments than you have." It was meant to be a stab at his lifestyle, but it wasn't a very good one.

"I know."

His attitude fired her anger because she wasn't as naive as he thought. "You don't know everything."

"No, I don't. If I knew everything, I wouldn't have asked you to come along."

That stung, and she couldn't help the quick tears that came to her eyes. Not wanting him to see, she turned away from him, picked up the empty paper plates and announced, "I'm going to get ready for bed."

"I'll try to get some water from the pump. You won't be able to flush the toilet without it."

How did he know all of these things?

She hated depending on his know-how, on his survival skills, but she had no choice. She just knew she was going to keep her distance from him until they got back to Thunder Canyon and civilization. Until they got back to Chicago, where everything would be ordinary again.

When Brad awakened the following morning, sun streamed in the cabin windows. The fire had gone out and the rooms were cold. Immediately he noticed Emily was still asleep, almost invisible cuddled inside the two blankets she'd wrapped around herself.

They'd gone to sleep in stony silence, and that had been his fault. He shouldn't have kissed her. He shouldn't have even *thought* about kissing her.

Still troubled by feelings he didn't understand, troubled by the effects of that kiss, he drew back his blankets and sat up. Fortunately he'd found extra covers in the closet, along with a sheepskin jacket and a down parka. Brad wondered if they belonged to Caleb or whoever had lived here before. It didn't matter. He was just glad someone had left them.

He'd slept in his clothes last night, in deference to Emily, not wanting a repeat of what had happened last evening when she'd caught him naked. He'd try to play it low-key, but the way her eyes had roved over him had unsettled him, raised his temperature and made him wonder what it was about this woman that suddenly got to him.

When he threw back the covers and stood, Emily's head popped up from under her blankets. "Where are you going?" She was sleep-tousled, and her voice was husky from awakening quickly.

Trying for a casual tone, he answered with, "After I brush my teeth, I'm going to try to dig us out. I know it's cold in here, but I think we should wait until I come back in to light the fire."

"But if we're leaving today—"

That's what she wanted and so did he, but he didn't think it was going to happen. "Last night when I brought in the bucket of water, we'd already gotten about four to six inches of snow. I'm not sure that car can handle it."

She looked totally crestfallen.

"As I said, I'm going out to assess the damage."

Quickly sitting up, she declared, "I'm going with you."

"Emily, there's no need."

"We're stranded here together, Brad. I'm going to do my part."

By now he'd realized she had a very stubborn streak. "Fine. You can wear that parka we found. It should keep you warm."

Before she could argue with him about that, he headed for the bathroom.

As they stepped outside fifteen minutes later, the sun gleaming off the snow almost blinded them. Emily held her hand to her forehead like a visor and turned in slow circles, scanning all of it. "I can't believe anyone would want a cabin out here. It's so deserted." The parka seemed to swallow her up, and she looked adorable.

"It's isolated, but there could be a neighbor over the next rise. There's plenty of creatures, too, if you look for them. I don't think I've ever been anyplace more...serene. Listen," he advised her.

When she did, a puzzled expression came over her face. "I don't hear anything."

"That's the point. Where else can you hear silence like this?"

Her gaze met his, and the powerful connection he'd felt last night when he was kissing her seemed to be there again. But then she broke eye contact and glanced at the car. It was snow-covered, and her expression fell.

"I found a shovel and broom out back last night. I'll

get them, then see if we can move the car." But he doubted that they'd be able to move it very far.

She motioned to the sun, whose rays were a welcome relief from the cold inside the cabin. "Maybe it will melt it all."

"Maybe it will," he agreed, yet he knew snowmelt from the mountains could cause more problems. It was the reason the creek was already running full.

For the next half hour he shoveled around the tires of the car, while Emily used the broom to brush the snow from the hood and the trunk, then returned to the cabin for her camera. He was aware of her shooting photos of the scenery.

After he'd also shoveled the snow away from around the car, he gazed down the half mile that led to the bridge.

Taking the car keys from his pocket, he said, "I'm going to see how far I can get."

Before he could stop her, she'd climbed in the passenger side.

"Afraid I'll leave you behind?" he asked with a chuckle.

"I'm not taking any chances."

Although the remark might have been joking, Brad sensed Emily didn't trust him. He'd sensed that in the wall she kept around herself since she'd become his secretary. Last night that wall had slipped, but now she was evidently sorry about that.

After a cough and a sputter, the car started up. But as soon as Brad left the area he'd shoveled, he was spinning his tires. When he glanced at Emily, he saw her expression—it was near panic. "This obviously isn't going to work. We'll have to try something else."

"What else is there to try? We're stuck."

Their contact last night made it easy to lay a comforting hand on her arm. "Caleb knows we're here. He'll get us out if we can't manage to get ourselves out."

Suddenly her face brightened. "You have a cell phone, don't you?"

"I tried it last night. I couldn't get a signal up here in the mountains. This morning when I turned it on, the battery had run down."

Her expression looked so forlorn, he joked, "I'll have to give you an even bigger bonus after this trip."

Her large green eyes went wider. "Why? Because of that kiss last night?"

He knew she thought he was a ladies' man, but the idea that he'd up her bonus because of the kiss really irked him. "It was more than one kiss, and you were as involved as I was. But, no, that's not the reason I'll give you combat pay. I think you deserve overtime for being stranded where you obviously don't want to be."

Then he exited the car before he gave into the temptation to kiss her again.

Inside the cabin once more, Brad lit the fire so they could warm up. It was almost noon, and he decided to make scrambled eggs on the Sterno burner. Emily was skeptical, and it took a while, but eventually they sat down to a lunch of scrambled eggs and buttered bread. As she had the night before, she added fruit to her meal while he finished a candy bar and thought about their options. There weren't a lot of them, and he considered his comment to her this morning. There *could* be a neighbor just over the rise—a neighbor with a four-wheel-drive vehicle. Just as Caleb had purchased this cabin during the gold-rush siege, other people had also discovered Thunder Canyon and the surrounding area. He'd heard a movie star had even purchased a ranch near Caleb's new ski-resort project.

The summer Brad had spent in Montana with his friend James, he'd learned survival skills. He knew how to tell direction from the angle of the sun, the growth on the trees, landmarks he would designate.

Emily was trying to scrub the frying pan with water from the bucket and soap she'd found under the sink. She hadn't said much since they'd returned to the cabin, and he was sorry he'd been so gruff before. He didn't want to hurt her feelings. He didn't want to take advantage of her.

He didn't want to be attracted to her.

That more than anything made him say, "I'm going to go exploring this afternoon. Maybe I can find somebody who lives closer than we think."

"I'll go with you."

"No. I can go a lot faster without you and I want to get some ground covered." He could see the sun had slipped behind a cloud. In the mountains, the weather could change from minute to minute.

In a gentler tone he suggested, "You stay here, stay warm, keep the home fires burning. Though if you can help it, try not to use more than one log, okay?"

"Brad, this isn't a good idea." She looked downright worried.

He stood and went to the kitchen. "Are you afraid to stay here alone?"

"No! Well, yes," she finally admitted. "And I don't like the idea of you out there trekking in the cold and snow."

Taking her by the shoulders, he looked deep into her eyes. "I know what I'm doing, Emily. I spent a summer in Montana with a friend. We went backpacking for three weeks. What I didn't learn then, I've learned since on other backpacking trips. So you don't have to worry."

"I *will* worry," she said honestly, and he wondered how long it had been since somebody actually worried about him. That thought unsettled him just as Emily herself unsettled him. He hated to admit it, but for the past two days, being around her had made his life seem less empty. She soothed his spirit somehow, and he wasn't as restless.

The urge to touch her, the urge to kiss her again, was too much of a temptation. Stepping away from her, he said, "I'm going to wear the parka. It's warmer. Don't go outside unless you absolutely have to. Understand?"

"All right," she agreed.

Reaching to the counter for one of her PowerBars, he winked. "I'll take this along in case I get hungry."

When she gave him a small smile, he knew he had to leave—now. Too much about Emily Stanton was getting under his skin. A walk in the snow was just what he needed.

For the first hour Brad was gone, Emily did just fine—except for watching him walk away and disappear behind some pine trees. That's when her stomach sank.

Every fifteen minutes she went to the window and peered out, wishing he'd stayed in the cabin with her. Finally settling on the sofa, she read a magazine she'd packed in her suitcase. Then, still restless, she studied the titles of the books on the bookshelf and drank a can of juice.

But during the second hour the sky turned gray, the clouds seemed even more forbidding and the damp cold in the cabin seemed even damper without Brad. A tight knot formed in her stomach. He'd left at one, and by two-thirty she was worried sick. What if he'd slipped and fallen? What if he'd frozen to death? What if—

She couldn't stay cooped up. The fire had almost burned out, and she didn't know whether to add another log or not. The sheepskin coat Brad had worn that morning hung over a kitchen chair. Slipping it on, she thought she could smell him. She remembered how he'd looked in it—like a rugged outdoorsman. It was warm, and before she considered his warning to stay inside, she added her sweater under the coat, turned up the collar and went outside.

Snow was falling lightly and she had no idea what she was going to do. She just knew she couldn't sit still any longer.

Brad's footsteps were visible from the back of the cabin in a line that seemed to lead very far away. Trying to keep her sneakers from getting too wet, she stepped into each one of his prints, though it was a stretch. His legs were much longer than hers. Everything about him was so distinctly male. She couldn't erase the picture of him naked. She couldn't dismiss the erotic sensuality of his kiss.

With each step she took, the snow fell a little more heavily and wind began to blow. She had to turn back.

Gazing into the distance, she stared at the pine trees, wishing she could see through them. She stared so hard her eyes blurred and then she saw something…someone. At first she believed it was her imagination or a wishful mirage that she had conjured up. But then she recognized the green down parka, the fur-lined hood. He was walking in a straight line toward her and she didn't move. Not until he was about ten feet away.

Then she ran to him and threw her arms around his neck. "Oh, I'm so glad you're okay. I was so worried. You didn't come back and you didn't come back…."

The hood came down over his eyes and his face, but now he brushed it back and it fell away. He was looking down at her with hunger in his eyes and the desire she'd glimpsed there last night. Now it seemed to flame even brighter. "I'm back. I'm fine. Come on, let's get you into the cabin."

But neither of them moved, and she felt tears come to her eyes. "I was afraid you'd been hurt."

Although he'd told her he was fine, that wasn't enough. Her arms hooked around his neck, and he held her. Their breath mingled as he lowered his lips to hers.

The kiss was so hot she forgot it was snowing. The kiss was so desire filled her head swam. One minute she was standing there kissing him and the next he'd scooped her up into his arms and he was kissing her. Then he carried her to the cabin in much less time than it had taken her to walk in his footsteps.

Once inside, he kissed her all over again. Their lips

melded, their tongues tangled and their need for each other seemed to explode out of control.

Carrying her to the bedroll, he set her down there and knelt down beside her. "I want you, Emily."

"I want you, too." Making love with Brad had been in her dreams for months. Now they were alone together, needing each other. Couldn't she make at least part of her dream come true?

Unzipping his parka, he tossed it onto the floor beside him. She slipped off her coat and sweater and looked up at him with all the anxiety of the past hour and a half. "I was so worried about you."

"I worried about you, too, at the cabin alone. But I wanted to try to get us out."

He had been out hiking for her.

When she reached up to him, he bent down to her. This time the kissing was even more urgent. After he undressed her, he pulled a blanket over her. Seconds later he was undressed, too, slipping under the blanket with her. As he took her into his arms, she played her hand across his chest, loving the feel of his hair, loving the feel of *him*.

Any cold that had lingered from the outdoors dissipated in the heat of their passion as his legs tangled with hers. When his hand caressed her breast, she moaned with such pleasure that she didn't recognize herself. Every place he touched seemed doubly sensitized. Every kiss he planted on her lips, her neck and her navel made her sigh his name.

"What do you want, Emily?" he asked, finally stretching out on top of her, finally giving her some of the satisfaction she craved.

"I want *you*. I want you inside me."

He gave her what she wanted. The first thrust almost took her over the edge, but then he stilled, savoring their fit.

Brad had played her body to a fever pitch, and now it was demanding release. She couldn't stay still. When she contracted around him, he groaned. Raising her knees, she hugged his thighs and severed the thread of his self-restraint. Thrusting deeper and harder, he set a rhythm that became hers. She rocked with him until he slipped one hand between them and ignited her climax. The moment seemed to go on and on forever, and he kissed her until his release came. When he shuddered, she held him tight, never wanting to let him go.

But minutes later, as Brad pushed himself up on his forearms, then rolled off of her, she caught a glimpse of his face and knew she had to let him go.

As he lay back staring up at the ceiling, shame and regret and hurt filled her. And before he said something she knew she wouldn't want to hear, she asked accusingly, "Is this the way it happened with Suzette?"

Chapter Four

Brad's face had been somber but now his jaw set and he looked angry. "I have *never* had sex with a woman before without protection."

She found herself wanting to believe him…wanting to believe him with all her heart. She'd like to believe he'd wanted her as much as she'd wanted him and absolutely nothing else had mattered. Maybe at the moment she had mattered to him, but she was afraid it had been just for the moment.

"I can't believe I was that stupid." She sat up and dropped her head into her hands on her knees.

When she'd been seeing Warner, she'd been on the pill and she hadn't missed a day. But somehow she'd made it into that one-percent-failure ratio and had gotten pregnant. This time, however, if she got pregnant, it would be her own fault.

Sitting up beside her, Brad said gently, "If you get pregnant, you won't have to go through it alone."

How many men had told women that? She remembered Warner saying a kid wasn't in his plans. Brad probably meant he'd give her money, just as he'd wanted to give her an extra bonus. That's the last thing she even wanted to consider. "You mean you'd stick by me like you stuck by Suzette?"

"I am *not* the father of Suzette Brouchard's child."

"Then why did she make the accusation?"

"It really doesn't matter, does it, Emily? Because you're dead set on not believing me anyway. I don't know what I've ever done to you that you think I'd treat you shabbily or take advantage of you."

"You've never done anything to me," she admitted honestly. "But I've seen pictures of the women you date. I read the tidbits in the gossip columns. I pass personal calls on to you. Your relationships don't last much longer than a thunderstorm."

When he studied her face, she suspected an angry retort, but he didn't give her one. "You think what you want to think."

Then he was on his feet and pulling on his jeans. "That log isn't going to get us through the night. I'm going to try to find some kindling that might be dry enough to burn."

"You shouldn't go back out—"

"This time I won't be gone as long. It was a wasted hike. Tomorrow I'll try hiking *down* the mountain."

Ten minutes ago they'd been locked in the most intimate contact possible between a man and a woman. Now she felt as if they were miles apart. "Thank you for trying."

"No thanks are necessary. We both want to get on with our business in Thunder Canyon."

Stranded at the cabin, she'd forgotten all about the investigation. But at least if they ever got out of here, she'd have something else to think about besides the two of them.

She'd dressed and was putting a salad together for supper, complete with beef jerky and cheese, when Brad returned from outside with kindling. "I'm going to try this before I burn our last log. But if it begins smoking, we're going to have make do with what we have."

Make do with one log? Just how long would *that* last?

At least they had shelter. They had food and plenty of blankets. They'd be fine.

Yet when Brad's gaze met hers, she didn't feel fine.

As Brad lit the kindling, almost immediately smoke began billowing from the fireplace, as well as up the chimney.

He swore. "That's what I thought, but I had to try it. Come on. Get your coat. Let's go outside for a few minutes until the smoke clears."

Coughing as smoky air penetrated the cabin, she grabbed the sheepskin coat from the chair, shrugged into it and followed him outside.

Snow had stopped falling.

Brad glanced up at the sky. "It looks as if the weather's going to break."

"I wonder why Mr. Douglas didn't try to get

through to us today. He probably has an SUV or something."

"Even if he tried to get up here with an SUV, he would have had to turn back."

"Why?"

"Because the bridge is flooded from the runoff. We're good and stuck until he figures a way to get us out."

Her expression must have shown her fear and Brad swore again. "I thought you'd be better off knowing the truth of it. But Caleb *will* come get us. A man who could put together the ski-resort deal he just managed should have some kind of contact to get us back over that stream."

Emily was trying to keep from worrying. She was trying to forget what had happened in the cabin not so very long ago. She was trying to keep her feelings for Brad from growing stronger.

Turning away from him, she looked toward a band of snow-topped firs, then stilled. "What's that?" she asked in a low voice.

Brad came over to stand beside her. "That's a bull elk."

"It won't come any closer, will it?"

Brad chuckled. "I don't think he's too keen for our company."

"Maybe he wants food."

"Soon it will be calving season. Maybe he's just looking for some peace and quiet while he can find it."

That observation made her smile.

"Let's see if we can go back in. We don't want to get any colder than we have to. In fact, we should probably warm water for hot chocolate."

"When are we going to burn the last log?"

"Tonight. Before we turn in."

Although that made sense, she was still worried. What if Caleb Douglas didn't rescue them tomorrow?

She wouldn't think about tomorrow. Tonight would be complicated enough.

Emily didn't know what time it was when she awakened in the pitch-black cabin. The log had obviously long died out, and she was freezing. With two blankets doubled on top of her, she was still cold, and no matter what position she curled in, she couldn't generate body heat. She was wearing her sweats. Maybe if she put on more clothes...

In the stillness she assumed Brad was asleep. She didn't hear the rustle of his bedroll or the creak of the floor signaling a change in his position. He'd insisted she keep the flashlight beside her. Now she picked it up from the floor and switched it on with the beam directed at the bedroom. A few minutes later, she'd added a blouse and her sweater but couldn't get her jeans on over the sweatpants. The bedroom was even colder than the living room.

Returning to the sofa, she lay there, her teeth chattering, shivers skipping up and down her body. First she tried curling on her side, then she lay on her back, then she turned toward the sofa cushion cupping her hands around her nose, hoping her breath would warm her face. Finally she turned on her back again.

"Can't sleep?" a deep voice asked.

"I'm cold," she mumbled from beneath the covers. "I put on more clothes, but they're not helping."

There was a long silence until Brad said, "There is another option."

"What? Using the furniture to light the fireplace?"

He chuckled. "Unfortunately the paints and varnishes on the wood furniture would probably smoke like the damp kindling. It's a shame someone loves wrought iron so much. Lodgepole furnishings might have worked."

She didn't know how he could still be in good humor about this. Maybe he wasn't as cold as she was.

"What's the other option?"

"You could sleep with me and we could combine our body heat."

His suggestion generated a definite warmth just thinking about it. "That's not a good idea."

"We could keep our clothes on, Emily. I'm suggesting survival here, not sex."

Was she being a prude? Was she being ridiculous thinking he might want to have sex with her again? Had the union of their bodies meant anything to him?

It had shaken her world and told her in no uncertain terms that she could fall in love with Brad Vaughn.

When she didn't respond, his voice pierced the darkness again. "Think about it."

Then she heard the rustle of covers, as if he'd turned over...as if he were going back to sleep.

What had he said? *I can sleep anywhere.*

She didn't know how much longer she curled on the couch, trying to keep still, rearranging the covers, pulling her sweater tighter around her. Nothing helped. She just wanted the night to be over. To keep her mind off

Brad, she thought about the huge elk they'd seen that afternoon. She heard other noises and didn't know what they were. Was that a coyote howling? Did they have coyotes in Montana?

Finally she gave up. Anything would be better than her mind racing and her body shivering. "Brad?" she asked softly.

"Still can't sleep?"

"No. If I could only stop shivering. Is...is your offer still open?" She felt silly and embarrassed.

It seemed like aeons until he answered, "Sure. Come on down. I'd lay on the sofa with you, but I don't think either of us would have room to breathe."

He was so tall and broad shouldered and muscular. They'd never fit on the sofa.

Switching on the flashlight again so she could see where she was going, she saw him turn onto his side and prop himself on one elbow. "Take off that extra blouse and sweater."

Her gaze met his and her thoughts must have showed.

"I'm not suggesting you undress. Just get rid of those layers. I think you'll be more comfortable. You might want to ditch the sneakers, too."

She didn't know if she was being the biggest fool on the planet as she removed the sweater and blouse and kicked off her sneakers. Then came the real challenge.

Awkwardly she dropped to the bedroll beside him. He'd quadrupled the huge bed quilt underneath him and had doubled the wool blanket on top.

"Do we need my covers from the sofa?"

"Let's try it like this."

Switching off the flashlight, she wasn't sure exactly what position to take.

"Face the sofa," he suggested.

She did that and hovered on the edge of the quilt, as cold as she'd been before.

But then Brad's arms were around her, his chest and stomach were against her back and her backside was curved into his thighs. Seconds later she felt his arousal.

When she would have moved away, he said, "I don't seem to have any control over that, but I'm not going to do anything you don't want me to do."

That was the problem. With his arms around her, with his body pressed close to hers, she wanted to do more than sleep. But making love with Brad Vaughn again would eventually devastate her heart...because *she* thought of it as making love. He thought of it as having sex. That was a very big difference.

The floor was hard, but for some reason, with Brad's arms around her, she didn't mind it.

His warm breath wisped across her ear as he suggested, "Relax, Emily. Go to sleep. Hopefully the sun will come out and everything will be better in the morning."

Would everything be better in the morning? She couldn't undo what she'd done. She couldn't forget about Suzette Brouchard. She couldn't deny she was falling in love with Brad, and it was more than a crush. As their bodies generated the heat he'd predicted, she felt her thought processes slowing and comfort surround her. She felt warm in spite of the cold. Before she drifted off, however, one question plagued her. What if she was pregnant with Brad's child?

* * *

When Brad suggested Emily sleep with him, he'd known he was asking for trouble. If not trouble, a night of discomfort. There was no way he was touching her again, not sexually anyway. What they did had blown his mind. That hour-and-a-half trek must have frozen his brain as well as his good sense. His hike had reminded him there should be more to his life than work…work he didn't have a passion for. It had reminded him how his life felt empty sometimes.

So when he'd returned and Emily had flown into his arms, a fire had kick-started. She'd been sweet and soft and honest and utterly guileless, so unlike the women he usually dated. The truth was, he hadn't been thinking at all when they'd started kissing, when they'd started undressing, when they'd come together in a cataclysmic explosion he'd never experienced before.

Afterward, however, conscious thought had hit him like the proverbial ton of bricks. He had never *ever* slept with a woman unprotected before Emily. What was it about her that had made him forget about protection now?

During the early hours of the morning, Emily changed positions. Instead of facing away from him, she turned toward him—unconsciously, he supposed. Now she nestled on his shoulder, throwing one of her legs over his.

He held her loosely in his arms. Loosely, because his self-control was getting hard-pressed. Loosely, because he knew he couldn't be intimate with her a second time. They were wrong for each other, as he'd learned with Robin. If two people didn't grow up with the same backgrounds, there'd be a fatal crash along the road—either a clash of goals or desires or needs.

The problem was, the women he dated *did* have the same backgrounds as he did. Yet he hadn't connected to any of them the way he'd connected to Emily. What did that say about him? What did he have to change?

Although Emily didn't like being stuck here, he did. It was a retreat, a soul easer, and maybe he just needed to take more vacations to remote places.

Emily's hand moved across his chest, and he could feel the path through his sweatshirt as if it were a scalding trail of hot water. When she rubbed her cheek against his shoulder, he almost groaned. Shifting a little, he hoped she'd soon awaken.

After she rubbed her cheek against his shirt a second time, her eyes fluttered open. Their faces were very close together. If he just tilted his head…

He slammed the door shut on that thought.

Self-consciousness dawned in her eyes, and when she realized how she was curled up with him, she scooted away a few inches. "Sorry. I guess I must have rolled over during the night."

Now fully awake, she sat up. Immediately she felt the chill and rubbed her arms.

"Now you can put on that blouse and sweater again." He tried to keep his tone easy. He tried to forget that all he'd wanted to do all night was combine their body heat in a more intimate way.

Scrambling to her feet, she said with determination, "After I brush my teeth, we can get breakfast started. Maybe that will warm us up."

She was babbling fast, and he knew she was embarrassed about cuddling up to him.

"Take your time," he called to her retreating back. "It's not as if we have appointments lined up this morning."

Five minutes later, he used another Sterno burner to warm water for instant coffee and cocoa. Emily wasn't a coffee drinker, but he was. Just one more difference.

When Emily entered the kitchen, there was still a heap of awkwardness between them. She was silent as they poured cereal. She was silent as she sliced a banana. She was silent as they sipped their beverages in Caleb Douglas's mugs.

Brad wasn't going to let her withdraw from him like this. If she was pregnant, they were going to have to keep communication open.

She was sitting at the kitchen table in a stream of sunlight that shone through the window. She'd tied her hair back in a short ponytail, and the style emphasized the perfect oval of her face.

"You said you have two sisters and a brother. What do they do?" he asked, choosing a safe topic.

"Eric is a history teacher."

"How much older is he than you are?"

"Two years. He got married right out of college and he and Sheila had kids right away."

"They still live in Chicago?"

"In Lyle." There was a fondness in her voice as she talked about her siblings. "Elaine's a paralegal. She's twenty-three, and Lizbeth will finish college this spring."

"Why didn't you start college after high school?"

Sadness passed over Emily's face. "I had other things to consider first." There was pride in her words as she explained, "Eric put himself through school and he'll be paying off loans for a long time. I knew if I went to college, I wouldn't be able to help Lizbeth and Elaine. So I went to a trade school for professional skills for a year and then entered the workforce. After Lizbeth finishes this spring, I'll be able to take the courses I told you about. It might take me a while, but I'll get my degree eventually."

Considering what she'd said, he realized she'd sacrificed her own education for that of her sisters' and sacrificed her own goals for her siblings'. He didn't know if he'd ever met anyone who had done that. His respect and admiration for Emily went up a few notches.

When she became silent again, he asked, "Are you worried about being pregnant?"

She didn't answer him but rose from her chair and took her mug to the counter. Then she poured more hot water into it and finally looked over at him.

"What's going through you mind, Emily? Tell me."

For a second she still hesitated, then finally answered. "I was in a serious relationship before I came to work at Vaughn Associates."

"How serious?" Brad asked, picturing her with another man and not liking the picture.

"Serious enough for me to be on birth control. I wasn't careless about it, but I got pregnant."

That news hit him like a bucket of melted snow. "Do you have a child no one knows about?"

"No. When Warner found out I was pregnant, he

wanted nothing to do with me or the baby. He was one of the partners in the law firm, and I was simply a secretary. I didn't realize until then he had been using me. I was just an afternoon treat, not a main dish…if you know what I mean."

Sometimes Emily's honesty made him uncomfortable. "And the child?"

"A few weeks after he broke it off and I quit my job, I had a miscarriage."

"Emily, I'm sorry!"

When he saw quick tears come to her eyes at his words, he went to her.

"It was a long time ago," she murmured. Her back was straight and she took an herbal tea bag from the box, opening it slowly.

"But apparently it's not forgotten."

Letting the tea bag dangle in the mug, she turned toward him. "I'll never forget. When I found out I was pregnant, it was a blow and it was going to complicate my life terribly, but I wanted that baby."

They'd had sex yesterday, and he'd held her in his arms last night. Nothing on earth could have kept him from hugging her now.

It pleased him when she laid her head on his shoulder as if it was a relief to lean on him. He had the feeling she didn't lean on many people—that she was the one who got leaned on.

Wanting to keep the situation between them honest, he growled, "I never should have put you in this position again."

"*I* was there yesterday, too," she said softly.

A low hum sounded through the cabin's walls and windows, becoming louder with each second.

Emily leaned away from him. "What's that?"

"It sounds like a helicopter. Maybe Caleb has sent the Marines."

When they grabbed coats and ran outside, they saw a helicopter had arrived. After it landed in the large clearing beside the cabin, they ran to it and met the pilot. He had indeed been sent by Caleb.

"We just have to put everything into our suitcases, then we'll be ready," Emily told him, her mood buoyant.

And that's about all it took.

She and Brad hurriedly folded the covers that they'd used and put them away, cleaned up the kitchen leaving supplies they'd bought and zipped up their suitcases. Minutes later they were in the rear of the helicopter and the pilot was lifting off.

Emily had been overjoyed when the helicopter had finally landed, but now, sitting beside Brad, staring out the window and leaving the cabin behind, she didn't feel quite so happy. Her days with Brad there had been…special. This morning when she'd told him about the miscarriage, he'd been so incredibly kind.

Now, could they go back to being boss-secretary?

When she turned her head, she could sense Brad was studying her. If only she could crawl inside his head and learn what he was thinking. On the other hand, maybe she didn't want to know.

If she'd been entertainment, if coupling had just been his way of passing the time, her heart was going to get broken.

The pilot had told them he was taking them to Caleb's ranch, the Lazy D, and as they flew to Thunder Canyon, Emily concentrated on her bird's-eye view of it so she didn't think about Brad and what had happened at the cabin.

Brad leaned close to her, and in a voice she could barely hear above the whirring of the propeller, he pointed below. "That's all Douglas land. There's the mine entrance."

She could see there were three access roads leading to one particular spot.

After the helicopter covered more distance, Brad motioned toward the mine entrance. "The erosion hole the boy fell into, where the rescue workers found the gold, was over one of the tunnels much closer to town."

The helicopter buzzed over Thunder Canyon Road, and she saw the Douglas ranch. There was a fantastically large two-story house, barns, fences and cattle grazing everywhere. Apparently Thunder Canyon had received a minimal amount of snow compared to the area where the cabin was located in the mountains. With the sun shining, all that was left of the snow here were sporadic patches.

After the pilot landed to the rear of the huge house, Brad took both suitcases, not hearing of Emily carrying hers. The look he gave her was dark and intense and she wondered again what was going to happen next. What did she *want* to happen next?

Caleb Douglas met them outside one of the back doors and waved them inside. But Emily was concerned with making muddy footprints on expensive-looking rugs, which she decided had to be Oriental. Inside they stood in a large room with a fireplace, pool table and an assortment of sofas and love seats. That one room was bigger than any apartment she'd ever lived in.

She slipped her shoes off and Caleb looked at her questioningly.

"I don't want to mess up your carpet or floor."

"The housekeeper will take care of that." He studied them both. "You don't look any worse for wear. I'm sorry you two got stranded up there for so long. I figured the power would go out with the snow and the wind. I want to get a generator up there but just haven't done it. I've been busy with the ski project. Anyway, I drove up there yesterday but couldn't get across the creek in my SUV. The helicopter wasn't available until today."

After a quick look at Emily, Brad answered, "We're fine."

Caleb went on. "The bad news is, no rooms have opened up at the motel or the inn. The good news is, my wife's family left yesterday so you're welcome to stay here."

"We don't want to be in your way...." Brad began.

"This house is big enough. You won't be in my way. I also wanted to tell you I rented an SUV for you. Brought it in from Bozeman. You won't have any trouble getting around, no matter where you want to go, unless you want to cross the creek," he added with a wink.

A woman had slipped quietly into the room while they'd been talking, and now Caleb motioned her forward. "This is Tess Littlehawk, my housekeeper. She'll show you upstairs to your rooms."

Tess Littlehawk was a striking woman who looked to be in her forties. She had jet-black hair parted down the middle and bound in a thick braid. Her eyes were the darkest brown, almost black, and her broad face had lines around her eyes and around her mouth. She was wearing navy blue slacks and a matching tailored top with short sleeves that Emily guessed was a uniform of sorts.

"It's good to meet you, Tess," Emily said immediately.

"You too, miss," Tess responded.

"Take them up to their rooms now, Tess," Caleb ordered. "I'm sure they're going to want to get unpacked and enjoy some creature comforts after the past few days." He checked his watch. "After lunch, we'll meet in my den. I know you need an update on what's been happening here." Motioning toward the double doors that led out of the family room, he urged, "Go on now. If you need anything, just let Tess know."

When Brad reached for the suitcases, Caleb shook his head. "I'll have someone get those."

Brad picked them up anyway. "I'll take them up."

"Suit yourself." He saw Emily was carrying her laptop computer and a camera bag. "You might want to bring your computer along for our meeting—then you can type notes as we go. I'll expect weekly reports," he told Brad.

"That's what I intended," Brad assured him.

Minutes later they emerged from the family room onto more polished hardwood floors. Tess led them down a corridor, then into an immense foyer with a two-story-high ceiling. The sweeping staircase was also polished wood.

As she and Brad followed Tess upstairs, Emily saw mostly closed doors.

"This is the east wing," Tess told them. "Mr. and Mrs. Douglas are situated in the west wing. I haven't gotten all the rooms up here cleaned and swept yet, but these two are yours." She motioned to two open doors on the same side of the hall. "These rooms are connected by a bathroom. If that's not to your satisfaction, I'll have another cleaned in about an hour."

"It's up to you," Brad said, gazing down at Emily.

They'd just shared two days in a cabin with a single bathroom. "This is great," she murmured.

"Let me show you the setup." Tess led them inside.

The first bedroom was huge, with a king-size lodge-pole headboard and a burgundy-and-hunter-green quilt on the bed. Vertical wooden blinds were open at the windows.

Tess kept going and opened a door that led into an opulent bathroom. There were two vanities, two sinks, a huge shower and a Roman tub.

Quickly Tess went to the second door on the other side of the bathroom and opened that. When Emily saw a lilac-and-yellow room, she knew no place would be more pleasant to sleep. It was absolutely beautiful, with its white spread with lilacs scattered all over it, Priscilla curtains and maple dresser, nightstand and headboard.

"This is wonderful," she told the housekeeper.

"Would you like me to unpack your suitcases for you?" Tess asked.

"I'll do mine myself," Brad said. "Emily?"

"I'll unpack, but I will need an iron and an ironing board."

"I'll take whatever you need ironed down to my suite and do it. I'm sure that's what Mr. Douglas would want."

Emily had no idea what it was like to be waited on. She accepted the offer. She didn't know how busy she and Brad were going to be after their conference with Caleb.

"If there's anything else you need," Tess advised them, "just use the intercom. Press the button for room three. If I don't answer there, dial in the number on the pad by the phone. Just call that and my pager will beep."

While Emily was trying to absorb that, the housekeeper took another long look at Brad. "Mr. Douglas said that you were a private investigator."

"Yes, I am."

Emily thought the housekeeper was going to say more, but then she just gave them a tight smile and repeated, "Like I said, just buzz me if you need me. My rooms are behind the kitchen, so I'm always around."

Then she left Emily's room through the door into the hall.

"I'll get your suitcase for you." At the bathroom Brad stopped. "Are you sure this setup is fine with you?"

"Yes, it's fine with me."

"If you'd feel more comfortable about it, you can lock your door into the bathroom at night."

Then he went into the other bedroom, leaving Emily to wonder whether he was just being considerate of her feelings or if he was telling her they wouldn't be sleeping together again.

Chapter Five

Emily sat in Caleb Douglas's study in a tan leather chair, taking notes on her laptop. Every once in a while when there was a lull in Brad and Caleb's conversation, she admired the western sculptures sitting about—the cowhand on a horse, the cowboy on a bucking bronc—as well as the charcoal sketches of rodeo scenes hanging on the walls along with elk antlers.

After Brad's parting comment about keeping her door locked, he'd told her he'd go downstairs until she finished showering and then he'd take his. He'd wanted to get the lay of the land. Later, while she'd dressed, she'd heard him in the shower and remembered his musculature in the light of the fire.

She also remembered his strength and power as he'd made love to her.

"Emily, did you get that?"

Brought back to the present with a jolt, she realized Brad was speaking to her. "I'm sorry. Could you repeat what you said?"

He gave her an odd look. "The gold mine and the mineral rights to it were owned by Amos Douglas, Caleb's grandfather. He supposedly won the property in a card game."

"I thought the deed was in my safety-deposit box along with all the other deeds, but it wasn't," Caleb explained.

"Could another descendant of Amos Douglas have it?"

"I'm the last one. Riley has checked through all his papers, though he says he's never seen it."

"And you hired a lawyer to do a title search?"

"I hired an attorney in town. He found there's simply no record anywhere. I do have this, though." Caleb stood, went into the room adjoining the den, which Emily supposed was his study, and returned with an envelope. He handed it to Brad.

As Brad opened the envelope, Caleb warned, "Be careful. It's old."

Emily watched while Brad drew out a yellowed half sheet of paper.

"What is it?" she asked, more out of curiosity than for her notes.

"It looks like a promissory note. Someone owed Amos Douglas. Whoever it was agreed to pay Amos back twenty-five dollars a month. If the borrower missed a payment, the deed to this section of land..." He stopped and looked up at Caleb.

"That's the land where the gold mine's located," Caleb offered.

Brad continued, "The deed to this section of land plus the mineral rights would revert to Amos Douglas."

"Who signed it?" Emily asked.

"That's the problem." Brad ran his fingers along the edge of the paper. "I don't think this is torn, but it looks like the paper separated from the fold. It's over a hundred years old. No wonder." Brad looked up at Caleb again. "Do you think your great-grandfather foreclosed on this property?"

"It's not only possible, but likely. My father told me Amos was a shrewd businessman."

"Are there rumors about who this person was he foreclosed on? Where I'd have a place to start?"

"No rumors about the note."

"Searching the archives in town is probably the best place to start," Brad concluded. "Emily and I will head over there this afternoon."

"I also heard there's a reporter who's been asking questions," Caleb said.

"About the mine?"

Caleb looked discomfited. "This whole gold-rush thing has gotten bigger than anyone expected. A paper hired this reporter to do a story. I called him yesterday but he said he hasn't turned up the ownership. He wouldn't say much else. There was a baby crying in the background so it might have been a bad time. Maybe you can get more out of him."

"What's his name?"

"Mark Anderson."

"I'll call him today and set up an appointment." Brad stood and asked Emily, "Can you be ready to go over to the town hall in about ten minutes? I'd like to get there before it closes."

"Sure. Are you going to call Mr. Anderson?"

"Hopefully I'll catch him in."

Caleb handed Brad a scrap of paper. "There's his number. I hope you can figure out this whole mess. I know that land belongs to our family."

"I'll see what I can do."

Emily knew if anyone could get to the bottom of it, Brad could. When he was determined, he went after his goal, and heaven help anyone in his path.

From the street, Emily lifted her camera and snapped a photo of the town hall. As she and Brad walked up to the double doors, he said to her, "This could have waited until tomorrow if you're tired." She'd been very quiet since their meeting with Caleb.

"I'm fine."

He opened one of the doors for her. It was wood and heavy and it creaked.

Stepping over the threshold, she almost felt as if she was walking into the past. "This is one of Thunder Canyon's original buildings," Brad explained, then glanced at her because she didn't respond. "Are you thinking about our meeting with Caleb? Or are you thinking about our stay at the cabin?"

As they walked deeper into the reception area, they spotted a woman seated at a rough-hewn wooden desk.

"Both, I guess," Emily murmured, wishing he hadn't

begun this conversation here. He must have felt the same because his look told her they'd finish later.

Crossing to the desk, he nodded toward the nameplate—Rhonda Culpepper.

"Are you Ms. Culpepper?"

"Sure am. Can I help you?" she asked in a chipper tone.

"I hope you can help us," Brad returned with a smile. "I'm looking for the archives room."

Rhonda's face took on a perplexed look. "Why ever would you want to go down there?"

"It's in the basement?" Emily asked.

"Sure is, and everything smells musty. It's much older than I am," she added with a little laugh, then went on, "but I'm afraid you can't go down there. The room's always locked. There are original documents, you understand. We can't have people just poking in them. Our last archivist was making sure all the information was put into computers."

"Your last archivist?"

"Yes, Saul Rindos. He went to college to be a historian, then couldn't find a job. So we hired him. But fortunately for him and unfortunately for us, a few weeks ago he found a position in a museum—on the East Coast, mind you."

"Who's in charge of the room now?" Emily asked.

"Well, nobody exactly. I guess Mayor Brookhurst, if it comes right down to it. He has the key. He won't let anyone in there until we have an archivist. We have a new one coming—Harvey Watson. He's due in about mid-June."

"I think the mayor will let us in," Brad said to Emily.

"Oh, no," Rhonda protested. "I'm afraid he won't. Not right now, anyway. First of all, he won't let anybody in that room without an archivist present, not even just to look. He's paranoid about it and the history of this town. But on top of all that, he's taking his vacation. Went somewhere in Wyoming to see a friend, I think. Anyway, he's got the key and won't be back until the middle of the month. He has to be back for Caleb Douglas's groundbreaking ceremony for his ski resort."

"When's that?" Emily asked.

"May twenty-third, I believe. We have quite a reception planned afterward. Maybe you two can come?"

"I'm hoping we'll be finished our work here by then," Brad remarked. "Did the mayor leave a number where he could be reached?"

"He and his friend are doing some traveling. From what I understand, he wants nothing to do with phones or contact from us until he returns. Said he gets hassled enough here. Doesn't want to contend with it on his vacation. You can't blame him."

"You said the archivist was entering information into the computer. Any idea if he did it in a particular order?"

"Well, that's another of our problems," she confided. "The archives have always been stored in the basement. Years ago, back in the late eighteen hundreds I think, there was a fire. We lost many of the ledgers. Just a while back, when we didn't have an archivist, we had flooding. Boxes were emptied, material was shifted around. So to answer your question, I doubt if anything is in much order. That's why we need another archivist to continue the work of the last one."

Moving his hand across his forehead, Brad said patiently, "Thank you for your help. Who might the mayor report to if he does call in?"

"He has a sister, Elma Rogers. Her number's in the phone book."

"Do you mind if I mention your name to her?"

"Of course not, go ahead. In fact, I'll give her a call tonight to tell her you'll be talking to her. That way she'll know you're not trying to sell her something."

With the reassurance that the mayor's sister was indeed a very nice lady, Rhonda bid them a good evening.

Outside, Brad and Emily looked at each other and smiled.

"She was helpful," Emily insisted.

"As far as it went. I could use some real help. I made an appointment with Mark Anderson for tomorrow afternoon. He said he and his wife have a new baby and she usually sleeps in the afternoons."

At the mention of the word *baby,* Emily's face clouded. It seemed there were so many land mines where they were concerned.

Instead of dwelling on that, Brad suggested, "Let's walk down to that western-wear shop. I want to buy you a coat so you won't freeze while we're here."

"I'm not going to let you buy me a coat."

If he said she should consider it part of her bonus, he had a feeling he'd be in trouble. If he said he wouldn't miss the money, he knew he'd be in just as much trouble. So he said, "I want you to charge it to my expense account. If you hadn't come to Montana, you wouldn't need it."

Her nose wrinkled as she thought about the logic in that. "What about you?" she asked.

He was wearing his denim jacket. "I brought a couple of flannel shirts, so I'll be fine. Emily, let me do this, all right?"

She took a terribly long time to answer but finally she agreed. "All right. But just something warm. Nothing elaborate."

"It's up to you to decide whatever you want." He knew what he wanted to do. He wanted to kiss that frown right off her face. He wanted to hold her again as he'd held her through the night. But he knew that might not happen, not ever again.

After they stopped at the car and locked Emily's camera inside, they crossed to the western-wear store. The scent of leather was strong as they entered. But Emily didn't head toward the leather goods and jackets. Rather, she aimed for a rack that held the sign Women's Fleece.

Choosing a jacket from the rack, she tried it on. It was royal blue with black horses edging the zipper and armbands.

"You look pretty in that color," he said before he thought better of it.

Her gaze locked to his and she seemed to be asking him if he was giving her idle flattery.

After he stepped closer to her, he adjusted the stand-up collar on the jacket, his fingers brushing her hair. "I wouldn't have said it if I didn't mean it."

He couldn't keep from pushing a few strands away from her cheek. He couldn't help inhaling her sweet scent. He couldn't hold his libido in check anymore where she was concerned, and that annoyed him.

Backing away, he said offhandedly, "It's practical."

"Yes, it is. I'll be able to wear it in Chicago next winter." She looked at the tag on the sleeve. "And it's even on sale."

Her pleasure in that made him laugh. This was the first woman he'd ever taken shopping who considered a lower price to be better than a higher one.

Instead of taking Emily into his arms and giving her a hug and a kiss right then, he checked his watch. "We'd better be heading back if we want to get ready for dinner. Is there anything else you want to look at?"

Her gaze fell on a rack of western-style blouses. "I'll just be a minute." Moments later she was rifling through them. When she found a white one with a cowboy hat and lariat embroidered on one pocket, a horseshoe on the other, she smiled. "It will be a souvenir."

He knew better than to offer to pay for the blouse. Maybe he hadn't known Emily Stanton well in the six months she'd worked for him, but in the past few days he'd learned enough to fill an encyclopedia.

As soon as Emily met Adele Douglas later in the day, she was impressed.

"I'm so sorry I wasn't here this afternoon when you arrived," Adele said as she showed Emily and Brad into the dining room that night.

Adele had a warm and gracious manner. She wore

her blond hair in a chin-length bob and had dressed for dinner in a green, long-sleeved sweater and wool slacks. Everything about her was sophisticated.

"We invited our son Riley to dinner tonight, even though he needs no invitation," she said with a sly smile, beaming at her son.

Riley looked to be around Brad's age, with black hair, green eyes and a killer smile. He was almost as handsome as Brad. Almost. Emily knew she was prejudiced.

After Riley shook her hand and Brad's, they all seated themselves around the large cherrywood table. The buffet along one wall held two highly polished silver candelabra. In the buffet's center stood a silver tureen. Tess Littlehawk was ladling soup out of it. Emily noticed the housekeeper eyeing Brad and she wondered why.

"When I want a good, home-cooked meal, I come over here and let Tess feed me," Riley joked.

"He eats here most of the time because of working on the ski resort with me *and* living only a half mile down the road."

"I'm surprised you didn't invite Justin, too," Riley commented blandly.

An odd look passed between Caleb and Adele. Finally Caleb explained, "I have another son, Justin...Justin Crane. Actually, I knew nothing about him until a few months ago."

Emily could see that Adele looked uncomfortable but she recovered quickly. "Justin just married recently," Adele added bravely, rallying from whatever thoughts she'd been having. "He married a dear girl we'd raised most of her life and always thought of as a daughter. I'm sure you'll meet Katie and Justin sometime soon, at the groundbreaking ceremony if not before."

"The groundbreaking for the ski resort?" Emily asked.

"Precisely," Caleb boomed. "We're having a fine party afterward in the town hall."

"I'm hoping we'll have this whole mine matter wrapped up before then," Brad responded.

"What did you find out this afternoon?" Caleb asked.

"Not much. We can't get into the archives until the mayor returns."

"Why not?"

"Apparently Mayor Brookhurst doesn't trust the key to the archives room to anyone. I'm hoping it's not necessary. I'm not going to sit around and wait until he gets back. Emily and I have an appointment with Mark Anderson tomorrow afternoon."

"I hear he has invested in the *Thunder Canyon Nugget*," Adele offered.

"He has a good reputation as a writer," Riley commented. "Maybe he'll use those pages for something more than gossip."

Caleb laughed. "You young folk don't appreciate the power of knowing what's going on in the town."

Riley returned his father's smile. "I don't need to know whose horse ran away from his barn. Maybe Mark will concentrate on bigger issues."

"Such as the ski resort?" Caleb asked with upraised brows.

"I'm hoping we can pull in some high-caliber tourists," Riley admitted.

Adele, who was sitting around the corner of the table

from Emily, leaned over to her. "If they start talking business, you and I are going to start talking fashion."

Everyone at the table laughed and the conversation turned to the food Tess was serving, which smelled absolutely delicious.

After dessert, Adele showed them to a sitting room. Emily found herself in a striped love seat with Brad very close beside her. For the rest of the evening she had to concentrate hard to keep her mind on the conversation. He was wearing a tan, cable-knit sweater and hunter-green corduroy slacks. He fit right in here with Caleb and Adele and Riley. Emily knew she didn't. Her hair wasn't styled in the latest fashion. Her clothes weren't as fine as Adele's. She kept her nails trimmed and shaped, but they weren't manicured like her hostess's. This wasn't the life she knew, and she probably never would know.

Yet to Brad this was probably the norm.

When Tess asked if anyone wanted a nightcap a while later, Emily couldn't help but yawn. "I'm sorry," she said, embarrassed.

"You have no reason to be sorry," Adele assured her. "You must have had a terrible couple of days in that cabin with no power. Now maybe Caleb will get a generator."

"And do something about that bridge," he said decisively. "I'll have to get a civil engineer in to look at it."

The evening broke up then. After Emily and Brad bid the Douglases good-night, they headed for the stairs.

As they walked up in silence, Emily felt she had to say something. "Wouldn't you like to know the story behind Justin Crane?"

"How do you know there is one?"

"His name's different, and Adele looked uncomfortable when it was first brought up. My guess is there might have been an infidelity there."

"You'd make a good private investigator."

She glanced at him quickly to see if he was making fun of her.

"You would," he said seriously now as they reached the second floor. "You're intelligent, savvy and can read people well."

At her door they stopped. "I have trouble reading *you*," she admitted softly, hoping he'd tell her what was going on in his head…or, more importantly, in his heart.

"Ahh, Emily," he said with a sigh, running his thumb across her bottom lip, looking deep into her eyes. "You're a temptation. But I think we'll both be better off if we keep our minds on what we came here to do."

Was she a temptation he didn't want or need? So be it. "You're the boss," she retorted flippantly, as if the whole conversation hadn't mattered at all, as if his touch didn't burn and spark desire in every part of her body.

Opening her bedroom door, she forced a smile to her lips. "I'll see you in the morning."

Then she closed her door and leaned against it. She was going to lock all of her doors tonight, as well as her heart. Not to keep Brad out—but to keep herself from getting hurt.

As Brad drove to the new housing development on White Water Drive the following afternoon, he glanced at Emily taking in the scenery. She hadn't brought along her camera today. Yesterday when they'd walked down the raised sidewalk in Old Town, she'd snapped picture after picture.

"No photographs today?" he asked now.

"No, I'll keep my mind on what we're doing."

"Do you have more than one camera? Lots of photography buffs do."

"Oh, no. It took me a long while to save for that one."

"So that's why you handle it so carefully." He'd noticed how she held it, how she used it, how she carried it. He should have realized that if she was using her money to help her sister through school, she wouldn't have funds for more than one camera.

"What do you enjoy photographing the most?" he asked.

"People I love. Sometimes its hard getting candid shots of them. Scenery's a close second."

"What do you do with the pictures?"

"Some I frame for gifts, others that are good I donate to worthwhile causes—auctions and the like. I have two file boxes of them in my closet."

"Did you ever think of submitting them to magazines?"

"You haven't even seen them. How do you know if they're good enough?"

He shrugged. "I have a feeling anything you do meets a certain standard. You're that kind of lady."

Glad he didn't have to explain himself further, he pulled into the driveway of the ranch house on Wagon Wheel Drive. It was a white house, and as yet there were no trees planted anywhere—or grass, either, for that matter. It looked as if the residents might have just moved in.

After Brad parked in the drive, they exited the SUV and went up the walk. When Mark Anderson opened the door, they heard a baby squalling.

"I'm Mark," he said, shaking their hands and motioning them inside. "Sorry about the noise," he called above the crying. "I thought Marissa would be asleep."

Inside the house, Brad noticed it was cozy. There was a stone fireplace and a mantel with family photos in silver frames. The living room furniture was casual and comfortable looking and it all seemed to be brand-new.

Mark Anderson appeared to be near forty. He was around six feet tall, lean and wore his dark hair long. His wife, Juliet, looked to be more around Emily's age. Petite, she had brown eyes and long dark hair. But she looked tired right now as she juggled her baby from her arm to her shoulder.

"Want me to take her?" Mark asked.

"No, I'll go back to the bedroom with her. You have a meeting."

The baby was waving her arms now and crying so hard that she was red faced.

Emily approached Juliet and her daughter. "Would you like me to try? I'm Emily Stanton, Brad's assistant, and I have two younger sisters."

"If there's anything you know how to do to make her stop crying, go right ahead," Juliet said, a bit exasperated.

Fascinated, Brad watched as Emily took the infant from Juliet's arms. Holding the baby, she bent down to it, her hair hiding her face. She began making a sound into the baby's ear. It sounded like "Sssh, sssh, ssshoo." Over and over she did it until Marissa began quieting.

The little girl's parents looked on, amazed. As Emily shushed and rocked, the infant looked up at her. Mark asked, "What are you doing to her?"

Emily didn't answer, just continued making the noise and rocking for a few moments longer. Finally when Marissa was quiet, she smiled at the new parents.

"I heard about this pediatrician who made a video. Anyway, babies are comfortable in the womb. Coming out into the world is overwhelming. So when you make that noise in their ear and you rock them, they think they're back in the womb again."

"Why didn't they tell me that at the hospital?" Juliet asked, shaking her head.

"Maybe because they don't know or they've never tried it. I doubt if it's going to work every time, but it might work some of the time."

She bent down to the baby again and repeated the sound.

Little Marissa's eyes closed.

"Well, I'll be darned." Mark's face was a study in exasperation and appreciation.

"Would you mind taking her back to her nursery and laying her in her crib?" Juliet asked. "I'm afraid if you transfer her to me she'll wake up again."

"I don't mind at all." Emily checked with Brad. "Unless you need me?"

"No. Mark and I'll get started. Take your time."

As he watched Emily carry the baby down the hall with Juliet leading her, he knew she'd make a wonderful mother. She'd make a wonderful...wife? He didn't know where that thought had come from. A wife was the last thing he wanted. His mother's betrayal of his father had made him certain from an early age that marriage was a risky business. He'd been tempted to try it with Robin when he was too young and idealistic to know better, but she'd reinforced the idea that marriage wasn't in the cards for him.

"You have a beautiful daughter," he said to Mark, envying the man.

"I'm going to adopt her."

"I don't understand."

Mark motioned to the two easy chairs. Brad took off his jacket and settled in one.

Looking not at all embarrassed, Mark explained, "Juliet was seven months pregnant when I met her. I sort of ended up taking care of her, and after the baby was born, I figured out we belonged together. In fact, we just got married by a justice of the peace yesterday and we're planning a church wedding next month."

"You made that sound very easy."

Laughing, Mark shook his head. "Sure I did. Happily ever after *is* easy. It's getting there that's hard."

Getting there. A man had to want to get there to get there and had to believe there could be a happily ever after. Brad simply didn't.

That settled, he asked Mark, "So, what can you tell me about the Queen of Hearts gold mine?"

Chapter Six

As Emily stood at Marissa's crib looking down at her, her heart hurt for the baby she'd lost. Someday she wanted lots of kids...with the right man.

The little girl was sleeping now as Emily stepped away from the bed, glancing around the room. The walls were pale pink with a wallpaper border of dolls dressed in lavender, green and pink. The dresser and crib were a light wood, and there was a small, green, crocheted blanket hanging over the foot of the crib.

"This is handmade," she said in appreciation.

"My *abuelita* crocheted that. It's called a *covijita*. It's one of the few things I have left from my family. They're all gone now." She pointed to a bookcase that was rustic and scarred. "My father made that."

There was loss and grief in Juliet's voice but also

joy in the sentimental value of the gifts her father and grandmother had given her. Emily liked this woman already.

Glancing at the baby again, Emily said with a sigh, "I'd like to stay here all afternoon and watch her, but I'd better go in there. I'm supposed to be taking notes."

"Mark said Mr. Vaughn is a private investigator. Is that what you do, too?"

She thought about what Brad had said, that she might make a good one. "No. Not yet, anyway. I'm his personal secretary and assistant."

"Mmm," Juliet said.

Emily felt as if she had to explain further. "He thought if I came along on this trip, it would go quicker and we could get back to Chicago sooner."

"You must have had quite an experience being stranded with Mr. Vaughn in Caleb Douglas's cabin."

Staring at Juliet wide-eyed, Emily asked, "How do you know about that?"

"Even though we've had an influx of tourists, Thunder Canyon is still a small town. Gossip travels fast. That helicopter created lots of questions."

Shaking her head, Emily was embarrassed. "So everyone knows Brad and I were in that cabin? Alone?"

At that Juliet grinned. "Yes, and they've made assumptions about that."

"Oh, terrific! Just what I always wanted—a tarnished reputation. Brad and I are boss and secretary and..."

"Friends?" Juliet filled in for her kindly.

Feeling a blush steal into her cheeks, Emily couldn't lie to Juliet. "I guess. Sometimes I'm not sure. We didn't even know each other well before those few days in the cabin, but we got to know each other better there."

"I see sparks between the two of you," Juliet said with certainty.

About to deny it, Emily decided not to. "There might be sparks, but that's it. We're very different."

"Mark and I were very different, too. But we're very happy now."

"A child is a wonderful bond."

"Yes, Marissa is a bond, and Mark thinks of her as his daughter. So do I, but she's not. We were just married civilly yesterday and we're having a church wedding in June."

"You're kidding."

"No. Our love is very new, but it's going to last forever."

Although Emily wanted to believe in that kind of love, the kind her mother and father had had, she didn't know if she could. It was true she was falling in love with Brad. She could admit that to herself now. She never could have made love with him otherwise. But she didn't know if it had anywhere to go.

"I'd really better see if he needs me."

When Emily reentered the living room, Mark and Brad were still talking about the tourists who had come into the area and all the business Caleb's ski resort would bring in.

"I hope it will generate tons of advertising for the newspaper," Mark admitted. "That's what a newspaper needs in order to be profitable."

As Emily sat on the sofa, Brad filled her in. "Mark can find no record of the Queen of Hearts property on the computer. If the title *is* recorded anywhere, it's in a ledger in the archives."

"I just didn't get around to digging further," Mark explained. "Marissa was born, then Juliet and I moved in here and got married. With buying into the paper, I haven't had time to pursue the story or worry about old records. I did find two other leads, though. And the truth is, I'd like an exclusive if anything comes of them."

"It's a deal. What have you got?"

"There's an old prospector who lives out on Thunder Canyon Road. His shack looks as if it will fall down if you blow on it. He couldn't tell me much, and I'm not sure his ramblings can be trusted, but he implied that a woman owned the deed to that mine."

"A woman?" Emily asked. "Wouldn't that be unusual back then?"

Mark shrugged. "I just can't imagine how it's true if Amos Douglas won the property in a card game."

"It might not have been that simple." Brad told Mark about the promissory note.

"Now that's interesting."

"You said there were two possible leads," Emily prompted.

"Yes, the other is a woman named Tildy Matheson. Supposedly her grandmother was a friend of Catherine Douglas, Amos's wife."

"Besides your leads, I can also poke around at the historical society," Brad said.

"We might find out more about Amos Douglas there," Emily added.

"Is this Tildy reliable?" Brad asked Mark.

"Her memory's fading and she probably has stories handed down from her grandmother. But there's no way to know how they've changed in the retelling. Chasing down history is sometimes like trying to catch a wisp of smoke."

When Juliet came into the room, she was smiling. "Marissa's still sleeping."

"You might want to make a tape of shushing," Emily advised her. "Your voice and the sound could lull her to sleep when she's restless."

"You've got one smart assistant here," Juliet said to Brad, and Emily felt herself blush.

Whenever Brad focused his attention on her, it was as if she were the only person in the world—the only woman in the world. Now he did just that and she felt her whole body want to lean toward him, go to him, nestle in his arms.

"She's more than smart," he murmured.

His low voice led Emily to remember the husky sounds and erotic words they'd uttered to each other when they'd made love in his bedroll. From the sparks in his eyes, she wondered if he was thinking about that day, too.

"How would you two like to stay for dinner? Nothing fancy, just some carne asada and rice with a tossed salad."

Brad glanced at Emily, and she gave a little nod. She'd like to get to know this couple better.

"Sure, we can stay. I'll call Caleb and Adele so they don't expect us."

The talk before dinner and during it took many different roads. Mark had been everywhere and seen everything as he'd trotted the globe. His stories were engrossing. In the midst of the many topics of conversation, Emily pieced together that Juliet had come to Thunder Canyon alone. She'd only brought a few things and was waitressing at the Hitching Post, a local restaurant and saloon, when Mark had met her. Both of their lives had been changed drastically by that meeting. It was easy to see how happy they were. Mark was never far from his wife, encircling her with his arm, giving her a smile, touching her hand.

Later Emily and Juliet were loading dishes into the dishwasher when Marissa began crying again.

"This time she wants to be fed," Juliet explained. I'll do that in the nursery, then bring her out so she can join us. She's usually a contented baby."

"Does Mark help you with her?"

"Oh, yes. In fact, he's insisting that I pump milk and try to give her a bottle some of the time so he can feed her, too. That way I can catch a few more hours of sleep and skip a feeding."

About fifteen minutes later, Emily and Brad were discussing visiting the prospector when Juliet brought Marissa into the room. Her terry playsuit, pink with little kitties printed all over it, was still too big for her.

Instead of settling in a chair or taking Marissa to Mark, Juliet went over to Brad and sat beside him on the sofa. Time after time, as they chatted, Brad looked down at the little girl with a tender gleam in his eyes.

Finally Juliet asked him, "Would you like to hold her?"

"I've never held a baby before." His voice was

gruff, and Emily wondered what he was thinking about. Suzette's baby, maybe? The possibility he could be a dad?

"It's never too late for a man to get used to babies. Here, try it."

At first Brad was all thumbs, not knowing exactly how to hold Marissa. But with Juliet's gentle urging for him to support the baby's head, he took the little girl into his arms.

Emily wished she had her camera. The handsome man and the tiny baby would make quite a photograph. The expression on Brad's face was one she'd never seen there before. It told her that holding Marissa touched his heart in some way nothing else had ever done.

When he became comfortable with the infant, he ran his thumb across her chin and slipped one of his fingers into her tiny hand.

Marissa grabbed on to it reflexively and held tight.

Brad's gaze caught Emily's, and she felt herself in more turmoil at that moment than she had ever been in in her entire life.

Neither Brad nor Emily spoke much on their return trip to Caleb's. Emily knew the house would be empty except for the housekeeper. Caleb had told them he and Adele were going out after dinner.

Brad parked the SUV in the driveway. After he and Emily had gone inside and removed their coats, she wasn't sure what to do next. But Brad took her by the elbow and led her into the sitting room. "I'd like to talk to you about something."

She could feel his hand through the material of her

blouse. The sexual buzz between them was exceedingly strong tonight.

After Brad guided her to the love seat, she sat there beside him, curious as to what he wanted to discuss. Caleb's case? A trip to the prospector? Mark and Juliet? The two of *them*?

"I've been thinking about something," he began. "I meant what I said—that you would be a good private investigator. When we get back, I think it would be a good idea for you to work with Jack McCormick."

Jack was a senior investigator, in his fifties and very good at what he did. "In addition to being your secretary?"

"No, in place of being my personal assistant and secretary. It would be a promotion, Emily. Your salary would go up and you could possibly get into the investigative work itself."

A tiny voice inside her head screamed, *I don't want to leave you,* but of course she wasn't going to tell *him* that. It was obvious he regretted what had happened between them in the cabin and now he was trying to find a way out of it.

"If that's what you think is best." Her voice came out stilted but she couldn't help that. She'd thought they were getting closer. She'd thought they were really learning to know each other. But she guessed Brad could see their differences now even more glaringly than he had before.

Wrapping her pride around herself, she added, "I know Mr. McCormick's well respected and he can teach me a lot."

"Is it what you want, Emily?"

She couldn't tell Brad what she wanted because it was a dream she could never attain. *He* was a dream she could never attain.

Maybe holding Marissa had made him realize he didn't want to deny being the father of Suzette Brouchard's baby. Maybe he'd realized fatherhood wouldn't be so bad. Maybe he was thinking about her becoming pregnant and how that would affect them working together. Even if she wasn't pregnant, nothing would ever be the same as it had been before this trip.

As if he'd read her thoughts, he assured her, "I haven't forgotten what happened between us in the cabin. If you are pregnant, I'll stand behind you and support you however I can. I don't want you to be afraid of that."

"I'm not afraid, Brad," she said quietly. "I've been managing my own life for a long time now. I'll manage no matter what happens."

Then, because she couldn't continue this conversation, because she couldn't look at him without wanting to kiss him, she stood to leave. "I'm going to go up to my room now and type up notes on what Mark told us. Afterward I'm going to turn in. I'll see you tomorrow."

Trying not to run away from Brad Vaughn, she walked slowly out of the room and up the stairs. Although her feelings for him were growing stronger, she realized that she was just going to have to get over them.

Brad raked his hand through his hair and leaned back against the sofa cushion. *That* hadn't gone well.

Emily usually voiced her opinion. If she'd wanted to

continue to work with him, she would have said so, wouldn't she?

Ever since they'd arrived in Thunder Canyon, everything about Emily Stanton had gotten under his skin. It wasn't just her natural beauty that made him react to her. It was the essence of who she was—her down-to-earth nature, her compassion, her caring. When she'd held Marissa today and lulled her to sleep—

Brad had entertained visions of her carrying his child! What if Emily was pregnant?

He didn't have an opportunity to answer the question as Tess came into the sitting room. "Mr. Vaughn, would you like something to eat or drink?"

"No, thank you, Tess. I might go out for a walk."

"Before you do, sir, can I speak to you?"

"Sure."

Tess came over to the sofa, looking anxious. "Since you're a private investigator, do you ever find missing persons?"

"Once in a while we'll take on a client like that. Why?"

After she seemed to debate with herself, she answered, "I have a daughter who's missing. She was fifteen when she ran away. She'd be eighteen now. The year she left, I found this job with the Douglases, hoping to make more money so I could search for her. And I have. But traveling is so expensive and...I don't know where to go. But you...you probably have ways to find her. I have saved up some money and I wondered if you'd take on my case."

Without even asking how much money Tess had saved, Brad knew she could never pay what his agency expected. Somehow right now that didn't matter, but Caleb Douglas did. "I don't know how much the present case is going to tie me up in Thunder Canyon. Let me think about it and get back to you."

She looked happy he'd even consider taking her on. "I'd appreciate that. Are you sure you don't want something to eat or drink?"

"No, I'm going out for that walk."

Hopefully the Montana air would clear his head.

When Brad and Emily went looking for the prospector at his cabin on Saturday, to Brad's frustration, they couldn't find him. The conversation the night before with Emily had caused a strain between them that was palpable, and they talked little. On Sunday morning, Brad had intended to try to reach Tildy Matheson instead of searching again for the prospector.

However, after breakfast Emily requested the keys to the SUV.

"Where are you going?" he asked.

"To church."

After he was silent for a few moments, he said, "I'll drive you."

Before they left he phoned the number Mark had given him for Tildy Matheson, but no one seemed to be home and he turned off his cell phone. No answer... They were batting zero.

Dressing for church, Brad realized it had been years since he'd attended a service. He found peace settling around him as he drove into town. The steeple of the pretty white church reached high into the blue sky as clouds puffed around it. The building was located on north Main Street and although it wasn't as old as the structures around the town hall, the cornerstone noted that it had been built in 1910.

After Brad parked in the lot behind the church, townsfolk said their good mornings and strolled beside or in front of him and Emily, heading around to the front. Sun streamed through stained glass windows into the vestibule, creating rainbows on the tile floor. Two sets of double wooden doors led into the main body of the church. They were propped open, and Brad could see the pews were filling up fast. They walked up the middle aisle and found an empty spot at the end of the pew about ten rows back from the pulpit.

Brad had found his hand on the small of Emily's back as they'd walked up the aisle. An odd feeling of the rightness of being here with her confused him.

As they sat side by side in the pew, Emily leaned over and whispered to him, "Isn't this beautiful?"

He knew she meant the old wood and the stained glass windows and the interestingly carved pulpit that stood in the front. But all he could see was her face and the guilelessness in her beautiful green eyes.

"Yes, it is."

They were still gazing at each other when the organ music began. Startled, they reached for hymnals and opened to the hymn numbers posted on the board to the side of the front pews.

Discovering he remembered the old hymns, Brad's voice rose along with Emily's. Later he found himself listening intently to the minister's sermon about the bonds of family. He'd never known a close-knit family like the one the reverend spoke of. When he'd lived with his mother, he'd felt resentment that she'd broken her marriage apart. When he'd lived with his dad, he'd missed his mother and the softness of her presence in the big house. Over the years he and his father had become civilly polite to each other, but Phillip Vaughn had taken every opportunity to blame the collapse of the marriage on his wife.

Brad's mother had never talked to him about the divorce. She'd never defended herself. She'd never told him why she'd turned to another man. The odd thing was, she'd never remarried. After the affair that had torn their family apart, she hadn't even dated.

At the end of the service, the minister gave a blessing to the congregation, then made a few announcements. The second one made Brad's ears perk up.

"Matilda Matheson will turn eighty-five this month. In honor of this milestone and all of the work she's done for this church over the years, we'll have a gathering in the church hall on May twenty-fifth. Everyone is welcome, and if you can't find time to join us, you can bid her a happy birthday after services today."

He pointed to one of the first pews on the right side of the church. "She's wearing a special birthday hat her niece gave her for the occasion, so you can't miss her."

Brad took note of a large blue felt hat decorated with feathers and flowers, then leaned close to Emily. "We'll have to stop and introduce ourselves. Maybe we can set up a meeting."

"Do you want to hang back until everyone's wished her a happy birthday?" Emily asked.

"That's probably a good idea."

Although the rest of the congregation filed from the pews a few minutes later, after their row filed into the aisle, Emily and Brad lowered themselves to the pew once more. The church emptied amazingly quickly. Chatter in the vestibule was loud as they sat in silence.

"The reverend's sermon made me miss my family," Emily admitted in the hushed aftermath of the service.

"Do you see them often?"

"I live with Mom. I can help Lizbeth better with college that way and I think my mother's glad for the company. Lizbeth doesn't get home every weekend. She finds rides with friends when she can, though she'll be home for the summer next week. My brother and his family and Elaine and her boyfriend usually join us for dinner on Sundays. How about you? I know you see your dad every day at work, but that's not the same as just keeping each other company."

"My dad and I have never just kept each other company," Brad responded in a wry tone. "After my parents' divorce, I spent weekends with him. My mother would drop me off Friday evening after school and he'd take me out to dinner somewhere. But then he usually worked the rest of the night while I watched TV. Saturdays he took me with him to the office. And Sundays we were just sort of there together until Mom came and got me in the afternoon. I'm not sure that was keeping each other company because we didn't talk. After I began college, I didn't see him much at all."

"Don't you spend any *fun* time with him now?"

"Fun? I'm not sure my father knows the meaning of that word. We go to so many business dinners that I guess it never occurs to us to see each other outside of that."

Emily's eyes were large and sparkling, her voice soft as she asked, "And what about your mother?"

"I've always thought my mother was as complicated as my father. I went to school, did my homework and she'd have the requisite cookies and milk ready while I was doing it. She can talk about anything under the sun and fill up any silence. But I don't think we've ever had a serious conversation, not about anything that really matters."

"Like what?" Emily prodded.

"Like life and its pitfalls and rewards."

"Do you bring girls home to her when you're dating?"

That must have been some standard to Emily, so he answered honestly, "I did once. I met someone when I was in college and I brought her home with me for the weekend."

"Did your mother like her?"

"Actually, she didn't. Back then I thought she was against Robin for the same reason my father was. She came from a different side of life than I did. Her dad was the foreman in a clothing factory and her mother waited tables. My mother hadn't smiled much that weekend. She'd been polite to Robin but not completely welcoming."

"You said 'back then.' Do you see another reason now?"

"Maybe my mom saw a flaw in Robin that I didn't."

"I don't understand."

Until now Brad had never told anyone what had happened. Today, though, looking into Emily's honest face, he revealed, "My dad offered her money to stop seeing me. She took it and flew to the West Coast."

"Oh, Brad."

He shrugged. "I got over it. After all, I guess my father did me a favor if that's all Robin cared about."

"Your father should have let you discover it on your own."

Because Emily said that with such certainty, Brad asked her, "You advocate the school of hard knocks?"

"I'm not saying experience is the best teacher, but it's a good teacher. We learn from our mistakes."

"Oh, I learned from my mistakes. After that I didn't date girls from the wrong side of the tracks."

When he saw Emily's expression, he immediately realized what he'd said and how she'd taken it. "Emily, I didn't mean anything by that. That reference had nothing to do with you."

"My father was a blue-collar worker, too, but I don't think degrees of wealth have anything to do with integrity and moral fiber. I understand that you didn't want to risk the same thing happening again so it was easier to date women from the same circles you were in."

"Maybe I'm learning that was a mistake. Suzette had money of her own and now she's asking for more. I should have realized sooner how to find a woman with integrity."

He wanted to tell Emily that *she* was a woman of integrity, but after the remark he'd made, she'd think he was just trying to mend fences. He knew exactly what she was thinking—he'd slept with her but he didn't want to date her.

"The crowd is thinning back there," she said quickly in a soft voice.

Longing to put his arm around her, he wanted to draw her close and kiss her forehead and tell her she was the sweetest woman he'd ever met, though the most frustrating, too, sometimes. But he didn't have that freedom. Until this matter was settled with Suzette, Emily would believe he was an irresponsible playboy. Maybe he *had* been a playboy once, but this trip was changing his view of the world. And maybe it would change him, too.

After they walked to the vestibule, they waited until Tildy was finally alone.

Approaching her, Emily said, "Happy birthday, Miss Matheson."

Tildy's gray hair was straight and cut at her wrinkled double chin. She was stocky with substance to her and leaned on a cane. Her blue eyes twinkled as she asked, "Do I know you, child?"

"No, you don't. My name's Emily Stanton and this is Brad Vaughn. Mark Anderson spoke about you to us, and we wanted to say hello."

"Well, how kind of you. So many people have wished me well today. If all their wishes would just take away my arthritis, I'd be the happiest old-timer in town. I can't even do those front steps out there. I'll have to go out the side. But I guess that's a small price to pay for reaching eighty-five."

Brad stepped in then. "Actually, I tried to phone you this morning."

"You did? My niece picked me up to take me to breakfast before the service. In fact, I'm going home with her afterward. She's driving me to Billings so I can spend time with my sister."

Frustrated, Brad felt as if they were being stalled on all fronts. "The reason Mark mentioned you to us, the reason I called, is because we wanted to talk to you about whatever you know concerning the Queen of Hearts gold mine."

Just then a woman who might be close to sixty came up to Matilda Matheson. "Aunt Tildy, we should go."

Tildy introduced her niece Amelia to them. Then, returning to their earlier conversation, she told Amelia, "They want to come by and chat. I imagine I'll need to rest some when I get back on May twentieth. I don't travel as well as I used to. How about the day after that? You could come for tea."

Although Brad had wanted to get this trip over with as soon as possible, the fates were conspiring against him. Maybe he should stop pushing and go with the flow. Maybe he'd find the deed before Tildy returned and he wouldn't need to meet with her. However, keeping his options open, he said, "That will be fine. We'll call you when you get back and set up a time."

Emily smiled at Tildy. "You have a wonderful trip, Miss Matheson."

"Call me Tildy."

"We'll do that," Emily assured her.

As her niece took her arm and they walked back into the church to go out the side entrance, Emily asked, "We're going to be here until May twentieth?"

The twentieth was twelve days away. "I hope not. But it depends on how much progress we make. If you want to fly back to Chicago, I understand."

"No," Emily said quickly. "I mean, I said I'd help you with this and I will. Besides, Thunder Canyon is growing on me."

He had to smile…because it was growing on him, too. And so was Emily Stanton.

Chapter Seven

"**I**'ve never ridden a horse!"

As Emily stood looking up at the mount Caleb's foreman had brought into the corral for her, she felt total dismay. "Do *you* go riding?" she asked Brad, who was standing beside her.

"Not much anymore. I spent that summer in Montana years ago with a college friend. And I ride on vacations."

She fingered the camera strap on her shoulder. "I don't know if I should do this. What if I'm—"

"Pregnant?" Brad filled in, moving closer to her.

She nodded.

"You don't have to go riding. Don't do it just to impress Caleb. But if you want a taste of the experience, I'll help you into the saddle, and we can just walk our horses."

Thinking about it, she rolled the idea over in her mind. She'd heard that sitting on a walking horse felt the same as being in a rocking chair. Probably she'd never have the chance for this experience again. "Walking should be safe enough."

She glanced at the mount Caleb had chosen for her, a very old bay gelding named Calypso. "I'd like to try it. Maybe I can take more film of this beautiful scenery."

The foreman motioned to her to come closer to the barn. He'd left a hay bale there and was holding the horse beside it.

Brad's hand was on her shoulder as they approached Calypso, and she liked the feel of it there. Brad was so different here than in Chicago. Here he was a real person, not a rich man in a suit who could get whatever he wanted.

After she handed her camera to the foreman, she stepped up onto the hay bale. With care, Brad showed her how to put her foot in the stirrup and how to swing her leg over. In a matter of seconds, she was sitting in the saddle, feeling as if she were on top of the world. The horse lifted his head and then lowered it again.

Brad advised her, "Take the reins and get a feel for them. If you pull back, he'll stop. If you loosen them, he'll put his head down or go."

"Pressure on his flanks with your feet will also help push him forward," the foreman explained. "You'll get the hang of it."

Clearing her throat, she said to Brad again, "I just want to go slow. Nothing fast."

His gaze met hers and she saw that he understood.

When the foreman handed her her camera, she slipped the strap over her head.

As she did that, she noticed Brad running his hand up and down her horse's nose, scratching between his ears. He was comfortable with the animal. Too well she could remember him touching her. Her cheeks heated up and she took the reins in both hands.

A few minutes later, when Brad climbed into his saddle, Emily realized he more than remembered how to ride a horse. He looked as if he belonged on one.

After Caleb and Adele joined them in the corral, they mounted their horses. Adele rode a gray that was about the size of Emily's horse, while Caleb and Brad's steeds were larger and chestnut brown.

The walking motion of the horse was soothing. Emily felt more confident as the clip-clop of Calypso's hooves mingled with the lowing of nearby cattle and the chirping of birds. For a while they rode along the trail that followed the fence line. The scenery *was* awesome. Some of the ground was still snow-covered in shaded patches, and the firs were high against the immense blue canopy of sky. Breathtaking mountains stood in the distance, and Emily considered the fact that she certainly couldn't see scenery like this in Chicago.

When she glanced at Brad riding next to her, she felt a thrill just being here with him. She was actually glad they couldn't talk to Tildy until she returned. Emily wanted more time here with Brad.

When she heard the growl of an engine somewhere in the distance, she automatically gripped her reins tighter.

"You said you were in Montana years ago?" she asked Brad.

"On a ranch north of Billings."

"You seem to like it here a lot. Why didn't you ever come back?"

When Brad didn't answer, she glanced over at him.

The wind tossed his horse's mane, and he looked very somber when he finally responded, "I came out here that summer with a friend, James Lawson. We were roommates in college. I had to make some money, and jobs in Chicago were scarce and boring. I saw an ad in a magazine. The ranch needed hands and the pay wasn't too bad. It included room and board, so anything we made was pure profit. I think that summer was one of the most enjoyable of my life."

"Then why haven't you returned?" she asked again.

"When James and I were seniors, he found out he had leukemia. A year and a half later he was gone. I don't think I ever wanted to come back here without him."

Now she understood Brad's reluctance to return to a beautiful place where he'd only remember loss. His life hadn't been a joyride, either, and maybe that's why he kept emotional barricades in place. She felt as if she was really getting to know him now. "I'm sorry you lost him."

When Brad didn't respond, Emily understood that his loss hadn't diminished with time.

Up ahead Caleb and Adele crossed an access road. "I'm holding you back," she said to Brad. "If you want to ride ahead…"

"No. This pace is fine. I'm learning all over again

how it feels to relax. This has got to be the best way to do it. If you want to snap photos, I'll hold your horse."

Drawing up beside her, he took her reins while she lifted her camera from around her neck and took one shot after another. Suddenly she turned toward *him* and began snapping.

"What are you doing?"

"You're part of the scenery."

He shook his head. "That's enough, then, if you can't find anything better than me." When he handed her back her reins, their hands brushed and she gazed up into his eyes.

He said simply, "I'm glad you're here with me, Emily."

Not knowing how to react to that, she started her horse walking again, reins in one hand, her camera in the other.

The rumbling of a car grew louder and Brad frowned. "Whoever that is, they're going much too fast—"

The topless blue Jeep raced into view, speeding along on the gravel access road. It was occupied by four men wearing large hats. Immediately Emily stopped her horse. But before she knew what had happened, the Jeep backfired once, then again. Her mount reared up and took off at a run. When her camera fell to the ground, she hung on to the reins, scared out of her wits. Instinctively she wrapped the reins around one hand, trying to hang on yet pull back at the same time to make Calypso stop.

Nothing worked.

As she joggled in the saddle, suddenly Brad was racing beside her. He couldn't seem to catch Calypso's halter, so instead…

She felt more than saw him as he leaned closer to her and wrapped his arm around her. But as he pulled her away from her horse, her hand was still wound up in her reins and she felt her wrist wrench sideways.

Pain shot up her arm.

While Brad held on to her, she frantically wiggled her fingers. Finally the reins loosened, fell away, and Calypso raced ahead of them.

Practically in Brad's lap now, she held her breath until his horse stopped. Then he let her slide gently to the ground. Her legs were shaking so badly, she sank down onto the damp earth, trying to gulp in air as she heard the fading sound of Calypso's hooves.

Then Brad was beside her, his arm around her.

"Take it easy," he suggested. "Get a few breaths."

Finally her lungs seemed to work as she sucked in air and then sucked in more of it.

Bending over her, Brad's face was close to hers. The huskiness in his voice told her he was worried about her.

"I'm fine," she murmured, but as she braced her hand on the ground to scramble to her feet, she yelped. Her wrist hurt.

Brad rose quickly. "What is it?"

She knew she couldn't hide the injury from him. "My wrist."

"I'm driving you to the emergency room." Gently he took her hand in his. "Move your fingers," he ordered. When she did, he looked relieved. "I don't think it's broken. But I want you checked out."

"How am I going to get back?"

"With me." He'd tethered the reins to his horse around some brush. "Come on, I'll help you into the saddle. Believe me, I won't let anything else happen to you."

She believed him. "My camera…"

"I know where it fell." He lifted her onto the saddle and she swung her leg over the pommel. "I'll walk you over there before I climb on."

Five minutes later, he'd found the camera, handed it to her and swung up onto the horse behind her. His arms were around her as he held the reins.

With his lips close to her ear, his breath was warm on her neck as he asked, "Ready?"

She almost felt ready for anything with Brad. She knew she was beginning to rely on him, and that scared her most of all.

Thunder Canyon General Hospital was a relatively new two-story building, surrounded by a parking lot. Brad bypassed the main entrance and headed for the E.R., pulling in as close as he could to the emergency-room door. A few minutes later, he guided Emily under the covered portico.

She stopped and took hold of his arm. "I'll have to tell the doctor I might be pregnant. If you don't want to be around, I'll understand."

"I'm not going anywhere," he responded gruffly.

The emergency room had pale blue walls and a white tile floor. The waiting room was pleasant in blue, green and lilac, with tall windows that allowed the late afternoon sun to stream through.

After Emily registered, she sat and waited until her name was called. Then she was taken down a hall into a room with several beds where blue-and-white-striped curtains hung between each.

"Dr. Taylor will be in shortly," the nurse informed them with a smile.

"I'd better give this to you," Emily said to Brad as she realized she still had her camera around her neck. When she lifted it off, she looked at it and a gasp escaped her.

"What's wrong?"

"I think the lens is cracked. It is. Oh, Brad…"

Her voice broke and Brad realized this whole incident had caused more trauma than she wanted to admit. He also knew how much that camera meant to her.

"Let me see."

When she handed it over, he noticed the tears in her eyes, and instead of looking at the camera he put his arms around her and brought her close.

"It's okay. Maybe I can get it repaired."

"I doubt it."

He guessed how long she'd saved to buy that camera. He knew her pictures probably expressed a part of her that she was afraid to express on her own.

Putting his hands on either side of her face, he tipped her chin up to him. "I'm just grateful you're okay. If you *are* pregnant, I don't want anything to happen to our baby."

She gave him a little smile now. "I know."

"You're an amazing woman," he whispered, his lips hovering tantalizingly just above hers.

Temptation was so great, he couldn't resist. When he kissed her, it was as if he were coming home. They hadn't kissed since their stay in the cabin. They hadn't touched deliberately since they'd made love. He missed her kisses and her touching as if he'd been used to it for a whole lifetime. As his tongue danced with hers and she responded to it, he thought about their separate bedrooms with the bathroom in between. He thought about asking her into his bed again tonight. He thought about—

Someone cleared his throat.

When Brad broke away, there was a tall man with wavy blond hair and blue eyes standing in the cubicle. He was wearing a lab coat and a stethoscope and Brad supposed he was the E.R. doctor.

"I'm not sure that's the medicine I'd prescribe for a twisted wrist." His eyes were filled with amusement.

Brad instantly went on alert because the doctor was good-looking, but then he noticed the gold band on his hand and felt relieved. When had he developed a possessive streak?

Not giving an explanation for their kiss or why he was in the cubicle with Emily, Brad stated, "It's possible she might be pregnant."

His smile fading now, the physician extended his hand to Emily and then to Brad. "I'm Dr. Taylor. I'll examine your wrist, then if you want I'll page an obstetrician."

Emily nodded.

After the doctor took a hospital gown from a cupboard and handed it to her, he glanced at Brad. "When we're finished, I'll send someone to get you in the waiting room."

Brad wanted to stay but knew he had no right to. With a last look at Emily, with her camera in his hands, he left the cubicle and went to sit in the reception area, worrying about her in a way he'd never worried about a woman before.

An hour later a technician came to fetch Brad and take him back to Emily. She was dressed again, and the doctor had just finished wrapping her wrist.

Emily explained to Brad, "It's too soon to know for sure if I'm pregnant. The obstetrician told me I can have a blood test in a few days or use an early-testing pregnancy kit in a day or two."

Dr. Taylor focused on Brad now. "She seems fine except for her wrist. She preferred I not X-ray it, and that's wise under the circumstances. But I think it's just sprained. If it's not better in a few days, come back and we'll decide what to do. She told me what happened…about the prospectors in the Jeep." The young physician looked almost angry.

Crossing the room, Brad stood by Emily. "I guess that can be expected when there's a rumor of gold."

"People coming here for Caleb Douglas's resort are one thing. They're investing in the area and they're going to have a stake in our lives, too. But the fly-by-nighters who are just looking for an easy buck or a few nuggets of gold don't care what they do to our town."

"They help the economy, though," Brad pointed out.

"Yes, they do, and the sudden influx of revenue for everyone will help make improvements in the hospital. I guess we can't stop any of it now. I heard the gold mine even made CNN."

Brad felt as if he and Emily had been isolated from the real world for weeks—and it had only been six days.

"Thunder Canyon might grow faster than anyone wants it to."

"That's what I'm afraid of," the doctor agreed. Then he smiled. "But in the meantime, I'll just do what I do."

Turning to Emily, he added, "Being rescued from a runaway horse isn't an everyday occurrence. It wouldn't hurt to take it easy tomorrow. Keep ice on the wrist for the next twenty-four hours. A warm bath tonight might help relax you. If you have any unusual symptoms—dizziness, nausea, cramping—you come back in here. You hear?"

Although Emily nodded, Brad said, "I'll make sure she does."

At that, her gaze caught his and held.

Breaking eye contact, he walked her into the reception area and led her to a chair. "You stay here while I buy ice packs at the pharmacy."

"You don't have to do this—" Her voice caught.

"I know I don't. I also know you'd do the same for me."

With a smile that seemed to knock the wind out of her sails, he watched her as she sank down into a chair and picked up a magazine. She might be the epitome of the independent woman, but he'd found a much softer side to Emily Stanton, too. And he liked it.

When Emily and Brad returned to the Lazy D, Adele and Caleb were both solicitous and wanted to know what they could do to make her feel better. She simply smiled, gave them her "I'll be fine" speech and then said she was going up to her room to rest.

"Dinner will be ready in fifteen minutes," Adele advised her.

"I think I'll skip dinner tonight."

After she mounted the stairs, she made it to her room and lowered herself onto the bed.

Brad followed her. "I put the ice packs in the freezer. The doctor's orders said fifteen minutes every hour. He said a warm bath might help relax you, too."

"I just want to go to bed."

"Not going to listen to doctor's orders?"

She wrinkled her nose at him. "Don't parent me, Brad."

"Believe me, the last thing I want to do is parent you."

When she saw the glimmer of desire in his eyes, she remembered how he'd kissed her so tenderly yet with so much passion at the emergency room. Dealing with that on top of everything else was just a little bit too much.

"Just leave me alone, okay?"

Coming over to her, he hunkered down in front of her. "No, I'm not going to leave you alone. I'm going to draw you a warm bath. When you're finished, I'll put ice cubes in a plastic bag for your wrist until the ice packs are ready. So get undressed, put on a robe and come into the bathroom in about ten minutes. If you don't appear, I'll come and get you."

"You can be so arrogant," she mumbled under her breath.

Even though it had been low, he'd still heard it. Rather than being offended, he grinned. "I know I can. It's a great way to get my own way. Ten minutes, Emily."

After he disappeared into the bathroom, she heard water running in the tub.

She didn't know whether to laugh or cry. Whoever could have imagined Brad Vaughn would draw her a bath.

That was as crazy as this whole trip had been. But she did know Brad always got what he wanted and she didn't have the energy to fight him, so she did as he suggested.

He was still in the bathroom, standing over the tub, when she finally went in, her robe belted tight. Bubbles floated everywhere and the sweet scent of lavender hovered in the air.

"It's ready." He looked her over, making no move to leave.

"If you think you're going to stand here and watch me take a bath, you're sadly mistaken," she teased.

With a chuckle, he shook his head. "Somehow I knew you'd say that. I'll leave. But I won't be far away. Just yell if you need anything."

When he'd shut the door to his room partway, she laid her robe over a small settee and stepped down into the water. It did feel heavenly. Sinking beneath the bubbles, she let her head loll back, resting her bandaged wrist on the side of the tub.

For the most part Emily kept her eyes closed while she soaked, but every once in a while she'd hear Brad moving about in his bedroom. There was something totally intimate about having him close by.

Ten minutes later the water began to grow tepid. Shivering, she stepped out of the tub, dried off and belted her robe. Then she went to the door to Brad's room. "I'm going to bed now."

"Don't lock your door. I'll bring up the ice."

As Brad went downstairs, he thought about Emily's bath and how he'd wanted to join her in the tub. Then he remembered her body naked in the cabin shadows. It was an image he couldn't get out of his head.

When he entered the kitchen, he noticed Tess was putting the last touches on supper.

"How's Miss Emily?" she asked.

"Stubborn."

The housekeeper smiled, and then silence permeated the kitchen. Brad knew why. Tess wanted to know if he'd thought about taking her case.

In the midst of everything else, he had. He was stalled here in Thunder Canyon at least for a while. He might as well do something worthwhile with his time. Truth be told, Tess's case was the type of challenge he'd like to take on. "I've given some thought to finding your daughter."

"You'll do it?" Her face looked brighter than he'd seen it since he'd arrived.

"I don't want to give you false hope, Tess. I might come up with zero. It's been a long time and some people who don't want to be found manage ways to keep hidden."

"She left because she was rebelling. She wanted to find her own way and I wouldn't let her. But maybe now she's just too ashamed to come home."

He knew that often happened. "That still doesn't mean I can find her, but I'll try. I want you to write down absolutely everything you know about her—where she liked to go, what she liked to do, who she liked to be with. I want a list of names—any friends who are still around, anybody she talked to. I also want a list of stores where she used to buy her clothes, purses and shoes."

Tess looked puzzled. "Why?"

"Although she may have wanted to run away from her life, people have habits and certain preferences. If we do come up with a location or vicinity and we don't have an address, I never know what might help. So just do it, okay? Write a book if you have to. Even the smallest details are important."

"I'll do it tonight."

Feeling good about taking her case, not knowing where it was going to lead, he asked, "Can I have a tray for Emily?"

"Sure. What would you like? I can warm up something."

"I don't think she's going to go for a whole lot. Maybe a sandwich and a glass of milk?"

"Just give me a couple of minutes."

Ten minutes later, Brad was carrying a tray up to Emily's room along with a plastic bag of ice wrapped in a towel. For courtesy's sake, he rapped on the door.

"Come in."

She was propped up on three pillows examining her camera. "I hope somebody can fix it."

"After we get back to Chicago, I'll find someone who can. In the meantime, you might want to buy one of those disposable cameras."

"That's a good idea. I hate to miss shooting anything I might want to remember."

Their eyes caught and held. She'd snapped a few pictures of him. Maybe she didn't have as many regrets as he thought she'd have over what had happened in the cabin.

When he took the tray to the bed, he could smell lavender. Her skin was a pretty pink from her bath. She was wearing a pink flannel nightgown, and all he wanted to do was crawl into bed beside her and hold her through the night as he had the last night in the cabin.

Setting the tray on her lap, he advised her, "You'll feel better if you eat something."

"I know." She said it with so much resignation he had to smile.

"Just put your tray outside the door when you're finished. Tess said she'll pick it up."

Emily took a few sips of the milk and nodded.

At the door, he turned to her again. "I told Tess I'd take on her case." He'd confided in Emily that Tess wanted him to search for her daughter.

"Do you think you can find her?"

"I don't know. She's supposed to write up some information tonight. I'll see where that leads. In the meantime, I'm going to search for the prospector again."

"I want to go along."

"It would probably do you good to sleep late. But I'll check with you before I leave."

He hesitated only a fraction of a second before he suggested, "I want you to keep your door to the bathroom open tonight. I'll do the same with mine. If you need anything, then you can call me."

To his surprise, she didn't argue or protest. Instead she just murmured, "Thank you, Brad."

Before he kissed her and decided to crawl into bed beside her after all, he went out into the hall and closed her bedroom door behind him.

Chapter Eight

Late Sunday evening, Brad's cell phone rang and he wondered if the caller was his father. He'd talked to him when they'd returned from the cabin and also checked in with other investigators who were working on projects under Brad's direction. They all had his cell phone number.

"Vaughn here."

"Brad, it's Mark Anderson. Did you find the prospector?"

"Not yet. I'm going out searching again tomorrow. If he went off for the weekend, maybe he'll be back."

"Besides his hut, I also heard about a spot where he camps out."

"Can you give me directions?"

"Do you want company? It's rough trekking. We'll have to hike about a mile to where I'm thinking about."

Brad explained about Emily's runaway horse. "I'll pick you up around nine. If Emily's still sleeping, I won't wake her."

"Nine sounds good."

The following morning, Brad checked on Emily. She was curled on her side, breathing evenly, her one hand tucked under her cheek. She was all feminine and pretty and soft and he wanted to hold her again.

Just hold her?

There was no way he was going to wake her simply to tell her where he was going. Finding paper and pen in his room, he wrote a brief note and laid it on the bathroom sink where she'd be sure to see it.

Twenty minutes later, he'd picked up Mark and they were headed out of town.

"So what's this guy's name?" Brad asked.

"Miles Latimer. But everyone calls him Mickey."

"What does he do out here?"

"He digs in the ground for gold, pans the streams. He has a favorite spot. He told me where it is, but I forgot to mention it to you."

"He digs for gold with a shovel?"

"A pickax and a spade."

"Who's property is he on?"

"I think it's part of the disputed Douglas property, but no one keeps him from doing it. He's causing no harm. It's rugged land and thickly forested."

"You make it sound as if I should have brought my survival gear," Brad joked.

"You never know."

Fifteen minutes later, Mark directed Brad to take a gravel lane. "It's an old logging road," he said.

The SUV rumbled and jumped over dips and ruts and potholes until finally they came to a stop and could go no farther. "We walk from here," Mark explained.

After they hiked through pines, up inclines and over a flat area for about a mile, Mark pointed to smoke billowing toward the sky. "There he is. He has a fire going this morning."

"It got pretty cold last night. He stays out in the weather?"

"Weather doesn't seem to bother him."

"How old is he?"

"My guess is around seventy, maybe seventy-five. He looks about a hundred and twenty, though. Yo, Mickey," Mark called, announcing his presence. "I don't want to sneak up on him. If he's paranoid, I won't appreciate looking down the barrel of a shotgun."

In the clearing, a blue tent was a bright color of contrast against the landscape. A campfire was going about ten feet from it, and a man was hunched down at it.

"Do you mind if we talk to you?" Mark asked as he came closer to the man.

Brad could see that Mickey Latimer might have been a tall man at one time, but now he was stooped as he gazed into the fire. Dressed in jeans and a down parka that had seen better days, he also wore a leather hat pulled down over his eyes. The wide brim shaded his face and almost hid it. Ignoring Mark, Mickey poured coffee from a tin pan into a foam cup.

"Sometimes I think he's hard of hearing. Other times

I believe the gossip and think he's just senile," Mark explained to Brad.

Approaching Mickey, he hunkered down beside him. "I brought someone along who wants to talk to you, too. Do you mind?"

The old prospector gave Mark a look from under the brim of his hat. "Don't mind nothin'. I'm too old to mind anything."

Brad crouched down on the other side of the man. "Nice tent you have there."

The old man's eyes narrowed. "Don't you think about stealing it." As quick as lightning, he brought a pistol out that had been tucked in his back waistband.

"I wouldn't think of it," Brad assured him, giving Mark a look that asked if he really was dangerous. To make sure Mickey knew he was no threat, he sat on the ground beside him. "I'm not interested in your tent. I'm interested in what you know."

Mickey's focus went to Mark again. "What's he talking about?"

"Remember I asked you questions about the Queen of Hearts mine?" Mark asked.

"The mine. I have a mine."

Brad played along. "Where's your mine?"

Mickey motioned behind the tent. "Back there. Staked it out and everything. Do you want to dig with me?" There was a conspiratorial air about him.

"Maybe another time," Brad answered seriously. "I came to Thunder Canyon to find out if the Douglases really own the Queen of Hearts."

The prospector put a finger to his lips. "Shh."

Brad cast a look around him, then he caught on. "You know a secret?"

With a shrug, Mickey answered, "Maybe I do, maybe I don't. Maybe I remember things, maybe I don't."

"How old are you?" Brad asked.

The elderly man's face screwed up and he pushed back the brim of his hat. Brad could see his weathered countenance clearly now. It was long and lean and his eyes were blue and cloudy. His leather gloves were scraped and torn, and now he put a finger to his chin. "I don't rightly know. I can't remember. Maybe I have a birthday today."

Beginning to think they wouldn't get anywhere, Brad agreed, "Maybe you do."

"Don't want no birthday cake, though. It will rot my teeth. Did you come to give me a donation?"

"Do you take donations?" Brad asked, amused.

"Sure do. That's how I got my tent. That's how I feed my mule."

Brad hadn't seen any evidence of an animal around. "You have a mule?"

"Sure do." He pointed farther up the mountain. "A man up there keeps him for me. Keeps him warm when it's cold. Let's me sleep there, too, in one of the stalls."

Mark just shrugged as if he didn't know anything about all that.

"So tell me about the Queen of Hearts," Brad prompted, trying to get them back on the subject.

"You play poker?" the prospector asked.

"I have now and then. How about you?"

"Nah. I save what money I have. Rumor has it Amos won that mine in a poker game."

"And did he?"

"That depends on who you talk to. My granddaddy said he was an ornery old cuss."

"Amos was?"

"Yep. Didn't treat his wife none too good."

Caleb had mentioned Catherine Douglas in passing but hadn't seemed to know much about her. "What do you mean he didn't treat her well? Was he mean to her?"

"No one knows for sure. Back then women stayed because they had to." He looked Brad in the eye. "Now they don't have to."

The old man was right about that. He couldn't imagine Emily staying in any situation she didn't want to be in. "So what about the mine?"

"The mine. The Queen of Hearts." Mickey shook his head as he leaned close to Brad and whispered, "Women have the power."

"Maybe now they do," Brad said.

"Women have the power," Mickey insisted, looking agitated.

"A woman owned the mine?" Brad asked.

The man resumed his seat with his legs crossed in front of the fire, then he stared into it as if their whole conversation hadn't happened, mumbling, "Don't know for sure. Don't know nothin' for sure."

After another twenty minutes or so of talking to Mickey, or trying to talk to Mickey, of attempting to make sense out of his ramblings and their pieced-together conversation, Brad knew he wasn't going to get anything else.

Pulling out his wallet, he took out two twenty-dollar

bills and tucked them into Mickey Latimer's pocket. "There's a donation for you. Do you mind if we come back to see you again?"

"Might be here. Might not be here."

"We'll keep that in mind."

As Brad and Mark hiked back the way they'd come, neither of them spoke. Finally, in the SUV once more, Brad looked over at the reporter. "What do you think?"

"I think he's rambling, just like when I talked to him. I couldn't make much sense out of any of it."

"What do you think he meant—'Women have the power'?"

"It could be just something he picked up somewhere."

"He seemed to know a little history on Amos."

"Maybe. But maybe his memory is cloudy. Maybe he was confusing Catherine Douglas with someone else."

Brad repeated the phrase. "Women have the power."

Fastening his seat belt, Mark laughed. "That's true in my house. My life revolves around Juliet and the baby."

Thinking about acquaintances and colleagues, Brad wasn't sure he'd seen any successful marriages. However, he might not have looked very hard, either. His parents had colored the way he thought of men and women and marriage. His experience with Robin had colored it, too. But spending time with Mark and Juliet, he'd realized they seemed genuinely happy.

He'd never asked his mother why she'd had an affair or what it had meant to her. He'd never asked her why she hadn't married the man who'd come between her and his father. Brad had always believed everything his father had told him about his mom—that he and Brad hadn't been enough for her and she'd found something outside of the marriage, that she'd been selfish, only considering what *she* wanted. But as Brad grew older, he'd realized everything wasn't black or white. He'd also learned his father could be controlling and cold. Is that what had forced his mother into an affair?

He didn't like rethinking his entire life, but he understood that one of the reasons he was doing it wasn't just this trip to Thunder Canyon—he was rethinking it because of Emily.

As Mark checked his watch, he asked, "What are you doing for lunch?"

"I haven't decided yet. I was going to go back to the ranch and check on Emily."

"Why don't we stop in at the Hitching Post and get something. You might find a little taste of history there, especially when you look over the bar at the Shady Lady."

"The Shady Lady?"

"It's a painting of a woman who was rumored to own a brothel—Lily Divine. I was thinking you might run into some old-timers there who hang around and play checkers because they have nothing better to do."

"Let me give Emily a call. I'll tell her what we're up to."

When he took out his cell phone, he realized he couldn't wait to hear Emily's voice.

When Emily had found Brad's note, her heart had raced faster and she'd smiled. *It's only a courtesy note,* she'd told herself. Still, it was nice Brad had let her know what he'd be doing and that he was with Mark.

After she'd dressed, poured a cup of tea and gone to the sitting room with it, her wrist ached so she'd decided to delve into some of Adele's home-decorating magazines for a distraction. But then Brad had called and seemed to just want to talk. His concern for her had made her feel all warm and fuzzy inside. After he'd described Mickey and shared some of their conversation, he'd told her he was going to have lunch with Mark and bone up on some more of Thunder Canyon's history.

Now, still paging through magazines, the sound of Brad's deep baritone echoing inside her, she decided to return to her room and look at the notes she'd taken thus far. She could try to type one-handed.

However, when she neared the dining room, she heard male voices and stopped.

"I'm going to keep that mine one way or another," she heard Caleb say.

"You know I'll do anything I can to help you, Dad."
She recognized Riley's voice.

"No one is going to cheat me out of what is rightfully mine. I've paid taxes on that land for years. No assessor ever said anything about a title not being listed."

"It's not so odd considering how records used to be kept," Riley assured him. "Every descendent after Amos Douglas just kept paying taxes as his predecessor had."

"I wonder if Amos ever had the actual deed. A lot of deals were made by word of mouth back then."

"But you *do* have the promissory note," Riley reminded him.

"Yes, I do. The question is, did Amos foreclose? Apparently the rumor about the poker game was a myth."

"Thunder Canyon is full of legends, and that was just one of them."

Instead of making her presence known, Emily quietly slipped past the dining room and went into the kitchen for an ice pack. She and Brad would have to have a conference when he returned.

When he returned.

Her heart raced faster at the thought.

Typing with her right hand, her left helping now and then, was slow going. Emily was engrossed in correcting her mistakes on the laptop screen when there was a knock at her bedroom door.

"Come in," she called absently, making another correction.

After Brad stepped into the bedroom, her heart seemed to actually sing. He was wearing jeans and a denim shirt today, with the cuffs rolled back. The shirt was open at the throat and black hair swirled there. When she'd played her fingers through that hair, it had been so soft—

"You're back," she said lightly, trying to keep the pictures from playing through her mind.

"You shouldn't be typing," he scolded her.

"You brought me along to type up notes. I can't earn my bonus if I don't do that."

"Give your wrist a couple of days to heal."

"I needed something to do."

After he crossed the room, he sat on the bed, facing her. When his jean-clad knee brushed hers, she could smell his aftershave and also the scents of the outdoors.

So she wouldn't concentrate on how much she liked the shadow of his beard line and the way his eyes darkened when he looked at her, she asked, "Did you find out anything else?"

"I don't know what's fact and what's fiction and I don't know if the prospector is senile or cryptic. But I didn't find out anything more at the Hitching Post. I told you what Mickey said about women having the power. If a woman did own the mine, none of the old-timers playing checkers there had ever heard about it.

"Women have the power," he repeated as if he still wondered what the prospector had meant.

"What power?" Emily asked, amused.

But Brad wasn't smiling. He was studying her in a way that made her blush.

"You have more power than you can ever know."

"Because a man needs a woman to fulfill his needs?" she asked softly, wishing their time in the cabin had been more than a diversion for him.

"No. Because a man needs a woman to feel like a man."

Before they'd made love, Emily might have scoffed at that, but now she knew a woman needed a man to feel like a woman, too. In that cabin, as Brad had kissed and caressed her, she'd felt beautiful and desired and feminine in a way she'd never felt before.

The hum surrounding her and Brad in its erotic field wasn't coming from her laptop. She licked lips, which had suddenly gone dry, and couldn't break eye contact.

A nerve in Brad's jaw worked. His voice was husky as he said, "I did learn a few things about Amos Douglas from Mickey that I didn't tell you about on the phone."

Trying to follow the thread of conversation, she made her lips form the word, "What?"

"It's not going to help us any, but I learned he might have been a scoundrel. There's a possibility he mistreated his wife."

"That would have been Catherine Douglas."

Brad nodded. "I'll have to take you to the Hitching Post some night. It's an interesting place—part old-time saloon, part new-time grill."

"That's the place Juliet mentioned last night. She'd waitressed there. That's where she met Mark. It must have been hard for her, being pregnant, having to work with no family around."

"I think that's why she and Mark connected." Studying her again, he asked, "Do you often think about the baby you lost?"

Emily guessed Brad was remembering holding Marissa. Maybe he was thinking about Suzette Brouchard and her child. Maybe he was contemplating the idea of really becoming a dad. He'd already missed two years of that little girl's life, according to the article in the newspaper. She wished she could put Suzette out of her head. She wished she could put Brad's lifestyle out of her head and pretend he was just an ordinary guy and they were here together getting to know each other.

Her thoughts had scrambled to another direction be-

cause the miscarriage was still painful for her to remember. "I think about that baby every day. I wonder
if it would have been a boy or a girl, if he or she might
have had my brown hair or my eyes, been born tiny or
big." Tears came to her eyes as she shook her head.

Clearing her throat, she quickly changed the subject.
"I overheard Caleb and Riley talking."

After a moment of studying her, he asked, "About
what?"

"The mine. Caleb is vowing to keep it one way or the
other."

"I wonder how he intends to accomplish that if I find
out someone else owns it."

"I don't know. But Riley's on his side. I get the feeling he'd do anything to please his father."

"Parental approval," Brad said with a grimace. "It can
be a driving force."

"Has it been for you?"

"Wanting my father's approval has always been in
the back of my mind. When I was younger, I purposely
took a different road so I didn't have to deal with earning it."

"But you came back to Chicago to work with him."

"Yes, I did. My mother wanted me to. I don't think
she liked me being so far away and she simply pushed
the guilt button several times, reminding me my father
wouldn't be around forever."

"Are you sorry you came back?"

He ran his hand through his hair. "No, I'm not sorry
I came back. I think she was right. I should get to know
him before it's too late. But working with him, trying

to fit into the vision of what he wants me to be, that's something else entirely."

After a few beats of silence, without warning Brad took her laptop from her lap and closed it.

"Brad, I have to—"

"What you have to do is give that wrist time to heal." He took her hand in his and lifted the bandage. "Did you rewrap this this morning?"

His fingers on her skin started a burning heat that didn't stop at her hand.

"No," she somehow managed to say, even though her mouth had gone as dry as cotton.

"Do you want me to rewrap it? It's kind of hard to do one-handed."

Yes, it was. If she let Brad do it, it would only take a couple of minutes, maybe not even that long.

Already Brad was slipping the small clasp out of the fabric, laying it on top of the laptop computer. Then he was gently holding her forearm, unwrapping the stretchy bandage.

Searching for a coherent thought, Emily finally settled on saying, "What are you going to do this afternoon?"

"I thought I'd go into Old Town to the historical society and poke around."

"Want some help?"

"Sure, if you feel up to coming."

"There's nothing to do here. And if I don't think about my wrist, it doesn't hurt."

"Mind over matter?" he teased.

The bandage undone now, Brad put her hand on his thigh. Every nerve inside her rioted because she had touched him intimately there. *Mind over matter,* she repeated inwardly, as if the mantra could make his touch less volatile.

As he probed her wrist gently, he said, "It doesn't look as swollen."

"The doctor said I should only keep the bandage on a couple of days."

Brad proceeded to tuck the end of the bandage into her palm. When he began wrapping, Emily tried to pretend he was the doctor doing it. That didn't work at all.

Taking care with her and the bandage, Brad wrapped it over and under and around her wrist. Although he did it methodically and expertly, she noticed every graze of his thumb, every touch of his eyes on her, every change of expression on his face. There were tiny lines around his eyes. His black brows drew together once when the bandage buckled, but then he smoothed it and finally attached the small metal clasp.

"There you go." His words were light, but when his gaze held hers there was no lightness there.

"Emily," he murmured as he leaned forward.

She loved the sound of her name on his lips. She loved his claiming purpose as he stood and then pulled her up, too.

When his arms wrapped around her, he said, "I don't understand this chemistry between us any more than you do."

What made them want each other? What made her eager to catch a glimpse of him? What made her want to feel him inside her again? She knew this could only be temporary. She absolutely knew it.

Yet sometimes it simply didn't matter. His kiss was possessive and took her breath away. Brad took her breath away.

Totally engrossed in their kiss, Emily jumped when the phone beside her bed rang. Brad ignored it. He knew Tess always answered it. His hands were under Emily's top now, and she anticipated the feel of his fingers on her breast. It was a delicious anticipation. Their bodies weren't quite touching, and she wanted that, too. She wanted everything from Brad.

She was pulling his shirt from the waistband of his jeans when there was a knock on her door. "Miss Emily?"

Brad swore, rested his forehead against hers and then leaned away.

"Yes, Tess?"

"Telephone. She says she's your sister."

"How does she know you're here?" Brad asked, his voice deep, desire still simmering in his eyes.

"I called home after we arrived. When they can't get in touch with me, they worry."

Instantly she guessed that was a foreign concept to Brad.

His face was unreadable now as he tucked his denim shirt back into his jeans and then went to the door. "You'd better get that. Until you're ready to go, I'll talk to Tess to see if she has those notes for me on her daughter."

Then he was leaving Emily's room and she was picking up the phone, hoping the sound of her sister's voice would bring her back to the real world, remind her that she was Emily Stanton, secretary, that Brad was her boss. When they got back to Chicago, nothing would be the same as it was here in Thunder Canyon.

Chapter Nine

When Emily skipped breakfast on Thursday morning,
Brad wondered why. Her wrist seemed to be better.
She'd taken off the bandage now and was using it normally. But she'd been quiet the past couple of days and
he was concerned about her. Did she just want to go
back to Chicago and her life? Did she want to get away
from the tension between them as they slept in their
rooms at night? He was aware of her, just a bathroom
away, and that awareness gave him insomnia, as well as
dreams he couldn't act on.

For the past two days he'd tried to learn everything
he could about Tess's daughter. He'd made calls to contacts on the West Coast and he'd made local calls, too.
But Annie Littlehawk's best friend hadn't wanted to
talk to him. In fact, she'd hung up on him. He wouldn't

stop there, of course, but he would give her a few days to think about it, to think about helping him in the search. At the moment he felt stymied on all fronts, waiting for Tildy Matheson to return, waiting for the mayor to return. Today he'd decided to see what all the fuss was about at the Queen of Hearts mine itself.

Since Emily hadn't appeared at breakfast, he went looking for her and found her in her bedroom working on her laptop at the small reading desk.

"Still organizing notes?" he asked after he'd knocked on the door and she'd called for him to come in.

"Not for the case," she said with a frown.

He saw numbers on the screen and joked, "That looks more like a budget."

Smiling, she turned away from the computer. "It is."

"Yours?"

"Unfortunately, yes."

She seemed deflated somehow, and that wasn't like Emily. Their last kiss had put another wall between them, had warned him again to keep his distance, had made him search out ways to work alone instead of working with her, but he realized he still cared what she was feeling way too much.

"What's wrong, Emily?"

Avoiding his gaze, she looked as if she was about to brush off the question, but then her shoulders squared and she pushed her chair back. "Lizbeth called me on Monday."

It was the call that had interrupted their kiss that could have led straight to the bed. "Bad news?"

Emily pushed her hair behind both ears, as though

somehow straightening it could straighten out her life. "She was supposed to graduate this month."

"And now she's not?"

"She wants to change her major and go another year."

Beginning to see where this was headed, he took a step closer. "If she does that, you won't be able to start school."

"Not for another year."

"There's no way around it?"

After Emily glanced at the computer screen again, she shook her head. "Lizbeth already has more school loans than I'm comfortable with. She'll be paying for them the rest of her life. She'll have to try to get more financial aid, of course. I can't subsidize the whole year. But before she started, I told her I'd help her as much as I can, and I can't go back on my word."

"Even if that means putting your life on hold again?"

"Even if it means that."

Her expression was so troubled, he asked, "Something else is bothering you, isn't it?"

Standing, she avoided his gaze and went over to the window that looked out over fenced-in grazing land. "I'm wondering when it is going to be *my* turn. And that makes me feel so selfish."

Emily was probably the most *un*selfish person he'd ever met. "You expect too much of yourself. Blazes, Emily, you've been putting your own life on hold for how many years now? Resentment has got to go along with that no matter how much you love your sister."

Her eyes glistened as she murmured, "I don't want to resent it. I don't want to be jealous of Elaine finding a career and Lizbeth looking for hers. If I give, I want to give freely…with no strings and no regrets."

That's exactly how she'd given herself to him. But he was afraid she *did* have regrets.

In the course of their conversation, Emily had wrapped her arms around herself in a defensive posture, as if she expected judgment from him.

He crossed to her and gently clasped her shoulders. "You're Lizbeth's sister, not a saint. Don't beat yourself up for being human."

Dropping her arms to her sides, she sighed. "I was just trying to figure out if it was possible for me to go to a community college and at least start that way since my budget's going to be tight."

Before he realized what he was saying, he offered, "Let me pay for your college courses."

Emily's eyes went wide and she looked at him as if he'd suggested she do a striptease for him. "You can't do that."

He took a light tone with her. "Yes, I can. I'll be investing in your future."

Pulling away from him, she went and stood beside the desk. "I can't take your money, Brad."

"You haven't given this enough thought."

"It only takes three seconds to realize it's a bad idea. I don't know when I'd be able to pay you back. What if I leave Vaughn? Besides, I don't want to feel like I'm taking something from a man who—"

"A man you slept with?"

Her cheeks reddened. "Yes. I just can't do it, Brad. Things are complicated enough."

"Complicated how?"

When she didn't respond, he demanded, "Tell me what's going on in that head of yours, Emily."

She bit her lower lip, then finally blurted out, "I might be pregnant! You might already be a father and need to pay child support to Suzette Brouchard. Never mind this hum between us whenever we're in the same room. That's why I didn't come to breakfast this morning."

His suspicion that she'd been avoiding him was confirmed. "Maybe we should alternate breakfasts so neither of us goes hungry."

If he'd been hoping for a smile, he didn't get one.

"What do you want to do about it?" he asked seriously. "I can finish here in Thunder Canyon myself if you want to go home."

"I won't leave a job unfinished," she protested. "That's not the way I am. I want to know who owns that mine as much as you do. And I want to talk to Tildy Matheson. I think that will be fun. It's just—"

"It's just that you don't want to be in the same room with me."

Her lashes fluttered down and then she said very softly, "I want to be in the same room with you too much."

If he took her into his arms then, he could kiss her and maybe even lead her into bed. But that would confuse her even more and confuse him, too. They were in a world away here, but what would happen when they returned to Chicago?

He wouldn't take advantage of Emily. He wouldn't pretend they had somewhere to go when they didn't. She was the kind of girl who deserved a house in a neighborhood that had block parties. She deserved a princesslike wedding gown and a man who thought highly of marriage.

Moving toward the door and away from her was one of the hardest things he'd ever done. For whatever reason, Emily Stanton was like a shooting star that had exploded into his life. He didn't want either of them to get any more burned than they already had.

At the door, he stopped. "I think we both need an excursion."

Now her lashes came up and she lifted her gaze to his. "What kind of excursion?"

"We need to see this infamous gold mine that could put this town on the map. I also want to visit Annie Littlehawk's best friend. Do you want to go with me?"

She seemed to give the idea much thought. They'd still be together and that sexual hum between them would be ever present. But they would have the mine and Renée Bosgrow to focus on.

A smile finally spread across Emily's face. "That sounds like a great idea."

"How soon can you be ready to leave?"

"I'm ready now."

Ten minutes later they were in the SUV, driving down Thunder Canyon Road. They were heading toward the access road to the mine when Brad's cell phone rang.

"Vaughn here," he said as he kept his eyes on the road.

"Brad, it's Suzette."

The artificial sweetness in her voice turned his stomach. "You should be talking to my lawyer, not to me."

"Look, sweetheart, maybe the lawyers are the wrong way to go."

His jaw clenched when he heard the endearment. "Your lawyer started this whole thing."

"I realize that now. But I understand what this must be doing to your reputation."

"It's not doing anything to my reputation, Suzette. I'm not even in Chicago."

"Not in Chicago? Where are you?" Some of the sweetness had left her voice.

"I'm on a case, and in a minute or so the static is going to interfere with our signal. So you'd better tell me why you called."

"I just wanted you to know we can settle this whole thing without the DNA testing or results."

"I had the DNA sample taken before I left Chicago."

There were a few moments of hesitation and then she went on. "Even so. You know those results can prove you're the father."

He was about to protest heartily when she continued. "I'm sure we can come to an equitable settlement so you don't have to go through the embarrassment of the whole process."

"There won't be any embarrassment for me. I know what the results are going to say, and I have no intention of settling—not now, not later."

"But, Brad—"

Brad didn't know if the mountains were interfering

with the signal or the weather or simply the particular location he was driving through. But one moment she was there, the next moment she wasn't.

After a futile, "Hello? Suzette?" and no answer, he reclipped the cell phone onto his belt.

Knowing Emily had heard every word, he glanced over at her. "She wants to settle."

"And you don't."

"That's right."

He'd discovered that the man Suzette had lived with ever since Brad and she had broken up had gambling debts. He had a feeling Suzette had been bankrolling her boyfriend and now her modeling money had run out. He wasn't going to be a ticket to the easy life for the two of them.

After his call, Emily went silent. Brad wished she could trust him, could trust his word. But after what he'd let happen in the cabin, he could see why she was still in doubt. The thing was, the situation with Emily had never happened to him with another woman. He'd never before felt that overwhelming desire not only to be intimate with but to protect and look after a woman. He didn't understand the inclination at all.

Following directions Caleb had given him, Brad veered onto the gravel road that led to the mine. It had obviously not been used much until the past few months. It was rutted, uneven and felt like an amusement-park ride as they bumped over it.

As he rounded a pile of boulders Caleb had given him as a landmark, he spotted the mine entrance cordoned off by yellow tape about a quarter mile down the road.

No Trespassing signs were posted, and Caleb had told him the police did periodic drive-bys.

Brad slowed to get a good look around. Seconds later a shot rang out!

Brad braked fast, rocking them both against their seat belts.

"What was that?" Emily asked. "A backfire?"

Another shot broke the air and grazed the hood of their car. Brad no longer looked around for explanations. In a sputter of mud and a skidding U-turn, he headed for the way they'd come.

When he pulled over after the next bend, Emily asked, "What are you doing?"

"Sit tight," he ordered. "Keep the windows closed. If you see anyone, if anyone approaches you, hightail it out of here."

"And what are *you* going to be doing?"

"There's a pickup parked near the mine entrance. I'm going to get the license number. No one shoots at me and gets away with it."

"You're crazy!" She grabbed his arm. "Don't go back there. You could get hurt."

He saw worry in her eyes for him again, and in spite of the situation it made him smile. "I'll be back. Five minutes tops."

"I am *not* sitting here alone. I've been stranded in a cabin in a snowstorm, rescued by helicopter, shaken up by a horse and now shot at. That's enough for me. It should be enough for *you*."

Cupping her chin in his hand, he kissed her hard. "I'll be back."

Then he left the keys in the ignition, locked the door and ran to the side of the road under the cover of firs.

As Emily sat waiting, she tapped her foot, peered in every direction and constantly looked over her shoulder. She should drive off and leave Brad stranded here, but she'd never do that. In fact, if she found out he was in trouble, she'd drive right into it.

Each minute ticked by slowly. She counted them until finally Brad was running toward the SUV and knocking on the window for her to let him in.

She leaned over and unlocked the door.

Climbing inside, he started up the SUV and drove them as far as Thunder Canyon Road. Then he pulled over again and took hold of his cell phone.

In the next few minutes, he called 911 and told the dispatcher what had happened, giving him the license number of the pickup truck. After also giving the authorities his name and cell number, he ended the call.

Glancing at Emily, he asked, "Are you okay?"

No, she wasn't. Each one of his kisses affected her more than the last. Each touch of his hand, each one of his smiles, made her heart turn over. But she wouldn't let him know that. She wouldn't let him know she wanted her dream with him.

"I'm fine. But do you think we can stay out of trouble for the rest of this trip?"

At her tone, he laughed out loud. Then he undid his seat belt, leaned close to her and kissed her.

Brad's kisses were never the same, and this one was no exception. After his lips brushed over and pressed to hers, she parted her lips. But he didn't take advantage of that. Instead he nibbled at the corner of her lip, then ran his tongue over her upper lip, and she felt as if she'd melt into a puddle on the car floor.

Her moan must have told him that because she heard the low growl in his throat. She saw him prop his arm on the back of the seat to take some of his weight as he leaned in. She could feel his body heat and his desire as well as his hunger. It didn't scare her; it made her want. She wanted Brad again in a way that was so elemental, she didn't even understand it. She wanted Brad in a way that would fill up her life and fulfill her dreams. She wanted Brad...and she wanted more. Although she'd given him the impression she wanted to return to Chicago, she liked being here with him. She more than liked being here with him.

When his tongue finally slid into her mouth, she pressed against him with a yearning that had never been a part of her before this trip. She might have fantasized about Brad, but the reality was so much better than any fantasy. The reality was more than she'd ever imagined.

Her jacket was unzipped, and Brad's hands slipped underneath it. She could have protested. She could have shifted away from him. But that was the last thing she wanted to do. Her minutes with him were precious. His touch was something she'd never forget. When his hand moved over her breast, she could recall vividly every moment of their time in the cabin. One afternoon had been so erotically sensual, she didn't know if anything could top it. One night had been so safely protective, she never wanted to forget it, either.

Did Brad act like this with the models, actresses and

account executives he dated? Was she only a diversion because they were away from the city?

Her questions changed the kiss even though she hadn't voiced them.

He pulled away but didn't take his gaze from hers. "What are you thinking?"

"You make me feel as if I'm the only woman in the world. Do you do that with all the women you date?"

Slowly he leaned away from her and shifted back into the driver's seat. Staring straight ahead, he admitted, "You've gotten under my skin, Emily, and I don't know what to do about it. Because I'm not what you need."

"What do I need?" she murmured, almost afraid of his answer.

"You need a man who knows how to commit himself to one woman. You need a man who wants a gold band around his finger as much as you do. I spent my adult years doing everything I could do to stay disentangled from a woman's life. You need a man who will become totally involved in yours."

"You never want to get married? You never want children?"

When his gaze swung back to hers, she saw his answer. He made it definite when he responded, "It's never been in my game plan."

"You might already have a child," she reminded him.

"That's the thing, Emily. You can't even believe me when I tell you I'm not the father of Suzette's child. So I'm definitely not a man you want in your life."

He was deciding what she needed and what would be best for her life. That hurt her, and her hurt turned to anger. "I think it's more than that. I think I'm not the caliber of woman your father would approve of and that bothers you."

His jaw clenched. "That has nothing to do with this."

"I think it has everything to do with this. You're the boss and I'm your secretary. You live in a high-rise condo, ride in limousines and travel wherever you want. I'm just a nobody from Chicago who's never even been on a camping trip."

"You're mistaken."

She kept silent because she knew she wasn't.

A police SUV turned onto the access road, its lights flashing, and pulled up beside Brad.

Turning to Emily, Brad repeated, "You're wrong." Then he exited the SUV to tell the policeman what had happened.

Tears came to Emily's eyes, and she simply didn't know what to think anymore.

After Brad finished a brief but thorough conversation with the lawman, the officer drove toward the mine. Brad passed a backup police car zooming toward the mine and he wondered if Emily was ever going to talk to him again that afternoon. Whatever attraction they felt for each other was at an all-time high. As he headed toward Old Town, the life he'd led up to this point seemed to play in front of his eyes. He wouldn't give Emily false hope that his opinion of commitment and marriage would ever change.

All that said, he wished she'd talk to him. He wished they could recapture their earlier camaraderie.

To try to start dialogue between them once more, he mentioned, "This best friend of Annie's might shut the door in our faces."

"You said her name's Renée?" Emily responded stiffly.

"Yes."

Silence once more pervaded the car until Brad parked at the curb. As they walked up to the brick stoop, Emily kept her distance from him. No matter. His lips still burned from their kiss and his body hadn't altogether recovered. At the door there was no bell, but Brad let the brass knocker thump twice.

A teenage girl answered the knock. For the most part her hair was brown, but there was a circle of red on the crown of her head that looked chemically induced.

She was tall and thin and her green eyes glanced from him to Emily quizzically. "My mom doesn't have any more of those tin cups to sell," she said, assuming that's what they were there for.

"Tin cups?" Emily asked.

"Yeah, you know. With the prospector painted on the side. It'll be another week until she has more done."

Apparently Renée Bosgrow's mother was making an item tourists liked to buy. "We're not here for tin cups," Brad said. "Are you Renée?"

Now the teenager's eyes narrowed and she grew wary. "Who wants to know?"

He extended his hand to her. "I'm Brad Vaughn, and this is my assistant Emily Stanton. Tess Littlehawk asked me to find her daughter, and since you were her best friend, I need to talk to you."

"I was her best friend before she took off. But I told you on the phone I don't got nothin' to say."

"Even if you don't, I'd like to speak to you for a few minutes."

Renée took a step back. "Why?"

"Because I want to explain to you how it feels when someone you love goes missing."

Her expression changed a bit, only a bit, but Brad saw it and took advantage of it. "Renée, Tess Littlehawk has a hole in her heart because a child she gave life to can't be found. I don't know why Annie left, and I don't need to. I only know her mother needs to hear her voice. It's been three years, and she has the right to know whether she's alive or dead."

"Dead? Annie can't be dead."

Emily's quiet but steady voice asked gently, "Do you know that for sure?"

After a long pause, Renée shook her head. "No, I don't. I don't know where she is now."

"But she told you where she was going when she left?" Brad guessed.

As the wind played with Renée's hair, both the brown and red strands, she crossed her arms, plucking at the red sleeves of her sweater. "I promised not to tell anyone where she went. We were like sisters. I can't break my word to her."

"It's been three long years," he pressed. "You said you don't know where she is now. She's probably not anywhere near her destination of three years ago."

The logic of that seemed to sink in. "Did Mrs. Littlehawk tell you why she ran?"

Tess had written pages for him, revealing all. "She told me Annie hated being a cleaning woman's daughter and that she was dating boys Tess wasn't comfortable with."

"Comfortable with? She grounded her when she snuck out to see Ronnie."

"She didn't believe she should be dating yet," Brad said, standing up for Tess.

"Annie was a looker. She had boys all around her. Dating isn't something you suddenly decide you can do because you're old enough."

Brad realized that if he had a daughter that's exactly what he would do. He'd keep her locked up until a boy finally met his approval. However, he wasn't going to argue with Renée about when girls should date. "Tess was afraid she'd get in trouble."

"You mean her mom was afraid she'd get pregnant."

"Yes, I imagine she was afraid of that, but she was also afraid she'd get into a car with an older boy who had been drinking. Annie had done that and that's why she was grounded."

Staring down at the toes of her sneakers, Renée mumbled, "Annie wanted to be a model or an actress."

Now they were getting somewhere. That usually meant a trip to California. "She went to Los Angeles?"

Renée's eyes widened as if he'd just caught on to what made the world spin. "What makes you say that?"

"Give me a little credit. Isn't Hollywood the land of dreams?"

Looking across the street to a row of houses that was similar to the one she lived in, Renée admitted, "She didn't go to Hollywood."

When it seemed she wouldn't give them more information, Emily found a way to touch her on a different level. "Tess just wants to find out if she's alive and well. Think about *your* mother. What if she didn't know where to find you for three years."

Renée suddenly said again, "She *didn't* go to Hollywood."

"Then where did she go?" Brad asked, realizing again how good Emily could be in investigative work.

Minutes seemed to tick by until Renée shuffled her sneakers on the stoop and jammed her hands into her jeans pockets. "She used the computer at school and went to this chat room that a modeling school in L.A. set up. She couldn't afford the fees to go to the modeling school, but she got to be friends with another girl there—in the chat room. That's when she started making plans."

"Plans to go to L.A.?" he prodded.

"No. This girl—I think her name was Lena—lived in San Jose. Annie saved every penny she could for a year, and Ronnie took her to Bozeman. She bought a bus ticket to California."

"You know this for certain?"

"Yeah. Ronnie told me after he got back that day. He said she was crying and laughing all at the same time and couldn't wait to leave."

"Is this Ronnie still in town?"

"No. His brother lives in Portland. He went up there to live with him after he graduated."

"You don't know this Lena's last name?"

"No. I don't even know if Lena is her real name. You know how chat rooms go."

Unfortunately he did. He just hoped Lena was a girl who wanted to go to modeling school and not a predator preying on teenagers with dreams.

"Thank you, Renée. You've helped us a lot."

"You're probably right and Annie's not still in San Jose." That thought seemed to salve Renée's conscience. With that, she shut the door.

"What do you think?" Emily asked, looking up at him now.

"I think she told us all she's going to tell us. After three years, there's a possibility Annie's not in San Jose. But there's also a fifty-fifty possibility that she is. I have a place to start."

When a strand of Emily's hair blew across her cheek, he couldn't keep himself from brushing it away. His thumb on her cheek sent a jolt through him. "Emily, look. About what happened in the car—"

She shook her head. "Don't worry about it, Brad. I know where you stand. I won't misunderstand anything that happens between us."

In other words, she accepted their attraction to each other for what it was—chemistry.

Why didn't that make him feel better?

Chapter Ten

That evening, Caleb wouldn't take no for an answer and neither would Adele. The Montana Mustangs, a band they both enjoyed, were playing at the Hitching Post this one night only. They insisted Brad and Emily shouldn't miss the event.

As Brad rounded the SUV and opened Emily's door, she wondered why this felt like a date when it wasn't. Caleb had decided to drive his own car, but she wished he hadn't. Conversation would have been easier with the four of them.

"You just don't see a sky like that in Chicago," Brad said with appreciation as he helped her down from the SUV.

He was still holding her hand, and she didn't let go of his as she looked up at the black velvet sky, the almost full moon and the thousand pinpoints of stars.

"The sky might be the same in Chicago. We just forget to look at it."

His gaze dropped to hers, and when he studied her lips, they both knew what he was thinking. Instead of kissing her, however, he slammed the SUV door, then he tucked her hand into the crook of his elbow as they walked up the street and then took a step up onto the wooden promenade.

The Hitching Post sported a wild-west-style false front and looked like an old-time saloon. After Brad opened the heavy wood door, Emily could see that the floor was hardwood and at one end of the restaurant there was a long curving bar. Framed photos from the 1880s hung on the walls. The Montana Mustangs were set up near the bar and dance floor at the far end of the room.

After they hung their coats on a long rack, Brad leaned down to her ear and his breath whispered across her cheek. "Caleb said this used to be a saloon. It was renovated many years ago and turned into a restaurant, but you can see the history all around."

Emily saw history all right. There was a painting above the cherrywood bar, and the woman looked almost nude! She was a voluptuous blonde with a wicked grin, wearing a gauzy fabric draped over her breasts so that she wasn't entirely indecent. The effect definitely did not portray a proper lady.

A cash register stood at the end of the bar, and a matronly woman with silver-streaked hair worn in a topknot sat on a stool there. Almost smack-dab in the middle of the dance floor stood a contraption Emily didn't recognize.

"What's that?" she asked Brad.

As he eyed it, he grinned. "That's a mechanical bull."

"What do you do with a mechanical bull?" she asked almost to herself.

Just then the band member on guitar stepped up to the microphone. "Ladies and gentlemen, our bull-riding competition is about to start before our first set."

"There's Caleb." Brad's hand went to the small of her back as he guided her toward a table near the wall.

Caleb was grinning from ear to ear. "What do you think, Brad? I may be too old to get my bones shaken up, but you aren't. The prize is three hundred dollars."

Placing a restraining hand on her husband's arm, Adele shook her head. "Don't let him goad you. That machine's not much safer than the real thing."

"Adele, honey, you worry too much."

"If I remember correctly, when Riley was eighteen, he broke his arm falling off one of those things," Adele maintained with a stern look.

At the thought of Brad getting hurt, Emily gazed up at him. "You're not going to try it, are you?"

"Don't you think I'm in shape?" he asked with another grin that made her feel tipsy even without a drink. Remembering his naked body all too well, she decided his good shape wasn't part of this equation.

"You might be in shape, but that doesn't mean you won't get hurt."

"A bit of risk spices up life."

"A little risk can put you on crutches."

Laughing, Brad pulled out a chair for her. After she sat, he lowered himself onto the chair next to her.

"The Montana Mustangs bring that thing along for entertainment value," Caleb explained. "The bartender's always glad because he sells more drinks while the clientele work up the courage to go for the money."

Emily knew if Brad rode the mechanical bull, he wouldn't be riding it to go for the money. In fact, she wasn't sure why he would do it. Just for the thrill?

As the Mustangs played lively country music, one by one men with Stetsons, snap-button shirts and boots tried the mechanical creature. Most only lasted a few seconds. One or two almost made it to the end of the ride. A lean young man in his early twenties took his turn, and Emily winced as he was tossed onto the straw-strewn floor and landed on his shoulder.

He was slow to get up and she shook her head, muttering, "Stupid, stupid, stupid."

Brad's chair scraped against the floor as he stood. Leaning close, he rested a hand on her arm. "Watch how this *should* be done."

"Brad," she called as he strode toward the man-made machine that she believed should be declared illegal.

The band started a new tune as everyone clapped and Brad climbed onto the "bull." With a grinding whir it started slow and then sped up until Emily was clenching her hands together, her knuckles white. She couldn't believe Brad was holding on!

At least, one minute he was holding on and the next…he was on the floor, facing the stage rather than the bull!

The whole room applauded because he had stayed on a fair amount of time. But as he rose to his feet and seemed to be unharmed, Emily's relief was short-lived because he motioned to the bull again, indicating he wanted another go-around.

He was out of his mind. That was *her* verdict.

However, when Brad climbed on board again, Emily realized she shouldn't be surprised. Brad Vaughn was a man who conquered his mountains and always got exactly what he wanted. She didn't like the idea of him getting shaken sideways and backward and upside down again, but she had to admire his courage. His ride started again, and this time he not only stayed on, but as he raised one arm over his head, his body seemed to move in rhythm with the machine. To everyone's amazement, he lasted on the bull until the ride wound down and the machine turned off.

Most of the patrons in the Hitching Post got to their feet and applauded, including Caleb and Adele. Emily joined them, clapping as loudly as she could.

Returning to the table with a wide grin, Brad accepted the slaps on the back, the offers of free drinks and the praise for a ride well-done.

Emily was about to add her kudos to the rest when a woman in tight black jeans, a bright red shirt with buttons open to show cleavage and a white cowgirl hat approached Brad at the table. "You're new around here, cowboy."

"Just visiting," Brad answered nonchalantly with a smile.

"How about the first dance? Now that you've conquered that thing, they're going to move it away so everyone can have some real fun."

The fun this woman spoke of made Emily see green. She'd never realized she had a jealous streak. When she and Warner had been dating, they'd kept it low-key, secluded, away from the public. She realized afterward he'd wanted their relationship kept secret because he hadn't wanted to be seen dating a secretary in the firm. Even so, when she'd seen women with him in the law offices, she'd never felt this desire to scratch their eyes out. This woman in the cowgirl hat was entirely too bold, brazen and proprietary as she laid her hand on Brad's arm and stared up into his eyes with a coy look meant to lure him to dance with her.

Emily simply couldn't stand it. "He's dancing the first dance with me," she blurted, amazed at what had come out of her mouth.

At Brad's amused expression, she wanted the floor to swallow her up.

"Is that true?" the cowgirl asked, giving Emily the once-over. She eyed the white western shirt with embroidery, the ironed blue jeans, the flat leather shoes.

"That's true," Brad admitted as the bull was wheeled away, straw was swept up and the band started up again.

"Maybe I'll just have to cut in," the cowgirl stated.

"I'm not sure you want to do that," Brad responded with a wink at Emily. "She might look delicate, but I hear she boxes in her spare time. It would be a pleasure to dance with you," he said with a consoling smile, "but I promised I'd dance with Emily tonight, and I don't break a promise."

The cowgirl looked from one to the other and then

she gave a little shrug. "The good ones are always taken. See you around, cowboy."

Emily knew her cheeks were bright red. Her heart was racing so fast she could hardly breathe.

She was ready to sink into her chair and keep quiet for the rest of the night when Brad's arm went around her shoulders. "We told her we were going to dance so we'd better get out there and do it."

Couples were already on the dance floor. But they weren't standing in traditional dance poses, and Emily didn't understand the steps they were executing.

"I don't know how to do that," she whispered as Brad walked her to the dance floor.

"It's the Texas two-step and it's real easy to catch on to. Just follow me. You'll be fine."

Follow him. She was beginning to think she'd follow him anywhere.

At first Emily felt totally ridiculous. She didn't know how to dance the Texas two-step. She didn't know how to dance! Her feet seemed to want to go in every direction but the right one. But then Brad's arm tightened around her, his feet seemed to direct hers and they were moving around the circle behind another couple, amazingly keeping in step. Finding herself breathless, she realized it was because she could feel Brad's heat, inhale his scent, lean into his strong body. Everything about him shouted "fantastic male," and she wished she could get past the dizzying sensations of dancing with him, being with him...loving him.

When she almost tripped, Brad caught her. "Are you okay?"

No, she was definitely not okay. She was irrevocably in love with Bradley Vaughn. Not falling in love. Already fallen.

"Just learning the steps," she mumbled as they got into the rhythm of it again and she tried to pull the blinds on the realization that seemed life-altering.

They had finished the first dance when Emily felt a twinge in her side and then some cramping. Familiar with the rhythms of her body and its shifts and changes, she pulled away from Brad's arm. "I'm going to freshen up."

He cocked a brow inquisitively.

She simply smiled and slipped away, finding the short hall that led to the ladies' room.

Five minutes later, Emily washed her hands at the sink and wanted to cry. Her reaction was totally irrational. She should be glad she'd gotten her period—absolutely thrilled. It meant she wasn't pregnant. A baby now should have been the last item on her agenda. Yet she realized she hadn't yet bought a pregnancy test because she'd been nurturing the idea of a baby, getting used to it, anticipating a bond with Brad that would last a lifetime.

As she looked herself in the eye in the mirror, she saw the futility in all of it. Getting pregnant was the worst reason to have a connection to a man. It was the worst reason to think about a relationship. She'd known that for years. Her love for Brad had to rise or fall on its own merit. If he had feelings for her, she couldn't attach strings to them. If he had feelings for her...

She knew they would change and evaporate once they returned to Chicago.

With her purse under her arm, Emily practiced a smile in the mirror and returned to her table to pretend to enjoy the Mustangs for the rest of the night.

As she approached Adele and Caleb, she saw Brad talking to a uniformed officer. It was the policeman from the SUV that had arrived after Brad's 911 call from the mine.

By the time she reached Brad's side, the officer had moved away and was threading his way through the crowd.

She took her seat and waited for Brad to take his. When he did, she asked, "Did he catch whoever shot at us?"

"Yes, they did. After I called, they notified surrounding towns. Law enforcement in Livingston spotted the truck. It turns out there was a warrant on the driver for an assault charge. The good guys won this one."

"Because of you. Not just anyone would have had the courage to get that license number."

"You didn't see it as courage at the time," Brad joked.

"Yes, I did. But I was scared and you weren't. At least if you were, you didn't show it."

"I've had a lifetime to practice hiding what I feel."

When they'd arrived in Thunder Canyon, his guard had been solidly in place. But while here, she'd seen it slip now and then.

Caleb ordered another round of drinks, interrupting their conversation. As the Mustangs played, all Emily wanted to do was talk to Brad privately. They couldn't do that here. After munching on peanuts and sipping her club soda with its twist of lime, she danced the Texas two-step with Brad again.

When the song ended and the band began a slow

ballad, Brad turned her into his arms. "Maybe we can catch our breath on this one."

She doubted that. She absolutely couldn't let Brad hold her. She couldn't give in to her love for him because she knew it had no place to go. "I'd like to go back to the ranch," she said seriously.

His smile slipped away and he released her. "If that's what you want." His expression had gone stony and she explained, "It's not that I don't want to dance with you. I do. But we need to talk. Can we go?"

He relaxed some. "All right. Let's find our coats and I'll tell Caleb and Adele we're going back."

"The Mustangs too much for you?" Caleb asked as Brad brought her her jacket and she slipped it on.

"The Mustangs were great," Emily assured him. "But I have some notes I want to work on."

Caleb's brows arched and he looked as if he didn't believe her. "Don't forget to collect your winnings," he reminded Brad.

Brad nodded. To Emily he said, "I'll just be a minute."

Waiting by the door while he spoke to one of the band members, she studied the picture of the Shady Lady again. After Brad joined her, they went outside.

"Did they give you a check?" she asked.

After a short hesitation, he responded, "The Mustangs donate time and money to juvenile diabetes. The lead guitarist has a daughter with it. So I told them to donate the prize money to that."

It was becoming harder and harder for Emily to reconcile her old image of Brad with the new one that was forming.

As soon as they'd climbed into the SUV and fastened their seat belts, Brad asked, "Do you want to wait until we get to the ranch to talk or do you want to talk now?"

She didn't want to wait. She really didn't have that much to say. "I'm not pregnant. I got my period tonight."

After a few moments of silence, Brad started the engine, pulled out of the parking space and drove onto the main road. They'd driven about a half mile when he commented, "I suppose that's a relief to you."

"Isn't it a relief to you?"

"Actually for the past few days I was thinking of the possibility of being a father."

"Only the past few days?"

"Have I ever lied to you, Emily? Or misled you?" His voice was gruff with a hint of anger.

She thought about the months she'd worked for him and had to say, "No, you haven't."

"Then why would I start now?"

She held on to what she once believed about him because she was safer with that barrier between them. "Maybe because Suzette Brouchard could take you to court and use me as a witness. You want to make sure I'm on your side, and if you convince me to believe you—"

"Stop! We've spent almost two weeks together. Some of that time in very intimate contact. Just how do you think you would feel if I told you I thought *you* were lying to *me?*"

"I have no reason to lie."

"And neither do I."

Confused by her love for Brad, his reputation as a love-'em-and-leave-'em bachelor, feelings that she couldn't understand and she couldn't push out of her heart, she kept silent. Anything she said right now would only make matters worse. She knew if they didn't soon leave Thunder Canyon, her heart would be irreparably broken and she'd never be able to piece it back together again.

For the next few days, Brad tried to keep everything businesslike between him and Emily. His body yearned for satisfaction with her again, and he told himself it was simply a physical need that he could deny or take care of himself. But when she was beside him, taking notes, asking questions or just listening, he resisted the urge to take her into his arms. He resisted the urge to admit he felt closer to her than he'd ever felt to anyone.

While they waited for the mayor's return, as well as Tildy's, Brad left no stone unturned. After conferencing with Mark again, he went through piles of issues of the *Thunder Canyon Nugget* as far back as they went. He also spoke to the prospector again and with anyone else who might know anything about the history of Thunder Canyon, the Queen of Hearts mine or Amos Douglas. But he came up empty.

He and Emily were poking around at the historical society Tuesday afternoon when he got a call on his cell phone from his father. As Emily studied exhibits, he took it in an alcove.

"What in God's name are you still doing there?" Phillip Vaughn demanded.

Not for the first time in his life, Brad realized he didn't like answering to his father. "Look, Dad, if I could wind this up now, I would. If I'm going to take over the agency someday, you're going to have to learn to trust me."

"As long as I'm still the head of the firm, I call the shots."

That was the problem. His father was still head of the firm, and Brad wondered now if he would be until his dying day. It wasn't just answering to his father that bothered him, it was the type of cases that Vaughn Associates dealt with. He was still waiting for word from a California contact about Tess's daughter. What he would prefer was going out there himself. Then again, he had to rely on the people he trusted.

Glancing at Emily after hanging up, he saw she was standing in front of a display of a mannequin wearing a faded red satin dress that was trimmed with black lace. Ropes of fake pearls around the mannequin's neck, along with a black ostrich feather in its hair, accented the outfit.

"These clothes belonged to a woman named Lily Divine," she mused as he came to stand beside her. "You said she's the Shady Lady in the portrait."

"That's what I heard. She was supposedly the madam of a whorehouse."

Emily studied his expression, her concern now with him rather than with the artifacts. "Is everything okay?"

"My father expected us to return to Chicago by now. I was trying to explain for the third time why we were still here."

"I guess he didn't listen the first time," Emily said with a smile.

"If my father *ever* listened the first time, the world would stop spinning on its axis."

"You're not friends, are you?" she asked.

"Friends? Hardly."

He couldn't quite wrap his mind around that idea. He didn't think Phillip Vaughn was a friend to anyone, yet he did have his cronies who dined with him at the club and expensive restaurants, who played tennis with him. Brad had known true friendship with James, but since then it had eluded him—until this trip with Emily. It was odd, but he felt as if they'd become real friends.

"Are you and your mother friends?" he asked.

"Absolutely. I mean, she was a parent and all, gave us rules and guidelines, made sure we lived up to our potential. But she was always there to talk to. She helped with makeup and went to the movies with us. She's still a big part of my life. So are my sisters and brother, and I can't imagine it any other way."

The museum was shadowy, with not a lot of direct lighting. Brad gazed down into Emily's pretty face and watched her green eyes sparkle like emeralds. "We're so different, you and I."

"I guess we are in some ways. But in others…" She shrugged. "I think we're a lot alike."

Her conclusion surprised him. "How?"

"We work the same way. We analyze and think things through. We're both perfectionists. We both have a few walls, but deep down inside we just want to be accepted for who we are. And on top of all that—" she grinned up at him "—I think I've even grown to like Thunder Canyon and Montana."

Her expression was so mischievous, so genuine. He

cupped her chin in his palm and raised her lips to his. When he kissed her, she didn't pull away.

Until the beeping of his cell phone intruded.

Aware that a docent might interrupt them any second, Brad broke the kiss, gave her a wry smile and answered the phone.

"Vaughn here."

"This is Elma Rogers, Mayor Brookhurst's sister. He's back. He said he'll meet you at the archives room anytime you'd like."

Brad glanced at Emily. "How about in fifteen minutes?"

Twenty minutes later, if the mayor was surprised by Brad's impatience, he didn't show it. Unlocking the door to the archives room with his key, he turned the knob and pulled the heavy door open.

The mayor was in his fifties and dressed casually. A portly man with a handlebar mustache, he wore trousers with tan suspenders and a pale blue, long-sleeved shirt. The top of his head was bald and his graying black hair fell over his collar in the back.

"I'll have to stay with you," he said to them now in an apologetic tone. "These are all documents that need to be protected, and nothing can leave this room without my okay. Understood?"

"Understood," Brad agreed, eyeing stacks of ledgers, books and boxes. "Do you know if this is in any type of order?"

The mayor motioned to the left wall. "All I can tell you is that those ledgers are being entered into the computer."

"Do you know the years?"

"Eighteen eighty to 1920, but not all of them are

there. Our last archivist hadn't finished going through the boxes to find more. And, of course, there are those that were destroyed by the fire in the late 1800s and the flood more recently. From what I understand, there are gaps and holes. But you're welcome to look through all of it if you're careful."

Brad and Emily spent the next three *days* looking through all of it. They went through every box, every musty page, every book, newspaper and bound volume. They found some ledgers from the late 1800s. There were a few volumes from between 1890 and 1910, but none listed a transaction concerning the Queen of Hearts mine.

Finally at the end of their third day, Brad shook his head. "Tildy Matheson was supposed to return home yesterday. Let's call her and see if she'll let us come over this evening. She might be our last hope. It just doesn't seem possible if Caleb Douglas's ancestors owned this mine, as well as the mineral rights, that there's not a record of it somewhere."

"We're used to the tech age. Recording deeds was very different back then."

"Maybe. But I'm not ready to give up. I'll buy you dinner at the Hitching Post and we can call Tildy from there."

When Brad called Tildy from the saloon, she warned him not to eat dessert. Her sister had sent homemade oatmeal cookies with her, and Emily and Brad were welcome to share them.

Tildy Matheson lived in an old Victorian house. When she opened the ornate old door graced with a stained glass window, she was smiling. Tonight she wore a brightly colored blouse and slacks as she motioned them inside. "I'm so pleased you called. My family doesn't want to hear about old times. It's nice to talk to younger folk who do. Come on in."

Tildy's house was situated in Old Town, and Emily glanced around the interior, seeing at once that it was charming. Tildy obviously loved flowers. Her chintz sofa was covered with blue and green ones, and the drapes were made of the same material. The windowsills were hardly visible under small plants.

Crossing to the window, Emily took a closer look.

"African violets," Tildy explained. "I just love them. My neighbor took care of them for me while I was gone."

A Tiffany floor lamp brought rainbowed light into the room. Many of the furniture surfaces, including the bookshelves and the end tables, were covered with framed photographs.

"I put water on for tea. It should be ready now. I'll get it and the cookies."

As Emily helped Tildy in the kitchen, the woman chattered all the while. "I was just finished napping when your young man called. Traveling always tires me out for a while."

"Did you have a nice trip?"

"A wonderful trip. I appreciate every minute I have with my family. At my age I never know what the next day will bring. I just wish I could get around better. I don't go upstairs much anymore. Last year my niece insisted I turn my sewing room into a bedroom on this floor so I didn't have to do the steps. She was right. I certainly don't want to fall. But I miss not being able to wander into every nook and cranny of my house."

Emily admired Tildy's bone china painted with pretty pink blooms as she set three cups on a tray. "It was my grandmother's. It *is* pretty, isn't it? She had a fondness for flowers, just like I do. Just grab that can of cookies over there on the table."

After Tildy led Emily back into the living room, she spotted Brad studying the photographs.

"Some of these look quite old," he noted as Tildy settled herself in a fern-covered wing chair.

"They are."

After they all balanced their saucers and their teacups, Tildy asked, "Now, where would you like me to start?"

"Do you know Caleb Douglas?" Brad asked, setting his cup on the coffee table. Emily knew he didn't much care for tea.

"Everyone in Thunder Canyon knows Caleb Douglas."

"He's trying to prove his family owns the land where the gold mine's located."

"That gold mine. Such a hubbub over a few nuggets of metal."

"Mark Anderson told us one of your ancestors knew Catherine Douglas."

"Oh, yes," Tildy admitted proudly. "That would have been my grandmother." She pointed to the photographs on the bookshelves. "See that end photograph on the first shelf? That's my grandmother and Catherine."

Brad's gaze met Emily's and he stood, crossing to the shelf to pick up the photograph.

"That was taken in front of the town hall," Tildy explained.

Brad brought the picture to Emily so she could study it, too.

"We've been trying to find records from back then," Emily offered.

"It's easier to find stories," Tildy responded.

"What kind of stories?" Brad asked.

For the first time all evening, Tildy hesitated. "The kind of stories that are passed down in a family."

Emily could see Brad's focus intensify as he set the picture on the coffee table and seated himself once more. "Can you tell me about them?"

"I thought you wanted to know about the history of Thunder Canyon. There's a legend—"

Before she went off on a tangent, he intervened. "Caleb's ancestors are part of the history of Thunder Canyon, aren't they?"

"Yes, but there are some things people don't talk about much."

"Such as?" he prodded.

Gently Emily asked, "Isn't it better for true history to come out rather than something that's made up just because it sounds better?"

"I suppose you're right." Tildy's gaze met Brad's. "My grandmother used to tell me stories. She wasn't the type of woman to spread rumors."

"What stories did she tell you?"

Again Tildy hesitated. Finally she admitted, "That Amos Douglas wasn't the pillar of this community everyone thought he was. He abused his wife, and Catherine was afraid of him."

Tildy's statement landed in the room with a thud, and

Emily realized the Douglases might not be what they seemed. She held her breath and waited for Tildy to tell her story.

Chapter Eleven

"I guess I should start at the beginning." Tildy's gaze swerved from Brad to Emily. "I'm still not sure I should be telling you any of this."

"If it relieves your conscience any," Brad interjected, "I had already heard the rumor that Amos abused his wife."

"Where did you hear that?" Tildy asked.

"The old prospector, Mickey Latimer."

After Tildy thought about that for a few moments, she gave a shrug. "Stories came down to him, too, but like me he kept quiet. Now I don't think he remembers what he tells people and what he doesn't. What else did he say?"

"Not much else. When I asked him about the gold mine, he would just repeat, 'Women have the power.'"

"I don't know about that. Women in general had a

tough time of it back then. And many times they had to hide their true character."

"I don't understand," Emily said.

"My grandmother and Catherine Douglas were friends—*confidantes,* as they called it back then. Catherine told Grandma things she never told another living soul. She put up a good front, and few people saw through that. My grandma always told me, though, that Catherine lacked the courage to change her life."

"You mean by leaving Mr. Douglas?" Emily asked.

"Precisely." Tildy pointed to the picture on the bookshelf. "Over and over again my grandmother offered to take her in, but she simply said Amos would hurt my grandma and her family if she did that. Catherine wouldn't bring that harm on them. She was probably right. Amos was a scoundrel. He was wealthy and had a lot of power in these parts. And there wasn't an ounce of kindness in him. The way he got that gold mine was immoral."

"So he did own it?" Brad asked.

"It wasn't that simple. I don't know if you've heard talk about Lily Divine."

"Her picture hangs in the Hitching Post." Brad looked totally intrigued now.

Tildy wrinkled her nose. "Yes, it does, and I'm not sure how all that came about. But I do know she wasn't a prostitute or a madam."

"What *was* she?" Emily prompted.

"She was a lady trying to find her way in a world of men. She was smart and she was one of the few women to own land. *She* owned that mine."

At their stunned silence, Tildy continued, "She had also inherited a house from a madam. There were prostitutes around, of course, and lots of times the johns mistreated them. When that happened, Lily would nurse them back to health again."

"I can see how she'd get the reputation of being a madam," Brad muttered.

"The women in town knew the true story. But as I said, women weren't as vocal then as they are now. Pretty soon other women besides prostitutes came to her. Women who were being mistreated. But times got tough, and in order not to lose the hotel she had built across the street, she had to mortgage the gold mine property. She'd known Amos Douglas had his eye on the abandoned Queen of Hearts mine. She knew she couldn't get a loan through the bank, but she might be able to get one from Amos and she did. Only there were strict terms involved and when she missed *one* payment, he foreclosed."

Brad's gaze met Emily's and they thought about the promissory note that Caleb held in his possession.

"One payment and that old buzzard took the deed for the mine from her," Tildy related again indignantly.

"So Caleb *does* own it."

"It would seem so." Tildy sighed. "But I haven't told you the rest of the story."

Already on the edge of her chair, Emily found the history fascinating.

"One night, after all that happened, Amos went on a particularly bad rampage and Catherine got the brunt of it. She was pretty badly beaten. She didn't want to go to friends or relatives because she was afraid Amos would hurt them in some way, too. Even knowing what happened with the mine, she went to Lily because she thought she was her last resort. And Lily didn't turn her away. That woman had a kind heart. She nursed Catherine back to health and tried to convince her to leave Amos. But so many women in that position do the same thing—they stay. Catherine said she had to go back home. She didn't feel she had a choice. She told Lily she'd be grateful to her till her dying day, but then she returned to her husband."

"How sad," Emily murmured.

"I'll say it was. When I was younger, I would go through that old trunk up in my attic and think about the life women had back then."

"What's in the trunk in your attic?" Brad asked.

"Oh, I guess I didn't tell you. When Amos died, Catherine became rich in her own right. Of course, she left everything to their son—everything except her personal possessions. Her will stipulated that they go to my grandmother. So up in the trunk I have some of her clothes, pictures like that photograph over there, combs she wore in her hair. I keep her antique jewelry in my jewelry box, and I've worn it all my life. My grandmother gave it to me when I was a teenager. I'd be glad to get it if you'd like to see it."

"I'd love to see it," Emily said enthusiastically.

"This trunk," Brad mused, "you say it's in your attic?"

"Yes, it is. I've been wanting to give it to the historical society, but my niece hasn't found time to bring it down and I certainly can't get to the attic anymore."

"Would you mind if Emily and I look through it?"

With narrowed eyes, Tildy studied them both closely. Then she smiled. "You seem like upright young folk to me. Go ahead. By the time you return I'll have the jewelry out and more hot water for tea."

After Tildy showed Brad and Emily to the stairs, she instructed them, "If you go into the smallest bedroom, last one on the left, you'll see a closet. Just open the door and the stairs to the attic are in there. Be careful. They're narrow."

"We'll be careful," Brad assured her.

In a matter of minutes Brad and Emily found their way to the attic door. At the foot of the stairs, Brad flicked on the light switch.

He went up first and led Emily to a corner where an old trunk sat. The attic smelled musty, and there was a layer of dust across the trunk.

"No one's been up here in a while," Brad said as he examined the latch.

The trunk looked to be made of wood with leather stretched on top. It had hand-sewn edges. "Amazing." Brad ran his hand over it. "The historical society would treasure this."

After Brad lifted the lid, they peered inside. The trunk was about five feet long and three feet wide. Inside, clothes and photographs were tumbled together as if in its trip up the stairs everything had gotten mixed up. On the left side of the trunk, the material lining the inside was torn.

"Maybe someone could restore this," Emily murmured.

Seeing tears other places, Brad shrugged. "They might have to reline it."

Seated on the floor across from each other, they went through everything piece by piece. Emily held up a blue dress that had faded to purple. Its neckline was low cut, its sleeves full and puffy.

"What do you think?" she asked with a coy smile.

"I think you would have been the belle of the ball."

Brad's voice was low and deep and sent a thrill up her spine. There had been so much distance between them since she'd told him she wasn't pregnant over a week ago. Each day her love for him was growing and she wanted to be close to him, not have a wall between them. Yet that wall was protecting her.

"What's wrong?" Brad asked.

"Nothing."

"Emily?"

"I was just thinking about…us."

"And the fact that you're not pregnant?"

She nodded.

He looked as if he were going to lean toward her then. He looked as if he might kiss her. Instead he turned toward the trunk once more. "We'd better finish with this or Tildy will think we stole everything and escaped through the window."

As they sorted through each photograph, they studied the old clothes, the faces, the buildings in the background. Emily found a hand mirror of tarnished silver, a lady's parasol and a flimsy pouch made of silk hidden in the folds of a dress. Both the dress and the purse had once been green, but now they were faded and yellowed with age. The bottom corner of the purse was torn.

About to lay it back inside the trunk, Emily heard

something crackle. She ran her thumb and forefinger over the silk.

"What is it?" Brad asked.

"I don't know. I think there's something inside."

Prying open the drawstrings, she carefully slipped her hand in and pulled out another photograph. It was a cameo portrait of Catherine Douglas. Emily recognized her from the photograph downstairs. "She was a beautiful woman."

"And in the end apparently she got everything Amos owned."

"I wonder what happened to her? Tildy didn't say."

Emily laid the photograph on top of all the others. "I guess we should repack the trunk."

Carefully folding one of the dresses, Emily laid it in the bottom and folded another on top of it. The billowing skirt raised dust. Her fingers brushed the inside of the trunk as she lifted her hand to rub her nose, but her watch caught on the material of the lining and ripped it more.

"I'm ruining a historical treasure," she moaned.

"That lining is falling apart from old age."

Examining the new tear, worried about it, Emily thought she glimpsed something a different color than the wood. Hoping she wasn't going to do more harm than good, she eased her finger under the torn material. There was an envelope sticking to the wood. She didn't want to tear that, too, and she carefully extricated it.

Brad had been studying the photographs, but now he glanced up. "What do you have?"

"I don't know. It must have slipped behind the torn lining."

The envelope was old, brittle and yellow. Emily expected it to be a letter, maybe one Tildy and her mother had missed when they'd looked through everything. Who knew how long it had been lost inside the lining?

Reaching her hand down along the lining once more, she felt something else. It was thin, but she could feel its edge. Slipping her hand farther inside, her fingertips touched paper. Drawing it out, she saw it was a photograph of a man with a bushy mustache and a cowboy hat shading his brow. She had no idea who the man was, but wondered if it could be Amos Douglas. She showed it to Brad, and while he was studying it she opened the flap of the envelope and pulled out the sheet of paper inside. It was folded in half.

She saw *Queen of Hearts*. She saw *mineral rights*. Then she saw the transfer notice still in the envelope. When she spotted the line with the name of the landowner, she gasped. It was Lily Divine.

"What's wrong?" Brad asked.

After Emily handed him the deed, she perused the transfer notice and the date. In amazement she said, "Catherine Douglas transferred the mine back to Lily Divine!"

"Let me see that," Brad demanded.

After he examined all of it—Catherine's signature, the official embossing mark—he gave a whoop of success. "We did it, Emily! We *found* the deed."

Before she knew what was happening, he'd taken her into his arms and hugged her. She lifted her mouth to his and he lowered his to hers. The musty attic seemed to be heaven on earth. Brad kissed her with the pent-up passion he'd been suppressing for days, and she kissed him back with the same overload of desire she'd been denying. Neither seemed to be able to stop the onslaught of needs unsatisfied as they kissed harder and deeper and longer.

Then Brad was breaking away, looking down at her as if he didn't want to end the kisses but knew he had to.

"I'd better be careful with this." He waved the deed in front of them. "It survived this many years—I don't want anything to happen to it now."

No, of course he didn't.

"Emily?" his expression was suddenly sober.

"What?"

"This means we'll be leaving Thunder Canyon." He seemed to be waiting for her reaction.

The idea rolled through her and she felt shaken by it. Everything would change when they returned to Chicago. Everything. She wouldn't even be his secretary anymore.

Forcing a bright smile, she said, "You succeeded. Your father will be thrilled."

But that didn't bring an answering smile from him. "Yes, I guess he will be. But Caleb won't. He just lost a gold mine. Let's put all this away and go down and tell Tildy what we found."

Ten minutes later, they were showing Tildy the document.

"Land sakes!" she exclaimed, then sank into her favorite chair. "Lily Divine's the owner. If that don't beat all. My eyes aren't too keen anymore, but I think that's the year Catherine Douglas died."

"How did she die?" Brad asked.

"There was an epidemic of pneumonia that year. One day she was perfectly healthy, a week later she was dead."

"Maybe she had the deed transferred and never had the chance to give it to Lily," Brad surmised.

"She probably thought she was righting wrongs done to both of them. If Amos swindled Lily out of the mine to begin with, and Catherine was grateful for the care Lily had given her, it makes sense."

"The deed will have to be authenticated, of course." Brad added, "But I think we found the true owner of the Queen of Hearts gold mine. Do you know if she has any descendants?"

"She does," Tildy said with excitement. "Lisa Martin, her great-great-granddaughter."

"Do you know her?" Emily asked.

"No, believe it or not, we've never officially met. I know who she is. She has a pet-sitting business." Tildy examined the deed again. "This is so exciting. She just inherited a gold mine."

"Don't go spreading that rumor yet," Brad said with a wink. "The first thing I'm going to do is find an expert to have the deed authenticated. If it's as old as I think it is, then we'll inform Lisa Martin that she just inherited the Queen of Hearts."

"I wouldn't want to be in *your* shoes," Tildy said to Brad. "Caleb Douglas is going to be mighty put out about this, and that's an understatement."

"Caleb Douglas already has enough money and holdings to keep his descendants happy for a few generations. *If* they don't go through it like water."

"A man like Caleb Douglas always wants more," Tildy warned Brad. "Would you like to save the jewelry for another time?"

"Yes. I think we'd better be going. Lisa Martin is going to owe you a great debt."

"I didn't do anything."

"You could have tossed that trunk a long time ago."

Tildy gestured to Emily. "*She's* the one who had the good sense to look inside the lining. That tells me she's not deceived by outside appearances. You'd better hang on to this one," Tildy advised Brad with a wink.

Knowing she was blushing to the roots of her hair, Emily turned away and picked up her coat. Brad would be letting go of her, not holding on to her. She knew that in her soul.

Less than a half hour later, Brad and Emily were closeted with Caleb in his den. Brad handed him the deed with the transfer notice.

"This is a fake," Caleb boomed.

"I don't think so," Brad countered evenly. "Somehow it had slipped inside the torn lining of a trunk that dates back to the gold-mine era."

"You can't know that."

"Tildy assures us she inherited that trunk from her grandmother. She cherished everything that's inside it."

"Then why's it still in her attic?" Caleb blustered, looking as if he wanted to tear up the document in his hands.

In a flash, Brad took the document from Caleb. Emily knew he'd seen the same intent in Caleb Douglas's eyes.

"I'll hold on to this for safekeeping. Once we have it authenticated, we'll know what to do next."

Paling, Caleb looked trapped. "Lily Divine was a prostitute."

"That's not the story Tildy tells. She got that reputation because she helped prostitutes and watched over them like a mother hen, protecting them from abusive johns, caring for them when something bad happened. Apparently Lily Divine was a woman of character, ahead of her time. If this document pans out, her great-great-granddaughter, Lisa Martin, will inherit the gold mine."

"No," Caleb interrupted forcefully. "That mine belongs in our family."

"Your great-grandfather took unfair advantage of Lily Divine when she mortgaged that property to him. He didn't deserve it."

"You have no right to decide who deserves anything." Caleb's gaze went to the deed in Brad's hand and then his expression changed. "Look, Brad, why don't you and I talk about this reasonably. If you forget you ever saw this particular piece of paper, I'll make it worth your while...very worth your while. Anything you want—a share in the ski resort, shares in one of my other holdings or maybe you'd like five hundred thousand dollars in cash."

Although she was appalled by Caleb's offer, Emily held her breath waiting for Brad's response.

Brad's shoulders straightened, his jaw locked into place and he seemed much taller than six foot three when he responded. "You can take your money and your resort and your stock shares to your grave with you. I don't want them."

Carefully he folded the deed and transfer notice, slipped them back into the envelope and slid it into his shirt pocket. "I'm going to call a courier and make sure this gets into the right hands tonight. You'd better accept the fact that the Queen of Hearts gold mine simply isn't yours. Emily and I will be flying out tomorrow."

As Emily studied Caleb Douglas, she realized he looked like the most unhappy man she had ever seen. She was so proud of Brad and his integrity.

After she followed him out of Caleb's office, she laid her hand on his arm to tell him so. When he turned toward her, he still looked angry over Caleb's offer.

"I'm so proud of you."

"For not taking the money?"

It was so much more than that. "No. For being determined enough to find that deed, for telling Caleb where he could put his money, for handling all of it so well."

His expression gentled then as he slipped a hand under her hair. "I haven't handled *you* well. Something about you makes me forget common sense. We never should have had sex without protection. I never should have let you go horseback riding."

"I think we were both in denial, trying to pretend something hadn't happened when it had. I was as much to blame as you were."

Now both of his hands were in her hair and he was cupping her head, looking down at her. "Blame has nothing to do with this anymore. The chemistry between us is just too explosive to ignore, and maybe we should give in to it this one last night."

He could have started kissing her and carried her upstairs to a bedroom, sweeping her away. They both knew she was susceptible. But he wasn't doing that, and she suddenly realized that if he said he wasn't the father of Suzette Brouchard's child, she could believe him. Brad was a man of integrity and a man of honor, and tonight she wanted to love him one last time.

With a shaky smile she asked, "Your bedroom or mine?"

Forty-five minutes later, Emily sat in her bedroom brushing her hair. The shower was running, and she knew in a few minutes she and Brad would be together, at least for tonight. He'd made a call to a courier service in Bozeman after they'd left Caleb's office. Five minutes ago, she'd heard the courier's van drive away from the Lazy D ranch. In a few days, they'd know if the deed was authentic. Her instincts told her it was.

When the shower stopped running, she stopped brushing. Her suitcase was packed except for the clothes she'd left out to wear tomorrow for the trip home. Thank goodness her period was over. Thank goodness she had this one last night to pretend her dreams could come true.

As she laid her brush on the dresser, the door to her room opened and Brad stood there naked. This time she didn't turn away. This time she let her gaze roam over him, appreciating the muscles, the lines of his taut stomach, the curling black hair. The longer she stared, the more aroused he became.

"My bed's bigger." He held out his hand to her.

Placing her hand in his, she wasn't immune to the heat rippling up her arm nor the desire in his eyes. Leading her through the bathroom, he then let her precede him into his bedroom. As she quickly glanced around the room, she noticed he'd turned down the bed and placed packets of condoms on the nightstand. When his arms wrapped around her, he brought her close. He'd dried off, but his chest hair was still damp from his shower, as was the hair on his head. She could feel his arousal through her robe. She could feel the beat of his heart.

With his index finger under her chin, he lifted her face to his. "Are you sure?"

She'd never been more sure of anything in her life. She loved Brad Vaughn and tonight she was going to show him just how much. "I'm sure," she murmured.

When Brad kissed her, Caleb Douglas and the deed and Tildy and Thunder Canyon all fell away.

"I can't get you off my mind," Brad breathed between kisses. "I remember that afternoon in the cabin, the night I held you, and I feel different than before I came here."

"In what way?" she whispered against his lips.

"I'm not sure. I just know my life isn't going where I want it to and I'm going to change directions."

Then all thoughts of direction and work and Chicago were very far away.

Stepping back, Brad's hands went to Emily's belt. He untied it and her robe fell open. He didn't hurry to rid her of it. Rather, his hand brushed over and around her breasts, making her crazy with need. She reached out to him and ran her hands down his chest, over his stomach.

When he sucked in a breath, she smiled, and he laughed. "You've learned you have power, too."

"Not much."

"More than you know."

Sweeping her off her feet, he lifted her into his arms and carried her to the big bed, where he gently lowered her. She scooted over on the sheet and he came down beside her, facing her. Tonight he didn't hurry any of it. He took his time getting to know every inch of her. She took her time getting to know every inch of him. Where before they'd been frenzied and too hungry to wait, now Brad prolonged each caress to give her the most erotic pleasure she'd ever experienced. She explored his muscled thighs with her hands and lips and tongue, making him as crazy with need as she was.

Finally he admitted, "I'm beyond my limit, Emily, but I want to make sure you're ready."

"I'm beyond ready."

Smiling, he slid his hand between her legs to make sure, then took her lips with a searing kiss that burned through her whole being. No matter what else happened or didn't happen between them, she'd remember this night forever.

After Brad tore open the condom packet, she helped him roll it on. She did it slowly, teasingly, and he groaned.

"Just you wait," he growled.

Then he rose above her and entered her with such slowness, she wanted to cry. She was waiting all right—waiting for him to fill her. Finally he did.

In that moment, time stopped.

She felt whole and loved and cherished.

When he started moving inside her, pleasure began

building higher and higher until it was beyond any sensation she'd ever felt, brighter than any stars she'd ever seen, more encompassing than any feeling or desire that had ever overtaken her heart. Brad's final thrust tossed her over the mountain into free fall. His cry of release said he'd followed her.

She held on to him and he held on to her, and their landing was gentler because they had each other. With Brad's arms around her, with his body still connected to hers, her breathing slowed and so did his. Eventually he raised himself on his elbows and looked down at her.

"I'm glad we have all night. That wasn't nearly enough."

Emily knew exactly what he meant. But she also knew tonight would have to be enough, because when they returned to Chicago everything was going to change.

Chapter Twelve

On Monday morning, Emily reported to work early, not knowing exactly what to do. If she was going to be promoted, should she start working on anything that had come in while they were gone? On the other hand, she had yesterday's notes on Caleb's case to type up. That could take her a good part of the morning.

To her delight and dismay, Brad came in early, too. The night she'd spent with him in his bed had been heaven. Still, yesterday morning they'd awakened to the alarm, hurriedly dressed to drive to the airport on time and then flown away from Montana. Brad had said nothing about their night together and neither had she. He'd been perfectly clear about it from the outset. On her part, however, her love had grown along with her passion, and now she hated the thought of letting it go—letting *him* go.

This morning he'd greeted her and then had enclosed himself in his office. Now that door opened and he beckoned to her. "Emily, can I see you?"

Her heart pounded as she picked up her notepad and pen and went inside. "You won't need that," he nodded to the notepad. "I think you'll remember everything I have to tell you." He smiled at her then, but it was a forced smile and didn't light up his eyes.

"What is it?"

"I spoke with Jack McCormick this morning and explained how helpful you were in Thunder Canyon. I asked him to think about taking you on in a training capacity. He's willing and said he could use the help from someone as capable as you are."

"He's never worked with me."

"No, but he looked up your evaluations and he considers my recommendation a golden one. He knows I'm hard to please. So, as soon as you have the notes typed up on Thunder Canyon, finish up whatever else you think needs your final touches and tomorrow morning report to Jack."

"Tomorrow morning?"

"Is that a problem?" Brad asked.

About a ton of them, she thought, realizing this would be the last day she'd be working with Brad, the last day she'd spend any appreciable time with him.

She impulsively asked, "How would you like to have dinner at my mom's apartment tonight? It's a welcome-back dinner for me, and I'm sure she'd like to include you."

His gaze held hers. "Why are you inviting me?"

"It's a celebration for the work we did together, finding the real owner of the mine. It's also a thank-you for the promotion. We won't be...seeing each other much after today."

She knew she was only prolonging the inevitable, but she was so head over heels in love with Brad, she couldn't quite let go.

He hesitated long enough to tell her he was thinking about refusing, but to her surprise he finally responded, "All right. That sounds nice. What time should I be there?"

"Around seven?"

"Seven's good. I need the address."

Quickly she scribbled her mother's address on the pad, then tore the sheet of paper off and handed it to him. As he took it, she gazed at his long, strong fingers, remembering how he'd taken her out of herself as she'd welcomed him, remembering how tenderly they'd stroked her. Desolation overtook her because she knew he wouldn't be touching her in that way again.

"Can I bring anything?" he asked.

"No. Just yourself." Then she forced a bright smile and said, "I'll get those notes on Caleb Douglas finished as soon as I can," and went back to her own desk.

When she sat in her swivel chair, a tear rolled down her cheek and she knew she'd been an absolute fool to invite him to dinner.

Picking up the phone, she called her mother to tell her Brad was coming tonight.

Carrying the box wrapped with light blue paper decorated with a premade darker blue bow, Brad rang the doorbell to Mrs. Mary Stanton's apartment.

The intercom came on and an older female voice asked, "Yes?"

"Mrs. Stanton? It's Brad Vaughn. Emily invited me to dinner."

"Yes, she told us you were coming. Come on up. Everyone can't wait to meet you."

That wasn't what Brad wanted to hear. It had been a mistake to accept this invitation. But every time he thought about Emily going to work for Jack, his gut clenched. Every time he thought about looking out into her office and not seeing her there, he realized how important she'd become to his day-to-day work regime. When she'd issued the invitation to dinner, he'd known he should have refused, but when he was with her he felt taller, smarter and a better man. He told himself he'd merely woven some kind of glorified web about them since Thunder Canyon, and reality would come crashing through any moment.

It hadn't happened yet.

Stepping into the elevator, he pressed the button for the fifth floor. As the elevator rose, he had no idea what to expect when he reached the Stanton's apartment. Who else would be at this dinner besides Emily and her mother? Would Mrs. Stanton sense there was more than a business relationship between him and her daughter? A relationship he knew he had to sever, for Emily's sake if not for his.

When he rang the doorbell to apartment five-twelve, he was surprised when a man opened it—a man maybe a few years younger than he was. He looked a lot like Emily only his jaw was more square, his eyebrows thicker and he was much taller.

"So *you're* Brad Vaughn," he concluded in a voice that told Brad he wasn't overly pleased Brad had come to dinner.

Brad extended his hand. "And you're...?"

"I'm Eric Stanton, Emily's older brother." He gave Brad's hand a perfunctory shake. "She told us you were coming. We received the wine you had the store send us. It's expensive stuff."

"I thought your mother would enjoy a chardonnay."

"Mom likes wine that tastes like fruit juice, but she'll try it because you sent it. Come on in."

In a matter of minutes Brad was introduced to Eric's wife and two daughters, as well as Lizbeth and Elaine. He searched the living room, which was charmingly decorated in rose, peach and green with small porcelain figurines on top of most available surfaces.

Lizbeth must have noticed him glancing around. "Emily's in the kitchen. She's putting the finishing touches on dinner. Come on, I'll introduce you to Mom."

One of Brad's best traits was mingling and making conversation with strangers. He'd been doing it since he'd earned his MBA and worked on Wall Street making cold calls to potential clients. However, tonight he felt out of his element. Maybe he cared about what these people thought about him. That idea totally unsettled him.

Lizbeth was a pretty coed with light brown hair and a slim figure shown to its advantage in tight jeans. A good fourteen years older than she was, fatherly thoughts came into Brad's head—the jeans shouldn't be so tight, the blouse should button up a little higher, she shouldn't be wearing so much makeup.

"Is that for Emily or Mom?" She motioned to the package in his hand.

"Emily."

"I thought you'd say that." She grinned as they went through the dining room, with its table set in white ironstone china. "She's nuts about you, you know."

His quick glance made her toss her hair and shrug her shoulders. "Well, she is. And I hope you feel the same way about her. She doesn't deserve to get hurt again."

They stopped outside the closed door to the kitchen. "No, Emily doesn't deserve to get hurt," he said evenly. "No one does. But sometimes that's hard to prevent."

"Are you saying you're not serious about her?" Lizbeth's eyes were wide.

"I'm saying I shouldn't be having this conversation with you. We don't even know each other."

"Well, she told us all about you—what you do and all."

"What I do?"

"Yeah, being a private investigator. She said you tracked down that deed like a hound dog on a trail. She bet there wasn't anything you couldn't find. Like I said, she's nuts over you. But don't tell her I said that. She's pretending it's nothing special that you came to dinner, but she wore her best slacks and favorite blouse. So that's hogwash."

To change the subject, he focused on Lizbeth. "Emily mentioned that you were going to spend another year in college."

"I'm changing majors. It's hard for me to decide exactly what I want to do."

"You mean this isn't it? You still aren't sure?"

"I think I'm sure. CPAs make pretty good money, but I imagine it can get a little boring. I figured I'll try it."

Suddenly Lizbeth's airy attitude really annoyed him—not only that she was poking into his and Emily's personal lives, but that she was taking advantage of her sister and didn't even seem to mind it.

"You do know Emily wants to go to college herself?"

"Someday."

"Not some faraway day. Sometime soon."

His tone startled Lizbeth. "Well, I guess. She's getting older and all."

"She wants a worthwhile career just like you do. But she's put her life on hold and she sacrificed so you and Elaine could get through your schooling before she did. So before you tie her up for another year, maybe you ought to be sure about what you want to do."

Lizbeth looked at him as if he'd suggested she become an oceanographer instead of a CPA. Then she became defensive. "Emily's never said she didn't want to help me."

"Of course she hasn't. She's a good sister. She's reliable and she's dependable and she loves you. She sincerely wants to help you. But how long should she put herself second or third or fourth?"

After a few moments, Lizbeth cocked her head. "What happened to you guys in that cabin?"

Now he was the one who was surprised. "I don't know what you mean."

"Emily said you didn't even know each other before you left for Montana. And here the two of you are— she's swooning because you're coming to dinner, and you're…you're trying to put everything right for her."

He did want everything to be right for Emily. And as far as what happened in the cabin...

"We were put in a basic survival scenario at the cabin. We got to know each other very quickly."

"True character comes out in that kind of situation and all?" she jibed.

"Maybe so. Then we had the opportunity to work on an unusual case. It didn't seem unusual when it started, but Thunder Canyon is very different from Chicago. I think we both appreciated the differences."

"Emily never wanted to camp or go to Montana, but now when she talks about it... She got pictures developed and the scenery is gorgeous. She said she didn't just look at it, she felt it."

"She's right about that."

"You know something?" Lizbeth asked rhetorically. "Eric was all set not to like you, but I think you're okay."

With that declaration she pushed open the swinging door into the kitchen, and Brad followed her inside.

As soon as Brad stepped into the room and saw Mary Stanton, he knew she was a lady. Taller than Emily, she wore her salt-and-pepper brown hair in a sleek French twist. Her sweater and pants were an impeccable navy blue, in contrast to her daughter's pale pink.

When she extended her hand to Brad, she smiled. "Hello, Mr. Vaughn. Thank you for keeping my daughter safe while you were in Montana."

He looked for an underlying meaning to her words and found none. "She kept me on my toes."

Mrs. Stanton laughed. "I imagine she did. Emily can be quite creative. She's been telling me about her new promotion. I never thought of my daughter as a private investigator."

"She'll make a good one someday, if that's what she wants."

Mary looked from one of them to the other and capped Lizbeth's shoulder. "Let's you and I go see if everything on the table is where it's supposed to be."

"Mom, you had me check it—"

Nudging her youngest daughter into the dining room, Mary let the swinging door shut behind them.

"Hi," Emily greeted him brightly. She'd been tearing lettuce leaves and now she dried her hands on a towel and hung it over the handle on the oven. "I hope my family hasn't been too...daunting."

"Not daunting. Interesting."

"That they are. What have you got there? The wine's great. I told you you didn't have to bring anything."

He handed her the present. "This is for you. Sort of a Montana-wasn't-what-we-expected and a promotion gift."

Just looking at Emily—her silky brown hair, her wide green eyes, her slender figure in the pretty pink outfit— he was aroused and ready for another night in the bedroom. But that was the whole problem. Emily wasn't a torrid-affair kind of woman. She deserved a hell of a lot more.

Her fingers trembled slightly as she detached the bow from the gift, and he wondered if he truly affected her the same way she affected him. Taking care with the paper, she only tore it where she had to, then she set it aside on the counter and stared at the box.

"Oh, my gosh. You didn't!"

"I felt responsible for the other one being damaged."

"I took it to the camera shop so we could take the film out and salvage it. It was going to be expensive to fix it, so I was just going to wait a while. But this—"

Taking the lid from the box, she pulled out the camera in its leather case. Unzipping the protective pouch, she took out the piece of equipment carefully. "Oh, my gosh. It has *everything*."

"That's what the man said. So now there's no excuse for you not to take the very best pictures and submit them to magazines for consideration."

"You want me to be a P.I. *and* a photographer?"

"I want you to be whatever you want to be."

Her gaze met his, then she set the camera on the counter with the wrapping and gave him a hug. Dressed in a polo shirt and khaki slacks tonight, he could feel every one of her curves against him. He could also smell her perfume and breathe in her shampoo. He needed her too damn much. It would have been easy to kiss her. It would have been easy to prolong the hug. But neither would have been the right thing to do.

Leaning away, he said, "It's supposed to do as well indoors as outside. You might want to take a few of your family."

"More than a few. I bet Eric will want to borrow it for the kids."

"And you'll let him?"

"Maybe. But I have the feeling I'm going to be protective of this for a while. Thank you so much, Brad. You didn't have to do this."

"I know I didn't. That's why I wanted to."

"I want to show Mom, and we have to get supper out before it burns. I hope you like meat loaf."

He hadn't had meat loaf since he was a kid and his mother made it for him every Wednesday night. "Meat loaf sounds great."

Seated at the dining room table with her family, he realized the meal felt like a Norman Rockwell Thanksgiving. Dinner conversation was lively. The problem was, every time Brad gazed into Emily's eyes, he couldn't look away. And it seemed neither could she. They were seated across the table from each other, but that didn't diminish the magnetic pull he felt toward her.

Surprised he found it easy to talk to this family, Brad entered some of the conversations. Lizbeth went on about college and the people she knew there, and Elaine recounted colorful anecdotes. Eric was the only one who was particularly quiet. His wife and two children didn't seem to notice as they ate their meal with gusto, and then the two little girls ran into the living room to watch a DVD. When it was time for dessert, Emily disappeared into the kitchen to help her mother and Elaine. Lizbeth went to the china cupboard in the corner and removed cups and saucers, the sugar bowl and the creamer.

While she was doing that, Eric leaned closer to Brad and asked, "So, this trip to Montana—was it all business?"

"It was business," Brad answered without elaboration.

Eric gave him a penetrating look. "Emily went on and on about visiting a couple and a baby. You know, don't you, that she wants a passel of kids someday."

Brad hadn't known that for certain, but he'd guessed.

When he'd seen Emily with Marissa, he'd known motherhood was in her nature. Just the way she related to her sisters proved that.

"Emily will make a wonderful mother." Brad knew that in his soul.

Frustrated he wasn't getting more out of Brad, Eric continued poking. "She said she's not going to be working with you anymore. Is that true?"

"That's true. She's going to train with a senior private investigator. If she likes the work, she can get her license."

"You think she's really cut out for that?"

"One thing I don't do is underestimate Emily. If she decides that's what she wants, nothing will stop her. And she'll be good at it, too."

When Eric studied Brad, as if gauging his sincerity, Brad became irritated. "I'm looking out for Emily's best interests, too."

Finally Eric backed off. "I just wanted to make sure of that. She's tough and smart but she's more vulnerable than anybody knows."

Brad knew that's why he had to cut this off now. He couldn't say their last night together had been a mistake. It had been too intense and fulfilling to be a mistake. But that last night was going to make everything said and done between them now even harder.

After dinner, Brad stayed a while longer. It was the polite thing to do. Finally, though, he said his goodnights and then he asked Emily, "Walk me out?"

Not hesitating, she followed him to the door and out into the hall.

Her smile slipped from her lips as she looked up at him. An awkward silence settled between them. Finally she murmured, "Thank you again for the camera."

After a very long moment, he said, "You deserve the best, Emily, the best of everything." He took a step away from her.

"I'm not going to see you again, am I?" she blurted out.

"No, not like this. It's best for you if we don't. I don't have anything to give you. One day you'll meet a man worthy of you."

"I've already met a worthy man. You have more to give than you think. But *you* have to believe that. Up until now, you thought you *were* your reputation, and I'm not sure you considered being anything else. In Montana, I saw so many sides to you that you keep hidden."

Every word was going through him like a lance...because he could feel the truth in what she said. But she wanted a family, children—the very things he'd avoided all his adult life.

"Your life is about family. Mine isn't."

"Yours could be, too, if that's what you wanted. You think because your parents divorced, because you were shuttled back and forth from one to the other, that you don't know how to be a husband or a father. But I think you're wrong. With Juliet and Mark's baby..."

He couldn't let her go on with this. He couldn't let her think there was hope. "I held Marissa for fifteen minutes. That's not being a father."

"It's the *way* you held her," Emily protested with certainty.

"You're seeing what you want to see."

"And you're denying what you think you have to deny."

In spite of himself, he couldn't keep from touching her one last time. Reaching out, he trailed his thumb across her cheek and felt her tremble in response. He wanted to kiss her so badly that nothing in the world seemed to matter—not his career, not his money, not his reputation, not anything he'd valued before. If he kissed her, he'd be taking advantage of her. If he led her on, he'd be worse than the irresponsible playboy she once thought he was.

"I have to go." He dropped his hand to his side. "Tomorrow you'll start working for Jack. If you put your heart and soul into it, you'll be great."

"I think my heart and my soul are busy thinking about something else right now."

"Forget about me, Emily. Tell your mother and your sisters and brother I had a great time."

Walking away from her, he stopped halfway to the elevator. "And use that camera for the best pictures you've ever taken."

Fortunately when he pressed the button on the elevator, it opened immediately. He stepped inside, wanting to get a last glimpse of Emily. However, before he could glance down the hall, the doors whooshed shut and she was gone.

His heart told him to stay. His head told him to leave.

He *always* followed his head.

In spite of her stern lecture to herself—that Brad had to go his way and she had to go hers—Emily cried on and off throughout the night. She'd seen the real Brad in Montana, a loving, caring man who could make a commitment, say vows and live a happily ever after if he chose it. Happily ever after wasn't a fairy tale or a dream, it was a choice. When you had the right person beside you...

She'd found the right person, but the problem was *he* didn't think he was the right person. There was nothing she could do about that.

When she went into work the next morning earlier than usual, Brad wasn't there yet and she was thankful for that. She had to empty her desk, pack up her personal belongings and take all of it down to Jack's office.

She was removing an extra pair of shoes from her bottom drawer when Brad came through the door followed by a beautiful blonde and an older man in a three-piece suit. A younger man in a suit and tie tagged behind.

Brad opened the door to his office as he said to the blonde, "My lawyer has the DNA report. We'll be finished with this in five minutes."

Seeing Brad this morning was like a punch in the stomach, and Emily found it hard to take a deep breath. She'd lectured herself before coming to work that she might run into him. And she told herself that in the days to come that was a very distinct possibility, too. He and Jack often worked together. They consulted on cases. The gossip mill in the firm would keep her apprised of exactly whom Brad was seeing and whom he wasn't.

Sinking into her desk chair, she realistically thought about all of that for the very first time.

She couldn't do it. She simply couldn't do it. She

couldn't work in the same firm, hearing news about him, seeing him in the hall or even having to deal with him. She loved him too much for that.

There was no way she could accept this promotion. No way at all.

Studying the three boxes on her desk, she decided to take them to her car and head home. But first she would type up a letter of resignation.

With tears in her eyes, she knew the only solution to loving Brad was leaving Vaughn Associates for good.

Chapter Thirteen

Brad stood in his father's office, relieved the meeting with his lawyer and Suzette Brouchard had gone so well. Of course, when the proof was printed in black and white—

"So Brouchard admitted she and her boyfriend were just trying to get money out of you?"

"She said it was her boyfriend's idea. With the test results, knowing with one hundred percent certainty that I'm not the father, what else could she say? They thought if they put enough pressure on me, especially through the media, they could get a settlement before the DNA testing results came in."

With a shake of his head Phillip Vaughn sighed. "Women."

Right now Brad didn't want to hear about his father's views on the fairer sex. "There's something else I wanted to discuss with you."

His father's eyes narrowed. "What would that be?"

"I want to open a missing-persons division of Vaughn Associates. And I want to do pro bono work, as well as work for hire. As head of the division, I would decide which cases we would take on and which we wouldn't. If you don't want to consider that type of work for this company, then I'll open my own firm to specialize in finding missing persons."

Shock appeared to be the main sentiment on his father's face. "Why would you ever want to do that?"

Concisely Brad explained about Tess Littlehawk and her daughter. Then he added, "I'm flying to California this afternoon to follow up on a lead."

A very long silence echoed in the elegant office. After a long, thoughtful look at Brad, Phillip must have seen his determination and exactly what he'd lose if he dismissed the idea—a connection to his son.

He asked, "Will you put some facts and figures together and write up a proposal? If you do that, I'll consider it."

A few minutes later, Brad left his father's office and headed toward his own. Maybe he could borrow Emily from Jack just for a day or two. She was so good at collating information.

No, that wouldn't be fair. She was no longer his secretary, and he just had to deal with that. Whenever he thought of Emily, he felt as if he had a hole in his heart. He was trying to fill it by taking his life in a new direction, yet he knew he might have to stop into

Jack's office to see her. He might have to tell her his good news.

One of his contacts in California had turned up a shelter log with Annie Littlehawk's name in it. The man had a couple of leads, and Brad wanted to help him chase them down. Soon he'd have to leave for the airport.

When Brad rounded the corner to his office suite, he saw Emily's empty desk. The sight of it made him frown. He didn't even want to think about interviewing for a new personal secretary, but he knew he had to do it.

The white legal-size envelope lying in the middle of his desk caught his eye as soon as he entered his own office. When he picked it up, he saw his name written on the outside. It was Emily's handwriting.

His heart pounding faster, he took out the typed letter, read it and swore. It was impersonal, one paragraph, a letter of resignation and thanks for all he'd done for her.

There was no explanation for why she'd written it, and he suddenly knew exactly why. She wanted to put him and Thunder Canyon out of her life.

Brad thought about going after her, but what would he say? *I can't stand the thought of coming to work and you not being here? I hate the idea of you working somewhere else?*

With a blinding flash of insight, he realized his feelings had nothing to do with Emily quitting her job. Rather, they had to do with him not seeing her again and not seeing her every day.

What had he thought they were going to do? Have coffee together in the mornings before she went off to work for Jack and he opened his own division?

As Brad packed his bag that afternoon for his trip, he thought about Emily. As he boarded the plane, he thought about Emily. As he slept alone in his hotel room that night, he thought about Emily.

Brad's contact in California had done good ground-work in San Jose. After two days of following leads, Brad found Annie Littlehawk in a bookstore shelving books. When he introduced himself and insisted that her mother missed her terribly, she began crying.

"I can't go home," she told him as she ordered a soda at a nearby restaurant. She was a beautiful young woman, with long black hair and sparkling brown eyes.

"Tell me why not."

After a few moments of hesitation, she murmured, "It's not just that I ran away. I know that hurt my mother. But I did things I'm not proud of *after* I ran."

"Your mother needs to know you're well and safe. All these years she didn't know if you were alive or dead. That's heartbreaking for a parent."

"I can't believe she hired you to look for me. How could she afford that?"

"Let's just say fate put us together at the right place at the right time. You have to let her know you're okay."

Annie fingered the straw of her soda. "I didn't think she'd ever want to hear from me again. I caused her so much trouble. We fought all the time. I said things I never should have said."

"You think your mother hasn't made mistakes in her life?"

When Annie looked up at him with wide, miserable

eyes, she frowned. "She's a good person. She'd never intentionally hurt someone."

"Did you *want* to hurt her?"

"Yes! Because she wouldn't let me do what I wanted to do. She laid down all these rules and I didn't understand why."

"And now you do?"

Annie nodded.

"Then call her." He slid his business card across the table with Tess's information written on the back. "That's where she's living and working now."

As Annie looked torn, he advised her, "Don't decide right now whether you're going to come home or not. I can tell her I found you, but I'm sure she'd much rather hear from *you*. If you decide you want to fly back to Thunder Canyon, let me know and I'll make the arrangements."

"Why do you care if I go home?" she asked, looking perplexed.

"Because I'm learning how important family is, how important bonds are. You don't break them if you can help it. And if you do and you have a chance to fix them, it's important that you try."

Three hours later, taking the red-eye back to Chicago, Brad thought about his words to Annie. He thought about them as he let himself into his penthouse and felt the emptiness there. Making strong coffee, he didn't even try to get any sleep. There was something he had to do…something he should have done years before.

It was nine-thirty in the morning when he greeted the doorman at his mother's apartment building. After he took the elevator up to her apartment, he rang the bell.

Connie Vaughn was an attractive woman in her early sixties. Her gray hair was silvery and she wore it in a pageboy, as she'd done for years. Today she was dressed in a taupe sweater and slacks and looked more than a little surprised to see him.

"Did I forget a breakfast date?" she asked.

They were long past due for dinner or breakfast or…something. That was *his* fault. "No, you didn't forget. I need to talk to you. Do you have time?"

Her eyes became worried now. "I always have time for you."

Looking back, he knew that was true.

Going into the elegantly furnished living room, he took a seat on the sofa.

She sat across from him in an upholstered chair and asked, "New look?"

He'd showered and changed but hadn't bothered to shave. "No. I just didn't take the time for the whole works."

"What was so urgent?"

Now that he was here, he didn't quite know how to put it into words. "I've met someone."

His mother smiled. "Is that good or bad?"

"I'm still trying to figure that out. She's different."

"Different in a general sense or different from the women you usually date?"

Connie Vaughn had hit the bull's-eye. "Different from women I usually date. She was my secretary."

He didn't see the disapproval he thought he might as his mother asked, "Was?"

"It's a complicated story. We were in Montana together the last few weeks on a case. She resigned when we came back."

"If she was your secretary, then she doesn't have money."

"No, she doesn't. Money's not important to Emily."

"You're sure of that?"

"I'm positive. She's put her own life on hold so she could help her sisters through school."

"It sounds as if she *needs* money."

"No. I mean, I offered to pay for Emily's own college courses and she wouldn't accept it. She has a lot of pride and self-respect and insists on making her own way. She never coats the truth in pretty words, and I can usually tell what she's feeling," he went on, remembering every detail of their time together.

"Usually?"

"Right now—" Frustrated, he raked his hand through his hair. "I cut things off between us because I didn't think I wanted a wife and a family. Or maybe I just never thought I'd be successful at it and I don't attempt anything I can't succeed at. Now I need some answers. I realize that what happened between you and Dad colored my view of women and marriage and whether or not two people can share a life."

"What answers do you need?" his mother inquired softly.

"Why did you have an affair?"

When Connie stood, she went to the window to look down over the city. "I wish I could give you a *simple* answer, but there isn't one. There is an easy answer, though. Your father didn't give me what I needed."

Now she turned to face Brad. "I know that must sound ridiculous when we had everything money could buy. But I needed the intangible things that maybe women need more than men."

"Such as?"

"Time...attention...affection."

"But you were married!"

She laughed. "Oh, yes. My family had a hand in that. I'd just graduated from college when Phillip's family invited me to come stay with them for a weekend. My father and his father had been old college buddies."

"The marriage was arranged?"

"No, not in any old-world sense. Let's just say we both came highly recommended. At first I was fascinated by your father. He was so intelligent, so sophisticated, five years older than me and worldly. He intrigued me, and I mistook his ambition and drive to succeed for passion."

Not knowing if he wanted to set foot in that arena, Brad decided he needed to have answers. "I don't understand."

"I thought the intensity in Phillip's nature meant he could love deeply, that when he turned his energy on a relationship, it would be everything we both could want."

"But he didn't do that?"

His mother slipped her hands into her slacks pockets. "Your father could build an empire if he wanted to, but he couldn't talk to me. I fell in love with him. I thought if we got married and had a family we'd find what we needed together. That didn't happen. The more he worked, the more distant he became. That distance turned to coldness. He didn't know how to show affection and didn't want to learn. He wouldn't even consider counseling. So our marriage limped along until one day I met someone who looked into my eyes when he talked to me. He put his hand on my shoulder when I needed one there. He listened in a way I'd never been listened to before. I had been drowning emotionally and he saved me. So we had an affair."

"And Dad found out?"

"Yes. One afternoon we weren't careful and had lunch in a popular restaurant. One of your father's associates saw us. I don't know. Maybe I wanted him to find out. Maybe I wanted to push myself into making some kind of decision, and that's what happened."

As Brad honestly thought about his dad, he knew his father could be cold and distant. He'd just never pictured how that would play out in a marriage. He'd blamed his mother all these years for her lack of morals, for her infidelity to her vows. Yet hadn't his father broken their vows before she had by his attitude, by his neglect of her?

"Men-and-women relationships are complicated, Brad. They're never exactly what they seem on the outside," she counseled him.

"After you and Dad divorced, did you see the man you had the affair with?"

"No."

"Why not?"

Now she sat on the sofa again and folded her hands in her lap. "Because of you. I knew what you thought of me. I knew you believed I'd destroyed our family. At first you were resentful and defiant and sullen. I couldn't get a smile out of you for months. Do you honestly

think I would have taken a chance on losing you altogether by dating and maybe marrying this man?"

Never before had Brad realized what his mother had
sacrificed for him. He thought about Emily and what
she'd sacrificed for her sisters. Was that kind of selfless-
ness in women's natures?

Not all women. Just the special ones.

"What about now? Why haven't you ever gotten
married?"

"Cowardice, I guess. And I've become set in my
ways." She studied him for a few moments. "But I know
you have more courage than I do. I also know you've
dated a lot of wrong women, and maybe that's why
you've never asked me these questions before."

"Emily makes me think and question. She makes me
laugh. She frustrates me, yet she leads me to see life in
a different way. And…I love her. I *do* love her." He
could admit that now.

"Did you say she resigned?"

"Yes, and she's hurt because I cut her out of my life.
She has no reason to ever want to speak to me again."

"But you're going to find a reason."

Ever since he'd read Emily's resignation letter, he'd
felt as if he had a lead weight in his chest. Now he felt
lighter.

"Yes. I'm going to find that reason."

On Sunday afternoon, Emily was looking at the pictures she'd shot in Montana and the want ads lying beside her on the sofa. She had three interviews set up for
Friday. She had intended to look through the paper, cir-

cling more possibilities. But she'd picked up her developed pictures yesterday and she couldn't seem to put them away. The breathtaking Montana scenery tugged at a deep place in her soul. However, the pictures of Brad brought tears to her eyes. Her heart hurt and she didn't know if she'd ever get over him.

Reluctantly plopping the pictures on the coffee table, she picked up the newspaper, intent on finding a new job, when her phone rang.

"Hello? This is Emily Stanton."

"Emily? It's Brad."

Her heart pounded so fast, she couldn't catch her breath. Was he calling so she'd reconsider her resignation?

"Emily?"

"I'm here," she managed to say.

"I want you to fly to Thunder Canyon with me tomorrow."

"Tomorrow?"

"Yes."

"Why?"

"To finish what we started. A couple of things have happened. I found Tess's daughter. Annie's going to fly in and she and Tess are going to be reunited. I want to keep *that* meeting private. But then there's going to be a press conference, and the mayor would like both of us there."

"Why a press conference?"

"The deed was authenticated. Lisa Martin is the true owner of the Queen of Hearts mine. Apparently this story has piqued the nation's interest, and the press conference will be broadcast on CNN. The other networks might be there, too. Brookhurst says he'll tell us what he has planned when we get there, but he's adamant about you coming along. You're the one who found the deed."

"It was a fluke."

"A fluke *you* investigated. The mayor wants us *both* there," he repeated firmly.

When Brad used that tone, she knew he wouldn't change his mind. "And you want to leave tomorrow?"

"Yes. We'll have a meeting with the mayor after we arrive. The press conference will be held the following morning. Will you come along and finish this with me?"

She knew she shouldn't. She knew her heart was already broken and being with Brad would keep it that way. Yet she also couldn't resist the idea of seeing him again, being with him again. Besides, she did want to see Tess and her daughter reunited. That was the most important aspect of all this.

"All right. I'll come along."

There was a pause. Then he said, "Great. I have meetings tomorrow morning before our flight so I'll send a car for you."

"I can take a taxi."

"I'll send a car for you. He'll pick you up around nine-thirty. Our flight leaves at noon."

Before she had a chance to change her mind, he hung up.

Gazing at the pictures she'd taken of Brad, she knew this could be the biggest mistake of her life. Nevertheless, she had nothing to lose this time because she'd already lost her heart.

* * *

On *this* trip when Emily and Brad arrived in Bozeman, he rented a car. The awkwardness between them had hit an all-time high. Brad seemed to be mulling something over, and she'd left him to his thoughts most of the trip.

Now, as they drove into Thunder Canyon for their meeting with the mayor, she asked, "Are we going to check in at the motel first?"

"We're not staying at the motel."

"We certainly won't be welcome at the Lazy D."

"Actually, we're staying at the cabin tonight."

Her gaze jerked toward his. "Why?"

"The same reason as last time, actually. Everything's booked up. This press conference has brought people in from all over the country, including reporters, news teams and curious busybodies."

"And Caleb's letting us use the cabin?"

"I made a deal with him."

That surprised Emily. Last week she might have asked Brad what the deal was. But today she really had no right to know.

The meeting with the mayor was methodical as he went over the schedule for the press conference.

Then Brad said, "I'm picking up someone at the airport tomorrow morning. Is there a place we could use to have a private meeting before the press conference starts?"

The mayor thought about it. "You can use Conference Room A on the second floor. Would that be suitable?"

"That will be just fine."

Emily couldn't help but see that Brad looked worried. Maybe he was afraid Tess and her daughter's reunion wouldn't go well.

As they drove to the cabin, Emily asked, "I guess the creek water's gone down?"

"Yep. I had someone check it for us. Unless we get tons of rain overnight, we'll be able to get out in the morning." His gaze met hers. "Don't you want to get stranded again?"

She wasn't exactly sure how to answer that one. "I have job interviews on Friday. I can't miss those."

When Brad looked back at the road, his jaw was set, his mouth a tight line. Something was going on with him, but she had no idea what it was.

After they arrived at the cabin, she saw it was stocked both with groceries and with firewood. Apparently Brad wasn't taking any chances this time.

She motioned toward the logs. "We have plenty."

Dropping his suitcase next to the sofa, Brad motioned out back. "There's a generator hooked up now, too, so you won't have to worry about the power going out."

"I'm not worried." She wasn't—not as long as she was with Brad.

After they'd eaten a quiet supper with forced conversation, Brad realized he didn't know what the hell he was doing. He thought he'd planned this out, but being with Emily again had made him doubt his course. He didn't want her to think he'd brought her to the cabin again to sleep with her. That wasn't what this was about. But she seemed as jittery as a teenager on her first date, and he wasn't much better. He knew he couldn't just tell Emily he loved her. He had to show her. He had to make a public declaration so she'd know his intentions were true.

Tomorrow he'd find out if she loved him. If she wanted to spend her life with him. The suspense was killing him.

They sat in front of the fire listening to music. He told her how he'd found Tess's daughter and then he added, "I'm going to take more cases like Tess's."

"Missing persons?"

"Yes. Especially parents who can't find their kids. I'm starting a new division at Vaughn Associates just for that."

Her eyes became huge and wide. "Your father agreed to that?"

"He didn't have much choice if he wanted me to stay. I'll be head of the division. He won't be overseeing it."

Emily looked happy for him, yet there was deep sadness in her eyes, too, and he wondered if that was because they wouldn't be working together. They might be if all went as he'd planned.

As Emily stared into the fire for a few more moments, she said, "I guess I'd better turn in."

He hadn't touched her up until now because his self-control was at a premium. Although he wanted her in his arms, he wanted her there the *right* way.

When she stood, he stood with her and blocked her path to the bedroom. "Did you see the gossip column in the newspaper a few days ago—about Suzette and me?"

"Yes, I did. It was a public statement that you're not the father of Suzette Brouchard's child. I guess you're glad that's all over."

"I am. I just wanted you to know it was cleared up."

"Brad, I'm sorry I didn't believe you at first. My only excuse is that I didn't know you. Once we spent time in Thunder Canyon together, I realized that if you said you weren't the father, then you weren't the father. I knew that before we returned to Chicago."

Grateful Emily would never be anything but honest with him, he was touched deeply by her words. His lips longed to take a kiss, his hands longed to rove her body, but instead of doing either, he brought his hands to her shoulders and leaned in and kissed her forehead.

Huskily he said, "You have sweet dreams tonight, Emily. You should never have any other kind."

As she looked up at him questioningly, he just smiled and tapped his index finger to her nose.

Smiling back, she disappeared into the bedroom and closed the door.

Chapter Fourteen

When Emily took Tess to breakfast the following morning, Caleb's housekeeper was outwardly nervous. She couldn't seem to sit still, opening her purse for a tissue, pushing her food around, picking up her fork and putting it down again, wiping her mouth with her napkin.

Emily leaned across the table and patted her arm. "It's going to be all right."

"When I talked to Annie on Saturday, she seemed so hesitant about coming home again. I told her it didn't have to be permanently. If she liked California, I could go out there and visit her. Since Mr. Vaughn won't take any money for finding Annie, I have my savings."

"Your daughter might need to get the feel of Thunder Canyon again. I know it took *me* a while."

"She wasn't happy here," Tess said with a shake of her head. "Maybe I should move out there. I could. Maybe Mr. Douglas has a friend in California I could work for." Then she sighed. "He's still in such a bad mood these days because of the mine and all."

Ignoring Tess's comment about Caleb, Emily focused on Annie. "I think you should wait and spend a few days with your daughter and find out what she's thinking. You'll have to get to know each other all over again."

Tess took another bite of her eggs. "I guess you're right. My mind's just speeding ahead so fast I can't stop it."

All too well Emily knew what that was like. Last night as she'd lain in the cabin bedroom alone, hearing Brad move about out in the living room, her mind had raced, too. But it hadn't gotten anywhere.

She wondered why he'd asked her along. Simply because she'd been involved in the case and might want to see the conclusion? Although he'd told her the mayor wanted her there, that seemed superficial. Maybe this trip was Brad's way of saying a final goodbye since they hadn't done it when she'd resigned. Whatever the reason, her heart ached to be with him…really with him. He'd driven into Bozeman to pick up Annie at the airport, and she and Tess were supposed to meet him at the town hall in the conference room upstairs at ten-thirty. The press conference was scheduled for eleven.

Glancing around the Hitching Post, trying to absorb everything about it because she knew she wouldn't be back, Emily felt tears come to her eyes. Not wanting Tess to see, she quickly blinked them away, winked at the Shady Lady above the bar—a woman who'd had a lot more substance than the town had ever expected—and said to Tess, "I don't want to rush you, but we should be going."

Pushing back her plate, Tess gave Emily a weak smile. "Thank you for the breakfast. I just wasn't hungry."

Emily had taken care of the bill after the waitress had brought their breakfast. Now she left a tip and led Tess outside.

It was a beautiful end of May day, and the immense blue sky was cloudless. The temperature was already sixty degrees, and Emily's light blazer felt just right. She'd bought the pantsuit for her job interviews. It was a beautiful emerald-green, and the sea-foam blouse complemented it. Brad had appraised her that morning with a light in his eyes that usually meant he wanted to kiss her. But he hadn't.

She wouldn't think about that.

That morning Brad had dropped off Emily and Tess at the Hitching Post. Now they strolled leisurely through Old Town to the town hall. Already residents, tourists and news crews were spilling from the covered sidewalk into the street. The mayor had given both Emily and Brad passes so security would allow them inside.

Emily showed her pass to the security guard, keeping hold of Tess's arm. "She's with me," Emily said.

After the guard gave Tess the once-over, he nodded for them to enter.

Sitting at her desk, Rhonda fielded questions from men in suits and ties and women professionally attired. She'd be busy today.

Emily guided Tess toward the staircase to the left of the large foyer. It was the same polished wood as the floor, and Emily caught the scent of must and history as they neared the second-floor landing. Going down a hall, she spotted Conference Room A and opened the door. No one was inside.

With all her heart Emily hoped that Annie hadn't changed her mind and decided not to fly to Thunder Canyon.

There was a conference table and a few chairs, but Tess went to stand at the window. "All this fuss over a gold mine. Don't these people know what's really important?"

Emily knew what Tess meant. She knew what was important. Loving someone was important. "Lisa Martin's life might change completely because of this."

"Maybe not for the better," Tess murmured.

When the door to the conference room suddenly opened, Emily saw Brad first. He quickly stepped aside, letting a pretty young girl pass him.

Annie Littlehawk stood immobile in the doorway for a few seconds. Then Tess opened her arms to her daughter and Annie flew into them. Both women were crying, and Emily felt tears on her cheeks, too.

Crossing to the door, she gave Brad a wide smile. He put his arm around her shoulders, drawing her close.

Then he said in a husky voice, "Tess, Annie, you can stay here as long as you want. We're going to leave and give you some privacy. Mr. Douglas said he would send a car when you're ready to go back to the Lazy D. Just call the ranch."

When he and Emily were standing in the hall with the door closed, Emily smiled up at him. "I'm so proud of you for finding Annie."

"I had help." Taking his arm from around Emily's shoulders, he nodded downstairs. "We'd better get to the press conference. Mayor Brookhurst won't be happy if we're late."

When Emily and Brad entered the huge reception room, the mayor was already on the stage at the west end of the hall. He beckoned to them. After they mounted the steps, he murmured, "I can't get in touch with Lisa Martin, and no one knows where she is. I guess she'll find out she's the owner if she has her television tuned in to CNN."

There was a podium on the stage, which the mayor went to after he motioned Emily and Brad to the two chairs also on the stage. There was a handheld mike on a stand beside one of the chairs that they could pass from one to the other.

As soon as the mayor tapped on the podium, the

room went silent and all eyes were upon him. He introduced himself, knowing full well network cameras were shooting close-ups. Then he welcomed everyone and gave them a brief history of Thunder Canyon. However, he kept his speech short.

Finally he motioned to Brad. "Mr. Vaughn, a private investigator from Chicago, will now tell you how he and his assistant found the actual deed to the Queen of Hearts gold mine."

Emily noticed that Brad seemed very comfortable with the microphone as he made eye contact with the reporters and residents of Thunder Canyon, relating how he and Emily had investigated the ownership of the mine up until their visit with Tildy Matheson. Then he handed the mike to Emily, and she spoke about the trunk in Tildy's attic and the torn lining. The crowd listened with hushed fascination. Finally, when Emily had finished, Brad nodded to the mayor, and Brookhurst handed him something from inside the podium. It looked like a framed picture.

But it wasn't a photograph. Emily soon saw it was the deed, preserved and framed so nothing would happen to it.

The mayor announced, "The legal owner of the Queen of Hearts gold mine will be presented with this deed at the first opportunity."

"Who *is* the owner?" a reporter shouted out.

"The rightful owner of the mine was Lily Divine. According to our research, her great-great-granddaughter, Lisa Martin, will now inherit it."

Questions exploded. Many of them, about Lisa, couldn't be answered. Emily suspected reporters would be knocking on Tildy's door, as well as Lisa Martin's, as soon as the press conference was over.

As the questions eventually subsided, the mayor turned to Brad. "As far as the Queen of Hearts gold mine is concerned, we've concluded that part of the press conference. But Mr. Vaughn has something else he'd like to say."

Suddenly Brad stood with the microphone. Instead of addressing the audience, however, he turned toward Emily. Taking her hand, he drew her up out of her chair.

"Brad, what are you doing?" she whispered frantically.

"What I'm doing is acknowledging how I feel about you in front of the whole world."

Her heart galloped at triple speed as she looked up into his eyes, stunned by his announcement.

"I want the whole world to know how very special you are and how very much I love you. It was our trip to Thunder Canyon that made me realize how wonderful you are and how much I need you in my life."

Then he took a box from his pocket and knelt before her on one knee!

The room was silent again, everyone looking on and listening as Brad went on. "I'm taking the biggest risk of my life here today, Emily, because I don't know what you're going to say. But I felt I had to propose this way to prove to you how much I care about you. Pretty words don't mean a thing without action. So I'm taking action."

Opening the box, he held out a beautiful diamond in an antique white-gold setting. "I love you, Emily Stanton, and I want you to be my wife. Will you marry me?"

No words came to mind as tears welled up in her eyes. She looked at the ring and then she gazed at Brad kneeling on the floor before her…humbling himself before her. All at once she realized he'd planned his proposal this way to prove to her he didn't care if she was from a different background. He didn't care that her father had been a blue-collar worker. He didn't care that she didn't move in his social circle. He was on his knee before her to prove how very much he loved her.

Somehow she found the words she needed to banish the anxiety in his eyes, to assure him she felt the same way he did. "Yes, I'll marry you."

At her answer he was on his feet and folding her into his arms, kissing her with all the pent-up passion he'd been holding in check.

Applause rang out all around them.

When Brad broke away from her, he took the ring from the box and slipped it onto her finger. Then he took her hand, led her from the stage and on a dash through the reporters and residents of Thunder Canyon. They were going too fast for anyone to stop them.

She ran beside him to the parking lot, asking, "Where are we going?"

"To the cabin."

"I can't believe Caleb is letting you use it again."

Two reporters followed them and were now close on their heels. Brad said, "I'll explain after we get there. Come on."

In seconds they'd hopped into the SUV and pulled out of the parking lot with a screech of tires.

They veered onto Thunder Canyon Road. Still stunned, Emily mused, "I thought we were going back to Chicago today."

"Can you spare a few days with me? We have a lot to talk about."

Happiness began in her heart and filled her whole being. "I can spare a *lifetime* for you."

Taking her hand again, he laid it on his thigh, and that's where it stayed while they drove to the cabin.

Once there, they climbed out of the car and went to the doorstep.

Brad scooped her into his arms. "Finally," he sighed.

"Finally what?" she asked with a coy grin.

"Finally you're mine."

She held her ring up to the sunlight. "Is that what this means?"

"You can bet your life that's what it means."

Opening the cabin door, he carried her over the threshold. After he kicked it shut with his foot, he took her to the bedroom and gently set her on the bed. With a quick shrug he ridded himself of his suit coat, then unknotted his tie and tossed them both to the bedside chair.

Beside her on the bed, he held her face in his hands. "Do you know how much I love you?"

"Tell me," she murmured.

"It about drove me nuts last night to sleep here with you and not sleep *with* you. I wanted you to know this trip had nothing to do with sex. This trip was about you and me and the life we're going to have...the children we're going to have. We're going to spend a few days here planning and dreaming because this is *our* cabin now."

"You're kidding!"

"Nope. I made an offer Caleb couldn't refuse. This is going to be our getaway when life gets too demanding. It will be our vacation spot. When we have kids, I guess we'll have to build on to it."

After he helped rid Emily of her jacket, he began unbuttoning her blouse.

Her fingers worked at the buttons of his shirt. "What made you change your mind? About marriage, I mean. That night at my mom's apartment you seemed so definite—"

His fingers stilled. "I was definite because I was denying what I felt. I thought if I sounded definite I'd be able to convince myself. When I walked away from you that night, my heart hurt, and when I found your resignation on my desk, I knew I couldn't abide the thought of you being with anybody but me. I went to find Tess's daughter and realized how important family was. After I came back, I had a long talk with my mother and I understood things I'd never understood before."

"About your parents' breakup?"

Tenderly he took her hand in his and caressed her palm. "Yes. She sacrificed her happiness to keep me in her life. I think over the last couple of years I realized that cars and trips and work couldn't bring happiness. I was restless and dissatisfied and unfulfilled until I came here and got to know you. Then my attitude and perspective changed. Maybe I finally grew up."

Seriously he said, "I know I put you on the spot at the press conference. If you have any doubts about marrying me, any doubts at all, we'll wait until I've proven to you there are no reasons for doubts."

During their stay in Thunder Canyon, Emily had learned that Brad was a man of integrity, a kind man, one who would know the value of a vow and stand by one for the rest of his life. "I don't have any doubts."

"If you want to go to college, we can make sure that happens. If you want to work with me and find missing persons, I'd like that a lot."

"I've been thinking about getting my private investigator's license. Working with you sounds like a wonderful idea. I'm absolutely sure about our future together. I do have one request, though."

"What?"

"Will you make love to me until I believe everything that happened today is real?"

"Your wish is my command."

Then Brad was kissing her and holding her and undressing her and loving her.

Emily's dream burned away in the fire of their passion, and she wasn't sorry. Because the reality of Brad loving her was so much better than any dream ever could be.

* * * * *

MILLION-DOLLAR MAKEOVER

BY
CHERYL ST JOHN

A peacemaker, a romantic, an idealist and a discoursed perfectionist are the words that **Cheryl St John** uses to describe herself. The author of both historical and contemporary novels says she's been told that she is painfully honest.

Cheryl admits to being an avid collector who collects everything from dolls to Depression glass, brass candlesticks, old photographs and—most especially—books. She and her husband love to browse antiques and collectibles shops.

She says that knowing her stories bring hope and pleasure to readers is one of the best parts of being a writer. The other wonderful part is being able to set her own schedule and have time to work around her growing family.

Cheryl loves to hear from readers. You can write to her at: PO Box 24732, Omaha, NE 68124, USA.

A psychiatrist's comment: In dealing with a thoroughly pedophiliac the words that Cruel St John uses to describe naturally. The author of both beautiful and contemporary novels, and she has been able that she is painfully hopeless.

She'd admit to being afraid of nothing but collecting everything from dolls to Depression Glass. Plus candlesticks, old photographs and—most of all—books. She and her husband live in a roomy antique-filled collectibles shop.

She says and I love all her stories, bring important stuff for characters is one, on the best part of being a writer. The other wonderful part I brought able to set her own schedule and have time to enjoy a world her growing family.

Check I love to hear from readers. You can write to her at PO Box 2473, Ontah, NY, Ont 21-US1.

Chapter One

"This news conference is the biggest thing that's ever happened in Thunder Canyon," the local news announcer said over the murmur of the crowd behind her.

Lisa Jane Martin glanced up from peeling the cellophane from a frozen entrée to check out the television screen. "Yeah, well, get on with it and maybe we can still see the sports and weather."

Overwhelmed by sightseers and the influx of tourists, she'd been wishing this whole gold-mine thing would blow over so Thunder Canyon would get back to the quiet norm she appreciated.

At the sound of her voice, her two golden retrievers scrambled to their feet, nails scraping against the aged wooden floor, and vied for the same space in which she stood. Joey, the brown who always looked as though he had a smile on his face, tried to wedge his way between her knees and got caught in her ankle-length skirt. "Chill, Joey."

Piper, the blonde, noticed the extra attention and squirmed closer, stepping on her foot.

"All right, all right. Sit."

Both dogs obeyed immediately. She went to a covered bin on the back porch to scoop out two bowls of dog food and placed them on the floor just inside the door.

The sound of crunching nearly obliterated the reporter's next softly spoken announcement. "The gentleman in the blue suit is the mayor's assistant. Since we've spotted him, it leads us to believe the mayor will be arriving on the scene at any moment."

Lisa poured herself a glass of milk and glanced at faces as the camera panned the crowd. A few of her pet-owner clients caught her attention. "Are people really taking this seriously? I know I had a fork out."

On the counter beside the television was a stack of mail, including a couple of registered letters she'd been ignoring, and she picked one up. "I don't think they send a letter if you've won the lottery. Do they? They phone you, probably."

That would have been a problem, too. She'd been having trouble with her antiquated answering machine for a couple of weeks and knew she'd been missing messages from clients. A new one just wasn't in the budget.

She glanced at the return address on the envelope and discovered the street number for the courthouse. Last time she'd had to sign for something, it had been a notification of reassessed property taxes and an adjusted fee. The real adjustment had been eating tuna for three months to make ends meet. She tossed the envelope back on the pile of mail.

The house had been a steal, so she couldn't complain. She'd inherited half upon her grandmother's death and bought the other half from her old aunt Gert's estate after the woman had passed on eight years ago.

Lisa had come to live here with her gran and her aunt Gert when she was twelve and her mother had died. Only minimal changes had been made in all those years. She kept the dark woodwork, faded wallpaper, hardwood floors, crocheted doilies and vintage furniture well cared for. The house was her link to family and familiarity, her haven and her security. It was the only place she found solitude and escape from the stigma of being the descendent of a town pariah.

"The crowd outside Town Hall waits breathlessly for the true owner of the gold mine to be announced. Over the past months, gold fever has swept the town. Here's Mayor Brookhurst now."

Portly and balding, the mayor sported a handlebar mustache that came in handy each year when he starred as the sheriff with the Olde Time Players who put on skits during the summer festival. Because of his penchant for melodramatic acting, Lisa had trouble taking him seriously now.

"This day will go down in Thunder Canyon's history!" he predicted. "The economy of our town is about to take a turn for the better. We all knew the mine owner could be someone among us. And it is! We have a millionaire living in our midst!"

A buzz of excitement shot through the crowd gathered downtown. Lisa shook her head at the foolishness of the people who thought they were going to get rich quick.

"Humans are born into their lives and have to make of it what they will," she said to the dogs. "Nobody hands anybody a fortune on a platter."

At the ding of the microwave, she took out her dinner and seated herself at the chrome-and-red-Formica table.

"First I'd like to acknowledge and thank Brad Vaughn and Emily Stanton. These two were instrumental in the discovery of the mine's ownership. Without their investigation, we'd all still be wondering."

"Or not."

At her voice, Joey looked up and smiled.

She raised her glass of milk in a toast.

"After much researching of the Queen of Hearts claim," the mayor said, "it has been documented and proven that ownership over the years went from the original filer to Bart Divine to Lily Divine, who later became Lily Divine Harding."

The name of her infamous ancestor caught Lisa's attention. The bite she'd taken stuck in her throat and she laid down her fork. Lily Divine, Lisa's great-great-grandmother, was reputed to have been the owner of a brothel in Thunder Canyon; rumors abounded to this day.

Lisa's attention focused on what the man was saying.

The mayor held up a framed document and continued. "Lily mortgaged the deed to Amos Douglas in 1890. Proof has been uncovered that after Amos's death, his wife Catherine intended to return the deed to Lily, but the paperwork was never filed. Here's what this all boils down to, ladies and gentleman. Lily Divine was the legal owner of the claim at the time of her death."

"Wow, boys. My great-great-grandma owned a gold mine. I hope this doesn't mean people are going to ask me about it. Or about her." Unease slid into the pit of her belly at the thought of being singled out. She'd spent her whole life avoiding the rumors and the stigma surrounding the legend.

The camera zoomed in for a close-up of the mayor, and a hush fell over the crowd. "Today we know that the rightful owner of the Queen of Hearts gold mine is… *Lisa Jane Martin,* a lifetime resident of Thunder Canyon and the only living descendent of Lily Divine Harding."

The last bite Lisa'd taken swelled to the size of a grapefruit behind her breastbone and wouldn't come up or go down. She choked and tried to breathe, to swallow, to do anything but strangle. She stumbled to the chipped porcelain sink and ran a glass of water. She must have heard wrong!

After two glasses of water, the bite went down. She grabbed a paper towel and wiped her chin. When her eyes stopped watering, she turned back to the TV.

Reporters were vying to ask questions and *her* name kept being mentioned! It was definitely her name. She stared and turned up the volume just in case her hearing had been affected by her near choking death.

"So far Miss Martin hasn't responded to our attempts to reach her."

Her gaze shot to the registered letters. *Oh, crap.*

"But we've learned her address and she will be contacted immediately."

"Oh, no." She was going to throw up. There was nothing worse than attention. Nothing. Lisa went *out of her way* to go unnoticed. She'd always been an introvert. Always.

She'd have to escape before they found her. She yanked her denim jacket from the back of the kitchen chair and shrugged into it, fighting with the collar that stubbornly turned under.

Grabbing one of her four key rings, she stared at the keys to dozens of homes. Homes with pets counting on her for their daily walk or for their food and care while their owners were away. She couldn't run out on her animals. They'd be unattended and no one would know.

There were three dogs in her fenced-in backyard right now, pets in her care during their owners' trips. She couldn't just leave, and she had no one to take over for her. She wandered blindly toward the front of the house wondering how she could avoid this. She'd had to live down Lily Divine's reputation her whole life. Gran and Aunt Gert had been sympathetic and accepting, but they were her father's family, not her mother's. They hadn't shared the black mark of a hussy forebear.

Reeling with confusion, Lisa paused in the hall and leaned back against the papered wall.

Piper came to comfort her first, and she bent forward to receive his devoted concern. Joey followed, finding her ear and giving it a swipe with his tongue.

She had just dried her ear on her sleeve when the doorbell rang.

Her gaze jerked upward.

The dogs barked.

Without thinking, she headed for the entrance. Both dogs ran ahead of her, and she tripped over Piper, catching the doorknob to steady herself. Instinctively she opened the door.

People. A lot of them. Flashes went off, blinding her. A dozen cameras whirred, and boom mikes swung over the heads of the reporters who crowded her front porch. She realized her mistake too late. Barking frantically at all the strangers, her dogs darted out into the throng.

"Have you been following the story of the Queen of Hearts?"

"What are you going to do with the money?"

"Miss Martin, look this way. Are you planning to mine right away?"

"Over here, Miss Martin! What's your favorite charity?"

"What about environmental protection?"

Frazzled, Lisa tried to see over and around the inquiring reporters in hopes of spotting her dogs. Even if she had an answer, she wouldn't have spoken in public—and definitely not before a television camera.

"Piper! Come!" She pushed her way through the crush and down the porch stairs. "Joey! Heel!"

"Miss Martin, just a few questions, please."

She spotted traitorous Joey making friends with a blond woman in a black pantsuit with pink trim. His tail wagged and he was smiling at her. Lisa made a lunge and grabbed his collar. "Heel."

Piper, obviously the smarter of the two, had a photographer backed up against the trunk of her oak tree and was growling menacingly. She'd never seen him bite anyone, but this fellow would have made a good start, judging from the camera on his shoulder.

After seizing Piper, she dragged both dogs back to the house, across the porch, then slammed and locked the door in the wake of the television and newspaper personnel.

"I hope you boys did your business out there just now, 'cause we're not opening that door again."

The doorbell rang and she covered her ears at the shrill barks that followed. "Get off my property! I'm calling the police!" she shouted through the door.

The doorbell didn't ring again, but the porch floor creaked, and an occasional peek through the lace curtains revealed that several curious information seekers still waited out front to catch her. Eventually she would have to let the dogs out the back. Eventually she would have to feed her clients' dogs. Sooner or later she'd have to go for groceries or starve. The stomach ache that had come on wasn't from hunger, though. It was a sick vulnerability that ached all the way through to her innards.

The phone rang.

For a minute she just listened to the persistent jangle. She'd had so much trouble retrieving messages, she'd gotten fed up with the hassle and had turned off the machine. The phone continued to ring.

If she had caller ID, she'd know whether it was a pet owner or a reporter, she thought belatedly. Until this moment she'd always thought paying to know who was calling—when you could just pick up the phone and see—was a ridiculous expense.

Lisa walked to the kitchen and picked up the receiver on a bright yellow dial wall phone. "Hello?"

"Miss Martin," the male voice said. "This is Mayor Brookhurst's assistant. Congratulations! The mayor would like to invite you to Town Hall so we can present you with the deed to the Queen of Hearts and get a couple of signatures. Just official red-tape stuff but necessary. We thought this would be a good time because the local newspeople are still on the scene."

"I'm not walking out my door."

"Excuse me?"

"I don't know how there could be any reporters left there, because they've overrun my yard and my porch and are trampling my petunias."

"It's a lot of excitement, isn't it? Thunder Canyon's never had so many tourists. I'm told we'll be on the national news this evening."

"I don't want to be a news story—national, local or late breaking. Nothing. And I want these guys out of my yard."

"But, Miss Martin, this is a huge story. You've just inherited a gold mine."

"I don't want it."

"But— But—" He sputtered for a moment. "I'm sorry, but it's yours."

She hung up.

Another peek revealed cars and news-station vans parked along the tree-lined street and people milling in her front yard, the shadows of the boldest haunting her front porch.

The backyard entered her thoughts, and she bolted through the house to look out the window in the rear

door. A few casually dressed men walked the perimeter of the six-foot chain-link fence, from inside of which
the collie and the sheltie barked. The dachshund wagged
his tail and ran in circles.

Lisa ordered her dogs to stay while she opened the
door and called to the others. "Brigette! Monty! Aggie!
Come in!" She made kissing noises, and the three dogs
darted inside. She promptly shut the door and locked it.
She wasn't about to open a door again without a good
reason.

The visiting pets found the food she'd put out for
Joey and Piper, and a growling match ensued until she
got out more bowls. The crunching intensified. *Oh, dear.*
Poop. Poop was a good reason to open the door, but she
wouldn't think about that until the time came.

Her phone rang again. She considered taking it off
the hook, but something drove her to pick it up and
listen.

"Lisa? Lisa, this is Emily Stanton. I've been involved
in the case of finding the owner of the mine."

Lisa remembered seeing the woman introduced on
the news.

"I'm right outside your front door. I promise to respect your privacy. I'd like to do whatever I can to
help you. We need to talk, and there are some legal
matters that need your attention. Can we talk?
Please?"

"I'm not talking to any reporters."

"I'm not asking you to. I'm asking for a few minutes
of your time to go over this situation. Just the two of us."

Lisa didn't say anything.

"Tell you what—I'll call the mayor right now. He'll contact the sheriff and have the newspeople removed. Does that show my good faith?"

"You could do that?"

"I'll do it right now."

Ten minutes later Lisa saw half a dozen sheriff's vehicles pull up alongside the other cars on the street. Officers spoke to reporters and ushered them away from Lisa's yard.

Lisa craned to see the woman standing near the front door. She moved to the foyer and called, "Emily?"

"I'm still here."

Lisa opened the door six inches to peer out. A young woman with straight, shoulder-length brown hair and green eyes gazed back at her. Lisa opened the door and Emily slipped in as a camera whirred.

Lisa closed the door and locked it.

Five dogs surrounded Emily, and her eyebrows rose in surprise. "Oh, my. You're a dog lover."

"Yes. But they're not all mine. I pet sit."

"I think I heard that somewhere. Your business is called Puppy Love?"

She nodded. "It seemed like I was always taking care of someone's pet when I was in high school. It just sort of turned into my livelihood."

"So, you bring pets home with you?"

"Only by special arrangement. Normally I go to their homes. I walk dogs during the day when their owners are at work, or I go a couple times a day when people are on vacation."

They glanced at each other in the awkward way people who don't know each other do.

"I work for Vaughn Associates," Emily said. "At least, I did until just a little while ago when my boss proposed to me on television."

"I must have been choking during that part. Congratulations."

"Thank you. Anyway, we're a private investigation firm hired to track the gold-mine heir." She gestured toward Lisa as she corrected, "Or heiress."

Lisa gave her a weak smile. "I don't want a gold mine."

Lisa noticed Emily's glance at the hallway slide to the living room. So what if her house looked as though it had been furnished and decorated fifty years ago? It had. She liked it this way.

"No, really, I like my house and everything just the way it is."

"We're talking a lot of money here," Emily said. "I don't want to tell you what to do, but...lives could change. We're talking about the economy of Thunder Canyon. About not only how your life can be enriched but what you could do with the profits. Think about it, Lisa. Haven't you thought of things you would do if you had money? I have. I'd be able to pay for my younger sister to finish college. And I've always thought I'd start a scholarship for young women. Isn't there something you've always dreamed you could do if you had the resources?"

Lisa shrugged. "The humane societies are underfunded and understaffed. I'd build an animal shelter. A no-kill facility where pets could live if no one adopted them."

Emily smiled. "You can do that now."

"Are you sure this is all…legal? This is for real?"

"It's for real. You own the Queen of Hearts. Caleb Douglas's experts have assessed a substantial vein. Because of all the gold diggers swarming the area, the Douglases arranged security some time ago. You'll be responsible for taking that over and making arrangements for how you want to proceed with the mining."

Just the thought made Lisa feel panicked. "I don't know anything about mining."

"There are people to help you. I suggest you hire a lawyer first thing. Someone with your best interests at heart, someone you trust. Then a financial manager."

Lisa passed a shaking hand over her eyes. "It's too much to think about."

Emily leaned over the back of the sofa to peer out between the lace curtains on the window. "The only car left out front on this side is my rental. The mayor has ordered the press to stay off your property and on the other side of the street. I'll take you to Town Hall, and you can file a restraining order against the press. Then I'll stay with you while you sign the deed papers. Okay?"

Lisa didn't know that she had much choice. People were not going to leave her alone until this was taken care of and the news blew over. "I'll put the dogs in their kennels."

Emily nodded.

The afternoon passed in a blur of meetings and legal talk. Lisa was placed in touch with the Montana Mining Association, several environmental agencies, The Office of Historical Preservation and the Bureau of Land Management. The operational and engineering issues would have to be decided, and she hadn't a clue what to do. Head spinning, Lisa just wished she could evade all the publicity and trouble.

She took Emily's advice and hired a lawyer. A woman Emily recommended. Bernadine Albright was more than willing to clear her afternoon schedule to meet with Lisa. Holding the press at bay, Emily drove Lisa to the lawyer's office.

Complete strangers were excited and animated, congratulating her and bringing her soft drinks and cups of coffee. The inheritance and the experience seemed unreal. Complicated. Overwhelming. She didn't want her life to change.

Lisa had too much to absorb and think about, and this was all happening too fast. More than anything else she feared was the fact that her life was never going to be the same.

Riley Douglas handed a stack of papers to the secretary who'd just arrived at their downtown building for the day and strode down the hall to his father's office.

At sixty-six, Caleb still had a thick head of silver hair and a physique toned from keeping a hand in the working operation of his ranch. He'd kept his recent bouts with heart disease a secret from their colleagues and the community, and Riley was one of the few to recognize fatigue and stress taking a toll on the man. Right now Caleb's face was red with anger. Riley picked up the phone and punched in a number. "I'm calling Dr. Simms. You're not supposed to be getting riled up like this."

Focused on this latest ghastly situation, Caleb waved

Riley's comment away. The enormous black-lacquer armoire was open, the television tuned to the local news yet again. On Caleb's desk was last evening's paper as well as today's special morning edition, both displaying the pages which relayed the gold-mine story.

"We've got to do something," Caleb insisted. "That's been Douglas land for four generations. No bohemian dogsitter is going to take it away from us."

Waiting to speak with the doctor, Riley watched footage of the young woman for the hundredth time. First they showed her chasing two dogs out her front door. Dressed in a long skirt, tennis shoes and a denim jacket, she was a fashion casualty if he'd ever seen one. Her dark hair could use an extreme makeover, as well, parted on one side and sprouting wild ringlets that fell to her shoulders.

She stared at the camera as though she'd been caught committing a crime, then jerked into motion, calling her dogs. She tripped over the huge beasts, tripped over the hem of her wallpaper-print skirt, then retreated back into her house and slammed the door.

"Doc, can you spare a call to my father's downtown office? I'll never get him to yours. He's taking his blood-pressure medicine, but I don't like the way he looks. Thanks." Riley hung up and kept watching.

The next video clip was taken as Lisa Martin and Emily Stanton approached Town Hall. With swinging dark hair, Emily was cool and professional, guiding the dowdy heiress through the crowd of reporters on the street and into the building, with the assistance of half a dozen police officers. This little town had never seen so many law-enforcement officials. The state patrol and the sheriff's department had been on call since early reports of the gold strike had been leaked months ago.

The following shot was of Lisa Jane Martin riding in the passenger side of a silver Chrysler Intrepid as Emily pulled away followed by a camera crew. They'd shown these same clips over and over since the night before. Reporters had used every rags-to-riches phrase they could come up with and had dubbed the Martin girl Cinderella.

And then came the picture someone had culled from a past Thunder Canyon High yearbook, a photograph of a dark-haired girl who looked vaguely familiar. According to the caption under the likeness, she'd graduated two years behind him, so it was possible he'd seen her in the halls. Nothing remarkable about her. Nothing that would have garnered more than a passing glance.

She was either divorced or never married, he guessed, since her name was still Martin and she lived in the house where she'd lived with relatives since her mother's death. After one day of news, he knew more about Lisa Jane Martin than he did about the women he dated.

"She's single," he said thoughtfully.

His father finally removed his gaze from the television. His eyebrows rose and a glimmer of hope sparkled in his eyes. "Yes. Yes, she is."

Chapter Two

Lisa opened her eyes and stared at the plaster ceiling. Saw the same two cracks that had been there the day before and the week before that and the month before that. She sat up, and beside her both retrievers woke and yawned. Joey placed his front feet on the floor first, stretching with his hind feet on the bed, then slowly stepped down. Piper bounded from the bed in one leap and danced in front of her while she stumbled to the bathroom. "Hold on a sec."

A few minutes later, she peered out the curtained window of the back door, let the three dogs out of the utility room and loosed all five into the backyard. The click of a shutter reached her through the morning stillness. She couldn't see anyone, but sun momentarily glinted off a distant object. There was a wooded area behind her house, and it *was* possible someone could wait out there with a telephoto lens. "Get a life!" she shouted and shut the door.

While she made coffee and poured orange juice, she watched the dogs through the window over the sink. They seemed unconcerned with anything other than their morning sniff-and-pee routine, so she guessed all was clear.

She turned on the television, looking for her morning show and instead saw her own image plastered across the screen. She raised one hand to her hair in horror.

"Oh, my. Oh, my." The Lisa on the screen looked as if she'd been struck by lightning coming out of the Salvation Army store. Her goal had always been anonymity, but her appearance called attention by its very weirdness.

The clips of her with Emily emphasized her drab fluffiness next to Emily's clean lines.

What could be so interesting that all those feet of film were being taken of *her?* A million dollars, she gleaned from the commentary and shook her head. She still had no concept of her inheritance.

The next image induced a groan. She'd always detested that high school picture. While other girls' parents had forked over an arm and a leg for touched-up studio work, she'd found the very least expensive photographer in the area. She'd never thought it would make a difference. Who would see it after all?

Lisa flipped channels. The very same picture was plastered on CNN footage. *Only a few million people had seen it.*

Mind reeling, she turned off the TV. The real problem was how she was going to take care of her pets today without being followed. She had filled out paperwork for a restraining order and the judge had signed it. The press was required to stay a hundred feet away from her and out of her yard. She had twelve homes to visit this morning, then meetings with the security people and the mining association in the afternoon.

She let the dogs in and they ate while she fixed herself breakfast. She slipped on her neon-green garden boots and washed out the kennels and runs, filled bowls with water, then locked the dogs into the shaded runs for the day.

After showering, she considered her wardrobe. Whatever she donned, it would be on the news tonight. A pretty mind-boggling concept. There wasn't much choice. Only long skirts hung in her closet, so she chose one and dressed, found a white ball cap to hide her hair and donned a pair of sunglasses.

Her rusty old green Blazer started with a puff of smoke, but it started, and she pulled out of her drive. A glance in the rearview mirror showed three SUVs with satellite dishes following her.

She'd seen clips of Madonna, J.Lo and Gwyneth Paltrow being hounded by reporters, and she'd wondered how they ever managed to go anywhere in private. That she was facing the same problem today was surreal.

Having an audience took the joy from a task she usually enjoyed. Caring for her pets, walking the dogs and knowing they were getting attention, was normally rewarding. Today she felt as if she were under a microscope. And she was. She took three dogs at a time in her Blazer, walking them on leashes through the park and politely picking up after them with plastic bags, which she disposed of in trash barrels.

"Heiress picks up collie poop," she said to herself. "Film at eleven." Jake, the collie in question, barked at the cameraman across the street. The dog's owner drove to a nearby town to work and paid Lisa to walk the animal once a day during his absence. Lisa scratched Jake's ears. "Unnerving, isn't it, to do your business with paparazzi watching? Maybe a talent scout will discover you and you'll be the next fast-food icon. You like tacos?"

Dogs eventually walked and cats all fed, Lisa drove home to grab a quick lunch. A new white Expedition pulled into her drive behind her, and a forty-something woman got out. "I saw Aggie on CNN last night! You, too, of course."

Lisa nodded. "Smile. You'll probably see yourself tonight."

Barbara Cooper, owner of the dachshund in Lisa's backyard, glanced around and fluffed her hair with her fingers. "Are you serious?"

"'Fraid so. Did you have a good trip?"

Barbara tugged the front of her shirt neatly into place and followed Lisa into the house. "It was work, what can I say? Did Aggie behave herself?"

"A sweetheart, as always."

When they reached the kitchen, Barbara took a check from her purse and handed it to Lisa. She was one of Lisa's longtime clients, though they'd never had a personal conversation until now. "So you own the gold mine?"

Lisa nodded. "That's what they tell me. It's official, because I signed all the paperwork yesterday. It's still not real, though."

"What are you going to do?" Barbara asked as they walked out to the backyard.

After handing the woman Aggie's retractable leash, Lisa opened the kennel door and the dachshund shot out. "What do you mean?"

Barbara knelt and scooped up her pet. "Surely you won't be taking in dogs anymore. I don't know where I'll find someone else I trust who really cares for Aggie the way you do."

Lisa petted Aggie's head. "I can't imagine not taking in my dogs," she replied. "They're like friends who come to see me."

Barbara fastened the leash on the dog's collar and set her pet down. "We'll see. Somehow I don't think you'll be interested next time. You'll be busy."

"Doing what?"

"Spending money. And I won't blame you. That's what I'd be doing." She walked toward the side gate. "Well, congratulations. And thanks."

Lisa watched her go, checked the water dishes and fixed herself a peanut-butter-and-potato-chip sandwich.

When she walked out her front door, a dark blue limo waited at the curb. The driver, who'd been standing beside the rear door, tipped his hat. "Miss Martin."

She took several steps forward. Mayor Brookhurst had told her he'd work out the details of her meetings. "This is for me?"

He nodded. "Yes, miss. Mr. Douglas sent me for you."

Everyone in Thunder Canyon knew of Caleb Douglas. Even Lisa, who shied away from people and the places they gathered, had heard the talk. Occasionally Lisa cared for Adele's enormous poodle, but she'd never run into Caleb during any of her visits.

Gran had never had much use for the man or his high-handed wife, but because of their wealth and property holdings, none could deny the Douglases were pillars of the community.

"You're taking me to the security meeting?"

"Yes, miss."

There had been talk recently about how the Douglases had come to claim ownership of the Queen of Hearts mine. She'd learned from Emily that the Douglases had hired her firm to prove their legal claim, but that the investigation had proven otherwise.

Whether she liked it or not, Lisa was up to her neck in this gold-mine business. She was going to have to be better informed, she concluded, slipping inside the limo and seating herself on the soft leather as the driver closed the door. She had a lot more questions for Emily.

She surveyed the elegant interior and marveled at over half a dozen sparkling glasses set into wells on a minibar. Absently she wondered what was a good peanut-butter chaser. Noticing then that the driver was smoothly driving out of Thunder Canyon, Lisa experienced a touch of apprehension. She tapped on the Plexiglas divider. It rolled down silently and the driver asked, "Yes, Miss Martin?"

"Where are we going?"

"To Mr. Douglas's office at the Lazy D."

"Oh. Okay."

The countryside was beautiful, so she enjoyed the scenery. Horses grazed behind miles of white fence, and seed-tipped hay fields waved in the sunlight. Finally they passed through a gate proclaiming the Lazy D ranch. Since Lisa looked after Adele's dog while the couple vacationed, she was familiar with the grandeur of the home. Instead of heading for the circular drive where the main home, guesthouse, foreman's cottage and bunkhouse sat, however, the driver took a road that wound away. Did Caleb have offices elsewhere?

After another half mile, she was getting ready to tap on the Plexiglas again when the driver pulled to a stop before a sprawling stone house and got out to assist her.

"Go on in, miss. Mr. Douglas is expecting you."

Lisa hesitantly climbed the stairs and opened the door. She entered into a huge foyer. Shiny wood floors reflected a massive hall table beneath a chandelier. Definitely not the same stuffy decor as the other place. "Hello?"

"Miss Martin."

She turned, expecting the silver-haired man she'd seen on the news. Instead a younger man, tall with black hair and intense green eyes, greeted her. Her immediate reaction was that she should turn and run right back out the door, but her feet were rooted to the spot. He wore a sport jacket, white shirt, jeans and boots. Casual attire, but on this man they made her feel even more inappropriately dressed. She'd have taken off her ball cap, but her hair was matted to her head by now.

She did slip off the sunglasses and drop them into her denim handbag. She felt exposed in his presence...vulnerable. And she didn't like it.

He strode forward and extended a hand. "Riley Douglas."

In the flesh. He was taller and leaner than she remembered from school, his features sharpened to devastating virility by the past ten years. He looked even better than he had then. "I know—I mean, yes."

She took his strong, warm hand for an instant, and then he released hers.

"I was expecting...your father."

"He'll be along. I handled all the security for the mine, so I thought I should bring you up to speed and answer any questions. He does want to meet you later, though. Come on back to my office. I asked you here early so we could get acquainted and go over a few things. Once the security team arrives, there won't be much chance for us to talk privately."

Lisa followed him down a hall bordered on one side by floor-to-ceiling windows that let in the sun and offered a stunning view of the ranch.

She'd been expecting dark wood, but his office was all black leather, chrome and glass. On a counter in one corner, two coffeepots were just finishing perking, but he gestured to the wet bar. "Care for a drink?"

This was a good-old-boy operation, she surmised, and probably a good many deals were negotiated over drinks. If his associates drank in the limo, as well, how did anyone make it through meetings sober?

"No, thanks."

"The wine's been breathing for about fifteen minutes," he said.

Lisa glanced at the bottle sitting in a bucket of ice.

Several others stood at the ready on the bar nearby. She did enjoy a glass of wine now and then, and the labels on those bottles indicated he hadn't picked them up at the same grocery store where she shopped. And he'd already opened one, she rationalized.

"Sure. Thanks."

He picked up the bottle and poured a stemmed glass three-quarters full.

She accepted the wine with a twinge of regret, because she knew she wouldn't drink a whole bottle, and it looked expensive.

"Does it suit you?"

"What? Oh." She tasted the white wine. It was better than anything she'd ever tried. "It's excellent."

He poured himself a tonic water and gestured for her to sit on one of the black leather sofas. She did, and he sat across from her.

"I'm glad we have this chance to meet."

No surprise that he didn't remember her. Having skipped fifth grade, Lisa had been a young freshman. She'd noticed Riley Douglas right away and secretly admired his good looks and popularity. She'd been his assigned tutor for chemistry, and spending two evenings a week together had afforded more than enough opportunity for her to develop a full-blown crush. He'd always been polite and friendly enough, though distant. She hadn't been his type then any more than she was now, and he'd easily dismissed their relationship after he'd passed his class.

It had been okay then. It was okay now. "Yes," was all she said.

"Would you like to go over the arrangements I had worked out with the security people? You might prefer to hire a company of your own choice, but we've used Weber Security exclusively for the last eight years. I can recommend them highly."

"Exactly what needs to be protected? I don't have any idea."

"Do you remember how this whole gold-mine thing came about?"

"Vaguely."

"In February the son of the high school coach disappeared."

"I remember that. The Stevenson boy was found in the mine shaft and rescued."

Riley nodded. "And a rescue worker found a gold nugget. That started the gold fever. On more than one occasion after that vandals broke into the cordoned-off mine site."

"I saw news reports that some of them were injured. The clinic was hopping."

"Things got pretty crazy. Anyway, that property had been counted as part of Douglas holdings for generations, but suddenly our ownership was questioned. Believing our claim would be verified, we secured the area. We've had a perimeter guard and armed security at the site round-the-clock since mid-February, in part to protect what we thought was our property as well as to prevent any more mining injuries."

Security guards. Oh, my.

"Now that the investigators have proven the land belonged to Lily Divine—and, in that case, to *me*—all along, will you want to be reimbursed for those costs?" Lisa was beginning to question the wisdom of coming here, of talking to a Douglas without her lawyer. "I think I should call my lawyer. May I use your phone?"

"Of course." He gestured to the desktop. "I assure you I wasn't thinking of reimbursement."

"It would seem only right," she insisted.

"It's petty, Miss Martin, and I won't entertain further discussion in the matter."

She raised her eyebrows. "Excuse me." She punched numbers, and Bernadine Albright took her call immediately.

"You were wise to call me, Lisa. I'll be right there. Don't agree to anything until then."

Lisa hung up the phone. "She's on her way."

Riley raised his glass. "Good decision. Until she arrives, we'll get to know each other a little better."

Lisa didn't want the wine to go to waste, so she accepted another glass. She glanced out the double glass doors that opened onto a brick patio. In the distance she saw a modern red barn. "Is this where you live?"

"And work. Built the house a few years ago."

"You run the ranch?"

"I help. My father is the hands-on rancher. I'm the financial manager. Over the past couple years I've devoted myself to expanding our real-estate ventures."

She remembered reading about him going off to college and later coming home with a degree in finance. Lisa walked to the doors and looked out over the pastureland where several horses grazed.

"Do you ride?" he asked from directly behind her.

Goose bumps rose on her shoulders and arms at his nearness. "I used to ride when Mr. McKinley had his stables north of town."

"Poor old nags." Riley chuckled. "They were long in the tooth and not much for looking at."

"Not everyone has his own breeding stock in the backyard," she replied.

He shrugged off her comment. "Maybe you'd like to come out and ride sometime. Anytime. Consider it an open invitation."

Riley Douglas was only one of the many people who'd suddenly found it in their hearts to befriend her. Funny how people who hadn't given her the time of day a week ago were now pursuing her attention.

She definitely questioned this man's sincerity. She may have inherited a gold mine, but she hadn't gotten any better looking.

She moved back into the room and studied the pieces of artwork. Modern paintings and a few sculptures. No photographs. She couldn't recall hearing mention of Riley ever marrying. Sometimes local gossip had him paired with one particular woman or another, all of them out of her league. Why his marital status should matter was questionable, but she sure was wondering.

"Did you do your own decorating in here?"

He nodded. "Is it that obvious? Pretty hit-and-miss, actually. I just pick up things I like when I'm traveling."

The place seemed a little sparse and modern for her taste, but what did she know? She hadn't spent money on more than a plug-in air freshener for her house in the last five years. And the only stuff she picked up while traveling was dog poop.

There was a knock at a side door, and it opened without Riley's consent. A thin woman wearing a dark green pantsuit carried a tray of small sandwiches into the room and placed it on the low glass coffee table. Lisa caught herself imagining setting anything edible on a table this low in her house.

The woman turned to the counter area, where she disposed of coffee grounds and set out several glossy black mugs, each one with a fancy *D* on the side.

"Do you need anything else, Mr. Douglas?"

"This looks great, Marge, thank you."

After she'd gone, Riley gestured to the food. "Help yourself."

Lisa perched on the leather sofa and looked over the selection with interest. Riley politely waited until she made a decision, then seated himself and picked up a napkin and a couple of sandwiches.

The thick chicken salad had chunks of walnuts and sliced grapes, and Lisa wondered how many she could consume without looking like an oinker. They sure beat her peanut-butter-and-potato-chip special.

Riley refilled her glass, and she felt a lot more comfortable here than she had at first. If he was trying to soften her up for something with food and wine, it was working. It was a good thing she'd called Bernadine. She was going to need a designated driver.

Her lawyer showed up a few minutes later. When Riley poured the woman a glass of brandy and offered her a sandwich, she met Lisa's gaze with a knowing look. But she ate and drank as their discussion got under way.

Riley showed them the contract he had with Weber Security and explained the situation. "Weber is willing to switch the contract over to your company without a hitch. Have you incorporated?"

"Lisa and I are working on that today," Bernadine said.

"This is all happening so fast," Lisa told him. "There's so much to do and to understand."

"Hiring Ms. Albright was wise," Riley told her. "And having her present when you make decisions is to your benefit. But in addition I believe you're going to need a financial manager."

Emily had told her the same thing.

"*And* an advisor," he added. "Someone to help you with investments. Someone who knows the markets and can help you manage and save money."

Lisa glanced at Bernadine, who nodded. "He's right. I can look over the legal stuff, but money management and investment are out of my field."

"Is there someone like that around here?" Lisa asked.

"A manager and an advisor are two different jobs." Riley eased back comfortably on the sofa. "I'm a manager, and I'd be the best man to work with."

"But isn't that a conflict of interest?"

"How so? You pay me for my services and I make money off your money. I'd be doing the best I knew how, just like I do for my own holdings and my father's."

"Do you have the time? Surely you have a lot on your plate right now. I've read about the ski-resort project. That has to be a huge responsibility."

"Thinking the mine was a Douglas property, I had already cleared time to handle it. This way I'd still be involved, but in your employ."

Those words perked her interest more than all the others. "You'd work for me?"

"More or less. Yes."

The concept was just too delicious. Riley Douglas, son of one of the richest families in Montana, working for the town dog walker, the great-great-granddaughter of Thunder Canyon's infamous Lily Divine. Lisa wanted to giggle. She held her exuberance inside with considerable fortitude, so it came out as more of a hiccup.

Bernadine glanced at her.

"Excuse me." She hid her smile behind a cocktail napkin.

"Think about it for a day or so," Riley suggested. "We'll talk again. How's that?"

"Unbelievable," she replied.

"What's that?"

"It's doable," she answered. "But you said it was two jobs. What about the investment part?"

"I work with someone who's always on top of things. You could either hire him or ask him to recommend someone. Phil Wagner has advised my father and I for several years, and I can hook you up. He's a savvy market man."

Riley did seem to have the know-how and the contacts she needed. His willingness to participate was flattering but a little unnerving.

Caleb arrived next, dressed in a western-cut sport jacket and a beige Stetson. He hung the hat on a rack inside the door and joined them.

"Dad, this is Bernadine Albright."

"We've met," Bernadine said, and extended a hand. Caleb leaned forward to greet her.

"And you're Lisa Jane Martin," Caleb said before Riley could introduce her. He took in her appearance with keen interest. "I guess the cap is your disguise?"

"It must not be working. You knew who I was."

"I've seen you on television. Is my son being a good host?"

"As hosts go, he ranks right up there with the best I've known." No man had offered her heavenly chicken sandwiches or plied her with wine before, so Riley was the best so far.

The security team arrived then. Lisa was disappointed that the rest of the time would be devoted to actual business, but the hard edges of Weber Security's facts and figures were softly rounded by the incredible buzz she'd acquired.

Craig Murphy headed the organization and had a manner of making people feel that he was in charge and that things were taken care of. Lisa liked and trusted him immediately. He showed her the initial police reports, maps detailing the whereabouts of his people at all times and a list of the men working the mine and explained the success of their plan thus far.

"These are the arrangements you made with Mr. Douglas?" she asked.

"Yes," he concurred. "And if this strategy works for you, we'll continue without change or interruption and simply switch the contracts over to you."

"We're not sure exactly how that's going to work

yet," Bernadine told him and explained their need to incorporate. "There are a lot of things still being worked out."

"Tell you what," Riley said. "Let's leave it the way it is for the time being. I'll pick up the tab. As soon as Miss Martin has her corporation set up and some money in her accounts, we'll do the new paperwork then."

"And reimburse you then?" Lisa asked.

"Only for services from this date forward," he answered.

"We'll need a simple agreement in writing," Bernadine added.

"Fine by me," Craig said.

Lisa and Bernadine concurred and accepted Riley's offer.

The meeting ended, and Lisa was one of the last to walk out of his office behind Bernadine. Riley and his father accompanied them.

"I'm glad we had this opportunity to meet," Caleb said.

"Likewise." She pulled out her sunglasses and slipped them on. "We meet with the Montana Mining Association this afternoon."

"Feel free to call me anytime if you need an opinion or advice," Riley told her. He gestured to the limousine at the curb. "Your ride."

"I'm riding with Bernadine from here, thanks."

She got into the lawyer's crème-colored New Yorker and glanced out the window at the two men who watched the car pull away.

"What kind of feeling did you get?" Bernadine asked.

Her feelings for Riley Douglas had been adolescent yearnings she'd outgrown years ago. "Why? What did you see?"

"Well, with Caleb I'm not sure that what you see is what you get, and I suspect the apple doesn't fall far from the tree."

"You don't trust Riley to manage us?"

"That's the odd thing. He's a hell of a financier, and we'd be missing out on using his genius brain for handling money if we didn't hook up with him. I *would* trust him as your manager. He knows what he's doing. But he probably has an ulterior motive, and we'd better have our loins girded for whatever that may be."

"What might his motive be?"

Bernadette cocked a brow at her. "Hello?"

"Money."

The woman merely nodded as she drove.

"Forewarned is girded, right? We let him do his money thing, and we watch for anything fishy."

"Watching is good," Bernadine replied.

Lisa thought about all the times she'd watched Riley Douglas. Watched him frown as he struggled with chemistry homework; watched him stroll the halls with that distinctive swagger; watched him on the football field as cheerleaders swamped him. Watching Riley was no hardship.

The interesting thing this time was that he was actually paying attention to her, knew her name, had sought her out. She didn't have any illusions that his interest was in anything other than the glittering gold mine she'd inherited, but the attention was, to say the least, flattering.

She might as well enjoy her new status. Who knew what would come of it?

Chapter Three

So much for the ball cap and the sunglasses. Lisa sat cross-legged on her sofa, her Lean Cuisine Mexican dinner in her lap, and stared at the television. Tonight's recap showed her hosing out the dog runs with untamed morning hair, wearing a pink tank top with yellow polka-dot pajama bottoms and the neon-green rubber boots.

"You people suck!" She sat her dinner on the coffee table and got up to stomp across the room to the front door. She turned the bolt lock and flung open the door. "You suck! Don't you have anything better to do?"

Her neighbor, Mrs. Carlson, had been setting her sprinkler to water her rose bushes, and she straightened to stare at Lisa. She always stared at Lisa, always seemed to be censoring her every coming and going, so the stare was nothing new.

"Oh, hey, Mrs. Carlson."

Piper tried to wedge past Lisa's legs, so she closed the door to keep him in and went back to resume her place. The last image on the screen was the high school picture again, just before the news moved on to footage of a water-main break downtown. Thank God there were a few disasters to occasionally take the focus away from her.

Joey burped from beside the sofa.

Lisa lowered her gaze to the empty tray where her burritos and rice had been. The tray had barely been moved, but it looked as clean as any of the dishes in her cupboards.

She met the dog's gaze and he smiled.

"Real funny. Now I get to eat peanut butter again. That was the last dinner, and I don't want to go to the store."

She ransacked the cupboards and finally ate a handful of trail mix and poured out the expired milk.

"Okay, tomorrow I'll go to the store."

Piper laid his head on her lap when she sat at the kitchen table and opened the phone book.

"I'll get you a chewy, but none for Joey."

At his name, the retriever padded into the room and stood watching her with expectation.

"Don't complain to me about heartburn, you pig." She got up, dialed the phone on the wall and ordered a pizza.

"Lisa Martin?" the voice on the other end of the line said. "Awesome! I just saw you on TV."

"Yeah."

"That's really cool, you owning the mine and all."

"Yeah, cool."

"We'll get your pizza there right away. You want any bread sticks or a two-liter or anything?"

She remembered a couple cans of beer in the back of her fridge. "No, thanks."

An hour later, she'd eaten her fill of her pan-fried-crust pepperoni pizza, finished a beer and was watching one of her favorite romantic movies. A comfort night she'd needed badly.

Here in her private haven, she was in her zone. The dogs had edged their way onto the sofa on either side of her, and she stroked their ears and heads.

As the movie drew to an end, she blinked back tears and drew a deep breath. "Oh, my—Joey, you *dog!*"

Now her tears weren't brought on by sentiment but by the Mexican dinner the canine had consumed.

She herded both dogs to the back door and stepped out for fresh air. "You're not sleeping with me if you keep that up."

Her boys ran along the fence and sniffed. Piper growled deep in his throat. Lisa glanced at the dark sky and the woods behind the house, not liking the constant feeling of being observed. "Suppose they have infrared, too?" She waved for good measure. "Let's go back in, boys."

Their tags jingled as they joined her.

The Super Saver Mart opened at seven the next morning, and Lisa was in the parking lot waiting for the doors to be unlocked. The television vans were parked at the farthest sides of the lot.

A newer car pulled up to a front slot, and the driver glanced toward the building. Just a customer, Lisa assured herself.

She'd showered and fixed her hair before cleaning the runs that morning and she'd found a skirt that looked less like wallpaper than all the rest. Her denim jacket fit nicely, but her tennis shoes were simply the most comfortable for grocery shopping.

After glancing at her reflection in the rearview mirror and knowing her hair was hopeless, she caught sight of someone unlocking the doors from inside the store and got out of her Blazer. She refused to turn and look at the television vans as she hurried to the door.

An SUV was coming through the parking lot, as well.

It was cool inside the market, and someone was adjusting the piped-in music. Lisa got a cart and passed Joseph Martinelli building a display of boxed macaroni dinners. "Morning," the store employee said.

"Morning."

Lisa decided to stock up on nonperishables so she wouldn't have to come back for a while. She filled her cart quickly and headed for the checkout, where she glanced with trepidation toward the magazine racks. None of them sported her picture, of course, but she sympathized with Kirstie Alley, who'd been photographed at her least flattering moments. She pushed her cart on past.

The two women checkers spotted her and one said something to the other. Lisa had seen both of them in here for years and neither had ever voiced more than the total of her purchase.

Today, however, the woman checking her out said, "Beautiful morning, isn't it?"

Lisa nodded.

"Did you find everything you needed? This is the best buy this week. I got some of these nectarines the other day and my son loved them."

"They do look good." Lisa dug in her wallet for her debit card.

When she glanced up, a tall, dark-haired man was making a purchase in the other lane. She'd recognize Riley Douglas anywhere, even without his sport jacket. Buying his own groceries? How unlikely was that?

He accepted a plastic bag from the checker and turned to leave, then noticed her.

The woman was bagging Lisa's groceries.

"Well, hi," he said easily. "You're out early."

"Had to get my worms."

He gave her a blank look.

"Never mind. What brings you into town?"

He raised his bag, which clearly held only one small item. "Allergies are kicking up. Had to pick up something."

And he didn't have a prescription for that? Or a personal assistant to run his errands? He looked fine to her. No watering, itchy eyes or runny nose that she detected.

"Uh-huh. Well, I hope it does the trick."

"Carryout on five, please," the checker called.

"I'll get this," Riley said and took charge of the cart. Lisa glanced from the woman to Riley's back and followed him and her groceries out the door.

"You realize you're on *Candid Camera*," she said as they crossed the parking lot.

He glanced toward the media vehicles. "Not so candid. Is it like this everywhere you go?"

"Pretty much. They'll probably go in and interview the checker now, and tonight's news will feature my supper menu."

"Yeah, how was the pizza last night?"

She blinked. "You read that this morning?"

With a grin, he nodded.

They had reached Lisa's Blazer, and she used the key to unlock the back door. It opened with a squeak of metal, and a few flakes of rust fell to the pavement.

"I got rear-ended once," she said. "This door's never been the same." She'd used the insurance money to pay her vet bill instead of having the dent pounded out, but she didn't feel the need to share that detail.

Riley set her bags in the back, glancing at the items on top. "What kind of wine goes with rawhide strips?"

"Those aren't my dinner."

"No kidding." He finished loading her groceries and pushed the cart into a return area. "Have you been to the mine yet?"

She shook her head. Oddly enough, she wasn't even sure where the Queen of Hearts was located.

"Want to take a ride out there and have a look at your property?"

Couldn't hurt, could it? She'd been curious but too self-conscious of the stares. She gestured with her thumb to indicate their observers. "They'll follow, you know."

Riley didn't look toward the media vans. "We could lose them."

"How?"

He appeared to be thinking for a moment. "Drive out to my place. They'll follow. We'll leave your vehicle parked and take another one."

"But they'll see us leave."

"Trust me. I'll figure it out."

She shrugged. "Okay. I have to get my groceries home, then take care of a few pets. It might take me a couple hours."

He reached into his pocket and took out a tiny phone, which he flipped open. "What's your cell phone number?"

"Don't have one."

He closed the phone. "Do you have a piece of paper?"

She rummaged through her purse and found a receipt and a pen.

He jotted something down and handed both back. "That's mine. Call me when you're leaving."

She put the pen and note in her purse and got into her car.

An hour and a half later, none of the dogs questioned had answered when asked if they were having any allergy symptoms.

She stopped by the McGills' to feed their cats and change litter boxes. She asked Sassy and Callie about allergies, as well, but after being rudely ignored, she returned home, freshened up and made an attempt to tame her hair.

If she changed clothes, Riley would think she was

trying to impress him or that she cared what he thought. She wasn't and she didn't, so she wore what she had on.

Lisa called Bernadine to make sure she wasn't making a tactical error. "I'm going to see the mine site with Riley Douglas. Do you think there's a problem with that?"

"Sounds innocent enough. Unless he tries to get you to sign something. Or tries to get you naked."

Warmth infused Lisa's cheeks even though she was alone. "I wouldn't sign anything. And he's not going to try to…do the other thing you said. What made you think that?"

"You're a rich woman now. Some men find that very attractive, if you know what I mean."

"I do know and I'll be wary."

"If I was you, I'd be expecting men to fall all over me."

"Thanks for the warning, but it's not like I don't suspect ulterior motives. Let's see, last ten years, no men seeking me out. Now, today, suddenly man pays attention. I can figure it out."

"Okay. Good."

Her next call was to Riley to let him know she was leaving her house.

Lisa would rather have believed Riley was just a nice guy offering to help, but their history made her assume otherwise. She drove to the Lazy D, followed by the news vans. They parked out on the road when she pulled into his drive.

Riley led her out the back door, where his assistant, Marge, waited in the driver's seat of a Lexus. "Get down in the front," he told her, and she ducked down on the passenger side while he got into the rear and did the same.

Feeling as if she'd been zapped into an old *Dukes of Hazzard* rerun, she prayed Marge wouldn't be driving through fields or jumping any waterways. "Where are we going?"

"I'm taking you to the garage at the big house," Marge replied. "I come and go from this place all day long, so no one will think anything of it."

A few minutes of blissfully sedate driving later, they pulled into a darkened building, and an automatic door lowered.

"Thanks, Marge," Riley told the woman.

She smiled and handed Lisa a straw hat. "Anytime."

Riley led Lisa to a red sports car, held the door for her and, after pressing a garage-door opener, guided the car out into the daylight. "Put that hat on."

"If we're avoiding the newspeople, I shouldn't need it." She tossed the hat on the backseat.

No cars followed as Riley took a back road. "This way is longer, but we'll avoid the cameras."

"Works for me."

She couldn't help noticing the shape of his long fingers on the gearshift or the way his jeans stretched taut over his thighs as he drove. He was as appealing as he'd been in high school, sexier even, and the fact wasn't lost on her. That *naked* word that Bernadine had used still disturbed her, especially when she thought it in his presence.

Riley knew a back route that brought them out farther north on Thunder Canyon Road. He headed south.

"One of the first things on my agenda was to have a chain-link fence built around the entire area, including the sinkhole and the mine entrance, to protect all the land where the mine sits."

"Think it's necessary?"

"Would you lock up a million dollars or leave it out?"

"Good point."

He took an unmarked road. Four times, brown-uniformed men stationed along the way stopped the car, and each time Riley showed his identification. It wasn't long before they reached the entrance to the mine.

Two more uniformed men walked out of a canopy-style tent and approached the car. Lisa was surprised to see them carrying pistols in shoulder holsters. Their belts held walkie-talkies and nightsticks. "Looks like they're ready for an invasion."

Riley walked around to open her door, but she'd already stepped out.

"Mr. Douglas," one of the uniformed men greeted him. "I didn't recognize the car."

"We're incognito."

The guard looked Lisa over then, and recognition dawned. "Gotcha."

"Miss Martin's come to look over her property."

"It's been quiet all week," the man told them.

"That's what we like to hear."

The entrance to the mine had obviously once been completely closed up, but boards had been removed and replaced with steel beams to take the load from aging timbers.

"Is it safe?" she asked.

"Up front, it is. It's only been shored up for six hundred feet so far. We won't go farther than that."

He entered a trailer situated nearby and returned with two yellow hard hats with lights affixed and carried a high-powered flashlight. He handed Lisa one of the hats, which she placed on her head, then he led the way into the mine.

The beams from their hats bounced off the walls, creating bouncing shadows as they entered and looked around. The interior was larger and cooler than she'd expected, and lights had been strung from posts. It was obvious that a lot of work had already been done to add support and safety features. As the tunnel led them increasingly deeper and lower, their steps echoed eerily in the stillness. Lisa imagined the primitive conditions that had once existed and pictured the original owner, whoever he'd been, carving out these walls.

They walked as far as the improvements extended, and Lisa stared into the yawning darkness beyond. Nothing glittered or gleamed or screamed *gold* to her, and the musty-earth smell was stronger. Growing up, she'd read too many Nancy Drew novels to feel comfortable in the bowels of a mine. "So, somewhere in there is a lot of gold, eh?"

Her voice carried through the darkness in a ghostly echo. It took all her courage not to move closer to Riley.

"That's right," he replied, speaking softly. The low timber of his voice sent a shiver up her spine. "A vein was discovered when a rescue worker was found with the nugget after Erik Stevenson fell into the mine a few months ago. Our experts' analysis showed the vein stretches back at least another three hundred feet beyond what's been exposed and branches considerably downward."

"And this mine was thought to be played out?"

"Apparently. And forgotten over the years."

"I wonder how my great-great-grandmother came to own it."

"Apparently her father, Bart, was the second owner. He may have purchased it or won it in a card game. No way to know for sure. Upon his death, she inherited it."

"Wasn't there a story about Lily losing the mine to your ancestor?"

"One story says she owed money to Amos Douglas and he took the land as payment."

"And the other?"

"The other says he foreclosed on her property and took it."

"Aren't there records?"

"That was over a hundred years ago. People didn't exactly have to keep information for income taxes."

"So how did the fact that I owned the deed come to light?"

"Emily Stanton and Brad Vaughn did all the digging on that. Apparently, as one of their last efforts, they had a talk with Tildy Matheson."

Lisa knew who the old woman was.

"Her grandmother was good friends with Amos's wife, Catherine. Tildy offered to show them papers and pictures that had been in her attic, and among her grand-mother's things was the deed to the mine—signed back over to Lily Divine Harding."

Lisa glanced up at Riley. It was difficult to see his ex-pression with the light on his hat glaring into the dark-ness. "And that's a legal document?"

"More legal than anything we Douglases can come up with."

She'd displaced him from ownership of a gold mine. "And how do you feel about that?"

He seemed surprised at her question and didn't immediately form a reply.

"Sorry. Dumb question."

"No. I just didn't want to sound insincere when I answered."

She noticed he didn't say he didn't want to *be* insincere, just that he didn't want to *sound* that way.

"Let's head back," he said and directed the flashlight beam back the way they'd come. He moved around her, brushing her shoulder with his chest. The heat from his body was a pleasant surprise in the cool interior of the mine. "I tried every way I knew to prove ownership to the land. I couldn't do it. You're the owner. Those are the facts."

And on the surface he'd been helpful and informative rather than resentful. The darkness at her back made her uncomfortable, and she didn't let him get too far ahead of her. "What's in this for you?"

He glanced at her, and she had to squint against the beam of light. He reached up and switched it off, then did the same to hers. "I've offered to manage your business. You're coming into a lot of money. If I work for you, I'll make money, too. Plain and simple."

Sounded too plain and simple. Maybe Bernadine was right.

Lisa blinked as they reached the mouth of the mine and the bright sunlight. While Riley returned their hats to the trailer, she found her sunglasses in her purse and slipped them on.

Riley drove her back to his place, where she thanked him, then headed home in her Blazer. There was more that she needed to know. She knew very little about her ancestor. Legend had it that Lily had run a bordello in Thunder Canyon, and apparently the museum held historical artifacts from that time. In all these years Lisa had never visited. She'd never wanted anyone to see her there.

There was one less news vehicle across from her house when she reached it, and she took that as a good sign that things were settling down.

That night the clips of her at the Super Saver Mart were brief, and the anchorwoman moved right along to a story about a grant for the library and a literacy program.

Lisa peered out her front window as her pork chop cooked on her indoor ceramic grill. She was boring, anyone could see that. Eventually they had to lose interest and move on. She wasn't going to suddenly do something exciting.

She had more meetings scheduled the next day, and Bernadine would be picking her up. Maybe afterward she could slip away unnoticed to go to the museum.

That evening she planned her escape and packed a canvas tote bag with a change of clothing and a scarf.

The following afternoon Lisa wished Bernadine goodbye and slipped into the restroom of the courthouse, where they'd been filing papers. She changed clothes, tied the scarf around her hair bandanna-style and put on her sunglasses like a spy in a James Bond movie.

She exited the building through a back door and walked several blocks to the museum, which used to be an old schoolhouse. The building was centered on an acre of land that had once been the school yard. Lisa glanced in both directions, but no one had followed her.

She entered the reception area.

A woman greeted her. "Do you have a membership?"

"No."

"Admission is six dollars."

Lisa paid the amount and accepted a brochure.

"As you enter, the room to your left holds displays of mining equipment and information about the history of Thunder Canyon and local industry. There's a Native American display and a pioneer-life section.

"As you see, in the center area are groupings of furniture arranged to look as they may have at one time."

Lisa glanced at the roped-off sections, her gaze wandering toward what she really wanted to locate.

"The room to the right holds personal items used by our town founders and the more infamous inhabitants of Thunder Canyon. Enjoy your visit. If I can be of any assistance, just ask. Please sign the guest book and visit our gift shop before you leave. All proceeds go to the historical society to support the museum."

"I will, thanks." Lisa wanted to head directly for the room on the right, but instead she nonchalantly moseyed among the pieces of furniture, entered the large room on the left and studied the displays.

The picks and scales and claim deeds were of timely interest since she'd just seen the inside of her first mine. Black-and-white photographs, enlarged and displayed on foam board, brought the miners to life with real faces. Someone, once upon a long-ago time—probably her ancestor, Bart Divine—had toiled in the depths of the Queen of Hearts with sweat and hope and then had apparently given up. She was curious about those times and increasingly curious about Lily.

The museum lady was nowhere to be seen and no other visitors were in the building when Lisa peeked across the center room. She made her way past settings of chairs and sideboards and a cast-iron stove holding a kettle to enter the opposite room.

A quick survey showed her the window she'd come to see, and she hurried closer. A mannequin dressed in a dance-hall costume stood to one side in the exhibit. The red satin dress was trimmed with black lace and had been scandalously revealing for its time. Long ropes of pearls hung around the mannequin's bare neck, and a black ostrich feather had been affixed to the dark wig.

Lisa drew her gaze to the objects displayed in the case and their descriptions: a tortoiseshell hair comb studded with rhinestones, several perfume bottles, a fan edged with Chantilly lace and trimmed with black purling braid and a fancy pair of black silk garters, each with a gilt buckle and a rosette of satin taffeta ribbon.

Her attention was drawn to a pair of photographs. One was of the inside of the infamous Shady Lady saloon. A bartender in a white shirt with black armbands stood behind the polished mahogany bar. On the wall behind the bar were rows of liquor bottles and glasses, and center stage was a painting.

The caption under the photo claimed that the portrait

was of none other than Lily Divine herself. The likeness was too small for Lisa to make out any features, but the most obvious thing to note was that the woman who had posed for the portrait was bare except for something sheer draped across her hip and hiding only minimal secrets.

Lisa read that the painting was property of the Hitching Post and still hung over the bar. She'd heard talk of the portrait before, of course. In high school, coarse comments had been made, along with inquiries as to whether she was as stacked as Lily Divine, but she'd been too embarrassed to go see for herself.

The last photograph was a picture of her great-great-grandmother. Dark-haired and fair of features, she stood on the white-painted stairs of a house, dressed in a very average-looking skirt and a blouse with a high lace collar. She shaded her eyes with one hand and wore a gentle smile.

Her expression struck Lisa as one of a woman sure of herself. Confident. Poised. A woman who knew her place in her world.

Somehow those qualities had been lost in the gene pool, she thought. Lisa stared at the picture for a long time. In all these years she'd never come here because she'd been embarrassed. Ashamed of Lily Divine's reputation and legacy. Her aunt and grandmother had rarely spoken of the woman, and when they had it had been in lowered tones of disapproval.

Lisa tried to make sense of Lily being friends with Amos Douglas's wife. If Lily had run a house of ill repute and Amos Douglas had been an upstanding forefather, how had the two women been acquainted?

There was more here than she was able to see on the surface. A big piece of the puzzle was missing, and something drove her to discover what that was. Maybe her own visit to Tildy Matheson was in order.

Chapter Four

"Riley, I didn't know you were coming by again today." Caleb Douglas spotted his son at the computer in the adjoining office. They had remodeled this downtown building where all the business for the ski-resort project was handled, but Riley worked from his home office most of the time.

"I needed to crunch a few numbers."

Ground-breaking for Thunder Canyon Resort had been set back by the gold-fever commotion and subsequent land disputes but was back on schedule.

The older man entered the room and closed the door behind him. Riley's mother had obviously chosen the shirt and tie Caleb wore, which coordinated with his tailor-made western-cut sport jacket. Caleb stepped in front of Riley's desk. "How are things going with the Martin girl?"

"She's about to hire me."

"You're going to have to push this a little faster. One more 9/11 scare will send gold sky-high. We need to be in place when that happens."

"It's coming together."

"The mining is moving forward. There's gonna be gold coming out of that hole by the ton."

"I said I'm working on it."

Caleb held up both hands. "Okay. It had better be good." He started to walk away, then stopped as if he'd had a thought.

"I'm meeting Justin for lunch. Care to join us?"

Justin Caldwell was the brother Riley hadn't known about until a month ago. Justin, however, had learned about Caleb two years previously and had schemed against the Douglases to get control of the ski resort through the investors. His scheme had worked, too. The manipulation and resulting takeover had nearly broken Caleb. But in the end Justin had experienced a change of heart and given control of the project back to Caleb. Now the two of them seemed to be downright bonding.

Riley grabbed a pen and jotted down a few numbers. "I have other plans."

"Well, that's a shame. I'd like to get my two boys together for a change."

"Yeah, that would be real nice."

"Riley, he married our girl, Katie. You're going to have to accept him."

Riley's parents had taken in Katie Fenton when she'd

been fourteen and her mother had died. Katie's mother and Adele had been college friends. Katie was the daughter Caleb never had, his darling. Riley had been in college at the time, but he'd grown to love her, too. More often than not, however—even though he was the only offspring from his parents' union—he felt like the outsider in the family.

"Your mother's talking about a get-together soon," Caleb said. "A family thing. Bring someone."

Riley watched his father leave the room. Finding out about Justin had been a shock. His father'd had an affair when Riley had been just a baby. Justin had been the result of that, and Riley and his mother were still coming to terms with the betrayal.

Adele was a strong, proud woman, and her position in the community stiffened her backbone when it came to handling tough conditions. Riley, too, was loyal to family and the Douglas name. He and Justin had formed a tentative relationship, but Riley still had issues.

Not liking it didn't change the situation. He'd worked hard for his position in the Douglas Corporation and he wasn't going to let any of that go to waste. His plan was already in motion.

Lisa found Matilda Matheson in the Thunder Canyon phone directory and called her to set up a visit. The woman had been warm and friendly on the phone and sounded eager to meet her.

The following morning after her a.m. dogs were walked and fed, Lisa drove to the library, changed her clothing in the restroom and left by the rear door, wearing the only pair of trousers she owned and a hooded sweatshirt. These devious evasion tactics were getting old fast.

Her destination was a fair distance, but she was used to walking and no one spotted her. The house she sought was a two-story blue-and-white Victorian in excellent condition. Roses climbed trellises on either side of the porch and a calico cat napped on the padded porch swing.

Tildy was a kindly old woman with a toothy smile and soft-looking gray hair. She welcomed Lisa into her parlor and offered her a seat on the floral-cushioned sofa. Crocheted antimacassars were pinned to the arms and backs of the pieces of furniture.

"I'm tickled pink to meet you, dear. I've got tea ready. It won't be a moment."

Lisa glanced around, noting vintage furnishings and lamps similar in age and condition to those in her home.

Tildy came back with tea and sugar cookies. The china was delicate rose-patterned chintz with worn gold trim.

"I'm ever so pleased to meet Lily Divine's great-great-granddaughter," she said, clasping her hands together at her breast. "But I'm curious to know what brings you here."

"I understand your grandmother was a friend of Catherine Douglas's."

"Oh, yes, dear. The two were confidantes."

"Emily Stanton shared some of the story with me. The part about how she and Brad came to discover the deed to the mine."

"That was a surprise to all of us. I'm delighted for

you, dear. Those Douglases don't need any more money and they certainly don't deserve the mine."

"Why's that?"

"Well, the way my grandmother told the story, Amos Douglas was a mean old coot, who beat Catherine on more than one occasion. Lily was always the one who took her in and nursed her to health."

Lisa tried to picture a woman in a red saloon dress sitting at Catherine Douglas's bedside but couldn't make the scene gel.

"It wasn't unusual for her to take in women who needed a safe place."

"And a brothel was a safe place?" Lisa asked with serious doubt.

Tildy waved away that idea with a frown. "My grandmother said the Shady Lady was a dance hall, not a house of ill repute. Still, as a saloon it was not a place where respectable women of that day would have worked."

"But all the stories and the Heritage Day celebrations portray Lily as a prostitute."

"Makes for a far more colorful legend and a more interesting historical character that way, don't you think?"

Lisa recalled the face of the woman in the old photograph at the museum and the ordinary high-necked blouse and skirt she'd been wearing. She could picture that woman taking in an abused wife. "How can I know the truth from fiction?"

"I don't know, dear. You're welcome to go through Catherine's things. Emily and Brad left the trunk in my extra bedroom. It was in my attic for years before they brought it down here."

"Thank you, Miss Matheson. I'd like that."

Tildy sat in a rocker before a lace-curtained window in the quaintly decorated bedroom while Lisa looked through the contents of the enormous trunk. The fabric of the old dresses was so fragile, she feared tearing it, so she moved it aside carefully. She found a tarnished silver hand mirror, a parasol and a faded green silk purse.

"I intend to donate these things to the historical society, but somehow I just don't get around to calling them," Tildy told her. "My grandmother inherited all of Catherine's belongings, and I've had them since I was a young girl." Her hand went to a brooch she wore on her flowered dress. "I've worn the pieces of jewelry all my life."

"I'm the same way with my grandmother's things," Lisa told her. "I've kept most everything."

"The trunk and its contents are in my will," the old woman told her. "The foundation will get them when I'm gone."

Lisa didn't know how to respond, so she smiled and nodded. Catherine had kept several journals, and she read the first few entries in one.

"You may borrow those if you like. I'm sure there's mention of Lily."

Lisa ran her hand across the aged and cracked leather cover of the book she held. "I'll be very careful with them."

"I know you will, dear." Tildy wrapped the journals in tissue paper and placed them in a small bag for Lisa to carry.

After another cup of tea and more of the best cookies she'd ever eaten, Lisa thanked Tildy and left her house. On the walk back to the library she experienced a wash of anger that those stories of Lily's supposed profession had been propagated over the years. Because of another woman's hypothetical lack of moral character, Lisa had been looked down on her whole life—when all along that could have been one big lie!

If there was a way to absolve Lily's name, she was going to try to find it.

The back door of the library was locked when she arrived, so she had to walk around front to get to her Blazer. Only one news van remained, and the driver appeared to be napping. Lisa started the engine and drove away without a tail.

She felt blissfully unencumbered when she stopped and took care of her afternoon pets, then drove home.

She let herself in and the dogs licked her senseless, then danced around yipping until she put leashes on them and took them out for a walk. The driver of a news van spotted her on her return and drove slowly alongside. "I'm reporting you to the police," she called. "I have a restraining order!"

The van dropped back and she hurried on to the house.

That evening she curled up on the sofa with one of the journals and read it from the beginning. It had been written during an early time in Catherine's life, and there was no mention of Lily. The second book, however, mentioned Lily a few times, referring to her home as a refuge. The dates of the entries were sporadic, and Lisa had the impression that Catherine had left out much of the true happenings of her life.

Emily had given Lisa her phone number, and Lisa

called it now, only to get a recording. Emily and Brad had done extensive research in looking for the mine owner, and perhaps she had discovered more than Lisa had thought to ask about.

She left a message, then tried to distract herself by baking brownies. Her grandmother's recipes were some of her dearest treasures, and these brownies especially reminded her of the warmth and comfort she'd received in this home during her formative years. Lisa poured herself a glass of milk and ate the brownies warm.

Emily might not return her call for hours or perhaps not even until the next day. She dusted the china hutch and sideboard in the dining room, admiring the dishes and thinking how similar her grandmother's things were to Tildy's. She still missed her grandmother, even though she'd been gone several years. Having her things was a comfort, just as the house was her link to family. Maybe part of the reason she was so curious about Lily was because she craved a family connection.

Later, as she was washing up the baking dishes, the phone rang.

"Hi, Lisa, it's Emily. I got your message."

"Thanks for calling. I have a couple of questions and I thought you could help me find answers."

"If I can, sure."

"I went to see Tildy today."

"She's a sweetheart, isn't she?"

"And the cookies are to die for."

Emily chuckled.

"She doesn't believe Lily Divine ran a whorehouse. Her grandmother told her differently."

"I got that impression, too. Of course, there's no official documentation to prove it one way or the other."

Lisa propped the phone under her chin and dried a spatula. "I guess prostitutes didn't exactly apply for a license to practice, did they?"

"It was a lucrative business back then. The saloons supported the city. In fact, the law often accepted payment to simply look aside."

Lisa thought about that. "And the lawmen probably frequented the places."

"Likely. It was a western mining town. Saloon owners got rich off the miners."

"Did you learn anything else about Lily?"

"Brad and I searched all the papers in the archives in the town-hall basement."

"That must have been fun."

"Actually it wasn't so bad. Lily's name came up a lot in later years, when she was Lily Harding. She was married to the town sheriff."

That news surprised Lisa. She leaned back against the counter. "I thought that was probably another tall tale."

"No. She was married to Nathaniel Harding, who by many accounts brought law and order to Thunder Canyon. Lily herself was a voice ahead of her time, speaking out for women's rights and later in their quest for the vote."

"You found articles in the *Nugget* that told about that?"

"We did."

"I think I'm going to go look through them myself."

"That's a good idea. We weren't really searching for

Lily's history, so there may have been information we overlooked."

"Thanks, Emily."

"Anytime. How are things going?"

"What? You don't know? I thought my menu and routine were public knowledge."

Emily laughed. I know about the pizza, but I was actually wondering about *you*. Are you handling all this?"

"It's pretty awful. I can't go anywhere without cameras following. I'm my own reality show and I'm boring. I did make some awesome brownies tonight."

"They'll find something else to interest them soon and you'll be old news."

"Not soon enough for me. Thanks again."

"Oh," Emily added, "one more thing I just thought of."

"What's that?"

"There's an elderly woman who lives out on the western edge of town, past Elk. Almost to the Douglas property."

"Emelda Ross," Lisa said. "She reads to the children at the library."

"That's her," Emily said. "You've met her?"

"Used to go to story time when I was a kid. My mother took me."

"Well, anyway, she has stories about the early days of Thunder Canyon that just don't quit. She was quite entertaining when I spoke with her. She might know more about Lily."

"Maybe I'll go see her. Thanks." Lisa hung up and glanced at the clock. It was too late to go visiting, but she would make a trip out to the Ross house soon.

* * *

They'd caught on. The next morning Lisa opened the back door at the library, and farther down the alley two reporters who'd been leaning against the fenders of their vehicles grabbed cameras and aimed the lenses at her.

"Come on, people! There has to be something going on *somewhere* that's more interesting than this." She went back inside and stood in the hall a moment.

She changed plans and walked out the front door and down Main. She didn't turn to look behind her, but she knew the vans were back there. All the buildings along Main Street sat side by side with covered boardwalks. When she reached Town Hall, the receptionist, a woman with black hair and a white streak over one temple, recognized her and accompanied her to the records in the basement. She showed her the basic layout and how to get started finding newspaper articles.

For a couple of hours Lisa scanned microfiche of the *Thunder Canyon Nugget.* More than once Lily had spent the night in jail for refusing to turn a woman over to her husband or father. Most of those incidents had been before Nathaniel Harding became sheriff, Lisa noted. There was only one account of the sheriff actually locking up the woman he would marry. One story told of a fire that had ravaged a property Lily owned, and there was mention of an auction Lily held to raise money for a fatherless family.

Again Lisa thought of the woman she'd seen in the black-and-white photograph. *Confident* had been her overall impression of Lily. Assured of her purpose.

Comfortable with her life choices. There was no doubt she'd owned and run a saloon. In fact, according to announcements in the *Nugget,* numerous town meetings had been held in her establishment.

Lily'd held her own in a time when women were considered inferior. Nothing inferior about Lily Divine. She'd raised her head high and marched to her own tune.

Lisa marched to her own tune, as well, but it was a quiet melody, written to blend into the surrounding sounds. She'd spent her whole life trying to be invisible.

She hated attention, and why was that? Was she inferior to others in some respect? Looks? Money? Yes. Yes.

Well, she had money now. Or at least she would have. Bernadine was rushing the paperwork. The Douglases had established an account to hold future profits from sales of ore from the Queen of Hearts, and the names were already being changed on that account. The thought of being responsible for a prospective million dollars or more plus employees and all that this inheritance entailed made her feel ill. She definitely needed all the help she could get.

Lisa walked out the front door of Town Hall and spotted the news vans. She was disgusted with herself for hiding because she felt inferior. She could hide because she didn't want the publicity, but feeling inferior was wrong.

Instead of heading back for her Blazer, she headed west on Main until she came to the Hitching Post. Old Town had been restored and reconstructed to look like the 1800s town it had once been, and true to the bar and restaurant's name, split-rail hitching posts lined the boardwalk.

Two cars were parked in front, and she glanced at her watch, noting it wasn't yet the lunch hour. The place was popular and would probably fill up with locals soon.

Her stomach fluttered as she opened the door and entered the building with unexpected awe. The Hitching Post had been here for forty years in its current form and sixty-plus years before the remodeling. Her great-great-grandmother had stood on these very floors and walked the same rooms and lived and slept in the attached house next door.

The floors were scarred wood, the varnished pine walls darkened over the years. Lanterns, tin signs, spurs and all number of western memorabilia hung from nails and dangled in the doorways. How many of these walls and items had Lily touched?

No one stood near the counter at the front, and Lisa could see the bar from the entrance. The sound of a slow ballad droned from a jukebox in the corner. Two silver-haired men played checkers at a table and a stocky, middle-aged man in a white shirt stacked glasses behind the bar.

Lisa recognized the enormous polished cherrywood bar from the photograph and approached. The piece was hopelessly scarred and several grooves had been worn deep in the wood, but it was still impressive. Behind the bar, in a place of prominence between mirrors and shelves of glasses and rows of liquor bottles, was the painting she'd come to see.

The place didn't get a whole lot of sunlight, which had

probably aided in preserving the portrait. It was bigger than she'd anticipated, but every bit as...provocative.

Clearly the same Lily Divine that she'd seen in the photograph was depicted in the artist's rendition. Reclining on her side, the woman faced the artist. If Lisa wasn't mistaken, Lily's curly dark hair had the same auburn highlights as her own, and similar ringlets framed her face. The similarity was as surprising as it was exciting. What other characteristics did they share?

This Lily had probably been in her twenties and was depicted adorned with...pearls. Period. Lisa definitely wore more clothing.

The woman wasn't the well-rounded type Lisa'd seen in nude paintings in art-history books, although she obviously had what it took in all the right places. No wonder Lisa'd been asked how she compared to Lily Divine. The chick *was* stacked.

Her breasts were clearly visible through a gauzy black veil that draped over one shoulder, and Victoria's Secret would have signed this woman in a heartbeat. The material gathered over her hip and discreetly shaded her pubic area.

Lily's legs were long and shapely, and strands of pearls circled each ankle. Lily Divine was a hottie.

"This your first look at the Shady Lady?"

"What?" Lisa glanced at the bartender who'd approached. "Oh, yes."

"We got postcards we sell to the tourists if you wanna buy one." He pointed to a rack on the counter by an ice machine. "A dollar. Want one?"

"Sure, thanks." She opened her purse.

He placed a postcard on the bar. "What'll you have to drink?"

"Um." She glanced at the card and then around the interior of the room, orienting herself. "Do you have root beer?"

He shook his head. "Cola."

"Diet?"

"Sure thing." He prepared her a glass of soda and set it on a cocktail napkin. "Two fifty with the postcard."

She paid him, and he gave her another look, recognition dawning. "Say, aren't you...?"

Lisa's cheeks warmed and she busied herself placing the picture in her purse.

The man snapped his fingers. "You're the heiress." His eyebrows shot up. "The gal who inherited the gold mine!"

She acknowledged his observation with a nod and the bravest smile she could come up with. "That's me."

"Then you're—" He stopped and pointed up at the painting. "You're the Shady Lady's kin."

She looked back up at the portrait. It had hung there for generations. No sense getting embarrassed about it now. She was after all linked through history to this establishment. "That's right."

"Well...congratulations."

She nodded her thanks and he moved away. Lisa sipped her soft drink while she studied the portrait. What a fascinating woman Lily had been. She'd been known down through the years as the Shady Lady, though there wasn't much proof that she'd been a prostitute. Actually this painting seemed to be the only tie to her not-so-proper past.

What exactly had the woman had to be ashamed of?

Not that body, that was for sure. Though the painting must have been scandalous in its day, one could see nearly as much flesh today watching a Super Bowl halftime.

The artist had captured Lily's expression so vividly that this was without a doubt the same confident woman as the one in the photograph at the museum. Her dauntless smile revealed her pleasure with life. Perhaps pleasure with herself or her accomplishments.

Lisa wanted the same confidence Lily had possessed. Why hadn't she inherited that? She wondered then about Lily's children and what had transpired down through the generations to make Lisa and her great-great-grandmother so different.

"Want something else?" the bartender asked, snagging her attention.

She'd finished her soft drink. "No, thanks. I'll be moving along."

She picked up her purse and left the Hitching Post. A couple of her paparazzi were out of their vehicles, chatting in the shade of a maple tree. They saw her and jumped to their positions to follow. She observed them for a moment and wondered what Lily would have done if she'd been in this same predicament.

It was several blocks back to the library where she'd parked, but instead of hurrying, she took her time. Along the way she passed the Clip 'N' Curl salon. She'd always thought it sounded like a place where you'd take your poodle, but it was the only hair salon in town. Judy Johnson usually cut Lisa's hair.

Lisa had gone to school with Judy's daughter, Jennifer, so she always got an update on Jennifer's charmed and perfect life with her charmed and perfect teacher husband and her charmed and perfect children—one girl and one boy, of course.

Lisa pushed open the door and the overhead bell rang. The smell of perming solution immediately burned her nostrils. One customer in rods was being neutralized and two others sat under dryers. A fourth was having her silver-blue hair styled into waves.

"Hello, Lisa," Judy called. "I'm doing a perm and a color, so it'll be another hour."

"That's okay. I'll come back."

She stood on the boardwalk and glanced up and down the street before continuing on to her vehicle.

As she drove home, she changed her mind about going back to the Clip 'N' Curl. She'd try something different for a change. If she thought her Blazer would make it, she'd drive to Billings and visit a salon. Or a day spa.

Some millionaire she was. She didn't even have a decent car.

Joey and Piper wagged their tails excitedly when she arrived, and she knelt to give them both attention before letting them out into the backyard.

The light on the answering machine was blinking, and the contraption actually cooperated, so she played her messages. One was from Bernadine saying she needed a few signatures. Another was from someone named Dave who claimed they'd gone to school together and was wondering if she'd like to hook up. She remembered him as the receiver on the football team. He'd sat beside her in Language Arts and had never so much as spoken to her.

The last recording made her heartbeat stutter when she heard the deep male voice. *The quarterback.*

"Lisa, this is Riley. Give me a call when you get in. I want to ask you something. Later."

She used great discipline in phoning Bernadine first and arranged for a quick meeting. Then she took the slip of paper on which Riley'd written his cell phone number and dialed.

"Hey, you called me back."

"Yes. You wanted to ask me something?"

"I did. Will you have dinner with me Friday evening? We can drive into Billings. I'll make reservations somewhere nice."

Was this a business dinner? Or…personal? Her stomach dipped. She wasn't into the whole dating scene, and if he was expecting her to be cute or coy, it wasn't going to happen.

"Is this…business?"

"Do you want it to be?"

"I just don't want to mess up our relationship as client and agent."

"You haven't hired me yet."

"Right. Well, you're hired." She paused a moment. "Now we have a working relationship."

"Good. So I'll pick you up Friday?"

She still didn't know his intent, but she surprised herself and said okay anyway. She hung up the phone and second-guessed herself while she looked for something to eat for lunch. Dinner at someplace nice. Just thinking about it almost made her lose her appetite. What would she wear?

Maybe she would go to Billings and do a little shopping. She had credit cards. She could even rent a decent car to get there. She was a millionaire, after all. Excited about the idea, she slapped together a peanut-butter sandwich.

Chapter Five

Lisa glanced around the inside of the New Beginnings
Day Spa searching for someone who looked like exactly
the person she wanted cutting her hair. She spotted her
giving a man in his twenties a cut. "Her."

"That's Miranda. Five minutes, hon."

Miranda had short hair, dark at the roots and a combination of blonde and red on the bleached ends. She wore
black high-heeled boots and dangling rhinestone earrings.

"I don't want to look like the old me," Lisa told her
ten minutes later. "I need a whole new look."

"What are you going for? Color? Surprise?"

"Anything will be a surprise. I just want to feel good.
I want to be…confident."

Miranda washed and conditioned her hair, combed

it back from her face and studied her. "Can I do your eyebrows?"

"Sure."

"You have a great face. I want to give you a look you can learn to do yourself. I can give you a good cut, just above your shoulders and sort of fringy around your face. We'll do some highlights to add depth. And I can teach you to straighten it yourself. Wait till you see the results."

Miranda went to work. She was serious about her job and about the look she wanted Lisa to achieve. She snipped and cut and colored, and Lisa began to have a few qualms about what she'd gotten herself into. She didn't want to look foolish when all was done.

Her fears were soon put to rest when the hairdresser spun her around in the chair to face the mirror. The pretty young woman she stared at didn't look anything like the frumpy old Lisa. No frizz, just shine and soft curl that flattered the shape of her face.

Lisa had picked a miracle worker. The result was amazing.

Lisa studied her reflection and couldn't believe the difference. "I love it."

But they weren't done. Miranda worked with her until she could use the products and the iron and get her hair straight and styled on her own.

"Now," Miranda said. "Makeup."

"I do okay."

"No argument. You said you don't want to look like the old you. You need a face for the new you."

"You're right."

"I'll go get the cosmetologist."

Makeup was one thing. Waxing was entirely another. But Lisa'd come for the day and the works and she was going to stay for the whole ride. Legs waxed, a manicure, pedicure and a signature on a credit-card slip later and she was headed for a shop several blocks away where the stylist had recommended she go.

Lisa entered the store, which had two levels and a main sitting area with a cappuccino machine. A slim young woman in a fashionable blouse and skirt greeted her.

"I'm Gwen. Miranda told me you were coming. You look fabulous. I have a few things I'd like you to try on. Did you have anything specific in mind?"

"Actually I did. I think I'd like something in red."

Bernadine nearly fell out of her office chair the next day when Lisa walked in after the secretary's announcement over the intercom. "Lisa? Oh, my gosh! You look *fabulous!* It is you, isn't it?"

"It's me." She did a little whirl before the woman's desk, showing off her trim two-piece suit and sexy backless heels. It was a completely new experience to feel attractive, and she was enjoying the feeling.

Bernadine got up to come around and stare, hands on her cheeks.

"Big change, huh?"

"Change? My word, more like a total metamorphosis! You're like one of those extreme makeovers." She reached up to touch a wisp of Lisa's hair. "This color is incredible."

"I was pretty bad, wasn't I?"

The woman looked embarrassed. "No, well, not ugly or anything, just…well, okay, not a very fashionable dresser and, um…. Not bad, though."

"It's okay. I know."

Bernadine inched closer. "Did you get collagen injections in your upper lip?"

"I'll never tell." She didn't have to reveal *all* her secrets. The professional she'd visited had assured her the enhancement was completely safe.

"*When* did you do all this?"

"Yesterday. *All* day. It was exhausting. But worth it. I've been enjoying people's reactions this morning."

"Who has seen you? Have the reporters seen you?"

"Yes, but I think they thought someone else spent the night with me, because they're still back at my place waiting for me to come out."

"Oh, that's funny."

"Not really. What if they think I spent the night with another woman?" She wiggled her shapely new eyebrows. "*You know.*"

Bernadine laughed. "That's *really* funny."

Lisa sat on one of the comfortable upholstered chairs.

"They'll figure it out soon." The lawyer gathered a few papers that were stacked on the edge of her desk. "These need signatures."

Lisa picked up a pen. "I hired him."

"Douglas?"

"Yes."

"That's good. We can get the contracts under way for his salary and percentages. I took the liberty of mocking up a couple of standard ones for you to look over."

"Okay. Can I take them to show him? I'm having dinner with him tomorrow night."

"Dinner? Remember what I told you."

"Trust me, I know. He's in this for the money."

"Hon, when we talked about this before you said you hadn't gotten any better looking. Obviously you were good-looking all along, you just weren't letting anyone know. Now... Well, be careful. He's going to be on you like fuzz on a peach."

"I'm a big girl."

"I hope so."

The reporters were smarter than Lisa had given them credit for. They'd figured it out. They followed her home with cameras rolling. This time she turned and waved, did a little runway turn for them and took a bow.

The local evening news showed her in her casual suit and sexy shoes. Even Lisa couldn't believe this Lisa on film was the same person they'd been following. She looked so good. So definitely not a wallflower. Once home she changed, fed the dogs and took them for a run. As daylight waned, she stared into the refrigerator and settled for a bowl of cereal.

She appeared new and different. But she was still the same boring person she'd been all along. She looked a hundred percent better, but she hadn't *changed*. Change on the outside was good, but a metamorphosis had to come from within to be a true difference.

Maybe she was fine just the way she was. She'd been happy with her life before, even with its simplicity. Dogs weren't complicated, and she didn't have to impress anyone. There *was* no one to impress, she thought glumly.

Lisa selected a video, started it and settled on the couch with a bowl of popcorn. Piper and Joey snuggled up on either side and ate an occasional stray kernel. She could change. She could be really exciting if she put her mind to it. And at long last she *did* have someone to impress.

Somewhere around eleven she fell asleep, and Piper ate the rest of the popcorn.

The following evening Riley pulled into the long, narrow drive with a hedge alongside and got out of his red Jaguar. It wasn't dark yet, so the cameras had a good view of him approaching the porch and walking up to Lisa's door. He knocked, and dogs barked immediately.

He could see the massive form of a canine through the lace curtain on the full-length leaded-glass door.

"Get back," Lisa said from inside.

Had she been talking to him? He took a hesitant step back.

The lock turned and she opened the door.

An enormous golden retriever growled menacingly while another barked.

"Joey. Piper. Hush." He thought the woman who spoke to the disturbed animals was Lisa, but he was torn between gaping at her and keeping both eyes on the dogs.

Couldn't do it.

She was wearing a red dress that had a slit clear up one thigh and exposed both her shoulders. The garment

fit her sexy, slender body as if it had been made for her,
and the shock of knowing she *had* a sexy, slender body
hit him full force.

"I'll need to touch you," she said.

He stared at her and fought the physical reaction her
words nearly launched. Dark hair with golden highlights framed her face—and what a face it was. Sable
arched brows, full shiny lips, eyes as blue and deep as
a summer sky. "Lisa?"

"They need to see you're not an intruder." She took
his hand and pulled him inside. Standing close beside
him, she said, "Put your arm around me."

Riley did as told, draping an arm around her shoulder, his fingers grazing her bare upper arm. She smelled
so good, he closed his eyes and *experienced* the feminine scent.

"See, he's a friend," she said. "Let them smell you."

Riley opened his eyes and took his hand away from
Lisa to extend it hesitantly toward the dogs. "You're sure?"

She nodded.

The darker-colored of the two padded right up and
sniffed the proffered hand, gave it a lick, then sat and
panted. The blond retriever kept his distance and
growled.

Lisa looked up at Riley and shrugged. "I've never
known him to do that. That's Piper. This one's Joey. You
boys be good."

She turned the lock and pulled the door shut behind
her. Riley watched every stimulating movement.

"You changed your hair." And your body and face
and everything else. "And that dress—wow."

"Thanks."

He hurried to open the car door. A smooth length of thigh was exposed when she sat. She adjusted her dress, and he closed the car door and cautioned himself.

It was probably bad manners to ask what she'd done to achieve this incredible new look, but he couldn't get past the fact that she looked nothing like the woman his father had taken to calling "frumpy" and "bohemian." Riley got behind the wheel and concentrated on starting the car and backing up when what he wanted to do was turn and soak her in.

The fact that *that* body had been underneath those awful skirts and jackets all along loosened a screw in his steely confidence. He wasn't used to being so unprepared.

And he'd definitely been unprepared to see her looking like this. Even less prepared to have a very noncerebral reaction.

"Sorry about the rude welcome."

His brain switched tracks and he was glad for the distraction. He couldn't afford to lose his edge. "That's all right."

"The boys are usually very friendly."

"I'm sure they are."

"They're protective of me."

"Sure." He pulled out onto the highway and headed toward Billings. "Lisa, you look incredible."

"Thanks."

"No, I mean, you look *incredible*. What… I mean, what…?"

"Don't say it. I was ready for a change and I did it, that's all."

"You're...beautiful."

She was too quiet and he knew he'd said the wrong thing at the wrong time, no matter how true it was. He glanced over to see her looking out the passenger window. She raised her chin a little, turned to face him and smiled hesitantly.

A beautiful smile, too. Familiar and yet so different. "Want some music?"

She glanced the dashboard. "Sure."

He flipped open the console between them. "Pick something."

A silver bracelet dangled on her wrist as she reached to look through the CDs. She flipped through The Flaming Lips, B.B. King and The Doobie Brothers to hand him one by Norah Jones. He gave her a sideways glance but placed the disc in the tray and pushed Play. Was there any meaning behind her selection?

The strains of a sultry song filled the interior of the car. Surely she didn't intend to seduce him. Or to be seductive. Riley tried to think of something to say to her that wasn't about how good she looked. Not much else entered his mind at the moment. "So, you like dogs?"

"Yes," she replied easily. "They're not as judgmental or as critical as people."

"Can't take one to a movie."

"My dogs watch movies with me all the time."

"Can't teach one to play chess."

"I don't play chess either, so that's never been a compatibility issue."

"So, in your opinion a dog is as good a companion as a person?"

"More so." She glanced at him and her forehead furrowed. "You don't like dogs?"

"I like dogs. At least, the respectable ones."

"Respectable?"

"Some breeds you just can't respect."

"What are you talking about?"

"My mother has the most foolish-looking poodle. It's four feet tall and its fur is cut into ridiculous pom-poms."

"Derek," she said.

"Oh, you know Derek. Then you can see how I just can't respect that dog."

"He's friendly and very smart. Well behaved, too. I've taken care of him a few times."

Riley shook his head in distaste.

"There, you see? You're judging him by his looks."

"Well…yeah."

"He can't help how he looks. It's his breed. And the way your mother has him cut."

He wasn't earning any points with this conversation. She was starting to take his comments personally. "Sorry. You're probably right."

She glanced at him. "What about horses?"

"What do you mean?"

"Do they have to be perfect in order for you to respect them?"

"Horses demand respect."

"How so? Their size? Because they're not as intelligent as dogs."

Riley held up a hand in frustration. "I'm sorry I brought up Derek, okay? I'll try to adjust my attitude."

"Just because I said something?"

"Yes."

She smoothed her skirt over her knees. "I won't even ask about your attitude toward women."

"Thank you."

She laughed softly, and he understood she was having fun at his expense. He wasn't used to his comments and opinions being taken lightly or challenged. This evening wasn't going in the direction he'd planned. Well, maybe the direction was okay, but the person in the metaphorical driver's seat was in question. He needed to keep things where he wanted them.

"My mother's planning a reception to celebrate the ground-breaking for the resort," he told her.

"I guess the ski resort is a pretty big deal, huh?"

"It is. It will bring tourists to Thunder Canyon for more than the summer months. Right now we rely heavily on Heritage Days and the cabins and trail rides, but all that's seasonal. This will bring in more revenue."

"I have a few pet owners in the new homes out north. New Town is expanding."

She hadn't even picked up on his lead. "The reason I brought it up was to ask you to attend the reception."

Lisa glanced over at him in surprise. "I really don't think I'd fit in."

"Your status is changing. You own property, significant property. And very soon, once that mine is producing, you'll be investing. As your manager, I'm going to suggest strongly that you invest a percent locally. Public relations is an important part of business."

"So you think I should attend the reception for PR purposes?"

"Partially."

She didn't ask what the other part was. Was he pushing her a little too firmly?

"All right," she said, surprising him. "When is it?"

He told her the time and date and they made arrangements.

A few minutes later they reached Billings and he drove to the restaurant where he'd made reservations.

When they'd gone to the mine, Lisa had opened her own door before he could get around, but this time she waited. He walked beside her to the building and held the door.

A hostess showed them to their table and brought menus.

Lisa's eyebrows rose as she studied the menu. She glanced hesitantly at their neighboring tables.

"Something wrong?" Riley asked.

"It's so expensive," she whispered.

"It's okay," he replied in the same hushed tone. "I'm good for it."

When the waiter came, Lisa ordered a steak with a baked potato and Riley asked for the same. He couldn't remember the last time he'd been with a woman who'd ordered a regular meal and not a salad or seafood.

"Have you looked over the wine selection?" the waiter asked.

"Would you drink wine if I ordered it?" Riley asked her.

"Will you cut me off before my face goes numb?"

With a grin he picked up the list and held it so they could both read it. "I'll make sure of it."

Something about the way she studied the list, running her finger down the columns, struck him as familiar, but he couldn't figure out why. They'd never done this before, never eaten out or read a wine list together. He shrugged off the feeling of déjà vu.

"Let's get this out of the way," she said and took several papers from her bag and unfolded them. "These are agreements my lawyer drew up for our working arrangement."

He read them over quickly. "She faxed me copies so I could read them ahead of time. Got a pen?"

He signed them with a flourish, and Lisa tucked them back into her bag.

"Well, that's official," she said, not sure whether to be pleased or panicky. He was working for her. Maybe it would seem real once she'd seen some gold.

The deep red Merlot Riley had ordered arrived, and the waiter poured a dollop in a glass for him to taste. It was dry and rich, an excellent blend of flavors.

After it was poured, Lisa tasted hers.

"Impressed?" he asked.

"I'm impressed by anything without a screw-on cap. How do you know which wine to order?"

"I've toured several wineries and I belong to an international club. I subscribe to a couple of publications. You learn the same way you learn anything else."

"Only if you can afford to try the really good stuff," she added.

He nodded in concession to her point. He didn't suppose dog walking afforded her the luxury to purchase vintage wines.

"I'm trying not to think inside the same parameters," she told him. "Small, I mean. Cheap. But my bank account hasn't actually caught up yet, so it's not easy to break away from the habits."

"I've given some thought to that problem." He set his glass down. "You have to have money to make money—it's that simple. There are expenses in getting the mining under way. People must be hired and fees paid and there are all number of things cropping up. In the old days, a miner got a grubstake."

"Someone gave him money for his supplies with the understanding that it would be paid back once the strike came in," she replied.

Riley nodded. "Yes. The Queen of Hearts is a sure thing. It's not even a risk. You have gold sitting there waiting to be extracted. I'd like to grubstake the expenses for you. Give you a substantial amount to get you started and tide you over until the mining is well under way. It should be less than a month before that happens."

"I can wait," she said easily and watched as the waiter came by and filled their glasses.

"But you don't have to wait," Riley continued once the man had gone. "You could have money for the things you need now. I've seen that bucket of bolts you drive. You need a better car."

She glanced aside, but he could tell she was thinking.

"All the meetings are taking you away from your regular job, so there's a dent in that income, right?"

She sipped her wine and said lightly, "No, I'm juggling time for my pets."

"You can think about it."

"I don't need to think about it. I already owe you for security and safety measures and who knows what all, I don't want to owe you for personal items, as well."

"It wouldn't be that much, Lisa."

"Not that much? A new car? Excuse me, a new car is much."

"Comparatively speaking. It won't be that much compared to how much you'll be generating from the mine."

"And I can wait. I don't like the idea of being in debt."

She hadn't added the words *to you,* but they were there just the same. He raised a hand to say he was finished talking about the advance. He'd made the offer. If she was too stubborn to see the practicality of it, that was her problem.

He changed the subject to advice on how to deal with the people she'd be working with from now on. As the meal was delivered, he poured them both more wine. It was obvious she enjoyed it. Turning their attention to the food and the conversation, the tension between them eased.

"Body language is an important part of communication in business," he told her. "And there are ways to gain an advantage."

"Okay, what are they?"

"To dominate another, take control of their time. Make them wait for you."

"Isn't that rude?"

"No, it's controlling an encounter."

"What if the other person tries to make me wait?"

"Counter it. Make him wait for you. And always

choose where and how you sit. Don't take a low chair, and if there's no choice, sit on the edge or stand."

Lisa cut a bite of her steak and asked, "They taught you this stuff in business college?"

A flash went off before he could reply, and Riley glanced over his shoulder to see a man with a camera just inside the room.

Lisa set down her fork and dabbed her lips with her napkin. She waved pleasantly and raised her glass of wine toward the intruder. "Did you get the label on our wine bottle clearly?" she called. "Because it's a very good vintage. I could turn it a little bit."

Riley glanced from her to the reporter, who was joined now by two others. The other restaurant patrons were staring.

He leaned forward. "Don't you have a restraining order?"

"Yes."

He reached inside his jacket and pulled out his phone. "Then I'm calling the police."

Lisa pointed to Riley's phone but looked toward the reporters. "He's calling the police," she called. "You might want to move on."

His call was answered and he gave the dispatcher the details.

"This is Miss Martin's restraining order," the officer said. "She needs to make the complaint."

He extended the phone. "You have to report it."

She accepted it without hesitation. "Hi," she said. "The paparazzi are interrupting my dinner. Could you speak with them? I think they'll go if you just talk to them."

She got out of her seat to walk across the room.

More flashes popped, but she walked directly up to the nearest man with a camera. "It's for you," she said. "The police."

Chapter Six

Riley stood and followed a few feet behind her. He watched the bizarre scene unfold and couldn't help glancing at the curiously staring diners. The reporters looked more uncomfortable at being called out than Lisa did at confronting them. No matter how unorthodox her method, she'd deftly turned the tables and had the situation firmly in control. Maybe she didn't need his advice as much as he'd first thought.

"Go ahead," she said to the officer on the phone. "I'm putting the offender on now." She pointed to Riley's cell phone and handed it to the man whose camera was now lowered. The other two men first zeroed in for close-ups of the newly transformed heiress, then trained their lenses on the one-sided phone conversation.

"Hello?" the man said uncertainly. "Er, yes. Chad Falkner. Uh-huh. Yes, I'm aware. Certainly. All right. Now, yes. Er, thanks."

He handed the phone back to Lisa and turned to the men beside him. "We're outta here or they're coming to arrest us."

"I knew you'd see reason," she told them, still speaking in a friendly manner. "Hey, none of us wants to be made a spectacle of, do we?" She put the phone to her ear. "Thanks, Officer. They'll be going now."

She flipped the phone shut and extended it to Riley.

He stifled the urge to laugh while he tucked it away, and a sudden idea occurred. He stepped forward. "Excuse me, but may I make a suggestion?"

The restaurant manager hurried toward them at that moment, a concerned look on his face. "Is there a problem? Would you like to use my office? Or perhaps your party could step outside so as not to disturb the other diners."

"Did you get *this* on film?" Lisa asked the young man who still aimed a camera.

"I did," he said.

"How about him?" she asked, indicating the reporter who'd spoken with the police and was clearly at a loss for what to say or do next. "Did you get him talking to the police?"

The same reporter nodded.

"Let's step outside for a minute," Riley said, finally taking control.

He and Lisa and the manager accompanied the three reporters out the door. They stood on the pavement in front of the building. Night had fallen and insects buzzed around the neon signs that lit their small gathering.

"I'd like to make a proposition," Riley began. "And Miss Martin, you call me out if this is out of line or if you don't agree. I suggest Miss Martin give you an exclusive personal interview—"

"Wait a minute," Lisa started to object.

"Let me finish," he insisted and turned back to the reporters. "An exclusive personal interview at a time and place of her choosing and at her discretion. Taped, not live. You will provide her with the questions ahead of time. She can refuse to answer any she wishes, and she'll be allowed to provide questions she wants to be asked. She'll have the right to preview the interview before it's aired.

"In return for this gracious gift of her time and the sacrifice of privacy, you will leave her alone for an entire week following the airing." He faced Lisa. "Miss Martin, how do you feel about this?"

She glanced from Riley to the reporters and replied without hesitation. "Sure."

"And you, gentlemen?"

The media people all needed permission from their superiors, but all three were eager for the opportunity. Riley took their names and numbers and gave them his business card in return. Chad Falkner smirked as though he'd been granted an interview with Julia Roberts.

"Now if you'll excuse us," Riley said, "we have a dinner to finish."

When they returned to their table, their plates were missing. "I had your meals kept warm for you, sir," their waiter said. He signaled, and a moment later their dinners were returned.

Lisa's hesitant glance took in patrons at other tables, then raised to his.

"That was the last thing I expected you to do," he told her. "Confronting them like that. You were great."

"I'm all about your pleasure," she said, picking up her fork.

The double meaning of that statement zapped other coherent thought from his head. She wasn't anything he'd expected her to be, nothing like the reticent young woman he'd planned to befriend and assist. "You keep surprising me," he said honestly.

"I'm surprising myself."

He studied her features, her shiny hair and the way the light glowed on her bare shoulders. He wasn't the one who was supposed to feel as if he was walking on marbles. He had to be very careful around this woman.

"I've begun asking myself what Lily would have done."

"Lily Divine?"

"My great-great-grandmother. I think there's a lot more we don't know about her. And a lot we think we know that isn't true."

"Like what?"

"She's famous for being the Shady Lady, but that was just the name of her saloon. I don't think she was a prostitute."

"How do you explain that painting over the bar?"

"I don't know. I don't know that I have to."

"The dresses? The saloon?"

She looked him in the eye. "You can hang fuzzy dice

around your neck and go stand in your garage, but that doesn't make you a car."

He laughed.

She laid down her fork and placed her napkin on the table. "I've been reading your great-great-grandmother's journals."

"Which grandmother?"

"Catherine Douglas. Amos's wife."

"I've never heard about any journals."

"Well, they belong to Tildy Matheson now. Remember you told me about Emily Stanton and Brad Vaughn going through things at Tildy's and finding the deed? Well, it seems Catherine left her belongings to Tildy's grandmother."

"That's strange."

"She plans to bequeath a trunk full of items to the historical society."

"It's odd those things weren't kept in the family," he said, thinking out loud.

"Many families don't have heirlooms because things get discarded before they're actually valuable or have much sentiment. It's fortunate that someone kept these things in good condition."

He could see that and nodded his agreement.

She picked up her glass and sipped wine. The recessed lighting flattered her dark hair and the sparkle in her eyes accentuated the feminine hollows of her collarbone and the curve of her shoulders. Riley noticed the way the red fabric was designed to loop over the top of each arm and drape suggestively across her breasts.

He didn't remember much about the painting of the

Shady Lady except those exceptionally appealing breasts. At some time or another, he'd bet every teenage boy in Thunder Canyon had been intrigued by that enigmatic woman from the town's past...and by her breasts. In the next heartbeat his thoughts took a natural turn and he imagined Lisa without the dress. The mental image was a complete turn-on.

"Would you like to see them?"

If he'd been standing, he would have fallen. *Here?* She was looking into his face, and he made himself meet her eyes. His heart pounded.

"Riley, would you like to see the journals?"

"Oh! Yes. I'd love to see the journals...thanks."

"If you don't have any other plans, you can come to my place when we've finished eating. What kind of business do we need to discuss?"

He gathered his senses. "State and federal regulators. Water-quality inspectors. Ladders and escape routes."

"You really know about all that stuff?"

"I'm educating myself on the aspects of mining so I can advise you."

"That's as impressive as the wine."

He filled her in on what the inspectors would be looking for the next day. "The rest can wait," he told her. "We've talked enough business this evening."

She smiled. "I agree."

Lisa'd had him figured out since day one. She took a swallow of the luscious wine and let the warm glow suffuse her insides and spread to her limbs. He'd been hell-bent on endearing himself to her, making his services indispensable, and truth be told, she didn't mind all that much. She needed the know-how, experience and quick mind he had to offer. She didn't mind the attention. But his ruse was so transparent, she'd have to be blindfolded in a dark, windowless room not to see it.

His surprise at her transformation was gratifying. More than gratifying. *Delicious.* She'd caught him off guard. Turned the tables on Mr. Cool. She was sure he'd intended to impress her with an expensive meal and this incredible wine and his charming company. But he'd been expecting to impress and win over the Lisa with the baggy clothing and the wild coils of hair, not this new and improved version.

She smiled to herself. Maybe he'd just have to try a little harder now. Seeing him give his all could prove... rewarding.

"What's so amusing?" he asked.

"Nothing."

He raised one ebony eyebrow in question.

"A girl can have her secrets, can't she?" She chuckled at that because it sounded so ridiculous to her own ears. But her pathetic attempt at flirting must have been pretty good because he smiled, too, and his gaze traveled her face and hair in an altogether appreciative and intriguing way.

Lisa had been determined to break out of her timid, boring self and become someone confident and exciting. So far so good. She had him fooled, anyway.

What would someone named Lily Divine do if she was finally given the chance to stir things up with a man she'd had the hots for since adolescence? Okay, not the hots necessarily. Back then it had been an innocent unrequited yearning. *Now* it was the hots.

Well, someone confident like Lily would probably cast inhibition to the wind and grab opportunity with both fists. "Do you want dessert?" she asked.

"Do you?"

"I have brownies, ice cream and fudge topping at my place."

A grin tilted his lips, drawing her attention to their shape. "More wine?"

The bottle was empty. She wanted to remember the rest of the evening. "Better not. I can't feel my nose."

He signaled to their waiter, signed for the check and accompanied her to the door.

It was full dark now, a luminous crescent moon bright in the summer sky. Riley placed his hand in the small of her back as they walked toward the car. The warmth of his touch suffused the fabric of her dress and ignited another glow inside her.

They reached the red Jaguar, and Lisa heard the whir of a camera. Riley had opened her door and she turned to face him, standing in the minimal space between his body and the interior. "Maybe my place isn't such a good idea," she said, and her disappointment was sincere. "I have to think about tomorrow's headlines."

"What about the ice cream? And the journals?" he asked.

She shrugged.

"I can lose those guys. And I know of someplace private."

"Where?"

He leaned close so he couldn't possibly be overheard. "I have a cabin outside town. No one except family knows about it."

His whisper created goose bumps down her arms and across her shoulders. She looked up at him in the moonlight. "Then you'd better go back in and order dessert to go."

A grin spread across his face and he ushered her onto the seat. He was only gone a few minutes. She'd seen the way the staff catered to him. They'd probably run for the dessert.

"What is it?" she asked.

"Chocolate-raspberry truffle sound all right?"

She groaned. Chocolate bribes were a no-fail tactic with a woman like her.

He chuckled and started the car.

Within minutes he'd led the news vans away from town and was driving north on Thunder Canyon Road. He sped up, signaled as though he was turning toward his ranch, then quickly turned off the headlights and traveled straight ahead.

"How can you see?" she asked.

"I know where I'm going."

"You'd better tell me you can see. This is making me nervous."

"Just a little farther and I'll turn the lights back on." He approached a row of trees, which must have been what he was looking for, turned onto a side road and stopped. He turned off the engine and got out.

"Where are you going?"

"I'm checking to make sure no one is following us."

She had known him in high school. His family had

been respected—as well as resented—in this town for over a hundred years. She didn't think there'd been any serial killers in the Douglas line, but she probably should have checked before coming out in the wilderness with him.

He walked behind the car and returned after a few minutes. "Okay, we lost them."

After turning the headlights back on, he drove back onto the road, traveled what she thought was north for another twenty or thirty minutes, then took a left turn and headed along a dirt road lined with trees and tall grass. A deer sprang out of the foliage, and Riley braked until the animal bounded from sight.

Lisa was lost now, couldn't have found her way back alone, and she'd seen too many movies to not have a twinge of discomfort at her predicament. "Where are we?"

"Northwest of our ranch."

Finally he drove into a clearing where a well and a couple of shingle-sided outbuildings stood. He pulled directly in front of double doors, then got out to open them, and Lisa peered into the garage-like structure. He drove in, turned off the engine and grabbed the carry-out bag.

After locking the place, he led her up a lighted stairway.

"This is darker than the mine," she said. She seemed willing to let this man take her anywhere. Why was that?

"We'll be upstairs in a minute." He took her hand, and most of her doubts dissolved at the warm, strong touch. Lily wouldn't have had second thoughts about this adventure. Lisa wasn't going to let cold feet put crazy thoughts in her head. At the top was a landing and another door, and he opened it, guiding her into a dark room.

Riley stretched her arm as he groped for something, and a moment later fluorescent lights came on.

Lisa blinked. They stood in a kitchen. A well-appointed kitchen with stainless-steel appliances, wood flooring and a pine table and chairs. The open floor plan revealed a living area with comfortable sofas and chairs and a stone fireplace. Probably not someplace a serial killer would take his victims. Besides, dozens of people had seen them together tonight and even more would see their pictures tomorrow. "*This* is your *cabin?*"

"It's made of logs."

So it was. "How can it be that no one knows this place is here? Who built it? And delivered the furniture?"

"I hired an out-of-state builder. Brought the furnishings in myself."

"The appliances, too?"

"Remember me mentioning my financial advisor, Phil Wagner?"

"Yes."

"He's a friend. He helped. He uses the place whenever he wants."

Money will buy just about anything, she thought to herself. Even respectability. Anonymity. "If I asked you to take me home right this minute, what would you say?"

"Before dessert?"

She grinned. She'd had to double-check, after all. "You have newfangled plumbing in this rustic place?"

"There's a tiny bathroom in that hall right there, another bath through a suite of rooms you'll see on your left."

Size didn't matter right this moment. She found the closest functional room and minutes later felt much better. In the maple-framed mirror Lisa studied a reflection she wasn't used to confronting yet. Just seeing her new self reinforced her confidence. No wonder Riley looked at her differently. No wonder she felt so different. The new and improved Lisa was a force to be reckoned with. A chick with a life.

All the hard work that had gone into straightening her hair, selecting her clothing and putting together her new look had been worth the time and effort.

She wasn't sitting home sharing snacks with her dogs tonight. As soon as that thought surfaced, she experienced a twinge of guilt. *Sorry, boys.* She really liked those nights, too. But tonight was her night to shine. Riley was sniffing out more than popcorn, and she was liking it.

Returning to the other room, she discovered Riley had softened the lighting and made coffee. Chocolate-raspberry truffle waited on two small white plates.

"I have a sauvignon dessert wine if you'd prefer," he offered.

"No, the coffee smells really good."

"Have a seat and I'll pour us each a cup."

He brought two mugs of steaming coffee and sat them on the low table.

Lisa savored her dessert, momentarily closing her eyes and indulging. "This is incredible. Have you had it before?"

"No." He observed her with a mixture of awe and uncertainty that she took pleasure in knowing she inspired.

One of the reasons she didn't want to drink any more was that she already felt as if she was watching a bold new Lisa living her life. It was an odd feeling, but the impression was liberating. The times, they were a-changin', and she had to catch up with them.

"So," she said to break the silence that had stretched. "Only your family knows about this place."

"And Phil."

"And your friend, Phil. Does your family drop by? Use the cabin?"

He finished the bite he'd taken. "No, none of them drop by. Or use the cabin."

"How big is your family?" She didn't recall him having any brothers or sisters.

"My mom's from a large family, so I have a lot of aunts and uncles. When they visit my mom, they stay at the big house at the ranch. I have an adopted sister, Katie."

"Are you close to her?"

"Always was. She married at the first of the year."

Lisa heard something peculiar in Riley's tone when he spoke of his adopted sister's marriage. "Do I sense some tension there?"

"You didn't read about Katie and Justin Caldwell? Or see them on the news?"

"You mean Katie Fenton, the librarian? I know her from the library, and yes, I read about her playing the mail-order bride in this year's Heritage Day celebration. Someone stepped in to play the groom because Ben Saunders was sick. Some big-business type from out of town. They got snowed in together at the museum."

"That was Justin."

"Oh."

"Come to find out Justin was in town to get back at my father for using and discarding his mother—and then turning his back on Justin."

Lisa didn't understand his meaning, so she waited for Riley to explain, if he was going to. Her brain was probably still a little dulled from the wine.

"Seems my mother had a difficult time when I was born. She found out she couldn't have more children and she got depressed. She was too disturbed to properly care for me. And she turned my father away. He in turn took his interest elsewhere and got Justin's mother pregnant."

"Oh." She was sure that wasn't an insightful response, but his disclosure caught her by surprise. "So... Justin Caldwell is your brother."

"Half," he clarified. "He undermined us with the investors we had secured for the ski resort and took control away from my father. Then he told him who he was and why he'd done it."

"That was deceitful."

"He thought he had his reasons."

"You're defending him?"

"No. He did that as retribution for things he felt were done wrong against himself and his mother. It was a terrible time for my father—and for my mother when she learned the truth. Our family suffered because of it."

"I'm sure there wouldn't have been a good way for you and your mother to find out."

"You're right about that."

"Adele is a lovely woman and she's always been very

kind to me. That's more than I can say for a lot of people in this town."

"My father locked himself in his study and
wouldn't talk to me or my mother. It was only Katie
he allowed in, and she's the one he told the whole sor-
did story to."

The hurt in that disclosure was obvious.

"He had given Justin's mother half a million dollars
so that he could keep the baby. But she took Justin and
the money and disappeared. Caleb wanted Justin to know
he wanted him and asked Katie to get him to listen."

"The whole thing must have been awful for you,"
she said.

He shrugged as though it was of little consequence.
"I give Justin credit for doing right in the end. When he
learned that my father did care, he ended up turning control of the ski resort back over."

"So the two of you are on good terms?"

"We're okay."

"What about Justin and your father?"

"Hell, they're golf buddies."

"And your mother?"

"She's accepted Justin. His birth wasn't his fault."

"Neither was yours."

He looked aside at that remark. "I've never talked
about this before."

She could understand why. "You managed to keep
most of this out of the news, obviously. I don't remember reading anything about it."

"No one really knew what went on, and my father
certainly didn't want the truth made public. He gave

enough information to satisfy them and not enough to paint himself in a bad light."

"But he's recognized Justin as his son?"

"Yes. 'From a previous marriage' was the slant the papers got when the story finally broke."

"But he's not older than you."

"He wasn't born here, and since no one doubted the truth, the facts weren't checked. Suits the Douglas family."

Lisa sipped the dark brew. "This is incredible coffee."

"It's a blend Marge orders for me." He stood and removed his jacket. "Want to take another cup and sit outdoors? The porch is pretty high above the foliage, so it's usually free of mosquitoes."

The porch extended along two sides of the cabin and was furnished with comfortably padded chairs and chaise lounges. The half moon offered a silvered view of treetops and dark distant mountains. Fireflies dotted the landscape and frogs chirped. Lisa stood at the railing and gazed out into the darkness. The seclusion and cocooning silence lent a sense of peace to what had been unusually crazy days.

"It's a fantastic view in the daylight," he said.

"I'll bet the boys would love it here. They'd chase squirrels and rabbits to their hearts' content."

"You're welcome to use the place anytime. Bring them and hide out if you like."

"I'd never be able to find it."

"I'd show you." His voice came from right behind her. "Think about it."

"You're always giving me things to think about."

"I have good ideas."

She turned to find him studying her. The light from the front windows illuminated his features. Her heart fluttered unexpectedly. Just nerves, she thought to herself.

Lisa could count on one hand the number of dates she'd had in her life. Each one had been awkward and the conversation had been stilted, and she felt exactly the same way now as she had on those occasions: out of place. Was this a date? What did couples say to each other?

Her heart sped up. What did more-than-dating couples say to each other? She couldn't imagine. She'd watched a hundred movies in which the man and woman flirted and talked and ended up in bed together, but movies were fantasy, and though she loved those cinematic escapes, she was grounded firmly in reality.

What would Meg Ryan say to Tom Hanks right now? What would Kathleen Turner say to Michael Douglas?

"What's your favorite movie?"

He glanced toward the mountains, then back at her. "I don't watch a whole lot of movies."

"You don't?"

"No."

"Why not?"

"I don't know. Just don't take time."

"But you've seen movies."

"Of course."

"Then what's your favorite from those you've seen?"

He shrugged, seeming almost uncomfortable at being asked.

"What came to mind when I asked?"

"Platoon."

Lisa resisted wrinkling her nose. She hated war movies.

"What's your favorite movie?" he asked.

"I have a lot of favorites. A whole case of them, as a matter of fact."

"You made me pick one."

"Okay," she conceded. *"Roman Holiday."*

"Audrey Hepburn?"

She nodded. "And Gregory Peck."

"What's so appealing about it?"

She thought it over. "The heroine escapes her real life and has an adventure with no one knowing her true identity."

"I see the appeal."

"You do? Have you ever thought you'd like to be someone else for a while?"

"Not really."

"Too practical to have fantasies like that, huh?"

He touched her bare arm and a shiver darted up her spine. "Nothing wrong with fantasies," he said.

Lisa closed her eyes and heard the thump of her heart. Felt the chug of her blood in her veins and the heat of his hand on her arm. What would Lily say now?

He ran his palm up her arm, found her collarbone with one finger and stroked it.

Lily probably wouldn't waste time talking. Or even thinking.

Lisa opened her eyes and deliberately stepped into Riley's arms.

Chapter Seven

Lisa had never known there were kisses like this outside the movies. His lips on hers awakened a need that had been dormant inside her for a long, long time. It was easy to press uncertainty aside and lose herself in the sensations. He was warm. And strong. But she didn't delude herself that he felt anything for her. She wouldn't even let herself wonder if he felt the same flooding warmth and physical hunger she did at this moment, because she didn't want to spoil her fantasy come true.

Riley parted her lips and curled his tongue against hers in a deep, mind-drugging foray. Lisa slid her hands up along the hard, warm plane of his shirt front, wrapped her arms around his neck and pressed her body against his.

This evening, this moment, in Riley's arms she felt desirable for the first time. She wanted to sink all the way into this experience, to finally know passion and feel good about herself.

With one palm she framed his jaw. The unfamiliar texture of his cheek sent a jolt of excitement through her nerve endings. He turned into her touch and kissed her palm, his mouth hot and wet and more erotic than anything she'd ever known.

With both hands she bracketed his face and pulled his mouth back to hers for another staggering kiss.

Riley flattened one hand on her spine. With the other he rubbed her shoulder blade, stroked her bare arm and then cupped her breast. Her nipples were taut and her body thrummed with tense awareness. She wished she wasn't wearing this bra. Lisa felt exhilarated and sluggish at the same time and she didn't know how long she could stand on her own.

Maybe she gave him some sign of her lack of stamina, because he moved them both so that her back was against a wooden pillar. By insinuating one knee between her thighs, he prevented her from slipping to the floor but at the same time created a new and more disturbing sensation.

With both hands free he explored the contours of her body through her dress and caressed her breasts as best he could above her body shaper, soothing one ache while he created another. "You're incredible, Lisa," he whispered. "So beautiful."

His words were potent, giving her confidence, empowering her. She had planned this, she thought with smug satisfaction. Orchestrated events to her liking. And it wasn't over yet. Plain Lisa Jane Martin had Riley Douglas right where she wanted him.

Well…*almost.*

With renewed strength she left his lips and straightened to the task of loosening his tie. When he reached to assist, she pushed his hand away and tugged it off herself, then unbuttoned his shirt. Underneath he wore a stark white T-shirt that almost glowed in the moonlight. She ran her hands over his chest through the soft fabric, and he eased back only enough to tug it off over his head.

She let her fingers hover over his skin for a moment, anticipating the warmth of his flesh. She heard his intake of breath and looked up to read expectancy and arousal on his shadowed face. Lisa's heart pounded with anticipation.

She touched his chest then, soft hair, warm skin, lean muscle beneath. With his hands at her hips he simply experienced her exploratory caress.

Senses filled to brimming with his textures and heat, she ran a finger over his lips, then leaned upward for more kisses.

As he obliged her, Riley found the zipper on the back of her dress and pulled it down, lowering the front.

The salesgirl had told her the black strapless corset was all the rage. Putting it on, Lisa had compared it to a sausage casing, but the end result had made the dress fit perfectly. Riley *was* looking at her as if she were a mouthwatering breakfast, and she didn't mind.

He took the support of his knee away, so that she had to stand on her own, and he leaned down to kiss the tops of her breasts where they spilled over the corset. The tingling sensation his lips created sent Lisa's blood pulsing.

He straightened and kissed her again.

What was expected now? What was she supposed to say? Or do? She refused to show her awkwardness about any of this. Would he ask her if she wanted to get comfortable? Would he invite her into his bedroom? That might ruin the spontaneity, but she couldn't quite see baring it all out here on the porch with a thirty-foot drop below.

The thought gave her a twinge of panic. "Can we go inside?"

"Sure." He took her hand and she held up the front of her dress as he led her easily into the house. He paused and looked into her eyes. "Upstairs?"

One word, but it was his way of asking if they were going to move forward with what they'd started, as well as her chance to call a halt if she chose.

The same word gave him her answer. "Upstairs."

He let her walk ahead of him up a winding black wrought-iron staircase. From behind he finished unzipping her dress and cupped her bottom as though he couldn't keep his hands off her.

At the top he pointed to an open doorway, and she preceded him into the bedroom. After turning on a bathroom light, he left the door open a sliver, permitting only a slim measure of light to escape.

His broad form was in silhouette as he came toward her. Lisa's heart thudded with swift and unexpected delight and she kicked off her shoes. She'd imagined moments like this a hundred times in her girlish fantasies, and now her dreams had come to life. Riley leaned over the bed and, with a swoosh of silken fabric, pulled back a dark coverlet.

She let her dress fall to the floor and stepped out of it. There wasn't a second left for awkwardness, because he reached for her and snagged her around the waist, pulling her down with him on the bed. The sheets were cool against her bare back. Satin.

"This is sexy, but let's get rid of it," he said, reaching to find the hooks on her corset. *Good luck,* she thought, but he found the fasteners and released her breasts from their confinement.

He definitely knew what he was doing when he found her hard, sensitive nipple with his tongue. Freedom was one thing, but indulgence, oh, indulgence was even better, she discovered with a shudder. *This* was what she'd been missing. *This* was what scriptwriters tried to convey on screen and novel writers attempted to put on paper. No one had ever described it well enough.

She had a lot to learn.

Riley lavished attention on each breast and then on her mouth again. She wasn't sure which one of them reached for her underwear, but they both gave a tug from a different angle and the cotton garment was tossed aside. Gwen had tried to talk Lisa into a thong, but French-cut briefs had been as far as she'd been comfortable going. At this point she didn't think Riley would have noticed or cared if she'd been wearing boxers.

And surprisingly the complete lack of clothing didn't matter to her. She'd shrugged off her inhibitions the moment she'd put on the red dress.

This woman made Riley so hot, he didn't know how he was going to last long enough to perform the act. She'd been turning the tables on him for days. Tonight she had turned him inside out. Showing up in that dress and with that look in her eyes—that look that dared him to try not to fall victim to her seductiveness.

He dipped his hand lower and found her slick and swollen.

She made a sound halfway between a laugh and a cry.

He kissed her again because nothing was enough. Her mouth was sweet and her reactions so artlessly real, he'd lost himself in their first kiss and didn't want to be found.

She set his senses ablaze. "Your skin is so smooth," he praised her.

She bracketed his face with both hands, as though intent on his words.

"Your breasts…"

"What about them?"

They were gorgeous. Full and sensitive. "Let me just say…Lily Divine passed on some incredible genes."

Her lazy smile tipped his equilibrium.

When had he lost control of this game?

When had Lisa Martin become someone he *desired?*

He didn't want to think about it. He shucked out of the rest of his clothing and took great care in kissing and stroking her, tasting the skin behind her ears and at her throat. He used his fingers to coax a series of surprised little gasps and had her raising her hips off the bed.

She grasped his shoulders so hard, her nails bit into his skin. "Riley," she said breathlessly.

"Yes?" He looked into her eyes in the darkness.

"Nothing. I just wanted to say your name."

"Say it, then."

"Riley Douglas."

He reached for the night table, found the box of condoms he'd placed in the drawer earlier and sheathed himself.

She touched his shoulder almost hesitantly.

Riley leaned over her and kissed her. She drew him down to her, eagerly accommodating his weight.

"Keep kissing me," she urged.

He did and guided himself, hoping he wasn't shaking as much on the outside as he was on the inside.

Lisa sought his tongue and took it into her mouth in an erotic imitation of what their bodies were straining to do.

"Relax, Lisa."

"Riley."

Was she just saying his name again? Entering her took a moment of intense concentration while he kissed her and purposefully eased his way.

Her body accepted him all at once, and she grasped his upper arms at the same moment, as though he'd just pushed past a resistance.

Dull recognition nagged at the back of his mind while extreme pleasure flooded his senses. "Lisa, what…?"

"Don't say anything." She wrapped herself around him and made him forget reason and thought.

All that existed in the moments that followed was the two of them floating on a sensual ocean of enjoyment.

Somewhere in the back of his mind he knew she was taking more from him than he'd ever intended to offer, but he couldn't hold back. He wanted to give her more and he wanted more of her. As though detachment hadn't been bred into him from birth, he wanted all of her. Riley felt as if he'd been missing this, even though they'd never before shared a bed.

She climaxed with a soft groan and a shudder, and he gritted his teeth to draw the pleasure out for her. When her body relaxed, he allowed his own swift release and then shifted his weight to her side and kissed her.

She met his gaze in the darkness, and he thought he sensed a question. He threaded his fingers through her hair, combing it away from her face, and caressed her cheek with a thumb. But she said nothing.

Lisa wrapped her fingers around his wrist and moved so she could lie comfortably and kiss him.

Time didn't exist as their hearts returned to a normal beat and the air-conditioning cooled their heated skin. Riley couldn't remember ever spending leisurely after-sex time with a woman before. He wanted to kiss her as much now as he had hours ago. And he was still enjoying it every bit as much as before they'd had sex.

He'd only had this place a few months, but he'd planned to keep the cabin to himself. He was glad it had been Lisa he'd broken the rules for. He was glad he'd brought her.

He ran his fingers through her hair, catching in the tangles they'd created together. He lowered his face to the crook of her neck and inhaled her scent—a scent more intoxicating than the wine—then placed slow kisses along her shoulder.

They lay with their legs tangled, and she sensuously rubbed the sole of her foot against his calf.

Riley rose over her and looked into her eyes before he kissed her. Within minutes he was ready again and she was smiling a welcome.

Lisa had dozed for a few minutes, but she woke to the unfamiliarity of the room and her bed companion. She had to go to the bathroom, so she got up and closed herself in the adjoining bath. The reality of what she'd done tried to burst her bubble of pleasure, but she fought it. She'd known full well what she was doing. She'd wanted this more than anything. She wasn't going to be sorry now. A minute later she padded out and gathered her clothing.

"I have to go home. The boys will need to go out."

Riley leaned on one elbow. "Can't they wait till morning?"

"I never leave them alone this long at night." She took her clothes into the bathroom and talked to him through the partially open door as she dressed. "Besides, we don't want to be seen returning to my place in the morning."

"You're right." The sound of sheets rustling accompanied a click as he turned on a lamp. She saw the light through the crack in the doorway as she stuffed herself into the corset.

"My God," he said.

"What?"

"Oh, my God."

"What?" She had her dress on and was struggling with the zipper. She opened the door to see what had upset him.

He stood beside the bed naked, his boxers in his hand. "Why didn't you tell me?"

"Tell you what?"

"That you were a virgin, Lisa." He raked a hand through his black hair and it stood up in unruly waves. "I am so dense. I knew there was something I wasn't paying attention to. I'm sorry."

"For what?" Heart pounding, she turned back into the bathroom, found a comb in a drawer and tried unsuccessfully to tame her hair. Her inexperience shouldn't have to be embarrassing.

"For not knowing."

"What was to know? I didn't tell you because I didn't want it to be a big deal." Wherever she'd left her purse, she had a scrunchie. She moved through his room, ignoring him as he tried to step into his pants and follow her at the same time.

"It *is* a big deal." He grabbed his socks and shirt. "You'd never had sex before. I was your first partner and I didn't know."

She was ahead of him on the iron staircase. "I really didn't want you to know. And now I don't want to talk about it."

"Lisa."

"Please?" she said, finally pausing in the living room but not looking at him. "Please, Riley, can you just let it go?"

Behind her he was silent.

She picked up her handbag, found her hair tie and gathered her hair into a knot on her head. "Will you take me home now?"

"Of course. Whatever you want."

It was much more awkward putting their clothing and shoes back on than it had been taking them off. They descended the stairs and Riley opened the garage doors.

After he'd locked the place up, they were on their way back toward town. The ride was dark and silent, punctuated only by the burning looks she sensed him sending her way. She would never let him know how she really felt.

The streets of Thunder Canyon were deserted this time of night, and Riley drove directly to her house and parked in the drive.

One news van was parked across the street.

"Don't get out," she said. "I don't want the papers to have a picture of our good-night."

"Okay."

"Thanks for dinner. And the wine. And making those arrangements with the reporters."

He reached for her hand. "Lisa."

She looked at him finally. He was as handsome as ever. Mr. Cool. "We met before."

"Before what?"

"Before I inherited the Queen of Hearts."

His eyebrows rose in confusion. "We did?"

"Yes." Her heart chugged nervously, but she forced the words out anyway. "I was your chemistry tutor in high school."

For a moment she thought he was going to deny it, but then he nodded. "I remember having a tutor to get through that class. That was *you?*"

"It was me."

"Well. Funny how life comes around in a circle sometimes."

She didn't think there was anything funny about it. "Yeah."

"I'll call you."

"You'll see me at the mine tomorrow."

He released her hand and reached for her shoulder, but she opened the car door, turning on the overhead light. "Night."

Lisa hurried to her door, fumbled for her keys and let herself inside. Why she'd told him, she didn't know. She hadn't meant to ever let on.

Joey and Piper were excited to see her, sniffing her skirt and her feet to see where she'd been. She let them out back and peered around the corner of the house to see Riley's red car drive away.

Her first day and night as the new and improved Lisa had gone quite well, she thought, unwilling to acknowledge the awkwardness at the end. No one could possibly think this evening had been boring. It had been box-office, Julia Roberts exciting. Dogs petted and fed, she trudged upstairs, stripped out of the dress and got in the shower.

After she'd dried her hair and fought for a spot between her two pets in her bed, she relaxed against the pillows and sighed. At least now she did feel different. Still like a fake, but at least a more knowledgeable and experienced fake.

She smiled to herself. Experienced with none other than wealthy Thunder Canyon scion, Riley Douglas.

* * *

Lisa stared at the newspaper on Bernadine's desk the following morning. *The Shady Lady or the Lucky Lady?* the caption under two photographs read. The photograph on the left was a picture of Lily Divine that Lisa had never seen before. The dark-haired woman was garbed in the red dress now on display at the museum. Someone had retouched a black-and-white photograph to add color. Lily was smiling her confident smile and had been cropped out so that only the shoulder of the man beside her could be seen.

The picture on the right was present-day living color. Last-night color to be exact. It was Lisa in her red dress, smiling a self-pleased smile at the camera. A quick glance at the surroundings showed it to have been taken outside the restaurant.

One can see the resemblance between these two auburn-haired beauties, both residents of Thunder Canyon, both well-to-do women, both knockouts in red. Is there more than a physical resemblance between the two?

"What is that supposed to be implying?"

"Who knows?" Bernadine replied.

Lisa held the paper up for a better view. "Do I really look like her?"

"Well…yes."

Lisa smiled. "Not a bad thing."

"Not at all."

"What business do we have today?"

"We have a letter from a Logan Banks's attorney claiming that Logan is your cousin and entitled to his share of the Queen of Hearts."

"Never heard of him."

"Didn't think so, but we're checking him out anyway. We have to send a legal response."

Lisa poured herself a cup of coffee. "Isn't this about the fourth new cousin I've had?"

"Fifth. Great suit."

"Thanks. I did a little shopping. Oh, yeah..." She fished in her bag and pulled out the signed contracts. "He signed 'em."

Bernadine smoothed the papers on her desktop. "All the incorporation papers have gone through. We have our ID numbers and we're ready for business. Have you decided about Riley's loan offer?"

"Won't any bank in Thunder Canyon give me a loan now?"

"Bank loans require collateral. They'd ask for a share of the mine."

"Okay."

"The personal loan ties up less of your assets."

"But I don't want it to be personal."

"You don't want to owe Douglas."

"Exactly."

"Whatever you prefer. Want to have lunch?"

Lisa assured her she did, but added, "We'll have to be back for the state inspection at the mine this afternoon."

"What is it? Water quality?"

"It's basically a run-through of regulations since we're not pumping yet. They're going to check for proper storage of explosives, escape routes, ladders, marked ore shutes."

Bernadine turned to take papers from the printer on

the stand behind her. "Wow, you're really getting the hang of this."

"Riley's the one who's been learning it all and filling me in."

"A good right-hand man, eh?"

Right hand. Left hand. Good with both hands. Lisa simply nodded.

Bernadine took her to the Hitching Post for lunch. The place was filled with customers this time, and nearly all of them recognized Lisa. She was greeted with stares, wide-eyed interest and even a few friendly hellos.

Today's front page of the *Nugget* had already been framed and hung over the bar, near the painting of Lily.

"Well, if it isn't the Lucky Lady herself!" the bartender called from behind the polished cherrywood bar.

Several people clapped and cheered as Lisa and Bernadine made their way to a booth. Lisa smiled and gestured with what turned out like a parade wave—at least to her. Feeling silly, she dropped her hand.

Her cheeks felt flushed. "This is the first time I've actually let people see me," she said, in awe of their reactions. "I've been so caught up in hiding and running from the cameras, avoiding people in general, that I guess I just didn't know what their reactions would really be."

"You're the town celebrity."

"For now."

They ordered and ate. Occasionally someone stopped by their table to talk to Lisa or congratulate her. When Bernadine asked for their check, the waitress told her their lunch was on the house.

They headed for the mine in the lawyer's car, while Lisa grappled with her newly discovered status in town.

Lisa showed her ID to the security guards along the route, and when they arrived at the mine site, several cars were already parked there. Lisa recognized the Douglases' silver Town Car.

Riley was standing with a group of men, some in casual business dress, others in jeans and work shirts. He saw Lisa and Bernadine approach and turned to greet them. Her body tingled with intimate remembrance when he shook her hand.

He made introductions, and Lisa had to fight the urge to look up at him and gauge his expression. She'd dressed the part of a professional, in her navy pinstripe suit and white blouse. The men were treating her with respect, and she wasn't about to make a fool of herself by looking at Riley and revealing the emotions threatening to resurface.

He gave her curious sidelong looks she caught from the corner of her eye, but he kept up the professional front.

"What are they doing now?" she asked, shading her eyes against the sun. A group of men had moved away.

"Checking the pumps that will suck water from the mine's lower levels as we look for another vein."

"When will the actual mining begin?" Bernadine asked.

"As long as everything passes today's inspection, the mining will start first thing tomorrow."

A thrill of anticipation passed through Lisa. "It's really going to happen."

Riley nodded. "It is." He glanced at her. "You remember we have a meeting day after tomorrow?"

"It's on my calendar."

"You need to have a plan for how you're going to proceed with profits."

So much to think about and plan for, she thought. "Who knew a lot of money would be so much work to handle?"

"I'm going to strongly urge you to roll back initial profits into mine improvements and then acquire other mine properties in the vicinity."

"I'm sure you know best." There was no way Bernadine could know by their conversation or careful expressions that they'd been more than business partners last night. Nine hours ago they'd been naked and wrapped around each other like the strands of a licorice twist. The sun seemed warmer all of a sudden, and Lisa fanned herself with the checklist he'd handed her.

The men returned with their reports, and all were favorable. Riley thanked them and the different groups walked toward the cars.

"Lisa."

She stopped at Riley's call and motioned for Bernadine to walk on to the car ahead of her.

"I just wanted to ask how you were doing."

"I'm doing fine."

He glanced around. "We need to talk."

She refused to meet his eyes. She knew exactly what he wanted to talk about and she didn't feel the same compunction. "Poor timing, Riley."

"Not here. Will you meet me tonight?"

"I can't."

"Tomorrow, then?"

"I'll call you."

"Okay."

She walked to where Bernadine waited in the driver's seat of her car.

"What did you say to him?" the lawyer asked.

"Nothing."

"He looks like you told him his dog died."

"He doesn't have a dog."

"Hmm. Deduct points for that, huh?"

Lisa glanced from Bernadine to Riley as he strode toward his chauffeured car. Her stomach dipped a little at the sight of the man...at her intimate personal knowledge of the man...and at the indelible memory of what they'd shared.

She'd known going into that experience that it wasn't leading to a relationship. She'd been fine with that, as long as she had the experience...and the memory.

How did other women handle casual affairs? How would Lily have handled a lover? What should the new and improved Lisa do?

Lisa corrected her thinking. Riley was not her lover. He was a man to whom she'd been attracted. A man who'd never paid her the time of day until she'd inherited a fortune. And a man with whom she'd slept because she'd wanted to and because she could.

She could do anything she wanted. She could sleep with him again. She could choose not to.

She didn't *have* to do anything. Except be true to herself.

But there was something she could *not* do. And it was imperative she remember she was not Julia Roberts. She could *not* fall in love with Riley Douglas.

Chapter Eight

Emelda Ross's home was located on the western out-skirts of town. The only places farther out than hers were the ice rink and the Douglas ranch. Lisa still had unanswered questions in her mind, and the only person she knew of who was left to ask was the elderly lady who told stories to children in the library.

A dog barked from inside the house as Lisa parked and approached. The elderly woman peered out the door, then stepped onto the porch. A small Jack Russell terrier darted from behind the skirt of her long floral dress and yipped as Lisa got closer.

"Hi, fella." Lisa knelt and held out her hand.

The dog loped down the stairs and stood sniffing the air warily. It then trotted over to Lisa and licked her wrist and her fingers.

She scratched the animal's ears. "What's his name?"

"Dog. What's yours?"

"Lisa Martin."

"Lisa Jane! Well, why didn't you say so? Look at you! Come on in. I have applesauce cake."

She stood and climbed the stairs. Dog's nails clicked on the porch stairs as the pet followed her. "I tried to call, but only got a busy signal."

"I take the nuisance off the hook when I nap." Miss Emelda led the way into her house and ushered Lisa into a huge kitchen that was as outdated as her own. She cut slices of cake and poured Lisa a glass of milk as though she was still ten years old. "What are you reading now, Lisa Jane? You were never big on the classics, as I recall."

Lisa smiled as she said, "I like romance novels and cozy mysteries."

Miss Emelda chuckled. "I've read a few of those myself." She seated herself on a nearby chair. "I see your picture in the paper every day." She winked. "I especially liked the red dress."

"Thanks."

"What brings you clear out here?"

Lisa tasted the cake, paused in reverence and let her taste buds recover before she replied. "I've been digging into my great-great-grandmother's past."

"Aha. Lily."

"I visited with Tildy Matheson, and she had journals that belonged to Catherine Douglas. I read those, and what I'm reading and hearing are entirely different slants to what is commonly told about Lily."

"I've heard the old stories myself," Miss Emelda said

with a sage nod. "I had an aunt who was friends with the Hardings' daughter."

"Lily and her husband's daughter you mean?"

"Yes. Everyone still refers to her as Lily Divine, but she lived out her life married to a Harding. Their daughter would have been your great-grandmother."

"That's exciting. Did your aunt ever speak of the Harding family?"

"Oh, my, yes. Lily Harding was a headstrong woman, ahead of her time and subject for much discussion over the years. Seems she had a sorry lot in life before she came to Thunder Canyon. Not sure about the whole of it, but the story goes that she didn't think a woman's plight should be birthing a baby every year or being cook and laundress to a husband and his hired men. Lily saw too much abuse and too many women treated as property, and it was her mission to help women in need of a new start."

"Had Lily been mistreated herself?"

"That I don't know. All the stories I learned about her are from after she settled here. Lily's daughter said Lily inherited a bordello from a dear friend and turned it into a saloon and boardinghouse. When Thunder Canyon sprang up as a small mining town, she used a golden opportunity to make herself a modest fortune by selling liquor to the miners."

This story made more sense to Lisa. She listened with fascination.

"Now, Nathaniel Harding was a bounty hunter, a man tired of roaming, and he hired on to clean up the town and the saloons. Nate and Lily butted heads a good many times before they fell in love and got married. My guess is they butted heads a few times afterward, as well," she said with a wink.

"What a romantic story."

Miss Emelda chuckled. "Your favorite kind."

"Was Lily ever truly a prostitute?"

"I really don't know what her life was like before she took over the Shady Lady and met Nate Harding. And if'n it was true, she wouldn't have told her daughter now, do you think?"

"No. I guess not. But even if that was in her past— and I might never know for sure—she made a fresh start and did a lot of good in her life."

"She did at that."

"Thanks, Miss Emelda. You've been a big help." She stood.

The older woman bustled to remove their plates. "You know I like to tell stories about the old days. Maybe you'll be the one to pass this one on."

"I will."

"Take some cake home with you. I have too much and I don't get a lot of company. If I put it on this plate, you'll have to bring it back soon."

"I'll be glad to do that. And anytime you need someone to take care of Dog for you, you just call me." Lisa fished in her purse for a business card and placed it on Miss Emelda's counter. "That's what I do, you know."

"I don't go out much, but if I do, I'll call."

Lisa carried the plate of cake to her Blazer and waved to Miss Emelda and Dog. The old woman's stories had always delighted her in her childhood, and this one had

been even more special than all the rest because it revealed truths Lisa longed to know.

Even if she never knew the complete truth about Lily,
she was never going to be ashamed or embarrassed to
be related to her again. The woman had been smart
enough to run her own business, compassionate enough
to help other women, bold enough to think women
should vote and confident enough to wear a red dress.

Lisa smiled to herself as she drove toward home.

Among a dozen messages on her machine was one
from Riley: *"Lisa. Can we get together? Call me."*

His voice affected her as it always did, making her
stomach dip. Should they get together? That was the
question, but she didn't have a good answer. Lisa wasn't
about to take any chances with her heart where this guy
was concerned. She had to keep her wits about her and
stay one step ahead of his game. She wasn't hoping for
a happy ending with Riley Douglas. Maybe the wise
thing would be a friendly ending. The sooner, the better.

Riley tossed a signed stack of papers on Marge's
desk just as his cell phone rang. He reached in his jeans
pocket and dug it out. *Lisa.*

"Hey."

"Hi. You called?"

Marge glanced up at him. He stepped into his office
and closed the door. "Can we get together? How about
dinner?"

"We have a meeting tomorrow. We'll see each
other then."

"I know. This isn't business."

"I don't know, Riley." He sensed the hesitation in her voice.

She was giving him the brush-off? His head was so mixed up, he couldn't wrap a coherent thought around the woman. She'd shown up in that red dress and he'd lost his mind. What was wrong with him? He didn't get *involved.* He didn't lose his cool and he never, *never* deflowered virgins.

In his defense, he hadn't known she was a virgin until he'd seen the telltale signs afterward. It still made him a little weak in the knees when he thought about it. She'd waited all these years to have sex and then she'd chosen him. The fact stunned him. She didn't want to talk about it. Hell, she didn't even want to have dinner with him.

He got a little defensive. "Are you giving me the big kiss-off here? If I did something, let me know what it was, will you?"

"You didn't do anything I didn't want you to do," she answered.

"Are you talking about sex?" he asked.

"What are you talking about?"

He thrust his fingers into his hair and gripped his scalp in frustration. "I'm talking about you avoiding me now. *Since* we had sex."

"I'm not avoiding you."

"What do you call it when you hedge a dinner invitation?"

"I'm sorry, Riley, did we make some sort of a commitment that I don't know about?"

Her words gut-punched him more effectively than if

she'd been standing in front of him and swung a fist. He was sounding like a clingy high school girl, and she'd just given him the we're-just-friends line. He was swimming in uncharted waters here and he was concerned his sense of direction was going to get him lost. This had never—ever—happened to him before. "Never mind. I'll see you tomorrow."

Riley snapped his phone shut and stared at his office wall for a full minute, collecting himself. Fine. So she wasn't enamored yet. He'd be damned if he was going to let that deter him. Her lack of enthusiasm wasn't part of the plan.

But he still had a plan. And he was nothing if not persistent in getting what he wanted.

She couldn't help herself. Lisa hung the beige suit back on the hanger and dressed in a pair of black hipster pants with a cute silver chain belt and a blouse that only buttoned up as far as her cleavage. She had these Lily boobs, she might as well show them to their advantage.

Now the shoes took some getting used to. After living in tennis shoes, these backless little heels took some practice. But she was getting the hang of them. She'd spent an hour on her toenails last night and finally decided on red. Red went with everything and, well, it just plain looked sexy.

The bank loan Riley had helped arrange for her had gone through, and after their meeting today she was going to buy a car. She didn't know the first thing about car buying. Should she ask for advice? She was too frugal not to want to avoid being taken advantage of.

She drove the Blazer to the Douglases' downtown office, where Riley had asked her to meet him, thinking as she did that she wouldn't be driving the familiar beast much longer. No more breakdown worries. No more dead batteries in winter or repair bills she couldn't afford. The enormity of her new situation still took some getting used to, and she had to remind herself all the time.

A checkbook-size folder held closed with a rubber band lay on the console. Inside were all the coupons she'd clipped and filed and saved. For days she'd been looking at it, considering throwing it out, but had been unable to. Fifty cents was still fifty cents. Lisa laughed at herself and imagined the looks she'd get if she presented a coupon at the Super Saver Mart now that everyone knew she was the millionaire heiress.

She parked in the small lot and concentrated on walking smoothly all the way inside and up to the receptionist's desk. She did pretty well, if not breaking an ankle was any indication.

"Lisa Martin?" The slender, dark-haired woman greeted her with a smile. "It's so nice to meet you. I'm Connie Gray. Mr. Douglas asked me to show you right into his office."

Connie opened a gleaming wood door and ushered her into a room similar to Riley's home office.

Riley stood from behind a glass-topped desk. His gaze swept over her from head to toe and he seemed to struggle to maintain a professional expression. "Good morning, Miss Martin."

This was only the second time she'd seen him since

the other night, and she was bound and determined not to show any reaction or weakness. "Good morning."

"There are drinks set up on the table over there," Connie told her. "And I put out rolls and sandwiches. Please help yourself." She smiled and closed the door behind her.

"Is it just us?" Lisa asked.

"Yes. You look great."

"Thanks." She made her way to the long table and placed two of the delicate sandwiches and a cinnamon roll on a gold-edged white china plate. "Ever heard of disposable plates?"

"Connie takes care of all that."

"Like Marge does at your other office."

"Yes."

"Do they know each other?"

"Yes, why?"

She seated herself at a table and tried a sandwich. "Mmm, awesome chicken-and-walnut mixture." Then answered him with, "Just wondering. What are we deciding today?"

He brought a couple of folders and an envelope from his desk and sat across from her. Within half an hour he'd explained financial details regarding the mine's initial operation and advised her on the best courses of action. "You do still trust me to advise you, don't you, Lisa?"

"Do I have reason not to?"

"I give you my word I'll consider each action as though this was my own money. I'll use the best of my ability to steer you toward decisions that will benefit your corporation. I intend to show you every penny of income and expense and to offer you my best advice on generating profits."

"Your word is good enough for me," she replied easily. It was in his best interest to make her money since he wanted to share in it. She'd been born at night, but it hadn't been last night.

A roll and a cup of coffee later, their business was concluded. He was good at this money-managing stuff.

His intercom beeped and Connie said, "Mine foreman is on line one, Mr. Douglas. He says it's important."

Riley got up and stood beside his desk to push the speakerphone button. "Douglas here."

"Mr. Douglas." The man's voice was clear. "I couldn't reach anyone at Miss Martin's number. The two of you might want to be here when we haul this car out into the sunlight."

Riley met Lisa's eyes. "We'll be there."

He clicked off the phone and pressed the intercom button. "Connie, have the driver bring the car around, please."

"What's going on?" Lisa asked.

"This is it. The first of the ore. It's been right there waiting for us to have everything in place. Let's go."

"Oh, wow! This is exciting." Lisa pointed to the table. "Let's grab a few of those sandwiches for the road. They'll tide us over."

He watched her pile several sandwiches on a plate and cover them with a cloth napkin.

"What?" she said. "I'll return your napkin."

"Take all the napkins if you want. I don't care."

"Then what are you looking at?"

"You."

Lisa looked away, momentarily flustered. "Let's go."

They headed out past the receptionist and onto the street, where the chauffeur waited beside the Town Car. "Where to, Mr. Douglas?"

"The mine."

They got in and got settled. She placed the plate of sandwiches on the seat between them, and he looked out the window with a grin.

"Great picture in the paper. The one of you in the red dress," he said.

She hadn't minded it. She gave him a sideways glance and grinned. "It was okay."

He looked back. "Did you know the AP picked it up?"

"Associated Press?"

"Uh-huh. Chad Falkner made himself a pretty penny selling it to *People*."

"No way!"

"I'd watch for the next issue."

"Stop it." He was putting her on, and she wasn't falling for it. The thought of plain-Jane Lisa Martin's photo beside Jennifer Aniston's was ludicrous.

"So, we're on our way to see gold, is that right?"

"That's what's excavated from a gold mine."

"It's going to be real now." She looked out the window at the passing scenery, excited now in spite of herself. "What do you have on your schedule this afternoon?"

He thought a minute. "Paperwork for the ski resort."

"Anything you can work around?"

"Yes, why?"

She looked at him. "I want to go buy a car. Maybe you could advise me. I don't want to pay more than I should."

"Do you know what you want?"

"Not really."

He tapped his fingers on his knee. "Were you thinking of going to Billings? Are you ordering or buying from a showroom?"

She shrugged. "I have no idea."

"I'll come with you. We'll stop by the ranch to get my car on the way back," Riley said. "I rode in with my dad this morning."

"What about the Blazer? Won't I need it for the trade-in?"

"Lisa." He cocked a brow. "Get serious."

"What?"

"You're not going to get a trade-in on that thing. Besides, it won't make it that far."

"What will I do with it, then?"

"Call a scrap-metal dealer? Have a bonfire?"

She gave him a sideways look. It was fine for her to belittle her own vehicle, but she didn't like the verbal degradation coming from him. "I'll have you know that Blazer got me where I needed to go for the last ten years...*most* of the time."

"So it has sentimental value?"

"Some."

He tilted his head. "I hear you can have a vehicle smashed down into a coffee table."

"Now there's an idea."

They shared a laugh just as the driver pulled up to the last security point.

When they reached the mine, the flurry of activity amazed Lisa. There were workmen and trucks and all manner of tools and apparatus she'd never seen before.

The foreman dashed out to meet them. "It's up. Wait till you see!"

He led them to a metal cart filled with chunks of ore taken from the mine's interior.

"There you go, Lisa," Riley said, urging her forward. "There's your gold."

She stared at hunks of rock with gleaming fissures and exposed nuggets. Sunlight caught the exposed veins and gold glittered.

Riley asked for a hammer and knocked off a piece. Turning to Lisa, he held it out, then dropped it into her extended palm.

The chunk of gold he'd given her was as big as a plum and heavy. She held it out so the light caught it, then glanced at each person in the gathering. Smiles creased every face.

Someone let out a whoop, and the rest joined in. Lisa found herself swept into Riley's arms and spun around in a circle. When he set her down, the men crowded around her with excited congratulations. The whole thing still seemed surreal.

"Now do you believe you're wealthy?" Riley asked sometime later as they walked back to the car. "You owned the gold all along, but now you've seen it."

"It's more real, that's for sure." She still held the nugget.

The driver took them to Riley's, where they got his car. She dropped the piece of gold into her purse and selected a CD. Riley showed her how to load the unfamiliar machine and press Start.

"I think I'll get a car with one of these players."

The sandwiches ran out long before they reached Billings, and Riley drove through a fast-food place on the highway to order a burger and a soda. Lisa got a shake.

When they reached the city, he pulled onto the first car lot he came to, which happened to be a BMW dealership.

A young salesman spotted the red Jaguar and nearly ran out to greet them. "Hi! Are you looking for anything in particular today?"

"I just want to look," Lisa told the salesman pointedly.

"Go right ahead." The young man handed Riley a business card. "I'm Jamie. I'll be glad to help you if you have any questions."

Lisa test-drove half a dozen cars, but felt her eyes bug out of her head when she asked how much the price was on the one she liked the best.

"It's a *car*," she said to Riley, but the salesman was within hearing distance, so she lowered her voice. "I could pay the national debt with that much money. Or build a children's hospital."

"A hospital." Riley raised a brow and studied her.

"Well, a clinic. Hey, an animal shelter. Why on earth would I want to spend that much money on a car?"

"It's not just a car, Lisa, it's a BMW. Like mine is a Jag. It's going to cost more money than a midsize family sedan or an economy car. People buy them because they can afford to. A car like this is about image. You're a wealthy woman now. The cars you choose reflect you and the way you want to be seen."

"Afford it or not—image or no—it's a waste of money. I want to go somewhere where I won't feel like I'm throwing money away."

"It's not throwing money away, it's an investment."

"No, a stock is an investment. A car is transportation."

"Why'd you bring me, then? To make me crazy?"

"No, I read somewhere that a man can negotiate for a better deal than a woman. Did you notice he gave his card to *you*, when I'm the one who said I wanted to look?"

He tilted his head to indicate he had.

"*And* I brought you because I don't know cars."

At that remark he stared at her pointedly.

"I don't know cars, but I know I don't want one this expensive."

"Okay." He turned to the salesman. "Thanks for your help. We're going to look around a little more."

The next dealership was more like it. It still seemed an extravagance to buy a brand-new car when slightly used or even mildly dented would get her around just as well, but she fell in love with a new Blazer, gold in color.

"You said image, and this is image. It's *gold*," she said to Riley with a grin.

"But you've driven a Blazer for the last—how long?—twelve years? Don't you want something different? Sportier maybe?"

"I need four-wheel drive in winter. It's practical."

"I agree, but you could get both. This plus something sporty."

She directed her palm at his suggestion. "Don't. Uh-uh. One is plenty. Baby steps, remember?"

The salesman was nearly jumping up and down over

the sale with a check in full as payment, but when Riley started talking about two vehicles, she thought the fellow was going to hyperventilate.

"Easy." Lisa turned to him and explained in a serious tone, "I'm only getting the Blazer. Period."

The man looked to Riley, who shrugged. "She's calling the shots."

It took longer than she thought it should have for the transaction and for the service department to do their thing. She was itching to get the keys and her bill of sale.

"How about dinner?" Riley asked. "By the time we get back, they'll have your new wheels ready."

She had asked him to take time from his day to help her make this choice, though she'd pretty much made all the decisions herself. Riley was her measuring stick, however, and as long as she stayed just under his suggestions, she felt comfortable. She owed him for his patience. "Okay."

"Let's go make sure they didn't sell my car while I was looking with you."

With a grin Lisa joined him. The salesman had been disappointed when he'd learned Riley's Jag was not a trade-in.

"Where to?" she asked a few minutes later.

"What are you hungry for?"

"I'll eat anything."

"I've noticed."

She cast a frown his direction. "You'd rather take a picky eater to dinner?"

"Definitely not. Unless it was you. I just want to take you to dinner."

"Good cover."

"Yeah."

Lisa chose the restaurant—a casual steak house with a salad bar—and paid for their meals while Riley was using the restroom.

"Why'd you do that?" he asked as they took seats and the waitress handed them plates.

"You helped me today. It was the least I could do."

The waitress walked away.

Lisa leaned forward. "Besides, I'm rich."

She got up and went to prepare her salad. Riley followed and stood beside her. "This is a date, so I'm supposed to pay."

She barely glanced up from her plate of lettuce. "Who says?"

"Who says what? That it's a date or that I'm supposed to pay?"

"Both."

He made his salad and returned to the table with her. "You don't make anything easy, do you?"

She hoped not. It was her goal to stay a giant leap ahead of him at all times. She was not going to be sucked into his scheme. She'd always been attracted to him, so she had that working against her. She could never let him know how she really felt about him. But besides that she was having the time of her life.

"Remember this Saturday evening is the groundbreaking reception," he said.

She had forgotten.

"You agreed to come."

She nodded. "I'll drive myself."

Their dinners arrived. "Have you scheduled your interview?"

"I've been putting it off. I was thinking I'd call tomorrow and arrange it. If they keep up their part of the deal and leave me alone for a week, it will be pure bliss."

"You can always use my cabin. Feel free to take your dogs and stay as long as you like. There's only one lock—the one that gets you in through the garage—and I'll have a key made for you."

The offer was so tempting, she hadn't allowed herself to think about it. Time away from prying eyes would be welcome. Maybe she had a few qualms about returning to the place where she'd lost her virginity, but she'd have to deal with that eventually. "I don't know how I'd find it myself."

"I could take you out. Or lead the way." He looked up. "If you planned to take off during the week the reporters were leaving you alone, they wouldn't see you to follow."

She leaned forward. "The last day of the reprieve I could go out and take as many days undiscovered as I like."

He nodded.

Lisa laid down her fork. "How long can this last, Riley? I mean, wouldn't you think they'd be bored with this whole story by now?"

"There's something fascinating about the whole rags-to-riches story," he said, then paused with an apologetic look. "Not that you wore rags, but—"

"I get it."

"Your evasiveness is like an aphrodisiac to them," he said. Maybe he knew firsthand?

"I've heard of celebrities who go ahead and stop and pose for photos and then the paparazzi leave them alone because they got what they wanted."

He nodded as he finished his steak.

"Maybe this interview will have that effect."

"That's what we're counting on."

He had been a big help. She'd have been even more lost without him. But after what had transpired between them, things were more tense. Lisa had wanted what had happened. She was honest with herself—she could admit she wanted more. She just had to guard her heart. That was her first priority. If she could do that and still let him as physically close as she sensed him working toward, she would have it all.

"Saturday night," she said.

Riley had finished eating, and the waitress poured them cups of coffee. He smiled at the woman, and she blushed as she walked away.

"Saturday night," he prompted.

"Could you devise a way to come back to my place after the reception? You never did get to look at those journals."

He thought a minute. "You'll be driving yourself to the ranch, so they'll be following you home. What if I leave ahead of you and get to your place first? I can park a block or so away."

She dug in her purse, smiled when her fingers touched the gold nugget and came up with her extra key. "The dogs won't know you, so I'll leave them in their runs out back. You'll have to let yourself in the front."

She met his eyes and warmth diffused her face, neck

and chest. They were methodically planning a night together and they both knew it. Images of their last time snagged Lisa's breath and made her heart jump erratically. She was in control and she was not a coward. So much of her life had already slipped by that she wasn't willing to miss any more. She would only regret her actions if she let her heart get involved or if she didn't grab on to this opportunity.

Lisa didn't want any regrets.

Chapter Nine

It's All About Gold for the Lady In Red.

Bernadine had spotted Lisa walking an Irish setter in
the park, slid out of her car and run all the way, waving
a magazine.

Lisa gave the woman a wide-eyed once-over, taking
in her heels and taupe linen suit. "What's this all about?"

"My partner brought this to me. Look!" She showed
Lisa the front cover of *People* magazine with its usual assortment of stars and captions. In the lower left-hand corner beside Paris Hilton in a slinky pink gown was a picture
of Lisa in her red dress. Lisa looked twice, then grabbed
the magazine from Bernadine's hand to get a closer look.

"It's me." She looked up, then back at the glossy
cover. "Oh, my—it's *me!*"

"The story's on page nineteen," her lawyer said breathlessly.

Lisa flipped the pages until she came to the article that took an entire page. Half was a montage of color photos, the other half caption and text. "It's all about gold for the lady in red," she read aloud, her voice trembling. She went on to read the story, which played on local girl striking the mother lode. Lily Divine was of course mentioned, and there were quotes made by neighbors and people Lisa barely knew.

Mrs. Carlson was quoted as saying, "She's always been a shy girl. Keeps to herself and dotes on those dogs of hers." There was a small picture of her with Joey and Piper, taken from a distance, and it looked as though she was in her own yard. The biggest pictures were of her in the red dress—one with Riley at her side as they strode toward the cameramen outside the restaurant in Billings.

"Riley told me Chad Falkner sold pictures to *People*, but I thought he was putting me on." She closed the magazine and stared at her photo next to Paris Hilton's. "I don't *believe* this."

"You're a phenomenon, kiddo. Everyone aspires to win the lottery or the sweepstakes and become an overnight millionaire. You're an American dream come true."

"This is awful," Lisa said as the reality of this latest publicity hit her full force.

"What? You put Thunder Canyon in the spotlight."

"What does this mean, though? Will even more reporters come looking for me now?" She glanced around in dread.

Bernadine shrugged. "I don't know."

"Come on, Brinkley," Lisa said to the setter. "Let's get you home. I have phone calls to make." She headed for her new Blazer, and Bernadine kept pace beside her. "I'm going to schedule that interview Riley arranged. Will you be there?"

"Sure."

"Okay, good. And then I'm going to disappear for a while."

"You'll have to stay in touch with me. Where will you go?"

"I have a place in mind."

Bernadine handed her the magazine and admired the new SUV. "Nice vehicle."

"Thanks."

After taking the setter back, she went home and called Chad Falkner and the other local reporters to schedule an interview for the next day. She wanted the taping to take place in her home, where she was comfortable and where they could appease their fascination once and for all.

The salesgirl in Billings had given her a business card, so she called her and told her she needed something to wear on Saturday. The young woman had ordered a few things especially for her and offered to keep the store open for Lisa to try them on that evening. "Or I can come to Thunder Canyon," she told her. "No problem."

"No, I'll be there," Lisa told her. "I have a new car to drive now."

Gwen had specially ordered at least thirty dresses and as many casual outfits for Lisa to try on and showed Lisa as soon as she arrived. She had excellent taste, had picked up on Lisa's new metamorphosis and personality and had chosen garments accordingly.

"I saw you in the dress in the papers—and on the cover of *People*," she told her excitedly. "I told you that was a great choice."

"You did. I need something equally as..."

"Sexy?"

Lisa blushed. "Spectacular, anyway, for Saturday."

"Look at this." Gwen took the tissue from a slinky gown in shades of aqua and teal with tinges that shimmered pink in the light. "It reminds me of a butterfly," she told Lisa. "And so do you."

Lisa slipped into the dress and turned in front of the mirror. The garment dipped revealingly low in the back, and the side was slit up her thigh. Staring at herself, Lisa felt light and elusive—exactly the impression she wanted to convey. "You're a genius," she told Gwen. "I could never have shopped for myself this well."

"I also took the liberty of finding accessories," Gwen said hesitantly. "If I've overstepped bounds here, just say so. I can send back anything you don't want."

"Not at all. I need your help. I've never done this before."

"Lisa, you're beautiful. You look great in gorgeous clothes and you can afford the best. Allow yourself to enjoy this."

"I think I am. Thanks."

Gwen showed her the handbag and shoes she'd chosen, as well as sparkling butterfly pins for her hair. "What do you think?"

"That you've spoiled me and I'll need to hire you."

Gwen laughed. "That would be a dream job. I should be so lucky."

Lisa looked in the mirror again. "Think Paris Hilton has a personal shopper?"

"From what I've seen, she likes doing all her own shopping. She has a much different background and has always been a spoiled rich girl. Besides, designers are chasing after her to wear their stuff."

"I'm really getting into this," Lisa confessed.

"And why not? I heard about the big event Saturday night. I assume you're attending the ski-resort ground-breaking reception."

"Yes. I've never been around people like the Douglases and the mayor before. If I look good, I'll feel confident."

"You look good, honey. You definitely look good."

Dressed in her new clothing and driving her new Blazer, Lisa arrived at the Lazy D on Saturday night feeling more like Cinderella than ever before. She'd taken every measure she could to assure she'd look the part of the town's rich girl, but apprehension still fluttered in her chest. She pulled up to the house, and a parking attendant assisted her out, then took the keys to move her vehicle.

Lisa had been to the Douglas house before but never at night, when the windows were lit from within and strings of lights draped from posts to lead the way to the entrance. The door opened as she reached it, and a man in a tux motioned for her to enter.

"Good evening, miss."

She stood in the two-story foyer and glanced at the grand sweeping staircase, then at the room to her left.

Voices and the sound of stringed music carried out to the foyer.

Adele Douglas greeted her in the opening to the enormous room. "Good evening, Lisa," she said with a smile. "How nice to see you again. You're quite the news about town. I don't know when there's been so much excitement. You look so lovely, dear, I can hardly take it all in."

"Hello, Mrs. Douglas."

"Adele, *please*. Mrs. Douglas was my mother-in-law."

Adele had always reminded Lisa of a gracefully aging Meryl Streep in her serenity and quiet dignity. She was one person who wasn't treating Lisa any differently than she ever had. She'd always been warm and gracious.

Lisa recalled Riley's revelation about his father's affair and how Adele had only recently learned of her husband's illegitimate adult son. Only a classy woman such as this could forgive and accept and move on. "I never thought I'd be here for an occasion like this," Lisa admitted. "I'll have to have a moment with Derek before the evening's over."

Adele laughed. "You'll find him in the family room at the back of the house. It's his hiding place when we have company. I know he'll enjoy your attention, though."

"I'll look for him."

Caleb approached Lisa. He extended a hand and closed it over hers in a firm hold. "Riley told me you'd be coming. This is an exciting evening for us. We're finally going to see the resort take shape."

"I know Riley's excited about the project," she replied. "It's going to be a boost to our town's economy."

"That and the gold mine," he said with a wink. "You hold an important position now, as well, supplying jobs and channeling money into the community. Riley is the best man to help you with that. He's handled our finances for years now and he has a nose for making money."

"And spending it," she said under her breath.

She sensed someone at her side and turned to find Riley in a white shirt and black suit. His appreciative gaze told her the dress was another hit.

"There's nothing my boy doesn't know about finance," Caleb went on. "Trust him, and he'll steer you right. He's a good dancer, too."

The string quartet, which was set up in the corner, had begun a new piece, and Caleb gestured for Riley to escort her to the area set aside for dancing. Riley took her hand and led her to where Emily Stanton and Brad Vaughn danced. Emily introduced Lisa to her new husband.

Lisa hadn't danced since gym class in high school, but Riley put her at ease and smoothly led her in the steps. With one hand on her bare back and the other holding her hand, electricity sparked between them. He was more handsome than ever in his formal suit and tie. Looking at him made it difficult to breathe.

She was bold and confident when she'd made her plans, but when he held her like this, her self-assurance wavered. It took all of her considerable will to erect adequate barriers of protection. Riley was the demolition man, and she had to keep reconstructing the fortress that guarded her feelings.

"You do trust me, don't you, Lisa?" His voice was low and seductive.

"Of course I do." She trusted him to be persistent and persuasive. She trusted him to behave like the man he was born and bred to be. She trusted him to keep her on her toes.

"You're doing a number on me in that dress, you know."

"That's what I like to hear."

He glanced down, his gaze traveling to her cleavage. "I can't help wondering what you have on underneath."

Her nipples tightened, and warmth tingled in surprising places. "Shall I tell you?"

He was silent a moment. "I'll just keep wondering."

She smiled and glanced away. "Suit yourself."

For the first time she noticed that the two of them were cause for attention. Several curious looks were being cast their way. Adele and another woman were studying them with interest as they danced, and Lisa thought she spotted jealousy on a few female faces.

Her emotions ranged from pride to unease. "People are watching us."

"They're watching you. You're beautiful."

He'd told her that before. She glanced up, hoping to see the truth in his expression. He found her beautiful now, and yes, she had changed her appearance, but she was the same girl she'd been in high school—or even a month ago. He hadn't given her a second glance then. How much of the attraction was her transformation and how much was money?

"I did the interview Thursday," she told him.

"How'd it go?"

"Good. Bernadine came. I haven't been followed since. I wasn't even followed here tonight."

"So you think you have until next Thursday free and clear?"

She nodded. "Seems they're keeping their word."

"You can make arrangements with your customers and spend some time at the cabin, then."

"I think I will."

Riley changed the topic, filling her in on the identities of several of the partygoers. They ended the dance and he introduced her to his acquaintances. But underneath it all simmered the rising tension of what they'd planned for afterward. The night ahead never left Lisa's mind and she doubted from the looks he gave her that it left Riley's, either.

"Miss Lisa Jane," a man said jovially from beside her.

Lisa turned to discover portly Mayor Brookhurst. She'd met him face-to-face the day she'd claimed the deed.

"Hello, Mayor."

"You're the belle of the ball tonight," he told her. "May I have a dance?"

She glanced uncomfortably at Riley but said, "Certainly."

The mayor wasn't nearly as smooth a dancer as Riley. She didn't like suspecting that part of his reason in asking her had been to get close, but her dress was little more than tissue paper between her skin and the mayor's suit. It had been sensual with Riley as her dance partner. With the mayor it felt obscene.

After the song ended she excused herself as quickly as possible and sought out Bernadine, who was visiting with another woman.

"Lisa, this is Olivia Chester," the lawyer said. "She's our local ob-gyn."

Lisa greeted the pretty Native American woman she guessed to be in her forties.

"I've followed all the excitement about the gold mine," Olivia told her. Then she grinned and said, "Kind of hard not to."

Caleb approached Lisa then. "I have someone I want you to meet."

She excused herself and joined him. He led her to a small group. A young man and woman turned at his approach.

"Lisa, this is my son and his new wife, Justin and my adopted daughter, Katie."

"Lisa and I have met, of course," Katie told Caleb and greeted Lisa warmly. "Lisa has come into the library often."

"Nice to meet you, Lisa." Justin was tall and broad shouldered like Riley, his hair the same gleaming obsidian and his eyes held a similar intensity. The resemblance between the two half brothers was amazing. "I would have been able to recognize you without the introduction," she said.

"Both my sons are handsome devils, aren't they?" Caleb said proudly.

"That they are," Katie agreed, wrapping her arm around Justin's waist and smiling up at him.

Lisa imagined that Caleb had once been as tall and

virile-looking as his sons, too, because he was still a handsome man.

"Where is Riley, anyway?" Katie asked. "I never see much of him anymore." She spotted him, caught his eye and gestured for Riley to join them.

Lisa sensed Riley's unease as soon as he approached and stood with the group. She'd heard the pain in his voice when he'd spoken of this newly discovered brother. It had been plain that he still had a ways to go in accepting the situation.

Caleb behaved as though things couldn't have been more normal, however. "What a treat to have you all together. Adele and I are planning a family shindig soon. You're invited, Lisa. We'd love to have you join us."

"Well, thank you," she said uncomfortably. "I'll have to see if I can make it."

"Of course you can make it. You'll be there."

Lisa exchanged a look with Katie, who simply smiled as though she was used to the older man's overbearing manner.

"Excuse us now," Riley said. "I want to introduce Lisa to Phil."

Lisa met his friend and financial advisor, Phil Wagner, and while the two men stood talking, she slipped away and headed toward the back of the house.

Meeting all those strangers and trying to remember names and keep smiling was exhausting. The "family room," as Adele had called it, was an immense room with Oriental rugs, a pool table, fireplace, sofa and love seats.

At Lisa's entry, Derek—Adele's enormous white

poodle—roused from his resting place on the floor, sniffed the air hesitantly, then came forward to greet her with a lick.

"Hey, boy. How are you doing?" The white poodle wore a red bandanna around his neck and, as Riley had so adeptly described, his fur was cut into ridiculous pom-poms. Quite undignified for such a mannerly and handsome animal but not his fault, as she still maintained. Derek's fur was so thick, she had to bury her fingers in it to scratch him.

"Smart of you to find a quiet place to hide out. Wouldn't mind joining you, actually. You're smelling my dogs, aren't you? Wonder what they'd make of you."

She eased down onto the sofa and slipped off her shoes. Derek sat at her knees and seemed to enjoy her company and a lengthy head scratch by closing his eyes.

Sometime later the dog eased onto the sofa beside her, and they were enjoying the quiet time together when Riley found her. "There you are. Mother said I'd find you here."

"Derek and I are hanging out."

Riley glanced at the dog that barely seemed to notice his arrival. "What do you see in him, anyway?"

"He's affectionate. And intelligent. He's back here away from the crazies, isn't he? Don't give me your respect theory again. Respect is a two-way street. I doubt he thinks much of you either."

Derek opened eyes to slits to look at Riley at that moment, as though assessing the man.

Riley perched on Lisa's other side.

"So, Derek, what do you think of Riley?" she asked. "Would you trust him with your best rawhide strip? He could turn it into a steak for you. He has a way with investing." The dog tilted his head in keen interest as she spoke.

Riley chuckled and leaned forward to kiss her. She lifted her face to meet him. A sigh escaped her.

"You're a nut, you know that?" he said, gazing at her fondly.

"Be that as it may, I think you should give Derek a chance before it's too late for the two of you."

"How's it going to be too late?"

"Don't want him to hear this, but ogdays on'tday ivelay ongerlay anthay ifteenfay or osay earsyay."

"What did you just say?"

"You don't understand pig latin?"

"Sorry, I had a French tutor."

She leaned forward and whispered in his ear. "Dogs don't live longer than fifteen or so years. Your bonding is going to have to happen now."

She sat back and he studied her eyes with amusement flickering in his. "There's no one else I would do this for, you know that, don't you?"

She shrugged mischievously.

He turned and faced the dog. "So, Derek. May I call you Derek? It's come to my attention that I haven't given you a fair chance. I'd like to correct that. Can we be friends?"

The dog merely looked at him. Lisa had stopped scratching his head, and the animal looked expectantly from Lisa back to Riley.

Riley extended a hand.

Derek licked it.

Riley rubbed Derek's head.

"There, isn't that better?" Lisa raised up and kissed Riley's cheek.

He turned his face and reached his left arm around her back to bring her closer. Their lips met in a warm, melding crush of eager anticipation. His kiss had the same narcotic effect as the first time. She could easily become a Riley junkie.

A kiss wasn't enough. Two kisses weren't enough. She pressed her palm against the crisp starched front of his shirt and felt his warm flesh and hard muscle beneath. More. She wanted more.

She felt something warm and damp but completely out of place and realized Derek was licking her bare toes. "I think it's time to go."

Riley helped her to her feet and paused to address the dog. "Excuse us now. I'm not sharing her for the rest of the night."

She smiled and gave the dog a last affectionate pat.

Riley took her hand and they fled out the back door.

As they'd planned, Riley used one of his father's plain sedans and left first. Lisa waited fifteen tense minutes before following.

Surprisingly no one followed her. The reporters had been good for their word. Her heart pounded in a silly girlish flutter every time she imagined Riley at her house. Riley in her bed. But she calmed her giddiness and forced herself to think rationally. This was a temporary diversion. She was allowing him to think he was pulling one over on her. But no matter what, she would not let him know her feelings and she would not let her feelings get out of control.

She parked in her driveway and got out of her Blazer. At the back fence, the dogs whined. She walked toward the back, unlocked the gate and entered the yard.

She let the boys free from their run, and they ran in circles around her, pausing to sniff her feet and skirt and hands, keenly aware of the other dog scent.

"Be on your best behavior, boys. We have a guest."

She unlocked the back door and pushed it open. The light she'd left on over the sink partially illuminated the room.

"Riley?" she called.

"In here."

A light came on in the living room.

"I waited to turn on a lamp." His footsteps sounded in the hallway.

The dogs turned in that direction, and Piper let out an ear-piercing bark followed by a volley of others.

"Piper. Hush," she told him. "It's okay." Lisa hurried to meet Riley in the kitchen entryway, where she stood in front of him and turned to the dogs. Riley held a bottle of wine.

"Joey, Piper, you remember Riley. You met him once before." She took Riley's arm and leaned into him to show her pets the man was a friend.

Tail wagging, Joey came forward and sniffed Riley's trouser legs, then his crotch.

Riley took a wary step back.

"Sorry," Lisa said without embarrassment. One couldn't spend much time around dogs without becoming immune to their natures.

Riley extended a hand and Joey sniffed it, then allowed the man to pet his head and scratch behind his ears.

Piper, on the other hand, remained several feet away and growled low in his throat.

Lisa spent another five minutes coaxing the dark golden retriever to relax his guard and accept Riley, but the dog remained agitated.

Finally she ordered the animal to lie down on the kitchen rug and she got two glasses from the cupboard.

"Sorry they're not fancy," she said, indicating the tall, thin glasses with faded irises on the sides. She glanced at the bottle. "I don't have a corkscrew."

"I calculated for that." Reaching into the pocket of his suit coat, he pulled one out. "Brought one from the house."

"That's probably Piper's problem. He sensed you were carrying a weapon."

He cocked a brow to give her a skeptical look, then opened the wine and poured the glasses half-full. "What shall we drink to?"

Lisa blinked and studied him in the dim light. "I don't know."

He held up his glass and she did the same. "To second chances."

What he meant by that, she wasn't sure. He might have meant any number of things. His father and his half brother came to mind. He could be teasing her about Derek. Or he might be talking sex and toasting their second time together. Her stomach dipped at that possibility.

In the next second, the burning look in his blue eyes made her think that's exactly what he was talking about.

She sipped the wine.

He watched and did the same.

Riley took her glass and set both on the red Formica table. Without another word he pulled her into his arms and kissed her senseless.

Lisa met every brush of his lips and thrust of his tongue eagerly. She wrapped one arm around his neck and pulled herself closer.

Riley used his fingertips on the bare skin of her back to create shivers and raise her level of excitement. "You're not wearing a bra."

"You wanted me to let you wonder."

"I've figured it out. You couldn't be wearing one with this dress."

She'd let Gwen talk her into the thong this time, too. Lisa still had a surprise or two left.

"Why are you smiling?"

"You'll see."

"When?"

She reached up and loosened the knot in his tie until she could edge it away from his collar and off over his head. "Soon."

He took off his suit coat and she unbuttoned his shirt.

He wore the familiar white T-shirt, and she tugged it from the waistband of his trousers. He crossed his arms and yanked it off over his head.

Lisa pressed languid kisses against his chest.

"Where's your room?"

"Upstairs."

He picked up their glasses. "Lead the way."

Chapter Ten

She left the light on over the sink as well as the lamp he'd turned on in the living room and led the way up the shadowed staircase. She'd climbed these stairs hundreds of times, maybe thousands. Never with a man.

Well, no man except Wendell Carlton, the aged handyman her grandmother had occasionally hired to fix things. Wendell didn't count. Riley wasn't here to fix a leak or caulk a tub. Her knees got weak at the thought of him in her room.

After entering her bedroom, she turned on the painted-glass lamp on her dresser, knowing it would just barely illuminate.

Riley glanced at the antique furniture, the old-fashioned metal bed frame with its chenille spread and folded quilt. Her pillowcases were delicately embroidered and edged with crocheted lace. She knew how different her home was from his, how much their tastes contrasted. This was who she was, and him knowing it made her uncomfortably vulnerable.

He set the glasses on her painted night table and eyed her vintage bed. "Is that frame sturdy?"

"I guess we'll find out."

He grinned.

She turned so he could unzip her dress. He lowered the zipper and she stepped out of the garment, draping it over the cedar chest. She took a fortifying breath and turned back to see his reaction.

Riley was looking at her as if he couldn't drag his gaze away. Finally he spoke. "Wow."

She picked up her glass and let her gaze seduce him. "You're overdressed."

He sat on her bed to remove his shoes and socks, then stood and stepped out of his trousers. Still wearing a pair of snug-fitting gray boxer-briefs, he took his own glass and downed the liquid in one swallow. "Want more? I can go get the bottle."

She shook her head no, sipped her wine slowly, then set her glass aside and eased onto the bed. "Maybe later."

Riley kept a rein on his hunger. She knew exactly what she was doing. This woman strove to drive him crazy. She was a seductress in every way. If she'd told him she was a virgin, he probably wouldn't have believed her. But he'd learned firsthand. The thought still tied him in knots. And she wouldn't talk about it.

Something primitively male and possessive and old-fashioned puffed up inside him at the prideful knowledge that he was the only man who'd ever made love to her.

Just looking at Lisa now made his chest swell, and feelings he'd never known overcame him. The emotions weren't anything he wanted to acknowledge. They weren't anything he knew or understood.

She eased the covers back and stretched out on the bed.

But they were sensations that had begun to control him.

She was an anomaly, a siren and an innocent in one fabulous package.

She consumed his thoughts.

"Like the thong?" she asked.

"Love it."

"Now that you've seen it, I really want to toss it."

He laughed. "Go right ahead."

He loved her.

She eased the scrap of satin down her hips and legs and gave it a fling.

He lost a slat in the rickety footbridge between his brain centers, and his thoughts swung by a precarious thread. *Not part of the plan,* his head told him.

Doesn't matter, his body responded.

You're in perilous territory here. That word shouldn't have been in your mental vocabulary.

Just a slip. I didn't mean it. And I certainly didn't say it.

"What are you waiting for?" she asked.

"Just appreciating the view."

She propped her head on one hand. "Well, share the experience, then."

Riley stripped off his briefs and climbed onto the bed, not caring how small the mattress was or that the metal headboard creaked with his weight. All he wanted was to be close to Lisa.

A low growl thwarted his next move, however, and he raised his head to find the dark golden retriever right beside the bed, his ears back and his demeanor threatening.

Lisa rolled to the side of the bed and stood. "Piper, no. I told you Riley is a friend." She padded across the room and pointed out into the hallway. "Go."

The dog looked from his mistress to the man threatening his home, obviously confused.

"Piper. Go," she commanded.

The dog padded out and she closed the door, then returned to lie beside Riley.

A touch of amusement tilted the corners of her mouth, but her eyes were still filled with sultry passion. "I don't know what's wrong with him. Dogs are usually such good judges of character."

"Maybe he doesn't want to share your affections."

She tucked her hair behind her ear and asked, "You think I feel affection for you?"

Taking her in his arms, he outlined her lips with a finger, kissed the corner of her mouth and studied her features. "No, I just hope you do."

She'd told him they'd met years ago in school, but he only vaguely remembered the girl she'd been then. The fact that they'd met before explained the sense of déjà vu he'd experienced the evening they'd examined the wine list together, though. It was the way she'd told him that disturbed him. And the timing.

She'd said it the night after they'd made love as he'd dropped her off at her house, almost like a "so there" parting shot. She'd never mentioned it again.

"You're still just appreciating the view," she said. "Piper didn't spoil the mood, did he?"

"I like to look. The same way you like to say my name."

He thought she blushed.

"Go ahead. Say it."

"No, you can't make me now."

"I'll bet I can."

"You're on."

She said his name a dozen times with as many inflections over the next hour. He loved his name on her lips, loved her hair, adored the sounds she made when he brought her pleasure. He even loved her creaky bed.

Spent, Riley lay on his back, his skin damp with perspiration, and felt her heartbeat against his ribs. She drew lazy circles in the hair on his belly with one finger. He loved everything about being with Lisa Martin.

And he wanted to tell her.

"Lisa."

"Hmm?"

"I love you."

Her finger stilled. The sound of her ticking alarm clock filled his ears. He shouldn't have said it. He shouldn't have thought it. What had he expected her to do? Return the sentiment?

Initially yes, he had. He'd thought it would be an easy task to ingratiate himself and make himself invaluable. He hadn't planned to feel anything. He hadn't planned to care. Hadn't planned to mean it.

"I have a feeling that you've loved a lot of women," she said at last, her tone light.

He bit back an argument.

"Like you love your Jag and you love blackened steak a little rare. Like you love a really good vintage wine."

He didn't say anything, but his heart hammered.

She scooted upward on the bed with a creak of metal and sat with the sheets held against her breasts. The hair at her temples had turned to corkscrews.

"Tell me that's what you meant, Riley, because I don't want anything to happen to our relationship. We have to see each other at meetings, and you're contracted as my advisor. What we've already done is probably unwise and unprofessional...but I don't want it to be a big mistake."

He managed an easy smile that he didn't feel. "Of course that's what I meant. Actually you're better than wine, but my Jag? I'll need more time to think about that."

Lisa eased back against the pillows.

He'd passed off the uncomfortable moment with a stab at humor, and she seemed appeased. He should have his head examined. He should have his tongue glued to the roof of his mouth. He should *not* be letting feelings get in the way.

"Will you show me the way out to the cabin tomorrow?" she asked. "That is, as long as it's still okay for me to stay there for a while."

"Of course it is. Let me know when you're ready."

"I've had a couple of calls for interviews since the *People* thing. Did you see it?"

"Marge showed me. Are you accepting them?"

"No. I really just want this to blow over. I don't want to be on television."

"Maybe one big interview would satisfy the curiosity."

"That's what we thought about the locals, too."

"Your picture hasn't been in the *Nugget* for a couple of days now."

She picked at a thread on her bedspread. "I'll think about it."

"Lisa, did we graduate together?"

"No, I was a sophomore when you were a senior."

"A sophomore coaching me with chemistry? That hurts."

"A young sophomore, too," she added with a grin. "I skipped a grade in elementary school."

"Double ouch. Do you have any yearbooks?"

"Somewhere."

"Can I look at them?"

She got up and opened her closet, where she snagged a thick chenille robe and pulled it on. Then she pushed aside clothing and pulled out a couple of boxes. Inside the second one she found three volumes of the Thunder Canyon High yearbook and carried them back to the bed.

Riley reached for the lamp on the night table and switched it on before sitting back against the piled pillows.

"What do you want to see?" she asked, laying the books beside him.

"You."

"Oh, come on." She reached to take back the books, but he spread his hand on the top one and held the pile fast.

He glanced at the dates and covers and recalled having one the same. The volume was from the year he graduated. Opening it, he saw none of the youthful writings and scribbled good wishes that littered the pages of his. He quickly found *Martin, Lisa J.* in the directory and noted the three pages where her picture would be found.

In the first snapshot, sixteen members of the chess club smiled for the camera. He scanned the faces without recognition, then read the names listed below and found her. The same wild hair she'd had only a month ago, a concealing sweater and long skirt.

The second picture showed the library volunteers gathered around a display of presidential biographies. He picked her out this time, noting her shy expression and the way she stood behind someone else's shoulder.

"Which one has your graduation picture?"

"You've already seen it on TV."

"I'll find it myself."

"That one."

He opened the book she'd indicated and located her picture. Yes, he'd seen the picture on the news, but he hadn't known then that they'd met before. He studied the photo now.

Like a blurry image coming into focus, memories of Lisa watching him in the cafeteria, on the football field, in the library became clear. This was the quiet girl who had tutored him? He'd like to think he'd been too focused on learning the concepts and passing the class to get to know her. As the memories returned, the sting of conscience bit him.

"You worked in the cafeteria."

"Yes."

How had he not noticed her? Had he been that busy? That full of himself? So caught up in his social activities that a sophomore outside his circle was invisible?

"Don't try to figure it out," she said, as though reading his mind. "I worked at not being seen."

"Why?"

She shrugged. "A lot of reasons. The Lily thing was part of it—not wanting to draw attention. I didn't have clothes that were in style or hair like the other girls. I just didn't fit in and eventually it became my identity."

Lisa blushed and looked away as though she'd revealed too much of herself.

"And now? Who are you now?"

She took the yearbooks and moved them to the night table. "I'm not ashamed of Lily anymore. And I guess I can have all the clothes I want, huh?"

"What about guys? Boyfriends?"

"I can have all of those I want, too, huh?"

She'd deliberately sidestepped his question, not to mention implied that he wasn't her only option. The insinuation made a fist of anger rise in his chest. Anger. Possessiveness. Things he shouldn't be feeling. He had something to ask her and he was going to have to ask soon.

Her reaction to his hastily spoken declaration had been his warning to tread softly, however. The last thing he wanted to do was scare her off. This wasn't a sure thing yet.

"I'll just have to prove I'm enough." He slid a hand inside the robe and stroked the warm, soft skin of her waist and hip. "Think it'll take much convincing tonight?"

"Definitely. I've been having recurring thoughts of Orlando Bloom."

"Who?"

"Never mind. Convince me."

Riley was so large, he took up more than half the space in the bed. She woke in the dark with her body conformed to his. A glance at the luminous dial on her clock told her it was only a little after four. Lisa had never slept beside a man. She'd never shared a bed with anyone except her dogs, and the thought of them being closed out of the room gave her a twinge of guilt. She couldn't let them in now, not with Riley in the bed.

Getting up, she found her robe on the floor and tip-toed to the door. Piper lay in the hall as though guarding her room. At her exit, he scrambled to his feet. She pulled the door shut behind her, not risking the chance of another confrontation.

"Hey, boy." She bent to pet him before moving on down the hall and descending the steps.

Joey had been sleeping on the pile of blankets beside the sofa, and she told him what a good dog he was for sparing her furniture. Both dogs padded behind her into the kitchen.

She poured fresh water into their bowls and got herself a glass of milk. "Hope you're not taking this personally." She sipped her milk and glanced at their accusatory expressions. "I know having him here is out of the ordinary. But there's a lot to be said for new experiences. Ordinary can really suck."

Joey lay down with his chin on his front paws and blinked up at her. Piper glanced toward the doorway, as if he knew who she was talking about and didn't like being kicked to the curb one bit.

"It's not forever, guys, trust me. Please don't begrudge me this one thing for as long as it lasts. I had to know. I had to do something for me just this once."

Plumbing in the upstairs recesses of the house clanged. He was awake.

"C'mon, boys, outside."

They scrambled to the back door, which she unlocked before ushering them out.

"What are you doing up so early?" Riley entered the kitchen wearing his black trousers and carrying his shirt and shoes. His dark hair was endearingly messy.

"I just woke up."

He set the clothes on the seat of a chair. "I guess I'll head out."

"Want to stay for breakfast?"

"I couldn't eat this early. And I should be out of here before daylight." He slipped on the wrinkled shirt.

"Okay." She leaned back against the counter. "I'll pack a few things, buy groceries and be ready to go by this afternoon."

"Why don't you just drive out to my place when you're ready? I'll show you the way from there."

She was planning to spend time alone and knew better than to add complications, but she found herself asking, "Will you stay to have dinner with me tonight?"

A smile creased his cheeks as he sat to pull on his socks and shoes. "I'll do you one better. I'll help you fix it."

Lisa stepped forward and cradled his head against her breast. Riley wrapped his arms around her hips and hugged her tight.

She backed away then and he stood, finding his suit coat and fishing in his pocket for his keys. She walked him to the front door and stood watching as he headed down her street on foot in the dark. Several minutes later she was still watching from between the parted lace on the front windows when his Jaguar rolled by slowly. The taillights disappeared in the darkness.

Lisa was beginning to frighten herself with the thoughts and feelings she had difficulty controlling. The fact that Riley was pursuing her for the gold mine and that she was only turning the tables on him for her own satisfaction was getting harder and harder to remember.

He'd been her first crush, and as that had existed only in fantasy and dreams. All these years later he'd become her first lover. And the reality—the *physicality* of the man—was becoming her undoing. Physical pleasure and blooming friendship had combined with her new self-confidence to fling all those years of loneliness and emptiness in her face.

She didn't want to let go.

She didn't have to just yet.

She hadn't wanted him to move things forward, hadn't allowed him to take his scheme to another level. When he'd mentioned love, her foolish heart had wanted to hear the words, but her sensible head had warned her it meant the end. As soon as he made a move she couldn't counter, she would have to end this.

Originally, selfishly, she hadn't thought past that

first night. But after she'd made love with Riley—after it looked like the game could continue a little longer—she'd had to rethink her strategy and strengthen her defenses.

The deception felt wrong, but she justified her actions with the fact that he'd been the first to deceive. She'd been staying a step ahead of him all along, but now it felt as if she had to run to do that.

Lisa let the dogs in and climbed the stairs with them at her heels. They sniffed every corner of the room as well as her bed before climbing up beside her where she lay. She still had a couple of hours before she had to get up, and now she could sleep without Riley's presence disturbing her.

She didn't sleep, though. When daylight broke through her curtains, she was still awake, reliving their night together and hoping for more time.

Thunder Canyon was more quiet than usual for a Sunday afternoon, maybe because the sun climbed high and hot and baked the little town, chasing residents indoors. Lisa appreciated it, because no one seemed to pay her any interest.

Once she had her supplies loaded into the Blazer, she ushered the dogs into the back and cranked the air-conditioning. She checked the rearview mirror continuously, but no one followed her. She arrived on the Lazy D and at Riley's home without unwanted attention.

She rang the bell and waited.

Riley opened the door. The T-shirt he wore was damp with sweat and his face was flushed, his hair wet. His attention immediately focused on the length of her legs in the first pair of shorts she'd worn since she was a kid. "Wow."

Lisa's cheeks warmed at his appreciative reaction.

He grinned and gestured for her to come in. "I just finished riding and putting up a horse. Can you wait for me to take a quick shower?"

"Sure. I have to bring in the dogs out of the car." She led them in on leashes and cautioned Piper when he growled at Riley.

"Living room's that way. Make yourself at home. I'll be right back."

She ushered the dogs into the room he indicated. Sleek modern sofas and chairs, nickel-finish tables with glass tops and track lighting defined the room. Everything was plain and cold looking. "You guys would have to shed…and we'd need some real furniture to feel at home, wouldn't we?"

The dogs sniffed around, apparently finding nothing of interest because they just sat and panted.

Lisa tested a chair and then the sofa. "Not so bad, really, if a person didn't want somewhere to rest their arms." None of the pieces had armrests. "Probably cost a fortune, too, if I know Riley's taste."

True to his word, Riley returned in a matter of minutes, smelling like soap. His black hair was damp and combed into place. "Ready?"

Piper stood and growled.

"Sorry," Lisa said.

"It's not as big of a deal today, now that I have my pants on," he told her.

She ignored that comment. "Does this stuff really reflect you? Or do you have a decorator?"

He glanced around, seeming a little surprised at her question. "Well…I did have a decorator."

"For some reason I feel a little better about that."

He gave her a look that said he thought she was a fry short of a Happy Meal before turning away. "I have to get something from the kitchen."

She took the dogs outside ahead of him and loaded them back into the Blazer. Riley carried a small cooler out to his Jag.

Getting to his cabin took a little over a half hour, and she tried to remember the landmarks along the way so she could find the place on her own again—or so she could leave and return.

She parked in the double garage beside Riley and he led the way up the stairs. "Don't let that dog get too close," he called over his shoulder.

"I'm watching your butt," she replied.

"I know, just don't let that dog get too close."

"I don't know why he growls at you."

"He's going to like me tonight."

"Why do you say that?"

"Because I'm good at convincing."

She couldn't argue with that. She hadn't had a thought about Orlando Bloom all day.

After being released from their leashes, the dogs checked out every room.

"Do I have to take them down through the garage to do their business every time?"

"No, look here." He showed her into an enormous

suite where double glass doors led to a balcony. "You can use any room you like, but this side of the house is set against a hill. Those stairs lead up to the top, where there's a wooded area and a great view. C'mon, I'll show you."

Lisa called and the animals tagged after them.

Riley took the stairs first and Lisa followed. The dogs took some coaxing, but Piper came first and then Joey.

They came out on a flat expanse of land surrounded by woods and a sharp decline on one side.

"Can anyone get to the house this way?"

"No, it's too high above the roads and there's no path except deer trails. You're safe here."

"What about wild animals?"

"I'm sure there are some, so stay close to the steps if you have to come out at night. There's a flashlight beside the sliding doors. There's a cell phone plugged in on the kitchen counter, too."

Piper and Joey had taken off into the underbrush and returned with leaves clinging to their fur. She knelt and cleaned them off.

Joey brushed up against Riley, pausing to sit at his feet.

Riley scratched the retriever's head. "This looks like a fun hangout, doesn't it? Wait till you see what I have planned for supper."

After that they made several trips with Lisa's belongings and the groceries. Riley carried in the cooler and took out steaks and a familiar white take-out box.

"What's that?" she asked.

"That's *your* bribe. The steak is theirs."

"It's chocolate-raspberry truffle, isn't it?" She reached for the box.

He caught her hand and wrapped her arm around his waist. Lowering his face to hers, he said, "You don't want dessert first, do you?"

"Is that a trick question?"

He kissed her, and she leaned into the embrace.

From the other side of the room, Piper growled.

She started to say something, but Riley stopped her. "Don't worry. Tonight we're going to make friends."

He'd purchased three thick T-bone steaks, one for each of them and one for the dogs to share. "Don't tell me you don't feed them table food," he said. "It's just this once."

"Oh, I don't feed them table food," she pointed out. "Pizza and beer don't count. They're TV cuisine."

It only took Piper thirty seconds to warm to the offering Riley fed him in bite-size pieces as they sat on the deck and enjoyed the sunset. By the time his half of the steak was history, Piper was putty in Riley's hands. He licked his chops, then Riley's fingers, and burped.

"Same effect I have on you," Riley told her.

She took another blissful bite of her chocolate truffle and didn't argue. She did, however, resist burping.

They cleared away dishes and Lisa took the dogs up top to do their business while Riley lit citronella candles and opened a bottle of wine.

"You're going to turn me into a lush," she told him. But she accepted the glass and sipped.

"Do I need to lock my wine cellar while you're staying here?"

"Probably."

He grinned and pulled his canvas chair close to hers.

Piper propped his head on Riley's feet and groaned an exhausted sigh. She knew the feeling. The man had the ability to wear down the fiercest opponent.

"Is this how you negotiate business deals, as well?" she asked.

"Sometimes."

She'd seen the food and drinks offered for business meetings, so the suggestion wasn't far off.

Within minutes Lisa had moved to sit on his lap. Leisurely kisses turned hot and hungry, and she threaded her fingers into his hair.

"Lisa…" he said against her mouth.

She worked her fingers under the hem of his knit shirt and splayed her palm over his chest. "The answer is yes."

"You'd better hear the question first."

She smiled and tasted his mouth once more. This would be good. Anticipation shot through her nerve endings. Just being here where they'd first made love got her hot. He was going to invite her inside, maybe ask her to take off her clothes…suggest something exciting and erotic. "Ask away."

He touched her through her shorts and heat reached through the layer of fabric to make her squirm. He took his mouth from hers, pierced her with intense blue eyes and asked, "Will you marry me?"

Chapter Eleven

It took thirty seconds for Lisa's brain to catch up. When it did, a sinking rush of disappointment flooded through her chest and tears stung her eyes. To hide them she tucked her head under his chin and grabbed the front of his shirt. He'd done it. He'd moved so far out ahead of her, she wouldn't be able to catch up.

Her body still hummed with desire, but her heart and head had started erecting barriers. She struggled to find something sophisticated and witty to say, something that would diffuse the tension and leave them with the basics of their relationship intact. Nothing came to her. Nothing but a crushing sense of defeat.

"Why would we want to spoil a perfectly good thing?" she asked finally. "I mean, we have the best of everything right now, wouldn't you say? I'm not much at compromising, and you wouldn't want to share my lifestyle any more than I'd want to share yours."

"What are you talking about?" he asked.

Once again in control of her emotions, she straightened on his lap. "Think about it. Where would we live?"

"Does it matter?"

"Well, yes, it matters. My house isn't your style, and your house certainly isn't my style."

"You aren't planning to stay in that house, are you?"

"Why not?"

"Lisa, you're—" He cut himself off.

"A millionaire," she finished. "Rich. Yes, so I keep hearing. And so there must be something wrong with my home since I can afford better."

He shrugged. "I just assumed you'd build one."

"Because that's what you would do, Riley."

"We could build a home together. One that suits us both."

"It's foolish to talk about houses. It's foolish to talk about anything that permanent. What's the big rush, anyway? Things were going just fine." She pushed away and stood, walking to the railing and standing with a hand on a support beam.

"It didn't seem like such a bad idea to me."

Of course not—all his ideas were pure genius. "You don't need me. You were doing perfectly well before we met and you'll do just as well after—after this time together is over."

Ever since her ownership of the Queen of Hearts had been discovered, she'd felt as if she was being rushed and pushed in directions she wasn't prepared to go. The fact that she'd suspected Riley's true intent from the beginning didn't make it any easier to accept now that he'd brought his design out in the open.

"I was hoping we could take things to another level," he said, rising and coming to stand behind her.

"Why?"

He placed his hands on her upper arms and turned her to face him. "Why do most people get married?"

"We're not most people, though, are we?"

"I'm sorry for jumping ahead, Lisa. If you need more time, I'm okay with that. Just don't say no."

He lowered his head, and she was too foolish to turn away. She wanted this time with him, even if it would be their last. Raising a hand to his cheek, she returned his kiss.

Time wasn't going to fix this. Time wasn't going to wipe out her knowledge and make this sham real.

"Why don't we just concentrate on tonight?" she said finally.

If their kisses seemed tinged with desperation, she was the one responsible. If there was a sadness and finality to their lovemaking that night, it was because she had said goodbye in her heart.

They were more subdued, and fewer words were spoken between them than on the previous night. And even though no prying eyes would be there to see him leave in the morning, she didn't want to fall asleep beside him or wake by his side. She didn't want ownership of any more memories than those they'd already created.

Once he slept, she crept from his room down to the suite. She urged Joey and Piper up onto the bed with her, fighting the urge to take the boys and escape back to her own house. She had to stand her ground. She had to convince herself she could go back to life before Riley.

Lisa woke early to the smell of coffee wafting through the cabin. She let the dogs out and gave them time to run around the wooded area before calling them back in.

She found coffee in the pot on the counter and then located Riley on the front balcony. He had already shaved, showered and dressed in clothes for work. She joined him and studied the view. In full daylight the scene was indeed as breathtaking as he'd predicted.

"Sleep well?" he asked.

She glanced at him, sensing the new awkwardness between them. "I did. I see you're ready for the day."

He nodded. "I have a meeting with Justin this morning."

She looked at him curiously.

"He's involved with the resort."

"Oh. I wasn't aware of that."

He sipped his coffee. "You should have everything here that you need."

They were quiet for a moment, then Lisa broke the silence.

"I want to say something."

He turned and studied her. "Go ahead."

"I think from here on out we should keep things between us…professional."

Only the twitch in his jaw revealed any reaction.

"If you want to take back your invitation for us to stay here, I'd understand. I don't want to take advantage of you."

A look of discomfort crossed his features at her words. "Of course I don't want to take it back. You're perfectly welcome to stay here."

"Things just went a little too far, Riley. We had a good time. Let's leave it at that."

"A good time," he said, his voice flat.

"A *very* good time," she stressed.

His piercing green gaze flickered over the nearby woods, then back to her face. "I should probably forewarn you. I'm persistent."

"Your persistence won't do you any good this time."

"Persuasive, as well."

"I know."

She could tell there was an argument on his tongue, but to his credit, he held it.

"I'll call the cell number if I see any interesting news clips or if anything comes up," he said.

She nodded with a smile. "I'll answer."

There was a clumsy pause before he carried his cup into the cabin. Lisa followed in time to see him bend to pet each of the dogs. Picking up his sport jacket, he headed for the stairs.

She refilled her cup and observed from the balcony, as below, his bright red Jaguar could be seen through the trees until he'd roared out of sight and beyond hearing range.

She remained on the balcony until hunger drove her in to find something for breakfast.

Her well-planned getaway had lost a lot of its appeal overnight. She'd been alone with animals for companions her whole life and now here she was again. She'd made a huge effort to change herself inside and out and she'd done a damned fine job of it. Problem was she'd hooked herself up with someone she couldn't trust and whose friendship—or whatever it was—was only temporary.

But she wasn't going to worry or pine away her vacation time. She was going to rest, read, walk in the woods and go back to Thunder Canyon refreshed next week. Lisa set about that plan with renewed determination.

She spoke with Bernadine several times over the next few days. Occasionally she used the cell phone to call clients and double-check on her pets. Riley called twice regarding business decisions, three times about some trivial mention of her in the newspaper and once every evening just to ask how she was doing.

She missed him so much, she was tempted to ask him to join her, but she resisted the impulse. The lure, however, was too much when he called her Friday morning and mentioned he'd like to drive out the following night and bring dinner.

"I've missed you," he said, and his voice sent shivers along her nerve endings and made her nipples tighten. "I promise to keep things light. We'll just enjoy being together. Okay?"

Who was she kidding? She didn't have any resistance when it came to this man. She'd dreamed about him each night and thought about him every waking hour. How could she not when she was staying in his cabin?

"I'll bring dessert," he suggested.

That was low.

"Chocolate raspberry truffle."

She caved. "Okay."

That afternoon she took a long soak in the enormous whirlpool tub, thinking about the following night and smiling to herself because she'd brought along a couple of sexy new sundresses. She'd try one out on Riley.

After drying off and taking time to apply scented body lotion and paint her nails, she dressed in a pair of soft lounging pajamas and padded out to the kitchen to make popcorn. Riley didn't own a VCR or a DVD player, but she'd packed several books. The balcony was well shaded this time of day, and she was coming to enjoy the sounds of nature and the fresh air.

The cell phone on the counter beeped, so she checked it while the microwave ticked the minutes backward and the mouthwatering smell of butter filled the room. Maybe Riley was impatient and wanted to drive out sooner. It took her a few minutes to figure out which buttons to push, but she finally retrieved the message. The number on the digital display didn't mean anything to her, so she listened to the recording.

"Riley, where in blazes are you?" The voice belonged to Caleb, and he sounded perturbed. She should probably call Riley and tell him his father was looking for him.

"You dodged our meeting deliberately, didn't you? I'm starting to wonder what you're up to. What is taking so long for you to win over the dog walker? You losing your touch?"

Popcorn popped in the background, but Lisa's attention was riveted on the message meant for Riley.

"It shouldn't be that difficult, son. She's a nobody, and you're a Douglas. Charm her. Get into her pants— hell, knock her up if you have to. Just get a ring on her finger."

Numbness spread across Lisa's scalp in a horrifying confirmation. She'd known. She'd guessed from the very beginning. She wasn't stupid. But hearing the plan so crudely outlined was like rubbing salt in a fresh wound.

"The mine is producing," the recording of Caleb was saying, *"and where are we? Sitting with our thumbs up our asses, that's where. Don't avoid me, I don't like it. And don't waste any more time. I like that even less."*

The message ended with a click and a beep. Lisa stared at the phone before collecting herself enough to locate the off button and press it. She placed the handset back on the charger.

She's a nobody and you're a Douglas. That statement clanged around in her head for several jagged minutes. It was the truth. But as was the case more often than not, the truth hurt. Like hell in this instance.

Caleb had just confirmed what she'd known in her heart all along. She'd had Riley tagged the minute he'd shown an interest—before she'd transformed herself. Riley wasn't any better than the so-called cousins who'd been calling.

The fact that his father had been in on the plan all along cheapened what they'd done all the more, though. Had Riley gone back and reported to his father each time they'd been together? How sleazy did that make her feel?

She'd felt so smug in her ability to be the seductress and to turn the tables on him. She'd only been kidding herself that she was in control.

"You knew," she told herself. "This isn't a big revelation. You had his number from the beginning and you chose to play along. It's not like you've been tricked into thinking he loves you."

She took the popcorn from the microwave, grabbed her book and went out to the balcony. Joey and Piper followed and begged at her feet. She shoved Caleb's angry voice and superior tone out of her head and forced her eyes to the pages.

An hour later the two retrievers licked up the last of the popcorn from where the bag had fallen, and Lisa stared out across the wooded landscape. Dozens of plans formed in her head. Scenarios where she told off Riley in glorious eloquence. Scenes in which she won his undying love and devotion.

Should she still let him come to the cabin tomorrow night? Should she behave as though she hadn't heard the message? Or should she confront him now—call him this minute—and get the truth out in the open and over with? Or…she could be gone when he got here. She could take an extended trip and not tell him where she'd gone.

She could go someplace where people didn't know her or recognize her and see if she couldn't find a man who would be attracted to her *for her,* not for her gold mine.

What she could not do was be unprepared. Drift. Waver. She'd made up her mind to cool things off, then she'd gone and let him talk her into another night.

Get an upper hand, that's what she had to do.

Lisa went into the house and used the phone to make dinner reservations for the following evening. Then she called Riley's cell phone.

He answered, "Hey, Lisa."

He must have this number programmed into his phone. She wasn't savvy about this technical stuff, but she was figuring it out. "Uh, hi."

"What's up?"

"Change of plans. I made reservations at the Blue Moon in Billings for tomorrow evening. Meet me there at seven."

"Coming back early or just going out for dinner?" His voice brought back sensual memories. It probably always would.

"I'm heading back early. I've relaxed enough. I'm out of books and popcorn."

He chuckled. "Okay. You'll find your way back okay?"

"No problem. See you then."

Lisa had lain awake for hours trying to think of the very thing that would set Riley on his ear and show him she wasn't a puppet. The only fitting plan she could come up with was another man.

One small problem: there was no other man. Not that she couldn't find one. Offers came in daily, if her mailbox was any indicator. But for the most impact, it couldn't be just any man. It had to be one Riley would see as a true threat.

The next day she drove to Thunder Canyon and shopped for groceries before driving home. The house welcomed her like an old friend. She walked through the rooms comforted by the familiarity. The dogs seemed glad to be back, as well, dozing in a patch of sunlight that streamed through the dining room windows while she dusted and vacuumed.

Lisa sat with a glass of iced tea and read through piles of mail looking for something suitable, searching for just the right catalyst.

Finally she found him.

Phil Wagner. A formal letter with his business card almost scorched her hands. He wasn't married, was he? She didn't recall anyone accompanying him at the Douglases' party, but it would be easy enough to find out.

She needed a financial advisor, and Riley had recommended this guy. It was Saturday, but she took a chance and called him anyway. She left a message, mentioned she'd just returned to find his letter and would like to talk.

Fifteen minutes later, as she was putting away her clothing and toiletries, the phone rang.

"Phil Wagner here. I got your message."

"Thanks for calling back so quickly."

"No problem. What can I do for you?"

"I was wondering if it was too late and you already had plans for this evening. Riley and I are having dinner, and I was hoping you could join us. Your wife is welcome to join us, of course."

He chuckled. "I'm not married."

"Oh. Well, a date, then."

"I try not to mix business and pleasure."

"Probably a wise philosophy," she replied. "It's

really last-minute, so I'd understand if you can't make it."

"I can make it," he said after a second. "Give me the details."

"Can I pick you up around six thirty?"

"Sure." He gave her his address and she hung up.

For half an hour she fought down a rush of panic and guilt. After that passed she told herself there was no guarantee that Phil would even be attracted to her. He didn't have to —all he had to do was show up with her.

She took a few antacids and sat at the kitchen table. What a laughable creature she was. Her money would do any attracting that needed done—a sad fact to look forward to for the rest of her life.

Phil's his friend. You're playing with fire. You're playing dirty.

Oh? And what had Riley done? Played fair?

Two wrongs don't make a right.

No, but this one will sure be fun.

Revenge is not sweet; it's wrong.

This wasn't revenge. It was…turnabout. And turnabout was fair play. As long as her conscience was going to throw every cliché in the book at her, she was going to counter with a few, as well.

Her nails were already done, and she took her time straightening and styling her hair and applying makeup. She dressed in pale silver pants with a matching spaghetti-strap top and draped a sheer black shawl around her shoulders. It reminded her of the gauzy black fabric that draped over Lily Divine's hip in the painting at the Hitching Post.

Lily had been a self-made woman, a woman proud of

her accomplishments. What would she think if she knew the Queen of Hearts was producing gold and making Lisa rich? How would she see Lisa's actions? Apparently Lily had dealt with an overbearing Douglas, as well, so hopefully she'd be delighted to know Lisa wasn't letting the present-day Douglases get the best of her.

Lisa swallowed down her anxiety on the drive to Phil's. He lived in a nice condo in New Town, and she didn't have any trouble finding it. He was dressed in a pair of black slacks and a gray suit jacket and he greeted her with a smile.

"This is a nice change of pace," he said. "Going out to dinner with a pretty lady rather than a bunch of men."

"I learned from Riley that you wine and dine the people you want to impress," she said lightly.

He laughed. "Impress or coerce?"

Phil was nice looking in a young Jeff Daniels sort of way. There was nothing threatening or intimidating about him, and she didn't sense a superior attitude. He was just plain nice, and she wondered what he and Riley had in common.

"Just out of curiosity, what kind of car do you drive?" she asked.

"Business or pleasure?"

Okay, there was one similarity. "Both."

"I have a nice, sensible Camry. Silver."

"And for pleasure?"

"A black Chevy pickup with a bright red front bumper and red flames painted up the sides."

"I've seen it." A vehicle that flashy was hard to miss. He asked her about the recent goings-on with the mine, and as they got closer to their destination she explained several details about the initial extraction.

"Sounds like you've learned the business," he said as she pulled into the parking lot at the Blue Moon restaurant.

"I'm determined to keep up," she told him.

They got out and met in front of the Blazer. Lisa led the way in, glancing at her watch. Her stomach dipped in anticipation of what was to come.

Inside, a hostess directed them to a table where Riley was seated. The expression on his face when he saw the two of them was a priceless combination of surprise and confusion. Being the Douglas he was, however, he quickly masked his bewilderment and greeted both of them as though he'd known this was the plan all along. He stood, but Phil was already pulling out Lisa's chair.

Lisa sat and gave Riley a friendly smile while Phil took a seat on her other side.

With an envious look the hostess handed each of them a menu and inquired what they'd like to drink. "I'd like a bottle of wine, but Mr. Douglas will select it," Lisa said to the young woman.

Riley ordered a vintage cabernet, and the hostess left with a nod.

Lisa almost laughed at the absurdity of the situation. A month ago she'd never even been in a restaurant this nice, had never been seen with one handsome man, and now she was seated here with two.

"You seem in a good mood this evening," Riley commented. "Your vacation must have been refreshing."

"That's right, you mentioned you'd just returned home," Phil said. "Where'd you go?"

"A little getaway place you might know of," she replied. "Riley said you use the cabin occasionally."

"Riley's so-called cabin? It has more amenities than my condo. I'd been thinking I needed a retreat of my own, but he went to so much work, and the place is used so seldom, I figure why not take him up on his offer to use it."

"My boys loved it," she said. Then explained, "Three- and four-year-old golden retrievers."

"I've seen them with you in the photographs. They're beauties. I have a black Lab myself. He's almost five. I got him when he was six months old."

"What's his name?"

"MacGuyver. He'd been abused and was untrusting. Wouldn't even eat if I was in the room."

"Poor guy. He adjusted to you and your home, though?"

"Oh, yeah. Occasionally if I talk loud or shout—like during a Seahawks game—he starts shaking and tries to hide. But I just coax him out of it, and he's fine. He's a big baby, really. Sleeps on my sofa while I'm at work."

"Joey and Piper aren't allowed on the sofa, but they sleep with me at night. And I only have a full-size bed."

"Must be a little crowded."

Lisa chuckled and glanced at Riley. His jaw muscle was working so hard, he looked as if he could bite through the steel table leg.

Their server arrived with the bottle of wine, and Lisa gestured for her to have Riley taste it.

"It's fine," he told her, and she poured.

"Well," Lisa said, extending her glass. "To pleasant and profitable business transactions and to new friends."

The two men raised their glasses and they drank.

Phil steered the conversation to his investment suggestions, and Lisa listened with fascination. Occasionally Riley disagreed or had an alternative suggestion, but all in all the two men agreed on a plan for Lisa's venture capital.

At one point as she listened, her attention wavered to Riley and her thoughts drifted to the intimacies they'd shared.

Charm her. Get into her pants—hell, knock her up if you have to. Just get a ring on her finger.

Oh, he'd charmed her. More than that, he'd swept her off her ever-lovin' feet. As for getting into her pants, well, that had been mutual—she'd accessed his pants just as eagerly.

Knocked up? He'd wisely and safely used a condom each time they'd been together. At least he hadn't stooped that low—not that she'd have let him. She'd been hot, not stupid.

He'd suggested the ring. He'd gone beyond that, though, gone above and beyond his father's demands and professed love.

Looking at Riley now, Lisa wanted to cry.

She excused herself and found the ladies' room. She had no basis for self-pity, no grounds for feelings of betrayal. She'd been a willing participant from the get-go. And she'd known all along that he was deceiving her.

She hadn't just gone along with him. No, she'd initiated and prompted and used his determination for her own purposes. Lisa washed her hands and touched up her lipstick before heading back to the table.

The server brought their meals, and she ate her wild rice and salmon with an uncharacteristic lack of fervor. Even the wine lost its appeal and she declined a refill.

They talked a while after their dishes had been cleared. Lisa ordered slices of pie for the men and a dish of sherbet for herself. When the check came, she gave the woman her credit card and signed for their dinner.

Phil had been invited to a business dinner and seemed to take her payment of the bill for granted. Riley, on the other hand, looked decidedly uncomfortable.

Out of doors, the warm summer air skimmed Lisa's skin. She hadn't realized how cool it had been in the restaurant until she noticed how good this felt.

Phil reached to shake Riley's hand. "Thanks for hooking me up, buddy. I'll do a good job for Lisa."

Riley nodded, then glanced at her.

"Good night," she said.

She and Phil walked to her Blazer. She used her remote to unlock the doors, and Phil opened the driver's side for her.

Riley turned away, and several seconds later she saw the headlights on his Jaguar turn on. He was ahead of her as she pulled out of the parking lot and drove toward the highway.

His taillights disappeared in the distance, and she couldn't help wondering what he'd been thinking as they'd parted.

Phil talked about his Lab and asked her about Joey and Piper. It was always a joy to share stories with someone who shared her love of dogs, so they talked and laughed until she dropped him off at his condo.

"I'll be in touch, and we'll set up a meeting this week," he told her, sliding out and leaning in the open doorway.

"Sounds good."

He closed the door and Lisa drove away.

She'd shown Riley. She'd brought another man into the picture, but she didn't feel any better. Her plan didn't feel as rewarding as she'd imagined when she'd cooked it up. She didn't have the coldheartedness to actually lead a man on, so this business meeting would have to be enough of a ruse to prove to Riley that she wasn't hard up.

She pulled into her driveway, and her headlights lit the red reflector lights on the rear of a car. The Jag.

Riley was waiting for her.

Chapter Twelve

Oh, crap.

He wasn't going to take her rejection sitting down. Or by going home. Or by being avoided. He was going to confront her head-on.

She parked the Blazer and got out.

Every air conditioner on the block hummed in the summer night. Somewhere in the distance a dog barked.

Out of habit Lisa glanced around, not seeing any news vehicles.

Riley met her on the brick walkway to the house. "What was that all about?"

"What was what all about?"

"You know good and well what. We had a date."

Six nights ago he'd asked her to marry him. Tonight

she'd brought another man to what he'd thought was a date. He was probably a little angry.

"You assumed we had a date. I told you the other day that I wanted things to be professional between us."

"And then we spoke on the phone all week and I asked you out. You accepted."

"Well, I chose to keep things professional."

"So you asked Phil along?"

"He's a nice guy, isn't he?"

"I suppose you stayed to meet his dog."

Why hadn't she thought of that? "Is there some point to this conversation?"

"The point is you brought Phil along to tick me off."

She took her keys out of her handbag and approached her door. Not to tick him off, actually, just to wake him up. "I can have dinner with anyone I like."

Riley followed. "Don't act all innocent. You had an ulterior motive."

She unlocked her door, then turned slowly to face him. "And you'd know all about those, wouldn't you?"

"What are you insinuating?"

"Come on, Riley. I may not have been the best looking or most worldly woman you ever boinked, but I wasn't the stupidest. I remembered *you* from high school, got that? You never gave me a second glance until I inherited a gold mine. Hello?"

Insects buzzed around the light beside her door, so she stepped off the porch onto the sidewalk.

Riley had the grace to momentarily look guilty. "I don't think you're stupid."

"No? Then you think I would really be tricked into

believing you were paying attention to me for myself? I have the pictures, Riley, I know I looked awful."

"You didn't look awful," he denied without much conviction.

She snorted.

"Things just developed between us naturally," he said.

"And the fact that I had just inherited the gold mine you thought belonged to your family *never* had a thing to do with the attraction."

He looked slightly sheepish. "Maybe at first."

"At first? That's bull, and you know it. We both know it. Just stop with the act, will you? Could you just be honest?"

"Lisa, I didn't come here tonight because of the mine. That's honest."

"Really."

"Yes, really."

Behind her the dogs whined and scratched on the inside of the door.

"You might want to retrieve your messages from your other cell phone," she said. "The one at the cabin."

He blinked as though she'd changed the subject. "Why's that?"

"There's an urgent message from your father. Seems you ditched a meeting, and he wasn't very happy with you. He called that number and left an earful."

"What did he say?"

"Oh, he wondered if you were losing your touch since you didn't have a ring on the dog walker's hand yet. He had a few helpful suggestions. Charm her. Get in her pants. Knock her up."

If it had been daylight, she'd probably have seen a new color of green as yet unnamed by Crayola. But as it was, she simply read dismay at having been discovered in the tightening of Riley's lips and his tense stance.

"I have to give you credit, though," she said, gesturing with one hand. "You didn't try the latter suggestion." A flutter of panic battered her chest. "Unless you did something to the condoms beforehand."

"Of course not!" He threaded a hand into his hair and tilted his head back as though praying for deliverance. When at last he looked back at her, he said, "Lisa, I can explain."

"Of course you can. You're a master at getting what you want. It takes a strong person to resist your coercion. A *smart* person."

"May I please explain?"

"Do you deny you had a plan to get into my good graces?"

"No."

"Or that your plan included wining and dining and making me pliable?"

"No."

"Did it ever seem to you that I played along a little too easily?"

"I thought we were connecting."

"Did it ever occur to you that I was giving back to you as good as you were dishing out?"

He swallowed. "Were you?"

"Hello? The whole makeover, the dresses, the... *underwear?*"

"You've been leading *me* on? But...but you were a virgin."

"The word is not a synonym for *ignorant*."

"Lisa, don't you feel something for me?"

An ache swelled in her chest, but she fought it down to salvage her pride. What did he want from her? "Yes, I do feel something," she declared. "Sorry. Because now you have to go tell Daddy your scheme blew up in your face and that there won't be a wedding."

She turned and walked into her house, firmly closing the door and locking it.

Joey and Piper sniffed at her pant legs and licked the hand which still held her keys. She dropped them beside her purse on a table.

A light knock sounded on the door, as though he knew she was still on the other side.

"Lisa, let me in so I can talk to you. Please."

"Go away or I'll call the police and tell them I'm being harassed by a stalker."

He must have taken her threat seriously, because a minute later she heard his car start and saw headlights as he carefully backed out around her Blazer in the drive and left.

Well, there. That was it. She hadn't lost anything because she'd never had anything to lose. Rather, she'd saved her pride and her heart and had an experience she'd wanted in the meantime. No feeling sorry. No turning back. If anything, she'd come out ahead because she'd learned her strengths and discovered her sexuality. She'd held her own against a formidable deceiver.

If all that was true, why did she feel so empty?

"What do you say we go for a run tonight, boys? We're still in reprieve from the media and it's a pretty night."

She could buy a dishwasher. She'd always wanted one.

There really wasn't a place for one, so the cabinets would have to be redone.

Maybe it would be easier to just hire someone to do the dishes. And cook. Not a concept she was comfortable with.

She could buy a new house with a dishwasher and a housekeeper already built in.

Lisa shifted the heavy gold nugget from one hand to the other and set it back on the kitchen table.

The phone rang. She'd bought one with caller ID and had the phone company adjust her service. Riley again. He'd tried to call seven times that morning.

It had been three days since she'd seen him. Three days since she'd told him she was wise to him.

The doorbell rang. The dogs were out back, so they weren't underfoot to bark and trip her on her way to the front hall. Through the leaded-glass door she could see the brown uniform of the delivery man.

"Lisa Martin?"

"That's me."

"Sign here, please." The package he leaned up against the porch wall was six inches thick and about four foot by four foot square.

"Who's it from?"

"Um, Kincaid Restorations?"

"Never heard of them."

"Well, it's for you, miss."

She signed the electronic clipboard and carried the surprisingly heavy box into the house.

She had to get a knife to slice the strapping tape and cut open the end. She slid the packing material out on the floor. Between two thicknesses of foam and several layers of tissue and bubble wrap, she discovered a stained-glass window.

The exquisite piece was Victorian looking but not in a reproduction-type way. It was an antique. The individual pieces of blue, violet and green glass had been intricately leaded to create flowering wisteria and vines.

There was no note, no card, no invoice, and the absence of anything identifying the sender was proof it had been Riley. Who else? And since it had been Riley, that meant the bribe had cost a small fortune.

She couldn't keep it. She'd have to send it back. Or have it delivered to his address.

Lisa leaned the piece of glass up against the leg of a table, and the light from the front windows caught it. Colors spread across the wood floor and the wool rug like an incredible rainbow.

"How much does this suck?" she said to herself. "I get the first gift I've ever had from a man and I can't keep it. And it's really, really beautiful. And he knew I'd love it. The jerk."

Tears came to her eyes, but she blinked them away.

Several things still had to happen. She had to prove to Riley Douglas that she was not a pawn in his game. She had to come to some decisions on what she wanted for herself. And she still wanted to dispel the untruths about Lily.

First things first. Lisa waited until she knew school

would be letting out and drove to the high school. Little had changed since her days there. The outside had been landscaped and a bricked common area created. Inside there were new display cases and the offices had been remodeled to all-window walls.

After checking at the office, she was directed to a second-floor room where Ben Saunders taught.

The man was in his sixties, his hair grayer and his middle thicker than when she'd taken his class. He was putting away books in an oak storage unit at the back of the room.

"Mr. Saunders?"

He blinked and took in her slim skirt and off-the-shoulder pink blouse before smiling. "Lisa Jane! Don't you look just as pretty as all of your pictures. I'm surprised to see you here."

"I wanted to talk to you."

"Well, sure. Have a seat." He pulled out a wooden chair and gestured for her to take it. After she'd seated herself, he brought another and placed it across from her. "What's on your mind?"

"I know you're always involved with Heritage Day and the reenactments of Thunder Canyon history."

"Oh, yes," he replied. "I'm the chairman of the historical society's publicity and ways-and-means committees."

"And several people have mentioned that you're often found at the Hitching Post telling stories about the first gold rush and the early town founders."

He nodded. "There's always a lot of interest in our town history."

"Would you mind telling me the documented facts you know about Lily Divine Harding?" Lisa asked.

"Not at all. She operated the Shady Lady saloon. The operation did a booming business. It was one of three hurdy-gurdy houses in Thunder Canyon."

"Hurdy-gurdy meaning…?"

"Well, that there were women available to dance and, er, entertain the men."

"Do you know of any proof that Lily employed women as prostitutes? Are there letters? Arrests documented?"

He tapped a finger on his chin. "Actually, prostitution wasn't illegal at that time. But there was an organization called the Women's Temperance Prayer League. This group of the town's leading ladies condemned and protested the existence of what they called the 'dens of vice' and had a mission to shut them down. There are a few old meeting flyers in the archives."

"But those only prove that they were accusing the Shady Lady of being a den of vice. Has anything ever proven the fact?"

"Not to my knowledge," he replied.

"I borrowed several journals written by Catherine Douglas from Tildy Matheson."

Ben's eyes lit with excitement. "Emily Stanton—er, Vaughn, I mean—told me those existed."

"Tildy plans to bequeath them to the historical society upon her death."

His expression was intense as he said, "They should be carefully preserved."

"Catherine's things mean a great deal to her. She has treasured them. Catherine makes vague references to

Lily's house being a place of refuge and safety. Tildy's and Emelda Ross's stories back up the fact that Catherine Douglas was abused by her husband and often taken in by Lily."

"I've heard similar stories," he said. "There's a newspaper clip of a Polish woman named Helena who worked in the theater back east before escaping a bad situation with a man and coming to Montana. The article says that Helena found employment and refuge with a local establishment. I've suspected that establishment was the Shady Lady."

"Mr. Saunders, there's no proof that Lily was a prostitute or that her saloon was anything other than a dance hall, is there?"

He shook his head. "The theories have been elaborated over the years because of the painting. And the name of the saloon. It makes for a much more appealing story about the gold-rush days if our Lily was a colorful woman."

"Do you really think it would hurt commerce if the true facts surrounding Lily were made public?"

He shook his head. "I doubt it. After all, we have a present-day gold mine."

"I'd like you to put together all the solid facts regarding Lily, the Shady Lady and anything else relevant, and I'll have a book published for the historical society. You can be the author and take whatever is a fair share for royalties, and the rest of the proceeds will go to the foundation. How does that sound to you?"

His face crinkled with a smile. "It sounds fantastic,

Lisa. I can include photographs and documents from the archives. Perhaps quote from Catherine's journals."

"Okay, then this is your project. If you're aware of presses that do this sort of thing, I'll do the legwork."

"What kind of deadline do you want?" Ben asked.

"We'd like copies in our hands by next Heritage Day, right?" She thought a moment. "How about three or four months?"

"I can do that."

Lisa left the school feeling good about doing all she could to clear up speculation about Lily. They may never have proof of the real story, but at least they could give the facts and let people decide for themselves.

Lisa met Bernadine at the Hitching Post for lunch and told her what she'd come up with.

"That's great, Lisa. That's giving to the community, and they'll love you for it." She glanced at the menu. "What are you getting?"

"I don't know. A hamburger? We need a restaurant as nice as anything in Billings so we don't have to drive all that way for a real meal."

Bernadine laid down her menu. "You're right."

Lisa looked at her. "You really think that's a good idea?"

"I think it's a great idea. If we want to draw tourists to the resort, we'll need some classy places for them to frequent. Besides those on the resort property itself."

"Not anything stuffy, though," Lisa said quickly, getting into the idea with fervor. "Nice decor, maybe tin ceilings for atmosphere. Steaks. Good wine. Fabulous desserts. We'd need a good chef."

"You're getting the hang of this rich-girl stuff," Bernadine told her.

"It could be called the Claim Jumper. We could hang mining memorabilia, old photographs in keeping with the theme of the town and Heritage Days."

"You're really good at this."

"Dog Walker Turned Entrepreneur," Lisa said. "Notice how I think in headlines these days?"

"This is the kind of thing Riley mentioned," Bernadine told her, "when he recommended you put money into local ventures. He'll love this idea."

Lisa wasn't so sure Riley would appreciate anything coming from her right at the moment, but they were going to have to get past their...difficulties...and get down to business.

"I'd love to see his reaction," the other woman added.

"Yeah, I can't wait." Maybe this was it. Maybe this was how she'd show him she had her own mind and her own ideas and didn't intend to be pressured into other people's.

Lisa thought about the women in the movies with men troubles who always confided in their best friends. She didn't have a best friend. Bernadine was her friendly lawyer, but even if she was a friend, she certainly wouldn't have any experience that would benefit Lisa in her bizarre situation.

A confidant was an appealing notion at the moment, however.

A man stopped beside their booth just then, and Lisa glanced up to find Phil Wagner wearing an amiable smile.

"Hi, ladies."

"Hi, Phil," they echoed one after the other.

"I hear you're bringing gold out of the mine this week."

"Yep. Hope you're ready to make money for me."

"I'm ready. I've drawn up a five-year plan to go over with you whenever you have the time."

"I'll have the time this week."

Phil slid a PDA from his pocket and flipped it open. "Thursday looks good in the afternoon. Or Friday morning."

"Any lunches or dinners open?"

"Thursday lunch?"

"Perfect."

"Here?" he asked.

"There's the café and the lunch counter at Super Saver Mart."

"The lunch counter is good," Phil said.

They chose a time, and he moved away to pay his bill and leave.

"Another admirer?" Bernadine asked.

"Another business associate."

"Miss Martin?" Chad Falkner stood beside their booth, no camera in hand.

Lisa glanced around and didn't see any other reporters. "Well. I was wondering when I'd see you."

"Kept our end of the deal, didn't we?"

"Yes, you did."

"Did you see the picture I took in *People?*"

"Oh, yes."

"I was wondering if you have any kind of a follow-up statement to our interview or anything you'd like to share with the public."

Lisa thought a minute. "Actually I do. Have a seat and we'll talk. Have you eaten?"

Chad looked as if he'd been granted an audience with the queen of England. His expression was serious, and he sat beside Lisa with a look of sheer gratification on his face.

"I have a couple of new projects," she told him, "and I'd like people to hear about them from me. One of them is a book on Lily Divine for the historical society. Hopefully it's going to dispel some of the myths that have been perpetuated about her."

"Really?"

Bernadine leaned forward. "There will be press releases regarding Miss Martin's new ventures," she told Chad. "What would you say to seeing those first and hearing any other news she has to share first, as long as you keep your distance the rest of the time? The way you have been."

"I'd say yes. I can try to work out something with the other reporters so that they'll get the same accurate news after I've seen it. You might have to throw them a bone now and then and pose for a few pictures."

"I can do that."

"We'll have something written up for you about this book project next week," Bernadine told him.

"Great. What about the other projects you mentioned? You only told me about one."

"The other one is under wraps for now—at least until some more plans can be made. You'll be the first to know."

He stood and reached to shake both women's hands. "Thanks a lot."

"So, you're my publicist now?" Lisa asked Bernadine.

"No, but I have people who can work up press releases. Anything to keep those bloodsuckers off your tail."

Lisa thanked her and they finally got around to eating their lunch.

She had taken a huge first step toward her goal of clearing Lily's name to the best of her ability. She was handling the press without Riley now and she had come up with her own idea for a local business venture. That should show Riley she had a mind of her own. She still had to figure out what she wanted for herself, though, and that was proving more difficult than the other tasks.

First she'd thought she was happy the way she was and resisted change. Then she'd realized she wanted more and had broken out of her boring shell and tried to change everything about herself at once. She was discovering she was more creative and independent than she'd ever dreamed.

She'd even been enjoying talking to people and coming out of her isolation. Not everyone was out to wheedle a chunk of her gold mine.

"If I didn't have a gold mine anymore," she said offhandedly, "would you still want to have lunch with me?"

Bernadine's expression showed surprised but understanding, as well. "Yes, I would, Lisa. I think we're becoming friends, don't you?"

"Yes, I think so."

The more Lisa thought about it over the next day or so, the more she realized she'd been very judgmental of the townspeople. Sure, there were the crazies who called to convince her they were a long-lost relative, but there were also plenty of other people who were perfectly warm and friendly. She'd always considered that they'd looked down on her and ignored her, but she'd perpetuated that treatment. If she'd stood up to a few juvenile comments in school or had not been ashamed of being related to Lily, maybe things would have been different.

That kind of thinking changed her whole attitude. And scared her. And delighted her. She really had changed.

Riley stood outside Town Hall after a chaotic meeting with officials over the much-needed addition of more police officers, firemen and medical personnel. Ever since the onset of gold fever, the town had been overrun by would-be prospectors and sightseers. Good for the economy but a stretch to their fiscal budgets. The board had asked Riley to head a project to appropriate more dollars for these jobs.

Brad Vaughn paused beside him with a question about additional parking for Main Street shops. Brad and Emily had been married recently and had settled in Thunder Canyon. Brad had started a missing-persons investigation company and he took an active interest in town issues.

"The motels are inadequate for the influx of tourists, as well," Brad told him. "When Emily and I initially arrived here to investigate the mine ownership, we couldn't find anyplace to stay. Your father loaned us that old cabin."

"I heard that was a good thing," Riley replied easily.

"As it turned out, it was, but not everyone has that option. Especially since we bought the place."

"I agree. Even with the resort there will be middle-income tourists looking for an economy stay."

"Emily tells me the Martin girl was reluctant to claim ownership of the mine at first. From what we see in the papers, it looks like she's coming out of her shell now."

"She's come a long way. She wants to learn all she can and manage the monster that was dropped in her lap."

Brad faced Riley with a furrow between his brows. "I hope there's no hard feelings between us now—you know, because Emily and I made the results of our investigation public."

That comment didn't soak in. "What do you mean? You found the only documentation available. It's a legal document. I know we hired you to discover otherwise, but you did find the owner. Why would that create hard feelings?"

Brad gave him an odd look. "Well…" He glanced away. "No reason, I guess."

"No, speak up. In your opinion, why would I resent you?"

Brad seemed hesitant to speak but finally opened up. "When Emily and I found the deed, your father offered us money to keep silent about it being signed back over to Lily Harding. We wouldn't consider it. I thought you knew this."

The information burned in Riley's stomach like three-alarm chili. His father had offered Brad a bribe to keep Lisa's ownership a secret. If left to his own wishes, Caleb would have destroyed the deed and called the mine Douglas property without anyone knowing any different.

Shame heated Riley's flesh. "No. I didn't know. But thank you for your integrity."

"I wasn't sure where you stood," Brad said.

"I haven't been sure most of the time either," Riley replied honestly. "But the lines are becoming a lot more clear."

Brad extended a hand. "No harm done, then?"

"Just the opposite." Riley shook his hand.

He and Brad parted on the sidewalk, and Riley walked toward the street where his car was parked. Family loyalties ran deep, but bribery and deceit were family values he didn't want to condone any longer. He could forgive his father for his acts of adultery, but he had trouble with ignoring the pain his mother had suffered.

The story of Caleb offering Justin's mother money to keep him had always stuck in his craw. Had it made Justin feel valuable?

And now this. Offering the investigators money to hide Lisa's ownership of the mine. Equally as low-down and underhanded as Riley's devising a plan to win her affection and marry her so he could get control, wasn't it? He'd justified his actions by planning to leave her well off when he divorced her. What kind of warped thinking had that been? Why hadn't he rejected the idea when he'd first had it? Because he'd seen all his life how money and power got you what you wanted. What he hadn't seen—or wanted to see—were the far-reaching effects and the slow erosion of virtue when a person allowed this kind of manipulation.

This was the first time he'd admitted these things to himself. He'd never promised his father he would carry out the marriage. But he'd pursued Lisa as though he intended to make it happen.

What could he do to correct such a big, ugly mistake?

She wouldn't even take his calls.

He didn't know how to redeem himself or if it was even possible. But he knew he had to try.

Chapter Thirteen

Every day for the past week Riley had left a message on her machine. Every one-sided conversation had been similar. He wanted to see her. Wanted to talk to her. She was aware of her limitations and knew she was toast if she gave in to him. She would have to get past this and face him for business, but all in good time. For the time being, she checked in with Marge when she had a question or when there was something that needed a signature. Marge accommodated her by using a courier service.

Lisa went about her new life the best way she knew how. And she spent a lot of time thinking about where she wanted to direct her energy and her emotions. Dogs had always been her first love, and caring for them would always be important. Calls for walks and care had dwindled with her rise to local fame, though. Her clients assumed she didn't have the time or the inclination, and truth be told, it was becoming more and more difficult to juggle Puppy Love with her other business obligations.

She still loved her grandmother's house and couldn't imagine not having the security and memories it provided. One evening, out of the blue, the idea came to her that she could move this house to a more suitable location with surrounding land and a security enclosure.

Amazing how money could open doors and move otherwise unoiled gears. Her first phone calls were met by receptive people with the knowledge and skill to help her move the house. Calls to Realtors resulted in appointments to look at property.

Remembering something Emily had said to her the very first day they'd met, Lisa thought about the things she'd always thought she would do if she could afford to. Emily had said she'd pay for her sister's college. Lisa didn't have any siblings, but she'd given a lot of thought to things she would do with her money when she actually had an abundance.

Riley left a message for her to call the bank and verify balances. She did and her ears went numb. She was rich.

He was her financial manager. She needed to clear things with him, so she called Marge and asked her to leave him a message. Previously his secretary had caught on that Lisa didn't want to speak directly to him. Lisa told her she wanted to start a search for property and asked how much she could safely spend this month.

She wanted to implement a plan for an animal shelter, as well. Before she'd understood the magnitude of her inheritance, she'd had it in her heart that building a no-kill facility would be the height of her benevolent dreams. Now there was no reason it couldn't become a reality.

After explaining to Marge, she hung up feeling guilty and called her right back. "Marge, never mind. I'm sorry to have placed you in this position. I'll talk to Riley myself."

"No problem. He's right here."

She had expected him to return her call, not be standing by.

"Hello, Lisa."

"Hi. I want to move on a couple of projects, so I need to run them past you."

"Great. Want me to come over there?"

"We can talk over the phone."

"Whatever makes you happy."

She explained about looking for property and about the animal shelter.

"You'd better hold off on the shelter," he told her.

"Why?"

"You'd be doubling your efforts."

"How so?" she asked. "There's nothing like that in Thunder Canyon."

"But there will be. There's been land purchased."

"By whom?"

He paused only briefly. "By me."

Riley had already bought land for an animal shelter?

"One of the things I need to talk to you about is how to set it up and what features to employ. I thought we could visit a couple in nearby regions and get some ideas."

Lisa had to compose her thoughts to find her tongue. "*You* are planning to build an animal shelter?"

"Yes."

"Why?"

"I heard you mention it once."

"Is this some sort of manipulation technique?"

"No, it's going to be a gift. To the city."

"Why this particular project?"

"Because I know it's close to your heart. And that's where I want to be, as well. I was hoping it would show you I'm not the greedy, scum-sucking control freak you think I am. I admit I got close to fitting that description once, but I'm working at change. I'd like you to take over the project and have the final say on everything."

What did an animal shelter cost? she thought with skepticism. Only a fraction of a gold mine. If he sucked her in with this ploy, he'd still be a cool mil ahead.

"Will you do it?" he asked.

"If you're serious. But not if you think it changes anything."

The line was silent a moment too long. "Will you accept my apology so I can sleep nights?"

Why should he have a sleep advantage over her? "What, a conscience?"

"A conscience, a heart, whatever you want to call it.

I'm sorry. I can't go back and fix it. But I can show you I'm not that same person."

"By building an animal shelter?"

"By doing something I thought you'd respect me for."

"People earn respect, Riley."

"That they do. You earned mine."

She couldn't listen to this. She couldn't weaken. "We're business associates. I don't want to avoid your phone calls. I want to know that when your number shows up, you're calling about business. I want to know that when we see each other face-to-face, it's not going to be a test of wills. The manipulating and bribing have to stop."

"You're right."

"Why did you send the stained-glass window, then?"

"Because it's beautiful and I knew you'd love it. Why did you send it back?"

"Because it's beautiful, and I loved it."

"It doesn't go with my place."

She wanted badly to comment that nothing went with his place, but she held her tongue. "No more bribes."

"You say to-may-to, I say to-mah-to."

"Business. Period."

"All right, Lisa." The way he said her name with such sincerity and feeling hammered at her protective armor.

"I'm not kidding," she said and meant it.

"I know you're not. I agree to your terms. Thank you for calling, Lisa."

"We'll talk soon, then." She paused a moment too long. "Bye."

She hung up, satisfied with his promise but sorry

she'd had to wrest it out of him. No room for chances where Riley was concerned. Things needed to be as safe as she could make them. She was existing in a tissue-paper world—and it was raining.

The last thing Lisa wanted to do was attend the event at Town Hall on Saturday night of the next week. The Gold Fever Gala was being held in the huge reception room in the restored building. This evening had been planned in order to celebrate several things, including the boost to the economy and the production of gold from the Queen of Hearts, and to announce the plethora of projects which had been put in place.

As a popular Thunder Canyon daughter and the newly discovered heiress, Lisa had been invited as the guest of honor.

She had taken great care with her appearance, culling yet another divine red dress from the selection Gwen had pulled together for her. This one was calf length and slit up the side and left one shoulder bare. Tiny matching beads sewn on the fabric in leafy designs reflected the light.

A valet took Lisa's keys and the Blazer and parked it for her. Bernadine had offered to pick her up, but knowing her lawyer had a date, Lisa had refused.

Several people Lisa didn't know arrived just as she did. They introduced themselves and walked in through the double glass doors behind her.

Inside, the first person Lisa recognized was Emily Vaughn. She looked elegant in a deep-emerald gown that emphasized her sleek hair and dark eyes. Emily was quick to greet Lisa with a smile and a brief hug. "You look as though you're here for a roast."

"I'll try to compose myself. I'm still a novice at this social stuff. I expect to trip or sneeze on somebody's tie at any given minute."

"You're the woman of the hour, so try to relax and enjoy every minute while it lasts."

"I'll try. I feel like a big fake. I didn't do anything to be here. I'm only the mine owner because of my genes."

"Don't knock family money. Nobody ever says the Kennedys don't deserve what they have."

Lisa laughed. "I'll remember that."

A couple just inside the door to the reception hall greeted the two women. "Hi, Lisa. I'm Faith Stevenson, and this is my husband, Cam."

Lisa shook their hands. "Stevenson. You must be the parents of the boy who started this whole gold rush by falling into the mine."

Cam's brown eyes were as warm as his smile. "That's our claim to fame. It was scary, but it turned out well for everyone. Faith was the rescue worker who found Erik, and that's how we met."

"Well, congratulations. I'd love to meet Erik one of these days."

Bernadine was standing with Olivia Chester and a few other guests when Lisa spotted her. She gestured for Lisa to join them, and Emily excused herself and moved off into the crowd.

"You've met Olivia," Bernadine said.

"Hello again, Doctor."

"These are some of my colleagues." Olivia gestured to those beside her. "Christopher Taylor works in the E.R. and his wife, Zoe, is a resident."

"Nice to meet you."

"You, too," Zoe said. "I can see why red is your signature color. You look fabulous."

Lisa hadn't really thought of it like that. She'd chosen red dresses as a statement of pride about Lily, but she didn't mind the association. "Thank you."

The gathering broke up, and Lisa asked her lawyer, "Where's your date?"

"I thought he went to get drinks. I'd better go make sure he didn't meet someone else and forget about me."

More guests arrived and drinks flowed from bars set up in two corners of the room. Lisa was tickled to see Tildy Matheson had come to the reception. The woman was seated in an overstuffed chair, which had been situated for her comfort. Lisa pulled a folding chair close so they could visit.

"I already heard about the book project," Tildy told her. "Ben told me. I'm real proud of you for thinking of it. Catherine and Lily would be real proud, too."

"Thank you, Tildy. I'm grateful to you for helping me learn more about my ancestor."

Tildy glanced at the glass of wine a nearby guest held. "I could sure use a cup of tea. I don't suppose there's any to be had."

"I'll ask. You sit tight."

Lisa approached one of the corner bars. Two people

waiting in line moved aside so she could go first. "I'll wait my turn," she told them.

"Oh, no, you're the guest of honor. The guest of honor goes first."

"I just wanted to ask if there was any tea. Miss Matheson would like a cup."

"My wife carries a little tin with tea bags in her purse," the taller gentleman said. "I'll go ask her for one."

"They have a microwave in the back room," the other man said. "I'll go get a cup of hot water."

A few minutes later Lisa thanked them profusely and carried a mug of tea to Tildy.

"You're a dear girl," the old woman said. She blew on her tea and sipped it. "There's that nice Mark Anderson, the reporter who bought the *Nugget*."

Lisa glanced over at the dark-eyed man with graying hair at his temples. Bless Tildy for using the words *nice* and *reporter* in the same breath.

"He married that pretty Hispanic waitress from the Hitching Post, you know. He adopted her baby."

Lisa learned more local gossip at every event she attended. She could only imagine the speculation about her—and the talk regarding the times she'd been seen and photographed in Riley's company.

Justin and Katie Caldwell paused to greet the two women, and Lisa couldn't help glancing around for the rest of the Douglases. The room had grown full, and it was becoming more difficult to find people.

A ringing sound, like that of a glass being struck repeatedly with a utensil, resounded in the room and the crowd hushed.

Mayor Brookhurst stood on a podium, which had been set along one wall to elevate the speakers. "Attention, ladies and gentlemen! May I have your attention, please?"

Feedback from the microphone screeched and bystanders covered their ears.

Once the technical difficulties had been solved, the mayor proceeded. "Welcome one and all to our first Gold Fever Gala! Isn't this exciting? There hasn't been this much enthusiasm in Thunder Canyon for a good many years. I'm fortunate that the events of this year have taken place during my term. With everyone so happy and the town doing so well, maybe I'll get elected again just so I can bring good luck."

Soft laughter swept the crowd and a good-natured heckler told him democracy had nothing to do with luck.

"We're here tonight to celebrate our good fortune. The Queen of Hearts gold mine is in full production."

Applause rose in a resounding thunder.

"Our motels and restaurants, the gift shops, *all* the businesses have had more trade these past few months than in our history."

Residents clapped again.

"This evening there are several people we want to recognize for the parts they played in making this happen. We wanted to recognize Erik Stevenson's contribution, but his parents thought positive reinforcement for running away and hiding in the mine was a bad idea."

The crowd *Awww*ed collectively.

"But a donation to Erik's college fund is being made

on behalf of the Businessmen's Guild, and you're all sworn to secrecy until he's eighteen."

Lisa observed the smiles on Cam and Faith's faces. They hugged each other and went forward to accept the gift.

"This next award will be shared among several people who were each important in the events leading to our current boom. As you all know, Emily and Brad Vaughn were the ones who discovered the original deed to the mine. So, Emily and Brad, come up here beside me, please."

The couple made their way forward.

"Now, Brad and Emily wouldn't have come to Thunder Canyon at all if the Douglases hadn't paid for their investigation, so, Caleb and Riley, we want you in this group, too. Come on."

Murmurs went through the throng of guests. Caleb's silver hair came into view above the crowd, and then the rest of him as he stepped up onto the podium wearing his usual western-cut jacket. "Come on, Riley," he said.

Riley hung back and waved a dismissive hand. "I only wrote the checks. You found the team."

At his refusal to join them, Mayor Brookhurst went on. "Our next person of honor is the woman who kept the deed among her possessions for all these years until it could be claimed. Where's Matilda Matheson?"

A hubbub of chatter spread after her name was spoken, and after several minutes Tildy came forward, aided by Mark Anderson and Ben Saunders. They assisted her up to the platform. She was beaming with pleasure at the attention.

Riley lifted her chair into place, and she took a seat while the others stood beside her.

"Each of these fine people are hereby rewarded with a key to the city," the mayor said, and his assistant hung a large gold-foil key by a wide red ribbon around each of their necks.

Caleb looked at the mock key hanging on his shirt front and then aside as though he was sorry he'd come up for such pathetic praise.

"Now, that key doesn't really unlock anything," the mayor told them. "But whenever any of you want to be mayor for a day, you just bring your key to the Hall and the job is yours."

Laughter rippled through the crowd, and everyone clapped for those being honored. After pictures were taken, they dispersed back into the cluster of guests.

"Let *me* be mayor for a day and he'd never get hired again," Caleb said as an aside, and he received a few sidelong glances.

Oblivious to the comment, the mayor resumed his task. "Last but certainly not least, we have a special guest of honor we want to recognize right now. The people of Thunder Canyon want this young lady to know we're proud of her. Come on up here, please, Lisa Jane Martin!"

Lisa felt the warmth of nervousness climb her neck and face. This public recognition was so out of her element that if it had happened a month ago, she would have fainted dead away. She'd gained self-confidence in that month, however, and she was no longer ashamed of her connection to her great-great-grandmother. She held her head high and walked through the crowd.

Phil Wagner happened to be standing nearest, so he reached for her hand to help her. She held her skirt and stepped up on the riser.

Cameras snapped and whirred.

"Lisa, as owner of the Queen of Hearts, you've already shown that you're going to give back to our community. As docent of the museum, Ben Saunders is going to talk about the book project for the historical society."

Ben did indeed get up and share the details of the book he was authoring and that Lisa was publishing. "What we hope to do with this project is dispel the myths that have surrounded Lily all these years and present the facts. I'm honored that Lisa has asked me to do this."

After he stepped down and the applause quieted, the mayor looked at Lisa with a big smile. "We have another surprise to share. One of Lisa's first business ventures will be the Claim Jumper restaurant. Fine dining right here in Thunder Canyon."

The excitement over the announcements abated momentarily.

"In recognition, Lisa, we present you with this." He turned to where his assistant held out a box with the lid removed. From inside, Mayor Brookhurst took a gold tiara set with heart-shaped stones.

A few bystanders chuckled, but everyone clapped enthusiastically.

"You are now—officially—the queen of our hearts."

Smiling, Lisa stood still so he could place the tiara on her head, securing the combs in her hair.

Among the sea of faces, she spotted Bernadine smiling and clapping. Her date was a handsome fellow with a mustache and slightly graying hair.

Lisa's gaze locked with Riley's then, and the noise of the room faded away. Queen of their hearts was lovely. But she'd like to have a place in one special person's heart.

Congratulations were effusive, and she lost sight of Riley. She posed for pictures with the mayor and the other honorees.

An awkward hush caught Lisa's attention. It became clear that someone was saying something that had made people stop and listen.

Standing only five feet away with his hands in his pockets, Caleb Douglas rocked back on his heels. His next words were clear. "Why, she's probably the only trailer-trash royalty in the state of Montana."

No one laughed. His derogatory remark dampened the frivolous mood and garnered more than a few stares. A dozen sidelong glances were cast at Lisa to see if she'd overheard.

Her ears burned with anger. She wasn't ashamed of who she was or where she'd come from. It was the fact that he'd belittled her heritage and her family that got her feathers in a snit.

She turned a glare on him that would have scorched a lesser man. "I may not have been raised in a fancy house and waited on hand and foot," she told him. "But my grandmother and my aunt loved me and they taught me honesty and integrity. I wouldn't use another person's feelings to get what I want, and I would never encourage a child of mine to do the same."

Caleb seemed surprised by her show of grit and the way people had listened to what she had to say.

"I think that crown's gone to your head, missy," he said. "Just like the money did."

This wasn't the time or the place to vent her hurt and anger over the Douglases' manipulations, so she took a breath and counted to ten. Ten wasn't enough. She opened her mouth to speak, but before anything came out, Riley's voice interrupted her.

"Lisa's the last person who would let money go to her head," he said, speaking directly to his father. "She's the most genuine, unaffected and trustworthy person I know. That you could have anything ugly to say about her tells me you don't know her. If you did, you'd know someone with a lot of love to give and very little concern about what money will get her."

Riley turned, and Lisa met his vivid green gaze. His attention refocused on her.

"If you knew her," he continued, "you'd have to love her."

Lisa's heart staggered and she took several deliberate breaths to make sure she didn't pass out. This was worse than sneezing on someone's tie, but she didn't really care. She wanted to hear what he had to say.

"I got to know her," Riley said. "And now I can't think about anything else but loving her."

Tears welled up and clung to Lisa's lower lashes until she saw him through a watery blur.

Riley turned to the people beside him, as though explaining to a jury. "I deceived her when we met. I pretended to be interested in her when I was really only concerned about regaining ownership of the gold mine. My values were nothing you'd want to teach your children."

"What about now?" Heads turned to discover the voice that had spoken that question belonged to Adele Douglas, looking cool and sophisticated as always in a stunning silver dress. The crowd parted for her to move closer to her son. "What are you concerned with now, Riley?"

He glanced from his mother back to Lisa. "I'm concerned with convincing her I can change." His gaze was warm and beseeching. "With showing her I deserve a second chance."

"And?" Adele asked softly.

"And with proving that my love for her is real."

Lisa's blood pounded through her veins.

"I love you, Lisa," he said. "Please forgive me. Please marry me. Please...give me another chance."

In the silence that followed, you could have heard an itch. No one seemed to breathe as anticipation and hope electrified the room.

Lisa couldn't take her focus from Riley's face. His cheeks were high with color, but his eyes were pleading and sincere. She knew people were watching and waiting on all sides and she could imagine the look on Caleb's face, but none of that mattered at this moment.

The most unexpected image came to her unbidden. At that moment she saw Lily Divine's face as it appeared in her photographs and in the painting. Her great-great-grandmother's smile of contentment made Lisa yearn to share Lily's peace with her life choices. Made her desire the same assurance that she was being all she could be and leaving no breathing room for regrets.

Lisa's nerves had calmed and she was thinking with perfect rationality. She had no guarantee that Riley wasn't pulling the ultimate scam right at this moment. That he hadn't staged this for her benefit or even that his father hadn't been a part of it. But she didn't think so.

At last Lisa's gaze faltered and shot to Caleb where he stood. His face was red with anger and his green eyes shot lethal daggers at her. If he was in on a scheme, he would be much more pulled together and look less as if he would burst a blood vessel in his forehead at any moment.

Riley's expression didn't seem quite as confident as it would if he thought he'd pulled a fast one. In fact, she thought he'd begun to look decidedly anxious.

"I'll sign a prenuptial agreement," he told her, uncannily zeroing in on her last uncertainty.

"I can have one drawn up in five minutes." Bernadine's voice had come from several feet away. Her suggestion released the crowd's tension, and laughter rippled.

Lisa took several steps forward until she stood within an arm's length of Riley. "There aren't any guarantees," she said. "A hundred years ago someone bought a claim to the land where the mine sits, with nothing more than hope as a guide. Then somewhere along the line another somebody gave up. The gold was in there all along."

"I know this is a long-winded metaphor for something, Lisa, but could you speed it up and tell me how it turns out?" Riley asked.

She grinned. "It turns out that some things happen by chance. Like Erik stumbling into the mine. Like me being related to Lily."

"*Maybe* it's chance," Riley said. "But maybe it's not. Maybe there's a time and a reason for everything."

"Isn't that a Simon and Garfunkel song?"

"Not exactly."

She took a step forward and placed her hand on his arm. "In any case, I'd rather take my chances with love—and trust. I don't want any regrets."

Riley slipped his arm around her shoulders. "I'll see that you don't have any."

"You'd better make your second chance good."

"This time I love you."

She raised on her toes to meet his kiss. Riley wrapped his arms around her, and she clung to him greedily. She was never going to let go of this man again.

Around them the crowd cheered and whistled.

Lisa was so filled with joy, she could barely breathe. When the kiss ended, she glanced around at the smiles and tears on the faces of the people of Thunder Canyon. She had misjudged a lot of these people. And some of them had misjudged her, as well. She was big on second chances.

A movement caught her eye. Caleb had turned toward the door, and his wife watched as Justin and Katie broke away from the others to follow him.

"Your father hates me."

"Like I said, he doesn't even know you."

"I don't want to come between you."

"Right now there are a few value issues between us. If he wants to salvage his family, he'll come around. I'm not changing. And I'm not giving you up. Not for anything." His gaze rose to her hair. "You're the queen of my heart, too."

She remembered the tiara on her head. "What do you suppose the headlines will say tomorrow?" She glanced around. "Is Chad Falkner here?"

Riley gestured with a thumb over his shoulder. "Saw him back there. Why?"

"I'm wondering if *People* magazine will put my picture beside Queen Latifah's this time."

"Who?"

"Never mind. You're really going to have to widen your interests and take in a few movies."

"I'll take you all the time."

"We could open a theater! Or an old-fashioned drive-in. Wouldn't that be fun?"

"So, you'll marry me?"

"Yes!"

He squeezed her hand and smiled.

"I'm having my house moved, you know."

"I'll live there with you."

"Will you *not* bring your furniture?"

"How about my bed?"

"Okay, your bed. We'll need room for the boys."

Riley groaned.

Lisa laughed and he crushed her in a hug.

"Montana Woman Has Big Plans. My house at eleven."

"Local Heiress Gives Thunder Canyon Scion A Second Chance," he said against her ear. "Montana man has never been happier, and it has nothing to do with gold."

Epilogue

Lisa glanced around their new backyard—well, *acreage*, actually. Riley had convinced her to have her grandmother's house moved to this incredible forested site near a stream on a northeast section of Douglas land with a breathtaking view of the mountains.

No longer did she need dog runs to cage her beloved boys while she was away. This entire section of land had been fenced in so they could run for half an acre and back.

Today the area directly outside the back door was set up with enormous canopies and long tables in preparation for their housewarming party. The celebration had been Katie's idea, and she waddled between the kitchen, the two caterers' vans and the tables, making sure everything was arranged perfectly.

She and Lisa had announced their pregnancies at nearly the same time. Katie's baby was due in eleven weeks and Lisa's in ten. Lisa was delighted that her child would grow up with a cousin so close in age, an aunt and an uncle and even grandparents. This was the family she'd always wanted, even if some of the relationships still needed a little work.

The side gate opened and Justin and Riley carried flat boxes toward the tables.

"What're those?" Lisa called.

"More cakes," Riley answered. "The baker at Super Saver Mart wanted to contribute something to the festivities, so she made these this morning."

"Goodness," Katie said. "We already had four cakes."

"Don't worry that they'll go to waste," Justin told his wife. "Riley invited all the store employees and their families to stop by this afternoon."

Lisa laughed and gave her husband a hug, which was becoming more difficult with the size of her belly coming between them. Riley rested a hand atop her stomach and kissed her. "How's little Frodo doing?"

"His name's not Frodo," Lisa replied. After they'd watched the entire *Lord of the Rings* series together, he'd become obsessed with naming their expected child after one of the characters. Last week it had been Aragorn.

"You can name our next pet Frodo, not our child. We could agree on Sam," she told him for the hundredth time.

Excited barks sounded, and Riley stepped away from her to greet Joey, Piper and Derek. Derek had stayed with them a few months ago when Riley's father had been in the hospital for bypass surgery, and now Adele brought the poodle at least once a week for a sleepover. She claimed he needed the exercise and companionship, and Lisa's two retrievers were used to new canines sharing their space.

Riley knelt and gave each dog equal attention, scratching behind their ears and stroking their fur. He'd convinced his mother to let Derek's fur grow out of the ridiculous pom-pom cut.

"I told you this canine has more dignity and self-respect now," he said.

Lisa and Katie shared a look.

"What?" he said defensively. "Look at him. He's one of the guys now."

"He's no different, Riley," Katie told him. "Only his appearance has changed."

"Improved appearance does bring confidence," Lisa said.

"Are you people talking about the dog?" Justin asked.

Riley gave Derek a solid pat on the haunches and stood. "Lisa told me once that Derek only has so many years in him, so I'd better make the most of them."

"I guess that's true about anything," Justin said. "Like you and I, Riley. We don't have a past as family, but you've let me into your present and future."

Riley looked at his half brother. "Your birth wasn't your fault. I always understood that. I don't know what I resented more—the fact that our father was deceptive or that you forgave him so easily."

"I wanted a family," Justin replied. "More than I wanted to hang on to the anger."

The conversation had turned more serious, and the two couples glanced at each other.

"Riley's letting the Derek philosophy spill over to Caleb," Lisa said.

Riley nodded. "Seeing him in the hospital showed me we didn't have a lifetime to work through this stuff, so we need to do it now."

"Did he tell you he was sorry?" Katie asked. "It's tough to forgive when someone isn't sorry."

"Not in so many words," Riley answered with a shrug. "Right off I made it plain how things would be regarding my wife. He didn't know Lisa and he was judging her unfairly. Everything has always been about money with him."

Riley studied his beautiful wife, her eyes bright with the pleasure of life. Tiny ringlets of hair lay against her cheeks and temples. She bothered less and less to straighten it these days, but it didn't matter. She was all the more beautiful carrying his child.

"Once, it was all about money with me, too." He took her hand and brought it to his lips. "Until I found out money really can't buy love or happiness."

"Sure helped with all the extras, though." Lisa smiled and touched his cheek.

"I missed a lot by not looking outside my narrow, moneyed life," he said. "Thank goodness I had another chance."

"*We* have a second chance," she corrected.

Justin wrapped his arm around his wife's shoulder and they strolled away from the couple who'd become absorbed in each other.

Piper barked at a squirrel and the three dogs bounded away.

"I have a surprise for you." He took a red velvet ring box from his pocket and opened it before showing her what lay inside.

Lisa took the plain gold band between her thumb and forefinger. "It's beautiful, Riley! But I already have a wedding ring."

"It's not a wedding ring. It's made from some of the first gold mined from the Queen of Hearts. It's just…a symbol."

None of this would have happened if gold hadn't been found or if Lisa hadn't been proven the rightful owner. For once, losing had turned out to be the best thing that had ever happened to Riley Douglas.

Lisa slipped the ring on a finger and kissed him.

Her kisses were better than anything money could buy.

* * * * *

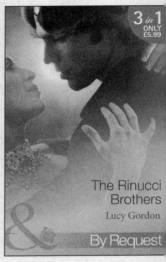

MILLS &
BOON

are proud to present our...

Book of the Month

The Accidental Princess
by Michelle Willingham
from Mills & Boon® Historical

Etiquette demands Lady Hannah Chesterfield ignore
the shivers of desire Lieutenant Michael Thorpe's
wicked gaze provokes, but her unawakened body
clamours for his touch… So she joins Michael on
an adventure to uncover the secret of his birth—
is this common soldier really a prince?

Available 5th November

*Something to say about our
Book of the Month?
Tell us what you think!*

millsandboon.co.uk/community
facebook.com/romancehq
twitter.com/millsandboonuk

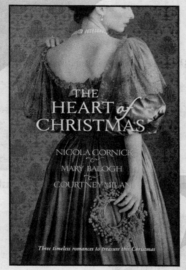
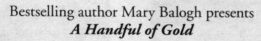

Meet Nora Robert's
The MacGregors family

1st October 2010

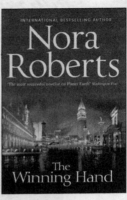

3rd December 2010

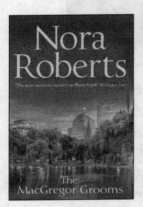

7th January 2011

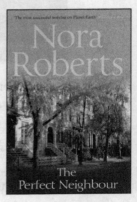

4th February 2011

"Did you say I won almost two million dollars?"

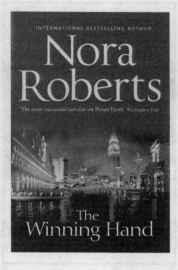

Down to her last ten dollars in a Las Vegas casino, Darcy Wallace gambled and won!

Suddenly the small-town girl was big news—and needing protection. Robert MacGregor Blade, the casino owner, was determined to make sure Darcy could enjoy her good fortune. But Darcy knew what she wanted; Mac himself. Surely her luck was in?

Available 3rd December 2010

www.millsandboon.co.uk

MILLS & BOON®
HAVE JOINED FORCES WITH THE LEANDER TRUST AND LEANDER CLUB TO HELP TO DEVELOP TOMORROW'S CHAMPIONS

We have produced a stunning calendar for 2011 featuring a host of Olympic and World Champions (as they've never been seen before!). Leander Club is recognised the world over for its extraordinary rowing achievements and is committed to developing its squad of athletes to help underpin future British success at World and Olympic level.

'All my rowing development has come through the support and back-up from Leander. The Club has taken me from a club rower to an Olympic Silver Medallist. Leander has been the driving force behind my progress'

RIC EGINGTON – Captain, Leander Club Olympic Silver, Beijing, 2009 World Champion.

Please send me ☐ calendar(s) @ £8.99 each plus £3.00 P&P (FREE postage and packing on orders of 3 or more calendars despatching to the same address).

I enclose a cheque for £ _____ made payable to Harlequin Mills & Boon Limited.

Name ....

Address ....

.... Post code ....

Email ....

Send this whole page and cheque to:
Leander Calendar Offer
Harlequin Mills & Boon Limited
Eton House, 18-24 Paradise Road, Richmond TW9 1SR

All proceeds from the sale of the 2011 Leander Fundraising Calendar will go towards the Leander Trust (Registered Charity No: 284631) – and help in supporting aspiring athletes to train to their full potential.